TILL MY LAST DAY

TILL MY LAST DAY

Book Two
Desert Hills Trilogy

Deborah Swenson

This is a work of fiction. Names, characters, places, events, and incidents are the product of the author's imagination and are used in a fictitious manner. Any resemblance to actual persons, living or dead, establishments, or events is coincidental.

Published by Nor-Mar Press 2024
normarpress.com

Designed by The Story Laboratory
Cover Design: Tabitha Lahr; Cover photos © Shutterstock.com
Cactus Vector: Designed by pikisuperstar, courtesy Freepik
www.WriteEditDesignLab.com

Disclaimer
There is a sensitive scene involving domestic abuse and a 21st-century domestic violence scene involving law enforcement that may be uncomfortable for some readers.

Any mention of medicinal plants in this book does not provide medical or naturopathic advice from the author. Its mention is used for the express purpose of this work of fiction only.

Although travel in 1880 was often dangerous, slow, and uncomfortable, train travel was expanding throughout the East and making its way to the Southwest. Still, much of the traveling needed to be completed by horseback or stagecoach. Our heroine's trip would demand far more time than I have indicated. I have taken the liberty to shorten her travel time to keep the book within a reasonable length.

ISBN: 979-8-218-96116-9
EISBN: 979-8-218-96117-6

This book is dedicated to

My loving and supportive parents
Norman & Marion
Who taught me anything was possible if I had *Faith*

⟅⟆

To a Loving and Strong Woman
'Nana'

⟅⟆

And to
The Sister of My Heart
Pamela K. Young

Acknowledgments

I WISH TO thank the following people for their support in making this novel a reality.

Jean Pennington and Tim and Sharon Zentler for their wonderful friendship, honest and open reviews, and being the best beta readers an author could ask for.

Janice Hurff, SPUR, and Will Rogers Medalion Award-Wining Author for her editorial assistance and friendship.

Betsy Randolph, 2021-2022 President of Women Writing the West and retired Lieutenant with the Department of Safety and Oklahoma Highway Patrol, for her expertise with law enforcement details.

Enedina Rojas Dumas, MSN, RN, Nurse Manager, University of Washington Medical Center, Seattle, Washington, for her help with Hispanic culture and language.

Krista Rolfzen Soukup and Janell Madsen of *Blue Cottage Agency*.

Corey Kretsinger of *MidState Design*.

Kelly Lydick with *The Story Laboratory*.

Tabitha Lahr, Cover Designer, with The Story Laboratory.

The supportive members of Women Writing the West and Western Writers of America whose writings bring the stories of the West alive.

"This is a time that is not a time.
In a place that is not a place
On a day that is not a day,
Between the worlds, and beyond . . ."

—GERRY MAGUIRE THOMPSON

TILL MY LAST DAY

⤳ 1 ⤳

BOSTON, MASSACHUSETTS,

DECEMBER 1880

Rebecca Young Ackerman

I WAS TERRIFIED.

Elliot was home making another of his late-night entrances, as his careless disregard destroyed the portrait of wealth he so carefully meant to depict for Boston's high society.

I gripped the arms of my chair as my fingernails dug deep into the fabric. I tried standing, but every muscle in my body stiffened.

Was this a dream? No! The sound coming from the foyer was real. Motionless, I envisioned the gaping hole the door handle had left in the wall. The last thing I wanted tonight was to face my husband.

Jaw clenched, I managed to push myself up. My feet were frozen in place as I anxiously waited for his usual acerbic outburst to commence. On other nights, I had persuaded him to go upstairs and sleep off the effects of the alcohol. But I sensed tonight I would not succeed, so I silently prayed that God would protect me and my boys from his wrath.

Until the pain registered, I hadn't realized I'd been clenching and unclenching my hands. I held my sweaty palms before my face and stared at the blood coming from the deep nail marks I'd created. I tried taking in several deep breaths to quiet my nerves, but it was futile.

Standing in front of the fireplace, I stared at my reflection in the mirror above the mantel and shook my head from side to side, not recognizing the woman staring back at me. She was a pale figure whose vacant eyes emanated unimaginable anguish. All because of Elliott.

Feeling as if I was falling apart, that familiar sense of panic rose deep within my chest as I rubbed my temples in an attempt to ward off an impending headache. I wanted to flee, but where would I go? With no family left, unless you counted my brother Caleb, who had been missing for five years, I knew running would do me no good.

Elliott knew all the potential hiding places in the house, leaving me no chance of escape. And thanks to his constant controlling ways, I had no close friends who would hide my boys and me. I needed a plan. But right now, more importantly, I needed to survive the night.

Chiming midnight, I visualized the hall clock with its large pendulum swinging deliberately back and forth. Tonight, its tone had a less calming effect than in the past. Instead, it deterred me from any reasonable thoughts. Was its solemn tone a foreshadowing of what lay ahead?

Back straight, head held high, I gathered what courage I had left and walked toward the hall. With only one oil sconce lighting the entry, the house was cloaked in darkness, and the only sounds heard were Elliott's raspy breaths and my taffeta gown swooshing over the hardwood floor as I made my way to the foyer.

Elliot Ackerman, the esteemed editor of Boston's leading newspaper, was drunk once again. Standing unsteady, disheveled, and inebriated in the dim light with shards of glass surrounding his feet, I watched as my husband swayed from one side to the other in an effort to remain upright.

Taking in the scene before me, I looked at the broken glass scattered about our intricately tiled entry. As on recent nights, I'd awaited his return from the club, where, of late, he spent more and more of his time.

Remaining in the shadows, he had not seen me yet, affording me one last minute of safety as he stumbled forward.

Then it started.

His crude bellowing could be heard up and down the three flights of the Brownstone, we called home. "Rebecca! Where the hell are you?"

For the past several months, I'd been living in constant fear of what would happen next. I should have been better prepared for Elliot's outbursts by now since each time he came through that door; he rendered fear and terror into all who dwelled within.

He reminded me of my father, an insufferable man who cared less about his family and more about money and his societal standing. My brother and I always believed he'd sent our mother to an early grave, not once looking back with an ounce of grief.

As my mother had done with my father, I, too, had catered to Elliot's needs, hoping he would change. But he never did.

Warily, I walked into the vestibule, where Elliot stood, breathing heavily. With his nostrils flaring and chest heaving, he leaned forward, splaying his palms on the round table. In its center stood a tall porcelain vase containing a stately display of fresh seasonal flowers. I watched it rock precariously back and forth, undecided if it was to remain upright or give in and topple to the floor.

Taking a chance, I crossed the gleaming black and white checkerboard tiles, ancient mystic symbols for good and evil, and grabbed the vase, hoping it would regain its posturing. My effort was to no avail as Elliot drew back his hand, brandishing his briefcase and heaving it forward. With an intense fevered stare, he yelled, "That takes care of your mother's precious vase."

Cursing silently, I screamed as flowers, porcelain, and water tumbled out of my hands, sending jagged fragments across the floor.

BOSTON, MASSACHUSETTS,

DECEMBER 1880

Rebecca

FOR NOW, WE were separated by the safety of the table, but I feared saying anything. Yet I took a chance, "Elliott, you're drunk." Raising my voice, I added, "You need to go sleep it off!" I wouldn't stoop to his form of vulgarism, so with great effort to remain calm, I pointed in the direction of the stairs.

Before I had a chance to turn away, Elliott leaned over the table and brutally slapped me across my face. My head snapped to the side, sending piercing daggers from my eyes to the base of my skull. Stunned and fighting dizziness, I pressed a hand to my face and the burning hot pain he'd created.

Vision blurry, I watched my husband struggle to remain upright when he slammed both fists on the table, exploding into a diatribe. His face was red with fury and his ear-splitting screams had me flinching.

"You don't talk to me like that, you harlot. Mark my words. I'll take my sons from you, and you'll never see them again."

Anger welled up inside me. I wouldn't let him get away with that. "They're my sons too!" I screamed back.

He may be their father, but I would never let him come between me and my sons. I couldn't believe I had once loved this man. When had he turned into this madman? Icy fingers ran up and down my spine as Elliott sent piercing daggers my way.

With hastened steps, I attempted to flee back into the parlor when his hand reached out, painfully grabbing my upper arm and jerking me around. I tried pulling away as his fingers tightened, but he held me firmly in place. I knew that come morning; if I survived, his grip would leave a reminder of his hatred.

My breath rushed out as he forcefully crushed me to his chest. He was close. Too close. Mere inches from his revulsion, spittle sprayed out of his mouth when he spoke, landing on my face. An image I wouldn't soon forget. Staring into his glazed eyes, which held such iniquity, I knew Elliot wasn't done inflicting his wrath.

My struggles were no use. Elliot was physically stronger than me. Before I knew it, he had one hand around my neck, the other pinching my chin to lift my head to his face. I sensed then he was going to kill me.

With a disgusting sneer, he slowly ran his fingers from my neck down my bare chest, then slipped a sweaty hand into the bodice of my dress and squeezed my breast. Staring into his hardened eyes, I gasped with pain and tried to push him away.

It was as if I was staring into the devil's blackened soul. Choking down the bitter bile rising in the back of my throat, I knew I had to get away. I looked around the room, seeking a way to escape, but Elliot held me too tight. I found myself gagging from the stench of alcohol and the acrid scent of his mistress' cheap perfume.

"Leave me alone! Elliot, you're mad!" The muscles in my free arm quivered with the strain as I continued to push back against his chest. Twisting, I struggled against his grip and screamed, "Elliot, you're hurting me! Let. Me. Go!" In one of Elliot's weak moments, I could finally swipe his hand away and shove hard against his chest.

Laughing wickedly, he stumbled backward and wiped his wrinkled sleeve across his mouth. Free from his grasp, I reached up and felt a wet sensation trickle down my cheek. The sticky warmth was my blood. Damn him!

Taking my hand away, I leaned forward and wiped the blood from my fingertips onto his jacket, a small act but an act befitting revenge on his once impeccable attire. Yet, it was a move I feared I would soon regret.

Lunging forward, Elliot grabbed hold of my upper arms. Digging his fingers deep into my skin, he violently shook me and yelled, "It's my husbandly right! You're mine to do with as I wish!"

Fighting back a primal scream, I closed my eyes and prayed, God, please let me live. "Let go of me," I yelled with all the fury I could rally, beating my fists against his chest.

Where is everyone? Why won't someone help me? With a burst of energy, I managed to twist and pull back from his grasp. Unfortunately, I didn't move fast enough as his hand swung out with another vicious blow to the side of my head.

Falling back in a billow of satin, I hit the newel post of the banister mid-back, causing shooting pains to run simultaneously down both arms. Slowly, I slid to the floor, where shards of porcelain from the shattered vase pierced the palms of my hands. Inhaling sharply, I held them to my chest, smearing blood down the bodice of my gown.

Dismissing the stabbing pain, I didn't have time to worry about my injuries since Elliot was making another move. Mercifully for me, he caught his left foot on one of the table legs as he rushed forward, sending him plunging to the floor. It gave me just enough time to find my footing.

But, in my haste, while hurrying toward the tread of the staircase landing, I tripped on the voluminous layers of my underskirts.

Get up, Rebecca! He's right behind you. I recognized that voice. But it couldn't be.

I fell forward onto the first step and landed on the rough woolen carpet. But before I could stand up, Elliot was able to stretch out his hand and grip the hem of my gown in his burly fingers. With a firm yank, he caused my steps to falter. My lungs burned as I once again struggled to be free.

Reaching back with my left hand, I held determinedly to the railing with my right and pulled with all the strength I had left. With the ripping sound of freedom, I wrenched myself from Elliot's deadly grasp, preventing me from falling back into the hands of a monster. Running up the steps as fast as my shaky legs would carry me, I didn't dare look back. I had to get to my room before Elliot caught up with me.

3

BOSTON, MASSACHUSETTS,

DECEMBER 1880

Rebecca

SWEAT RAN BETWEEN my breasts as I stumbled into the safety of my bedchamber. My hands shook as I slammed the door shut behind me, afraid I wouldn't be able to secure the heavy brass latch. Successful after several attempts, I leaned back against the cold wood, trying to catch my breath.

What just happened?

Beneath my feet, the floor vibrated. Elliot was getting closer. My eyes darted from side to side as I searched the room for a safe hiding place. It was either in my closet or out the second-story window, both of which would mean certain death. I was at a loss for what to do. But I wasn't ready to give up.

Not now! Not ever!

In my weakened state, I somehow managed to drag my dresser the short distance across the waxed floor, leaving deep gouges in the shining parquet, and secure it in front of the massive door. I prayed it would be heavy enough to keep Elliot out.

Rummaging through my 'what-not' drawer, I pulled out the Derringer my mother had given me years ago. Whatever possessed her then, I was ever so grateful now. I had no intention of killing my boys' father, but I would if it meant saving Porter and Daniel.

Exhausted and in pain, I dropped my head forward over my crossed forearms on the smooth dresser's top, unable to stop the salty tears from burning into the bloodied lacerations on my cheek.

～◦≶◦～

He's here!

Elliot furiously began pounding on my door, screaming loud enough to wake the devil himself. "Rebecca! Open this damn door! Now!"

Through the thick wood that separated us, I could hear his heavy panting and imagined his sizable body shaking with fury.

"I'm not done with you. You hear me!" he screeched, rattling the handle and continuing to pound his fists on the door.

I trembled as I watched the brass door knob move up and down. I had to think fast. "Get away from me!" I yelled.

"Let me in!" His pounding became louder and fiercer.

"Noooo!" I screamed. Hugging my arms to my chest, I still could not fathom what had set Elliot off tonight. At this point, I didn't care. I had done nothing to deserve this. My only concern was Elliot possibly going to our son's room and using them as pawns to get me to open the door. And it would work. But I couldn't allow it.

Leaving my room now would only allow Elliot, in his drunken state, the opportunity to kill me and leave my boys to his evil devices. I would have to trust Pearl to see to their safety. Maybe she already has, and that's why she didn't come to my aid. I could no longer put my boys through this. They might be young, but they had to know what was happening between their father and me.

Elliot left me no choice. I had to take them far away from here to a place where he'd never find us. But where? What I needed was to find my brother Caleb. Looking heavenward, I prayed, Dear God, show me a way out of here.

"Elliot. Get away from the door. You're drunk, and I'm not letting you in."

"Damn you, Rebecca! You'll pay for this!" He was probably right, but I was relieved when silence finally ensued. He must have conceded defeat from fatigue or intoxication. Either way, when I heard his retreating footsteps down the hall, I let out a long sigh of relief. Still, I was not about to let my guard down and open the door to check on his whereabouts.

Believing I was somewhat secure, I left the safety of the dresser and crossed to the far side of my room, where I commenced pacing back and forth between my bed and the wall. A brutal wind raged outside, causing the shutters to rattle violently against the house.

Pausing before the window, I pulled back the delicate lace curtains and pressed my bloodied cheek to the frosty pane. Peering down, I could barely make out the leafless trees in the courtyard bending to the storm's fury. My eyes followed one puffy snowflake as it whipped in circles, desperately trying to cling to the winter landscape. The scene below confirmed my fear. This path to freedom was out of the question.

A chill ran through my body as I stepped back from the cold seeping through the window casement. Without the light from the fire, the room was in total darkness. In my mind, a plan began to form. I had to get myself and my sons safely away from their father's volatile hostility. But first, I needed sleep before I made any rash decisions.

Giving into fatigue, I slowly slid down the wall to the floor and hugged my knees close to my chest. Come morning, I would set my plan in motion. In the meantime, my mind scrambled for answers as exhaustion won out, and I leaned my head against the side of the mattress. Inhaling the scent of Pearl's freshly washed linens brought me a moment of comfort.

Now wasn't the time to belittle myself. But I couldn't help it. I told myself I should have recognized the changes in Elliot's behavior. The past few months flashed through my mind, and I remembered when Elliot would come home irritably distant with bloodshot eyes surrounded by dark circles. At first, I thought he was having issues at work. But, of course, it was unacceptable for a husband to discuss work with his wife.

More likely than not, I didn't want to think the worst. I only thought if I loved him enough or I made a better home for him, he'd change back to the man I once cared for. But nothing I did or said changed his actions. His moods became more extreme, and his demeanor slowly morphed into a man I no longer recognized, trusted, or loved.

I needed a way out of this disastrous marriage.

4

BOSTON, MASSACHUSETTS,

DECEMBER 1880

Rebecca

WHEN I MARRIED Elliot, he'd received a large sum of money from my dowry. How damn ironic that he used that money to fund his illicit affairs. At the time, I chose to turn a blind eye to the whispering of the society ladies, or "Old Biddies," as I preferred to call them.

Oh, how they could gossip. I heard stories that most of the elite men in Boston had their so-called "outside activities." After all, my father had, and my mother never complained. Soon, I started putting the pieces together and understood why she never said anything. She had feared for her life. And rightfully so.

As a woman of the nineteenth century, I had no rights. My husband had legally taken over all that I owned. Although allowed, divorce was frowned upon and would be expensive. And to expose our dirty laundry in public was something I didn't want my boys to witness.

What little money Elliot gave me as an allowance, I divided for everyday expenses and hid the rest in my travel trunk that I had stored in the attic. Little did I know that that money would come in handy someday.

I had been Elliot's dutiful wife as I tried to save our marriage. I remember my father telling me that keeping her husband's home, raising our sons, and submitting to his conjugal rights was a woman's duty once married.

I no longer cared. I couldn't break through Elliot's dark moods. He had all the remaining household members on constant edge. They feared my husband, and I knew they whispered behind my back. The only solace in the house was the hours Elliot was away at work.

So far, I had been able to protect my sons, but I couldn't keep it up forever. We deserved a better life, a safer life. Oh, how I wished my brother Caleb were here.

"Becca, my dear," came the familiar voice I longed to hear again.

"Mother?" Looking heavenward, I asked, "Is it really you?"

"Yes, dear, it's me. Now listen. You must get the boys, yourself, and Pearl as far away from here as possible. Take the money you've hidden away, and remember you are the only one who can access what's in my safekeeping box at the bank as emergency funds."

Am I losing my mind? I couldn't believe I was speaking with my deceased mother. Shaking my head from side to side to clear the fogginess, I thought the two hits I sustained from Elliot must have addled my brain.

"Now listen to me. You need to leave this place as soon as possible. Today, if you can manage it. You and my grandsons cannot spend another night in this house with that madman."

What was I thinking? Hearing my mother was a comfort, so I continued, "Momma, what about the house? You loved this house."

"It's just brick and mortar. It no longer holds any sentimental value to me. You and my grandchildren mean more than this old house."

"You're right, of course. But I must figure out how to escape without Elliot finding out."

"Ask Pearl to help you. You can trust her."

I noted the catch in her voice as she added, *"Pearl helped me with your father many times."*

"I remember." If this really was my mother, I had to ask if she knew where Caleb was. Rushing out, I asked, "Momma, where is Caleb?"

She was gone. She'd left me with the one question I hoped she could answer. Did she know where Caleb was? Was he alive or, heaven forbid, dead? I couldn't think that way. He had to be alive. I needed him.

It seemed like an eternity since Elliot last pounded on my door. When in reality, it had only been an hour. Looking around my room, I realized I must have dozed off. My mother's words lingered in the back of my mind as I smiled for the first time in months, giving me renewed hope.

"I will get us out of here if it's the last thing I do."

❧

Pearl O' Callaghan

All the loud banging and yelling above stairs had me quickly donning my wrap and making my way up to Porter and Daniel's room. Rushing up the back servant's steps, I feared for Mrs. Ackerman's life, but I couldn't let that madman take our boys. They, too, had probably heard their parents fighting and were scared.

I needed to protect them at all costs. I knew Mrs. Ackerman would want me to put them first. I had been with Mrs. Ackerman since the day she married. I never cared for her husband, and I'm sure he knew what I thought of him. That's why I went out of my way to avoid contact.

Lately, when I was in his presence, the hairs on the back of my Irish neck stood up. He was a man I would never trust. And he certainly had proved himself tonight. Guardedly, I made my way up the steep, narrow stairway. Behind the stairwell, I heard the thundering footfalls of Mr. Ackerman as his feet pounded on the carpeted stairs off the main foyer.

Rushing into the boy's room, I closed the door quietly and locked it behind me. Both boys were huddled together in one bed, arms wrapped protectively around each other. I wanted to cry as I gazed at two pairs of frightened eyes staring back at me. Their fear was evident as tears streamed down their pale faces.

Porter looked up as he embraced his younger brother Daniel and asked, "Miss Pearl, what's happening?"

Intentionally ignoring his question, I instructed, "Boys, you need to get up. I'm taking you to my room." Pulling back the covers, I added, "Please hurry." Once out of bed, I gathered their blankets and pillows, pulling them behind me as we rushed out the door. Their little feet barely kept up with my rushed steps as we descended the back stairs.

Safely inside my room, I locked the door and then settled the boys in my bed. After this, I moved my heavy dresser in front of the door, praying it would keep their father out if he came looking for them. Without thought, I changed into a day dress in case we needed to flee the house quickly.

I climbed into bed next to the boys and felt the mattress give beneath us. Drawing Porter and Daniel into my arms, I ran a hand over their downy heads. I could feel their tiny hearts beating like a hummingbird against my chest. I could only pray that Mrs. Ackerman survived the night. If not. Well, I wouldn't think of that now.

I must have dozed off with one ear, carefully listening for Mr. Ackerman's thundering footsteps. Grateful, they never came. After terrorizing their mother, he must not have gone to his boy's room. He most certainly would have taken them if he had.

⁓⚬⚬⁓

Morning came, and I instructed the boys to stay in my room until I returned with their breakfast. I couldn't take the chance of bringing them upstairs if their father was still in the house. I needed to make sure Mr. Ackerman had left for the day.

Making my way up the back stairs, I found his door surprisingly ajar. Hesitating, I took a deep breath, lightly tapped, and waited. Thank heavens he didn't respond. Cautiously, I opened the door wider when my nostrils were assaulted with the smell of stale liquor, spent cigars, and cheap perfume.

The linens lay rumpled across the bed, and his night clothes were tangled in a ball on the floor. Ignoring them, I called out, "Mr. Ackerman. Sir, it's Pearl." I half expected to find him on the floor in a drunken stupor. With no response, I ventured further into the room. Propriety be damned, I searched his inner rooms and water closet. Failing to locate him, I heaved a sigh of relief and made my way to Mrs. Ackerman's room.

BOSTON, MASSACHUSETTS,

DECEMBER 1880

Rebecca

I ACHED ALL over, and stretching my arms above my head in an effort to ease the pain was pointless. Turning my head to the side, I knew this would be the last morning I would look out this window. I wouldn't miss it. It was no longer my home.

The storm had calmed, and beyond the curtain, I could see winter's pinks and purples of dawn breaking over the rows of townhouses in the city. I closed my eyes, thinking back a few short hours, and wondered how such a lovely morning could arise from such a dark and terrifying night.

It was wonderful to be wrapped in a cocoon of safety as I slid deeper under the warmth of my down duvet. I didn't want to get up, but I had so much to do in order to prepare for our journey of unknowns that lay ahead of us later today. Although my spirit was shattered, time was of the essence. We had to be out of the house before Elliot returned.

Throwing back the covers, I walked barefoot to the window for one last look. Placing both palms on the frosty pane, I looked down at the courtyard where Porter and Daniel had played just yesterday morning in the dusting of snow. These were happy memories for the three of us. Memories Elliot could never take away.

Deep in thought, I continued staring at the landscape. Once a contented wife and mother, Elliot's recent constant defaming and belittling remarks robbed me of my self-confidence. I had always tried to find happiness and the good in people. But he had stolen that spark of light within my heart and replaced all good in my world with apprehension, disquiet, and torment.

I feared I would never find myself again. Well, after speaking with my mother last night, no more. Today was a new day, and I was about to embark on a journey of taking my life back. Crossing the room, I stood before the mirror hanging on the wall. Absent the dresser, it allowed me to lean in close enough to see the damage Elliot had inflicted.

I wanted to scream. Staring back at me was the face of a battered and tormented woman.

Inhaling a jagged breath, only hoping last night had been a terrible dream, I carefully touched my fingers to the dried blood under my left eye. But my appearance told me otherwise. "Elliot, you'll never do this to me again! No man will!"

I jumped at the sound of a light knock on my door. Turning away from my reflection, I asked cautiously, "Who is it?"

"It's Pearl, Mrs. Ackerman."

"Just a moment, please." Brushing back my tousled hair, I ran my hands down the front of my dress I'd dared not remove last night. Aching muscles protesting, I gingerly moved to the dresser, pushing it slightly to one side. I made enough room to open the door just a crack. I wouldn't put it past Elliot to use Pearl to gain entry.

Reaching around the dresser, I opened the door, ready to close it if Elliot stood there. Peering at Pearl's face etched with concern, I asked warily, "What do you need, Pearl?"

Pearl replied in her light Irish brogue, "I came to check on you, Mrs. Ackerman. I heard the commotion last night and wanted to ensure you're alright."

Softening my tone, I responded, "I'm fine, Pearl. I appreciate your concern." Hesitating, I asked, "Is Mr. Ackerman still at home?"

"No, Ma'am. I believe he left early this morning without having breakfast." Pointing down the hall, Pearl added, "Before I came here, I checked his room to ensure he was gone."

Grateful my husband had left, I took a deep breath. But a sense of panic set in when I asked, "Pearl, where are the boys?"

Reassuringly, she answered, "They're fine, Ma'am. When I heard you and the Mr. arguing last evening, I brought them to my room. When I left to come here, I told them to stay in my room until I returned. They should still be there awaiting their breakfast."

"Thank God," I sighed, placing a calming hand over my heart. He had blessed me when he brought Pearl into my life many years ago. I knew she loved Porter and Daniel as if they were her own and would do anything to keep them safe from their father.

"Thank you, Pearl. You don't know how much I appreciate you taking such good care of them."

"Mrs. Ackerman, I love those boys and would do anything for them and you, especially when it comes to keeping them safe."

I noted her moment of hesitation before she continued. With her head lowered, she fingered her dress, "I'm sorry, Ma'am. It's not proper. I did not mean to be so forward with my thoughts."

"Nonsense, Pearl. You can speak freely with me. I'm so grateful you kept them safe." In another moment of panic, I rushed out, "Please tell me their father didn't get to them last night."

"No, Ma'am. But they won't speak to me. I believe they heard you and their father arguing and are still frightened."

The past twenty-four hours had us both on edge when Pearl added, "Mrs. Ackerman. I've worked for your family for a long time. I hope you trust that I will never betray you."

Leaning against the dresser, I soaked in Pearl's words and weighed my choices, which at this point were growing slim. With more effort than it took last night, I pushed the dresser to the side, allowing Pearl to enter my room.

Upon seeing my battered face, Pearl gasped and rushed to my side. I could tell she wanted to take me in her arms but hesitated. Instead, cursing under her breath in Gaelic, she took the floral porcelain pitcher and poured the day-old water into the matching basin. Dipping the edge of a cloth into the water, she gently wiped the dried blood on my cheeks. I winced.

"I'm sorry, Ma'am," withdrawing the cloth. Without hesitating, Pearl asked, "Did Mr. Ackerman do this to you?"

I nodded and turned away when I heard her swear out loud, "That despicable man!"

I agreed. But never had I heard Pearl use such language in my presence. Somehow, I knew deep down lay an Irish lass with more fire in her soul who would fight to the bitter end to protect us.

I don't know what possessed me to ask, "Pearl, do you believe in ghosts?"

"Of course I do! You know, we Irish never shun a ghost or ghostly tale. But why do you ask?"

In desperation, I looked into her eyes while taking her hands in mine. "Pearl, you must believe me when I tell you this. I, ah, it's hard to explain, but Momma spoke with me last night."

Was that a skeptical look on her face? Maybe I'd made a big mistake in telling her. Surely, with her Celtic heritage, one would think she believed in visits from the spirits. Or had she just said she did to appease me? I took another chance and continued. "She told me I needed to take the boys and get away from Elliot." Without stopping, I added, "She said I could trust you to help us."

"Your mother was a special lady who loved you beyond measure. Of course, I will help you and the boys in any way I can."

"I'm glad you believe me, Pearl. I was doubtful at first. But I heard Momma's voice as clearly as she was standing here with us now. You know I have to take the boys and leave here." I squeezed her hands tightly between mine and asked, "Will you help us?"

"I will do whatever is necessary, Mrs. Ackerman."

Drawing Pearl into my arms, it felt good to hold on to someone who sincerely cared about us. My mood was already improving when I asked, "What do I need to do first."

"Well, I need to get you and the boys fed. While I feed the boys, why don't you soak in a long hot bath and change into fresh clothes."

She turned toward the door when she added, "I'll tell them their mother is fine. While we pack, I'll send them to Mrs. Chatsworth to play with her boys for the day. She loves Porter and Daniel and is always willing to help. While they're gone, we'll start making plans."

"A hot bath sounds wonderful." I could use it to soothe away the physical pain. But it would take so much more for the emotional wounds to heal.

Pearl had just reached the door when I added, "Pearl."

"Yes, Ma'am," turning around, she answered softly.

"Thank you."

"Don't think anything of it, my dear." With a shooing motion, she added, "Now, go take that hot bath and come down when you're ready.

Without Pearl, I couldn't imagine how I would have survived over the years. She had been more than our housekeeper. She'd been my confidant, teacher, and shoulder to cry on. She'd been a mother to me once mine had passed and a strong Irish woman to reckon with if anyone tried any shenanigans in the house.

Shortly after losing her children to Scarlet Fever, she became widowed and never remarried. She wasn't prone to discuss that part of her life, and only I knew about it because Pearl had told me in confidence several years back. That's why I believe she took such care with Porter and Daniel, and I couldn't be more grateful.

6

BOSTON, MASSACHUSETTS, DECEMBER 1880

Pearl O' Callaghan

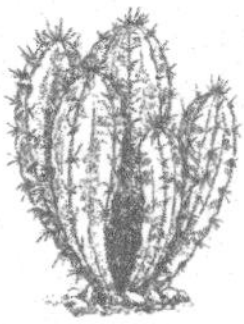

WHILE I WAS preparing breakfast for the boys, the bell on the front door rang. "Whoever it is can wait." Removing the pan of biscuits from the oven, I set them on the counter to cool and instructed Porter and Daniel to behave while I was gone.

Removing my apron, I placed it on the back of an empty chair and walked into the foyer as the door chime rang again. Muttering all the way, "I'm coming, I'm coming. What's your hurry?" Pushing in the loose pins to secure my hair, I ran my hands down the front of my starched black uniform, ensuring I was presentable. I never knew who would be standing on the other side of the door, and I had to remain presentable.

Reaching for the handle, I took a deep breath and hesitated, ready to do battle, just in case Mr. Ackerman had forgotten his key. Sighing with relief, I greeted the postman and signed for a special delivery letter addressed to one Miss Rebecca Young. Taking a coin from my pocket, I placed it in the boy's hand and closed the door without further conversation. "Someone doesn't know Rebecca is married."

I noted the return address was a town I'd never heard of, Yuma, Arizona Territory. "Now, who in the name of heavens does Mrs. Ackerman know in Arizona, of all places? Well, it's none of my business."

Hearing a commotion coming from the kitchen, I placed the envelope in my pocket and rushed down the hall, where I found Porter and Daniel arguing over a cookie. "Now, boys, I thought I told you two to stay seated at the table?" Looking contrite, I couldn't be mad at these two sweet boys I'd helped raise since infancy.

Gazing over the rim of my glasses, "You two shouldn't be eatin' cookies for breakfast. Those are for later. Now behave yourselves, or neither of you will get your favorite pancakes this mornin'. Understand?"

Wide-eyed, both boys stared back at me, smiling, knowing I would never deny them their favorite breakfast.

⤛⧫⤜

Leaving the dishes for later, I hurried the boys to their room to pack what they would need to spend the day at Mrs. Chatsworth's. Seeing their mother coming down the steps, they ran to her with open arms. She had concealed the bruising about her face well. She never needed to add to her beauty by using such frivolous powders. But this was the one time this expenditure paid off in covering up what their father's brutality had inflicted.

I watched Rebecca engulf her boys in a tender embrace as they excitedly told her about their plans for the day. I couldn't help but think about what their father would do to them if their mother weren't here to defend them. It was time the three of them left Boston for good.

"Pearl, I'll take the boys upstairs to pack for the day. You go back to the kitchen, and I'll be down shortly. In the meantime, I'll have

Amelia and Vernon take them to Mrs. Chatsworth. I presume you've had the carriage brought around?"

"Yes, Mrs. Ackerman," I replied, nodding my head. "It will be ready when the boys are."

◦◦◦

"I've made a pot of tea for you, Mrs. Ackerman. Let it steep a bit longer before pouring." Motioning toward a chair, Pearl added, "Why don't you have a seat, and I'll prepare your favorite dropped eggs on toast."

"Pearl, I haven't much of an appetite this morning. But thank you." Slowly lowering myself into the chair, I discovered my body ached in places I had no idea a person could hurt.

"Nonsense, Mrs. Ackerman. You must keep your strength up for those boys and the journey ahead."

Acquiescing, I tried eating. Truly, I was famished. After taking a few bites, I savored Pearl's simple fare.

Digging into her pocket, Pearl held out a tattered envelope. "Before I forget, the postman delivered this this morning. It looks to be a telegram. I noticed it comes from someplace in Arizona Territory."

Hands shaking, I stared at the brown, dirt-stained envelope for several minutes, not recognizing the script. Turning it over, I feared it conveyed news I dreaded hearing. Was it about Caleb? Was he dead? I couldn't handle such news right now. Caleb had to be alive. I needed him now more than ever. It had been hard enough these past five years, not knowing where he was.

I started easing my finger under the seal, then paused. Could my heart take more bad news?

Pearl must have recognized my unease. "Mrs. Ackerman." I looked up, not seeing her face. "Are you alright?" Holding out her hand, "Ma'am, your face has gone ghostly pale. Would you like me to open it for you?"

How could Pearl tell my face was pale behind all the bruising? "No. No, it's quite all right, Pearl. I'll open it." Palms sweating, I picked up the silver knife beside my plate and inserted it under the seal. Hesitating once again, I broke the thin wax closure and sent a silent prayer heavenward, hoping the message wouldn't break my heart.

Inside was a small faded sheet of yellowed paper folded into fours. Slowly unfolding the telegram as if to delay the news, it read,

12 Dec
Ms. R Young.
Come. Brother gravely wounded.
E Sweeney Yuma, AT.

Dear God! With my heart painfully pounding in my chest, I reread the missive several more times. Holding it out to Pearl, I tasted the salty tears cascading down my face. Finally able to move, I pushed my plate to the center of the table and stiffly stood beside Pearl, holding my breath as she read the letter.

My vision blurred, and I could no longer ignore the tears. Wiping my eyes unladylike with the sleeve of my dress, I feared I was too late, and my brother had died since the letter had been written.

Taking her hands in mine and squeezing them tightly, I said, "Pearl, I have to go to him."

"Of course you do," Pearl answered, pulling me into her comforting embrace.

"I've thought of Caleb daily since he left so abruptly five years ago. And I prayed nightly he would write to me, but he never did. I hope this is my chance to have him back in my life." Taking the letter from Pearl, I lowered my head as more tears flowed. "I didn't think it would be this way. I can't lose him again, Pearl."

Leaving the warmth of her embrace, I whispered, "I have to go. But first, I have to send Emily Sweeney a letter in today's post. Will you have Vernon take care of it for me?

"Wait! Mrs. Ackerman, I don't think sending a letter is a good idea. You don't want to leave any clues so Mr. Ackerman can track you down. You should wait until you have left Boston far behind."

"You're right. I didn't think of that. Thank you." Looking at Pearl's reassuring features, I asked, "Will you help me and the boys leave?"

"Of course, Mrs. Ackerman."

Pearl's face took on a pensive expression while worrying the hem of her apron through her calloused fingers. "What is it, Pearl? What are you thinking?"

Pointing to the envelope, she said, "Do you realize this letter is just what you need to get you and the boys away from here." Taking out a delicately embroidered handkerchief from the pocket of her starched apron, she began wiping the tears from my face. "Now. Enough crying. You have much to do to get ready. You're going to this Arizona Territory," she said, pointing to the letter I held in my hand.

Picking up the dishes from the table, Pearl instructed me to lay out clothes for myself and the boys. "While you're packing, I'll have Vernon take me to the train station to purchase your tickets. Mr. Ackerman won't suspect a thing.

"But I don't have any money. At least not now. Not until Vernon brings my trunks down from the attic.

"Don't worry about that. I've enough to purchase three tickets. You can wire me the money when you're safe in Arizona. Now hurry!"

"Thank you, Pearl. I love you."

⤨ 7 ⤩

Rebecca

I WAS ALONE in my room, but I still didn't feel safe. I kept thinking Elliot would come barging in and finish what he had started last night. I wouldn't cry. I had no more tears to shed as I wrapped my arms tightly around my waist and leaned my head back against the door, reliving the nightmare of his attack.

I only hoped the letter I firmly clutched in my hands was my saving grace. Maybe God was permitting me to free myself from Elliot's talons. Looking around the room, it dawned on me that this house had become my prison. I should have seen what he had done to me over the past year. But fear had made me blind to what was going on around me.

Elliot had me report my every move to him. I was allowed to go out only if Vernon or Pearl accompanied me. I had no friends. No one came to visit. He gave me a pittance of an allowance, which I only spent on my boys.

I should have known people were afraid of him. When I tried speaking, he cut off my attempts at conversation. My opinions mattered not.

He'd become a controlling husband who allowed me little to no freedom. His constant accusations that I'd lied and cheated on him held
no evidence. I'd never lied to my husband or looked at another man
the way I'd looked at him when we'd first married.

After last night's display of abuse, I suddenly knew why. He was
exerting his power and control over me. I'd been so stupid, hoping
my love could change who he'd become. I'd conformed to his will
and lost all sense of my self-worth.

Well, I'd almost been dead wrong.

Straightening up, I pushed away from the door, knowing I would
no longer be his submitting wife. As my mother had told me repeatedly,
"You're a strong woman, Rebecca, and a survivor."

I was ready to take that step in leaving Elliot.

So be it if I escaped with only the clothes on my back. Elliot
wouldn't get our sons! Rushing about the room, I pulled simple day
dresses from the armoire and undergarments from my dresser. Gazing
at the gorgeous gowns I'd once cherished in the early years of our
marriage, I would gladly leave them all behind. I doubted I would
need them in a frontier town like Yuma.

Closing the doors to the closet, I was shutting out my past. I had to
believe a better life awaited me and my sons in the Arizona Territory.
A knock sounded at the door as I lay my folded garments on the bed.
"Who is it?" I asked.

"It's Vernon, Ma'am. I've brought your trunks down from the attic."

Allowing him entry, Vernon placed two large trunks at the foot of
my bed. I was taking one for myself and one for the boys. Looking at his
aging eyes and graying hair, it was clear to me how much I would miss
this dear man. Over the years, he'd been so faithful to the boys and me.

"Mrs. Ackerman. May I say something, please?"

"Of course, Vernon."

"Yes, Ma'am. Are you and the boys going to be safe traveling
alone? Because I could always accompany you until you reach your
destination. I don't want anything to happen to you after the way Mr.
Ackerman treated you."

"Vernon. It's alright. We all know what Mr. Ackerman has become. It's why I'm leaving." I placed my hand on his forearm and added, "I promise we'll be safe traveling alone. I won't tell you where we're going because I don't want to put you or anyone else in harm's way. What I will say is I'm going to miss you so much. When I arrive at my destination, and I feel it's safe to do so, I'll send word to you."

"Thank you, Ma'am. The misses, and I would appreciate it." Brushing attic dust from his impeccable service coat, Vernon added, "I must tell you we will leave our employ here as soon as you are gone. I can't stay if you and the boys are gone. I'm sure you understand."

I only nodded my reply as he exited my room. Leaving Vernon and his wife behind was going to be hard. I only wish I could take them with me.

Securing the lock on my bedroom door, I opened the trunk to check the concealed pocket hidden beneath its bottom lining. I didn't think my house staff would steal from me, yet on the other hand, I wouldn't put it past Elliot. So, I needed to ensure that the cash I'd secretly saved over the past ten years was still there.

Carefully counting the money, I was reassured that it was all there and I could immediately pay Pearl when she returned. Looking at the clock on my dresser, I saw it was already ten-thirty, and I'd just finished packing when Pearl came home with our tickets.

"Mrs. Ackerman," Pearl spoke from the doorway. "I have your tickets. The train leaves in two hours. Will you be ready by then?"

So soon. I was speechless. Looking about the room I would never see again, I turned to Pearl and answered stoically, "Yes. Please have one of the house boys help Vernon bring our trunks downstairs."

"Yes, Ma'am. I'm going to make lunch before you leave and pack a basket for you to take on the train. I'm sure it will be a long first day, and the boys will be hungry. By the way, I sent a note to Mrs. Chatsworth earlier to ask her to feed the boys before we pick them up. I didn't tell her what your plans were. Only that we would both be busy until well after noon."

"You think of everything, Pearl. What am I going to do without you?" Suddenly, a thought came to me. Smiling, I had her attention. "Pearl."

"Yes, Ma'am."

I reached for her hands and asked, "Pearl, please come with us. I'm sorry you don't have any family here, and I surmise you won't stay and work for my husband." I silently prayed she would say yes. She would be such a comfort for the boys and me.

8

Rebecca

I'D TRIED PUTTING on a stoic front, but to tell you the truth, I was afraid to travel alone, knowing Elliot would probably come searching for us. If that was the case, I could send Pearl off hiding with the boys and lead Elliot on a trail following only me.

Patting the top of my hands, "Ma'am, you know I can't come with you. You and the boys will be fine. You're a courageous woman. Don't worry about me. I'll find other work here in Boston.

"Pearl. Please think about it." Hesitating, I added, "But I'll understand if you don't want to come with us." Placing my arms around her, I could feel her soft sob on my shoulder. I tried holding back my tears and was almost successful. Pulling away, Pearl turned and headed for the stairs before I could see her watery, red eyes.

After lunch, I was at least successful in convincing Pearl to change her uniform into a day dress to accompany us to the station. Once settled inside the hansom cab, I heard the crack of a whip and horses whinnying. Lurching forward, I grabbed onto the seat cushion, steadying myself as the emotional pain of the past few months lanced through my heart. I had to look back one last time. My eyes held firm to the brick-and-mortar Brownstone as it faded into the setting winter sun. I had no regrets about leaving. Using a hired cab meant the staff, except Pearl and Vernon, didn't know my plans. Doing so hopefully kept them safe from my husband.

Pearl sat across from me as we nervously watched out the cab's frosty windows for any signs of Elliot. Our first stop was to pick up the boys. Eagerly, they climbed into the carriage, unaware of where we were going. Once at the station, I would explain we were going on an adventure to see family out West. The less they knew now, the better it would be in the long run.

The cab rocked back and forth over the uneven, brick road when Porter caught my attention and asked, "Momma."

"Yes, dear." Looking down, I read his hesitation.

"Is Father going to be coming with us?" I wasn't surprised by his question, but the way he asked showed me his underlying fear.

"No, dear," I answered, smiling and running my hand gently over his crimson curls. "This is our special trip." One, I'm sure none of us would soon forget.

⌒⚬⌒

Arriving at the station with just minutes to spare, Vernon ensured our trunks were loaded into the correct baggage car. At the same time, the conductor helped the boys climb the steps to our private compartment. In the cold winter air, white, puffy clouds escaped past my lips as I mumbled a silent prayer, *God, please let us get away.*

Despite wearing my heavy woolen coat, I was chilled to the bone in the frigid December air. And it only became colder the longer Pearl, and I stood side by side on the platform. Pulling my collar higher, I tightened my thin scarf around my neck. I couldn't stop shaking.

Looking up into the train, I saw tears running down Porter and Daniel's cheeks while I hugged Pearl one last time. I knew we would never see each other again, and my heart broke into a thousand pieces. I didn't want to let her go.

Behind us, at the corner of the station, a loud commotion caught our attention. Stunned, Pearl and I saw a familiar man pushing through the crowd, knocking people over and heading our way.

"Oh, dear God," I screamed loud enough for Pearl to hear me above the steaming clamor of the train's engines. Grabbing her arm, I pulled her toward me. "It's Elliot. How did he know to come here looking for us?"

"Goooo!" Pearl yelled, pushing me toward the train. "Vernon and I will hold him off."

Pearl tried pulling her hands from my determined grasp, but I was steadfast in my grip. I pulled her forward with a firm tug, knowing Elliot would kill her if he knew she'd helped me escape.

Suddenly, the train started moving forward, and we found ourselves running away from Elliot. Our pace was just enough to throw us both off-balance. Panic set in, and I tried screaming for help, but not a word passed my cold lips.

I couldn't have Pearl slipping away under the massive steel wheels of the locomotive. So, I grabbed the handle to the stairs and gave Pearl's arm a firm yank. Thank heavens the conductor saw me struggling. Desperate, he grabbed hold of Pearl's free hand. Between the two of us, we pulled her up onto the platform just as the train picked up speed.

All three of us landed hard on the metal staircase with a thud. My dress was over my knees, and I shook so fiercely I couldn't breathe. Sitting there dazed, Pearl and I clung to each other as the landscape raced by. We had been saved from the violent vortex of wind that would have certainly sucked us both off and under our metal steed.

Had Elliot seen us? I prayed he hadn't. But, if he'd seen Vernon or Pearl, he would surmise the boys and I were on the train.

Now what?

9

TRAIN LEAVING BOSTON

Rebecca

WE ALMOST DIED.

Both Pearl and I were still shaking. With the help of the conductor, we made our way safely inside the car. From a gust of wind, the heavy door slammed behind us with a whoosh. Exhausted, Pearl collapsed in the nearest chair while I remained frozen inside the door. I tried wrapping my brain around what had just happened, but it was all unreal.

Finally, my feet moved, and I made my way over to Pearl. Kneeling in front of her, the vacant stare in her eyes told me she was just as stunned as I was. Taking her trembling hands in mine, I asked, "Pearl. Can you hear me?"

It took several moments before she replied, "Yes."

It wasn't like Pearl to speak so little. I turned to the conductor and asked if he could hurry and bring us a pot of tea. I was grateful when he nodded and went to do my bidding. I turned my attention back to my dear friend. "Pearl, we're safe. Are you going to be alright?"

Earlier that day, she told me she didn't want to come with us, and right now, I wanted to hear her scolding me in her Irish brogue. Her sitting there, unmoving as a cold granite statue, scared me. I feared she would never forgive me for pulling her onto the train. But what was I to do at that moment? I couldn't let her die at the hands of Elliot or the train's massive wheels.

Patting my hands, she finally spoke. "I'll be alright. Just give me a moment to comprehend what just happened." Looking about the room as if searching for something, she asked, "Are the boys alright?" Furrowing her brow, she leaned close and continued, "Did they see what happened?"

Upon hearing us talk, Porter and Daniel turned our way. It was obvious by their happy faces the boys were oblivious to our recent calamity. "I don't think they saw anything," I told Pearl.

"That's good. They have no idea what lies ahead, and I don't want them worrying unnecessarily."

The conductor, followed by a porter carrying a tray with tea cups and a steaming pot, entered the car. "Ladies, have you recovered from your ordeal?" he asked while directing the porter to place the tray next to Pearl.

"Yes," I replied. "Thank you for your assistance earlier. I believe we are in your debt for," lowering my voice to a whisper, I finished, "Saving our lives."

He whispered back, "I'm just glad I was there to help. Please tell your porter if you need anything else from me."

With that, he and the porter bowed and exited the car. Relaxing, I scanned the train's interior, appreciating that Pearl had wasted no expense on a Pullman hotel car for our exclusive use. She'd put my money to good use. A sleeping car equipped with an en suite and dining area allowed us to stay on the train during various stops. Also, within its comfortable confines, it would help us remain hidden from the public eye and Elliot's spies.

I stood to move about the car and admired its plush Rococo interior and brass accents. Running my hand along its opulent velvet upholstery, I couldn't help but notice its ample lighting. This pleasing car would make the first leg of our journey very comfortable for all four of us.

I walked toward one of the windows and watched the snow come down heavier since leaving the station. Like home, when I looked out my window last evening, I focused on one snowflake struggle as it fell from the gray heaven above, only to be swept away by the howling wind. I imagined each perfect crystal gathering in a cold white blanket on the frozen landscape in hopes of covering the secrets of the past. Like the snowflake, I, too, was on a journey hoping to melt away – never again to be seen by Elliot.

It was good we left Boston when we did, or we would have been caught in a nasty winter storm and unable to leave until spring. A horrible thought came to mind; by then, I could have been dead. Behind the frozen panes, the scenery rapidly transformed, giving me little sense of assurance that Elliot wouldn't be able to catch up with us. But I couldn't dwell on my fears.

I loved watching the boys' faces mere inches from the glass. Their childish innocence touched my heart as they stared at a new world. They had never been on a train before, let alone out of Boston proper. Elliot had always made excuses about his newspaper, so we never took any time away as a family.

Turning from the window, I sighed heavily. Pearl was sitting in one of the two overstuffed chairs, back straight, hands folded in her lap, her face void of expression. The tea untouched, I once again knelt beside her, taking her hands in mine. "Pearl."

She turned toward me, her eyes filled with unshed tears. "I'm so sorry, Pearl. I didn't mean to bring you along. I know you didn't want to come. I reassured her that she didn't have to continue traveling with us. "You can get off at the first stop, and I'll pay for your return ticket to Boston. You won't have to worry about us anymore."

Pearl's brows lifted as she remained silent. It was as if I could see the wheels in her head turning. Why wasn't she talking to me? "Damn it, Pearl, say something. Anything. Yell at me if you want."

Raising her hand, she gently stroked the side of my face, and I leaned into it. "I was so frightened we would both fall off and the boys would be left alone on the train. Oh, Mrs. Ackerman. I was so scared."

"Pearl, we were both scared. I did what was necessary to keep a catastrophe from happening. I'm just sorry I made you come along unwillingly." Brushing away loose curls from the side of my face, I stood, pulling Pearl up with me. "We'll figure something out before our first stop. Right now, let's get ourselves comfortable so we can relax. It's been an overwhelming twenty-four hours, and we're exhausted."

❦

Dusk rapidly descended, and I remained mesmerized by the train's clickity-clack and swaying motion. In the waning light, we made our way along the open countryside. Outside, the ground quickly became covered in a snowy carpet. I could barely make out a few lanky stalks of grass standing sentinel above the frozen landscape as the misty veil of steam from the train's engine billowed past our windows.

Sitting sleepy-eyed at the table, the motion of the train had Porter and Daniel yawning. I found myself picking at my food. It was excellent, considering it was train fare, but I was too tired to enjoy it.

It was time I put the boys to bed. Guiding them down the short hallway, I snuggled them side-by-side in the bottom berth, tucking a warm woolen blanket around them. I leaned forward, placing a kiss on the top of their downy heads. Before leaving the room, I heard the soft breathy sounds telling me they were already fast asleep.

Once back in the parlor, Pearl held out a fresh cup of tea to me as she sat in the overstuffed chair she'd occupied earlier. Taking it, I sank into the plush cushions and felt the tension in my shoulders relax for the first time today.

Looking over the rim of her cup, Pearl mentioned, "Mrs. Ackerman, I don't have any clothes to wear since I had no intention of traveling. Do you think we, I mean I, can take a chance in the first town and quickly shop for clothes and necessities?"

Putting my cup on the table beside me, I carefully considered Pearl's request before answering. "I think it would be safe enough if you got off at the next town, and I'll give you money for your ticket back to Boston."

"Well, that's what I want to talk to you about. I've changed my mind."

"You what?" I squealed. "I mean, you have!" I couldn't believe what Pearl was saying. "Do you really mean it, Pearl? You want to continue with us?"

"I've given it a great deal of thought. I have nothing or no one left in Boston. All I care about is right here on this train." Teasingly, she added," Besides, I can't have you go traipsing all over creation alone with two young boys, now can I?"

I jumped out of my chair, spilling our tea, and hugged Pearl while turning us in a circle. "You've made me so happy. Oh, Pearl, what an adventure this will be. I won't let the past hinder any of our journey."

Stepping back from our embrace, I added, "But we must remain vigilant for Elliot and any of his goons he may send looking for us."

"You are quite right, Mrs. Ackerman. But I think we can enjoy ourselves if given the opportunity. I've always dreamed of seeing the Wild West."

"Oh, Pearl," I responded teasingly, "Do you think the West is ready for us?"

We found ourselves grabbing our sides and laughing. It felt good, even if for a short time. Sitting back down, we devised a plan to allow Pearl to obtain clothing in the next town.

"Tomorrow, when we stop, I think it will be safe for you to get off and go into town. But only for a short time. I'll stay on the train with the boys. I can't have you taking a chance of being seen, though I don't think Elliot would be quick enough to have someone looking for us."

I tried swallowing the lump in my throat several times before I continued. Looking directly at her, I asked nervously, "Pearl. Promise me you'll come back to the train. Don't leave us now."

"Mrs. Ackerman. You need not worry. I'll come back. I'm going to see you safely through to your brother.

10

BOSTON, MASSACHUSETTS, 1880

Elliot Ackerman

A THROBBING HEADACHE had me leaving work early. I needed my medicine, which I had absentmindedly left on my nightstand that morning. I was stone-cold sober when I entered the house at three o'clock in the afternoon, the earliest I'd been home in recent months. Nothing was going right at work, and I couldn't handle listening to the reporters' sniveling complaints any longer.

An eerie silence greeted me when I opened the front door, which now had a board covering the damage I created last night. "Huh, Vernon, the old codger must have had one of the boys fix it. He's good for something," I mumbled.

Making my way into the foyer, I stared at the table, cursing as my foot still ached from the confrontation with its leg. Memories of last night flashed before me, remembering that Rebecca had once again pushed me too far. Shaking my head from side to side, I didn't understand why I continued to put up with her. But I wouldn't let last night's failure of trying to dispose of her hamper my future efforts.

Glancing toward the parlor, I yelled for my wife. "Rebecca!" I didn't hear the boy's usual laughter coming from upstairs as I waited for my wife to respond. Sometimes, those boys annoyed me to no end with their incessant racket. I despised having children. They were such troublesome creatures.

Normally, Pearl would have come out from the kitchen by now to see if she could be of service. But even she didn't appear. Frustrated, I yelled again, "Where is everyone?" Throwing my briefcase on the table, I tried yelling for Vernon. "Vernon, where the hell are you, man?" Again, no answer. This is strange. They can't have all gone out at the same time.

I noticed the fireplace in the parlor held no flicker of flame, and our saucy young maid, who always greeted me happily, was nowhere to be found. Walking further into the house, I made my way down the hall to the kitchen. Stepping inside Pearl's sanctuary, the usual aromas were absent. My jaw clenched, and my anger rose as I ground my back teeth. Making my way to my office, I heard or saw no one.

Rounding the banister, I raced up the stairs, taking two at a time. I paused on the top landing and clutched my chest as my heart thumped a painful rhythm. I instantly understood how foolish it was of me to think I was young enough to run up the stairs like that. There was a tightness there, and my left arm ached. I could barely hold onto the railing. Leaning forward, I sucked in large gulps of air. Was I dying? I damn well better not be. I had business to take care of.

I stared toward Rebecca's closed bedroom door as the pain eased and my heart slowly returned to a normal rhythm. Without hesitation, I knocked, awaiting a response. After several seconds, I knocked again. She can't still be hiding. This time, I knocked louder and called out while pounding my fist on the door. "Rebecca, open this door. Now!"

With each passing minute, I became angrier. Something was definitely amiss. Turning the handle, I was surprised it easily opened. A chill passed through me as I stepped into the cold room and found it neatly in order and the bed meticulously made. Although I no longer spent time in this room, I felt something had transpired since I'd left for work this morning.

Walking to my wife's armoire, I turned the handle, tugging, knowing it tended to catch. When I did, I stood staring at the many lavish gowns I'd purchased to present Rebecca to society. They were all there, but there were large gaps on each end. All her day dresses were gone. Without a second thought, I rushed to my boy's room to find it also empty of their clothing.

Furious, I stomped back to Rebecca's room and began rifling through her dresser. There was little left to search through. She had cleaned out most of her necessaries. Her silver brush and mirror, which she cherished from her mother, were gone. Her hair clips. Gone. She had taken all she valued except the jewelry I'd given her.

"Damn it!" My wife had escaped. Cursing, I marched toward the door. "I'll teach her she can't leave me." Walking past her dresser, I spotted an open envelope on its top addressed to my wife in handwriting I'd never seen before. Picking it up, I walked into the hallway to read it under the light of a sconce. The words caught my attention.

12 Dec
Ms. R Young.
Come. Brother gravely wounded.
E Sweeney Yuma, AT

Damn, she's gone after that brother of hers. By leaving, Rebecca was making a fool of me. I needed her mother's jewels and money to pay off debtors. And she is the only one with access to her mother's safekeeping box at the bank. Without her, I couldn't access the box her mother had hidden from her husband for years.

Rebecca had told me about them when we were first married. At the time, she was innocent and naïve, trusting me with her secrets. But I soon found out that she and her mother were shrewd women. "Well, you little harlot. You won't get away from me. I'll find you. And when I do, you'll wish you never left."

ొౕఠ

Rebecca

Pearl insisted I take the single room for myself while she slept with the boys. My room was spacious, with a full bed and two small windows that let in enough light and fresh air if desired despite the freezing temperatures outside. The water closet, although small, was a welcomed convenience.

Staring in the mirror hanging over the basin, the make-up I'd used to cover my bruises could not hide the deep purple along the side of my cheek. It sickened me to see the tint of blood showing through. Soon, it would turn green, then yellow as it faded. It couldn't happen soon enough. Just seeing it was a stark reminder of Elliot's violent nature.

Washing off the powder, I gently dabbed a clean towel over my face. Turning away, I didn't want to look at the painful reminder, so I climbed into bed and faced the window and the outside darkness. Closing my eyes, I tried letting the car's swaying motion calm me. Clickity-clack, clickity-clack. I hoped the repeating rhythm would lull me into a deep sleep. I needed to be alert come morning.

ొౕఠ

It was barely six-thirty, and Pearl and the boys were already sitting at the table when I entered our small dining area. I was so grateful to see a smile on Daniel's sweet face for a change. At six, he was so innocent and trusting. On the other hand, Porter sat stoically, staring at his empty plate.

He was too young at eight to carry the heavy burdens resting on his small shoulders. As his mother, I couldn't help but worry. My hope was this trip would brighten his outlook on life. He didn't say much but knew more than he let on about his father and me. Looking into his radiant green eyes, I hoped this journey West would be the best thing for all of us.

"Good Morning, my dears," I said, putting on a smile, as false as it may be. "Did you sleep well last night?"

Daniel looked so excited as he beamed at me, chattering away like an excited magpie. Not coming up for air, he proceeded to tell me, "Yes, Momma. I couldn't wait to get up. It's still snowing," he exclaimed excitedly, pointing out the window. "I saw horses and cows. Lots of cows. I've never seen a cow before. Have you seen a cow before? The houses outside look so small." Nodding his head, he added, "They're smaller than our house in Boston. Will we live in a small house like that? I hope so. Can I have a horse and cow, Momma?"

"Oh, my goodness, Daniel, so many questions. It's good to see you happy, but I'll have to give more thought to the cow and horse."

As the older brother, Porter rolled his eyes without saying a word. After being cloistered in Boston, it was evident that my boys had missed the real world. They had never been able to explore outside their four walls except when attending school or days in the park supervised by Vernon.

I took a deep breath and stared out the window at the passing scenery, relieved they would finally experience what real life had to offer, not just from their storybooks.

I had no idea what to expect on our travels West, let alone when we arrived in Yuma. Still, I prayed Caleb would be there and that I had made the right decision to leave Boston.

11

TRAIN TRAVEL

Rebecca

SLOWLY, THE TRAIN eased its way into Chicago's Central Depot. Although relatively short, the first leg of our journey had gone smoothly. I only hoped the remainder would be the same. After breakfast, Pearl rushed off the train to do her shopping for clothes and necessities. So, that left me to bundle the boys up against the cold December chill.

Palms sweating within my gloves, I exited the train, holding tightly to my boy's hands. Fear clutched my throat at seeing the alarming number of people within the station. I knew Elliot couldn't possibly have beat us here. Could he? I still didn't trust his underhanded connections. I had ignored his associations for far too long, and now I had to be ever vigilant if we were to make it safely to Yuma.

Without Vernon's assistance and watchful eyes, I had to take charge of seeing our trunks make it through to the next rail car. I pulled the collar up about my neck and pushed through the swirling icy wind. With the boys close to my side, we made our way to the baggage car as fat, puffy snowflakes drifted from a steel gray sky, alighting on our eyelashes.

Lifting his head, Daniel stuck out his tongue to catch the icy crystals and laughed. Ah, to be young again without a care. My grasp on the boy's hands tightened as a quivering in my chest almost had me stepping back onto the train.

"Momma, you're hurting my hand," Porter cried, looking up at me with concern.

I had clung to their tiny hands out of fear, not realizing how tightly I squeezed. "I'm so sorry, sweetheart." Loosening my grasp, I was determined to do this myself and avoid bringing our attention to strangers. I couldn't take a chance. I sensed Elliot had hired ears and eyes lurking in this town.

Securing our trunks for the next leg of our journey, the boys and I made our way into the station out of the freezing temperatures. After all, it was December.

Nervous, every five minutes, I found myself glancing at the large clock hanging on the station's wall in front of me. An hour, maybe two, passed as we waited. The tension in my back increased, and I worried that Pearl had decided to return to Boston. Working myself up into a tizzy, I let out a pent-up breath as Pearl rushed forward with an armload of packages. Why was I so worried? I knew she wouldn't leave us.

Thank heavens she had bought herself a warm coat. A wool knit scarf and warm mittens completed her attire. Seeing them, I wish I had thought to ask her to buy mittens for the boys. Just as I finished my thoughts, Pearl handed Porter and Daniel a package. Excitedly opening them, they beamed at seeing their colorful new mittens. Putting them on, they clapped their hands before me, showering me with their delight. Pearl handed me a similar package, and I gave her a grateful hug and kissed her icy cheek.

Now was the time to give Pearl another opportunity to return to Boston before I purchased the fourth ticket. I prayed her answer would still be no. So, taking her hands in mine, I looked deeply into her eyes and asked, "Now is your opportunity, Pearl. Do you want to return to Boston?" Before letting her answer, I proceeded, "I'll understand if you do. We'll be fine from here on out."

"Mrs. Ackerman, while I was shopping, I recognized I'd been so foolish. I thought I would be a burden to you, but I understand now you need me. And like I said before, I have nothing and no one to return to in Boston. And I certainly would never work for Mr. Ackerman again. The only reason I stayed as long as I did was because of you and the boys."

Looking down, I saw her take a shaky breath before proceeding. "So, I'd be delighted if you still want me to accompany you." Ruffling the boy's hair, Pearl added, "Besides, I'd miss my boys."

Wrapping my free hand around her arm, I smiled as we made our way to the station's ticket counter. This would be a more extended trip heading south, and I was glad to have Pearl along to keep me company and the boys in hand.

We had an hour to wait before the new train left. While sitting on a long wooden bench, my eyes darted from person to person within the massive station. An overwhelming sense of unease was settling in, and I felt the urge to flee when Pearl, recognizing my concern, laid her hand over mine. At that moment, I absorbed her strength and closed my eyes, imagining all four of us safe in Yuma. Without looking, I squeezed her hand gently, acknowledging her calming presence.

12

CHICAGO CENTRAL TRAIN DEPOT

Rebecca

BEFORE I KNEW it, it was time to board our new train. Thankfully, Pearl was coming along willingly this time, and I didn't need to worry about pulling her onto a moving rail car.

It was early in the day, but once inside the warmth of the parlor, the boy's cheeks bloomed a rosy pink, and their eyes slowly drifted closed. Grateful, Pearl escorted them to their room, settling them down for a nap.

My appetite had waned the past forty-eight hours, but now my stomach growled loudly, expounding my hunger. Fortunately, the train had yet to move, and I could order something light to eat. Maybe a cup of tea and a slice of toast would tide me over until the mid-day meal.

As I entered the parlor, I pulled the gold cord for our porter. Momentarily, a tall, elegantly dressed gentleman entered the car, asking for my request. Returning shortly after that, he placed a Chintz tea set with matching cups on a side table situated between two velveteen chairs. I thanked him, but before he excused himself, he went over the dinner menu to be served at seven this evening and then announced he would return with a light lunch at noon. Thankfully, Pearl could rest easily and didn't have to worry about our meals as we traveled.

Relaxing in one of the chairs, I gazed outside at the gray clouds hanging low in the sky, obscuring many of the city's buildings before they released their winter blanket, cloaking the car in early darkness. I fondly remembered, as a child, the silence of snow. Despite our father's absence for reasons we never understood, our mother ensured we led as normal a child's life as possible.

But the longer we sat on the tracks, the more nervous I became. The risk of one of Elliot's underlings finding us caused me to tense. Glancing out the frosted window, life as I knew it fell away. I was fascinated with snowflakes as I followed a delicate one drop from the top of the window, following it until it landed on the icy ground below. Then, poof, it was gone, joining the mass of snow accumulating on the boardwalk.

Drawn out of my daydream, I noticed a tall, handsomely dressed man in a wool overcoat and a Bolar hat staring up at me from the station's walkway. In the biting morning air, each breath he took came out in a puffy white mist, disappearing as it circled upward.

He'd recognized me.

My heart skipped a beat as our eyes connected. Abruptly standing caused me to spill my tea down the front of my gown. Swallowing back a muffled squeal, I couldn't pull my eyes away from the man as I burned his face to memory. He didn't look devious. But something about the way he stared at me had me shaking inside.

Without a doubt, he knew who I was. Somehow, Elliot had found us. Nodding his head as if to be congenial, he tipped his hat before breaking eye contact. As he turned to walk away, I caught a glimpse of shiny metal inside the left side of his jacket as it blew open in the frigid wind. He was armed. Was he here to kill me?

I was my own worst enemy. All I could think was Elliot had hired him. I could make myself crazy by playing too much into a momentary stranger's glance, and I couldn't let my thoughts wander in such a portentous direction. Yet, I had my boys to think about. Trying to repress my fears, I repeatedly thought that many men were armed for their protection.

Following his form, I watched him walk away with a pronounced limp on his left leg. He wouldn't be hard to recognize. As hard as I tried, I couldn't tell if he boarded the same train as us. Swearing under my breath, I had to find out.

"Mrs. Ackerman."

So focused was I on the man walking away, I didn't hear Pearl call my name. Before I knew it, she was taking her napkin, wiping the tea I'd just spilled down the bodice of my dress.

"Mrs. Ackerman," she asked again. "Are you all right? Your hands are shaking."

I shouted, "That man!" Pointing out the window, not taking my eyes off his retreating form. I was so close to the window that my warm voice produced a fog on the cold windowpane, blocking my view. "Pearl, he was staring at me as if he knew who I was."

A whoosh of air left the overstuffed cushion as I dropped down unladylike into the chair. Raising my voice, I could feel the heat blooming along my neck as I asked, "What if Elliot sent him to find us?" I was lightheaded, and the air around me became heavy. Unable to catch my breath, I feared I was on the verge of fainting. I'd never done so in my life, and I wouldn't allow it to happen now.

Gently patting my hands, Pearl asked, "Please calm down, Mrs. Ackerman. I'll call for the porter, and you can give him a description of the man so he can check to see if he boarded the train."

"No!" I answered abruptly. I was adamant we didn't draw any unnecessary attention to ourselves. Faking a smile, I added, "I'm sorry, Pearl. I'm just overreacting. I'll be alright." As long as I felt someone was following us, I had to remain vigilant. Holding the delicate teapot, I tried not to tremble while pouring a fresh cup of tea. I wanted desperately to lighten the mood, so I said, "Now, let's enjoy the moment before the boys wake up from their nap."

I couldn't fool Pearl. She knew how scared I was. But I was tougher than anyone knew. In my reticule was my Derringer. Even Pearl had no idea I'd brought it along. Pearl's smile wavered, and I noticed a slight tremor in her hand before she looked at me over the rim of her teacup.

Over the years, she had developed the ability to read my emotions and body language down to the fine details. I couldn't fool her, but at least I could try and play a better part in dispelling our fears.

⌒⋆⌒

PINKERTON AGENT

Benjamin "Ben" Reynolds

I'd finally located my assignment, and she matched perfectly the description her husband had given my superiors. My orders were not to apprehend but to follow the woman and the boys to their final destination and then report back to the agency.

Gazing at her through the train's window, I tried to remain a man only interested in a woman's rare beauty. It was hard to do when I saw the fear burning in her eyes.

Turning my head away, I couldn't help but think there was something unusual about her face. From what I could tell from this distance, one side had an odd yellow-green tinge to it. Was she ill? No, I'd seen that type of coloring before on battered women. But I couldn't be sure through the distortion of the wavy glass.

What monster had done this to her? Had it been her husband? At this point, I couldn't allow myself to jump to conclusions. In my line of work, I thought I'd seen it all. But seeing an abused woman was something that made me physically ill. And I wouldn't tolerate it.

Concerned, I needed to proceed cautiously, realizing Mrs. Ackerman may be trying to hide recent events the agency wasn't aware of. I was trained for this, and my time in the Army had taught me well, leaving me with years of raw memories that I desperately tried to forget. Yet, after all these years, the pain was still fresh. So, I would remain distant yet watchful.

Still, I couldn't help but think, what have I gotten myself into?

⤳ 13 ⤳

TRAIN TRAVEL

Rebecca

YAWNING BEHIND MY handkerchief, I asked Pearl, "Do you think you can handle the boys when they wake up? I'm so tired I can hardly keep my eyes open. If you don't mind, I'd like to take a quick nap before lunch."

"But of course, Mrs. Ackerman," Pearl replied, looking up at me with the smile I'd come to love. "The boys and I will be just fine. You go and get some needed rest. I'll check on them in a few minutes. I don't want them sleeping too long, or they won't sleep through the night."

"Thank you, Pearl. Please, wake me if I'm still asleep in an hour. I, too, want to be able to sleep through the night."

Standing, I walked to her chair and kissed her cheek. She was at least twenty years older than my twenty-eight, but she was a remarkably beautiful woman. Her skin was porcelain, and her soft, wavy hair held a scattering of gray, lending a regal quality to this gentile woman I loved.

Entering my sleeping compartment, I opened my portmanteau, remembering the letter I received from Arizona. Searching, I panicked when I couldn't locate it. I searched twice. No, three times, through each article of clothing, my jewelry box, toiletries, and the toes of my shoes. It wasn't there.

Next, I dumped the contents of my reticule onto the bed. Dread settled over me as I spread everything out on the satin spread. *It has to be here! I know I didn't pack it in our trunks.*

The letter was nowhere to be found.

Swearing under my breath, I remembered seeing it last on my bedroom dresser, but I must have forgotten to retrieve it as I left the room.

"Stupid, stupid, stupid!" I fumed. The letter was the only way Elliot knew where I was headed. If I left it on my dresser, I know he would have found it, and I am confident he would do anything his power allowed to find me and bring me back to inflict his final revenge.

Rebecca, dear. Please remain calm. If Elliot found the letter, you're far enough ahead of him. I'm sure you'll make it to Arizona before him.

"Momma, what if I don't? What if Elliot catches up with us? That man I saw outside the train in Chicago recognized me. He's working for Elliot. I know it!"

You can't be sure of that, dear. Now gather yourself together and tell Pearl.

Hunching my shoulders, it felt as if the narrow walls of the room were closing in on me. No matter what my mother told me, she hadn't convinced me that Elliot wouldn't catch up with us. Pacing back and forth, I pounded my fist on my leg. No physical pain would take away the mental anguish I was feeling.

Despite the cold outside, rivulets of sweat trickled between my breasts as all thoughts of sleep were abandoned. At this point, my nerves hung by a fine thread, remembering the man staring at me through the train's window. I hadn't imagined it. He worked for Elliot.

"Mother, you're wrong."

Calm down, Rebecca. You'll figure something out.

Walking down the short hallway, I held onto the walls as the car swayed from side to side. Its rhythm falsely reassured us that we were moving farther and farther away from Elliot's grasp. Pearl looked up as I entered the parlor, surprised I was back so quickly. Thankfully, she was alone. Not speaking, she stared at me, undoubtedly seeing the fear on my face.

"Pearl," I choked out, holding my hands out to her.

"What is it, dear?" Her face paled at seeing my distraught expression.

I had to tell her. And, if she wanted to disembark at the next station, she could. I wouldn't put her through what I could only surmise Elliot had planned for me. I'd have Pearl take the boys and find a safe hiding place until this nightmare was over. I had no one else I could trust them with except Caleb. But, he was still too far away, or heaven forbid, dead. Damn, what a mess I've created. It's all my fault. "No, it's not," I answered myself. "It's Elliot who created this mess."

My voice shaking, I rushed out my confession, "Pearl. I can't find the letter from Arizona. I thought I placed it in my reticule before we left, but it's not there. I've searched everywhere for it. For some reason, Elliot must have come home early from work and found the letter while he searched the house for the boys and me. He'll find us. I know he will."

Choking back a sob, I couldn't finish. I was so angry with myself. Turning to stare out the window, I continued in a hushed tone. "I must have left it on my dresser. That's why he was at the train station." Wringing my hands, I lowered myself into the chair next to Pearl. Sitting forward, I took hold of her hands in mine and said, "It's not a coincidence that man was staring at me outside the train's window. He has to be working for Elliot."

While I held her attention, I filled Pearl in on my plan. "Pearl, I want you to take the boys and get off the train at the next station and find a safe place to hide. I'll give you enough money to cover all your expenses. You should be able to find a nice boarding house that allows small children. Then, once I arrive in Yuma and locate Caleb, I'll wire you."

At this point, I was grateful for the cash I had secretly hidden away from Elliot over the years. It was proving its worth since Elliot surely would have blocked me from withdrawing any funds from the meager account he had set up for me. Plus, if I delved into my savings, it would give him a means of tracking my whereabouts. Now that he had that man following us, I guess it didn't matter.

Patting my arm, Pearl attempted to put a halt to my rambling. "Slow down, Mrs. Ackerman." She took a breath and continued, "The boys and I are not leaving you. If that man is looking for you." Pausing, she looked about the room. "And it's a big if. If Elliot hired him to retrieve you and the boys, he would have done so by now, and we would have never been able to leave Chicago."

"You're probably right, Pearl. But, I must find a way to keep us safe and out of that man's hands." The muscles at the back of my neck spasmed, and I could hardly hold my head up as Pearl continued.

"Now, this is what we are going to do." Pearl calmly laid out her plan, but I didn't hear a word she was saying as fraught as I was. I would have to trust her judgment in keeping us all safe.

Come nightfall, I was worn out from remaining hypervigilant throughout the day. I couldn't keep this up for another two thousand-plus miles. I needed to relax and enjoy the trip for the boy's sake. I owed them that much.

⌇⌇

With small stations between cities, our next big stop was St. Louis. The porter had told me when we left our last station that it was roughly three hundred miles and at least two days of travel if all went well. I was grateful to be moving further and further away from my husband. Now, if only I could lose the man I knew to be following us.

The Pullman car had been a blessing. It gave the boys enough room to run around during the day, wearing off their excess energy while helping them sleep through the night. What Pearl and I would do once we got to Kansas City was something I couldn't worry about now.

I had been forewarned in Chicago that these Pullman cars didn't run on all rail lines. But, until then, we'd enjoy its comforts and not fret about something we had no control over for our next venture.

Instead, I had a strange man following us. That was enough to keep me busy for the remainder of our trip.

Two days later, we pulled into the Kansas City station around nine in the morning, only to board another train soon after, taking us farther west. This time, our comfort was not a priority, as we would sit side-by-side and face-to-face in wooden pew-like seats. Sleeping upright would prove a challenge for Pearl and me. The boys, on the other hand, could fall asleep in any position and on any surface.

"All aboard!" yelled the Conductor. "Next stop, Fort Worth, Texas."

The train jerked backward, then forward, before it gained momentum. With the movement of the train, my stomach felt as if I would leave my breakfast in Kansas City. Gradually, its engine gained a rhythm and roared on. As far as the eye could see, we passed flatlands and rolling hills covered in a dusting of snow in one place and tall drifts in another.

Small settlements of what I found to be soddies dotted the landscape. It was a sight so different from Boston that I couldn't imagine man or beast surviving in this desolation. As the scenery outside the windows became bleaker, hours turned into long and arduous days. But the distance we'd traveled without being intercepted by Elliot or one of his henchmen put me at ease, albeit falsely. I knew beyond a shadow of a doubt he wouldn't stop searching until he had us in his grasp.

~☙ 14 ☙~

BOSTON, MASSACHUSETTS,

DECEMBER 1880

Elliot Ackerman

THE INTENSE RAYS of the winter sun glared through the ice-frosted window, waking me from a restless sleep, while below, on the cobbled street, I heard the familiar sound of pounding horse hoofs pulling carts filled with clanging metal canisters.

I needed my medicine.

Reaching out blindly for the nightstand, I came up empty-handed. "Now, where the heck is that bottle?" Groaning, I squeezed my eyes shut in pain and sluggishly rolled onto my side away from the blinding light.

What time is it? The clock over the fireplace chimed like the bells of St. Patrick's Cathedral, only intensifying the pounding in my head. I counted the clangs as they droned on. One. Two. Three. Four. Wait, was it only seven a.m.?

I didn't remember having a clock on my bedroom's mantel. Rubbing my temples with the heels of my hands, I willed the blinding pain behind my eyes to cease. It was no use. The aching had become more intense as the months passed and haunted me long into the day.

My doctor told me it was due to stress and my excessive thirst for spirits. What did that old quack know? The only spirits I longed for were a bottle of Boston's finest imported Irish whiskey and my liquid medicine.

Despite being in pain, my eyes flew open when a delicate hand drifted gently across my chest. Suddenly, I remembered I never made it home last night. Mystified yet pleased, I had no idea where I was, let alone the name of my warm and sultry bedmate.

Vaguely, I remember meeting her at last night's dinner party hosted by a wealthy business associate whose name I couldn't bring to mind. Grinning, what I did know was that I hadn't been too drunk to remember the passion we'd shared. I laughed, knowing Rebecca couldn't hold a candle to this blonde vixen lying beside me.

As my night companion stirred, her hand on my chest intuitively moved lower, immediately eliciting a tantalizing chill that I couldn't ignore from the base of my spine that rapidly moved upward, sending waves of pleasure to my brain. I shuddered, and my mind screamed for more of her magic.

But despite her most arousing and provocative ministrations, I sucked in a deep breath and grabbed her tormenting fingers in mine, unhurriedly pulling them away. As much as I despised social events, they did provide alluring comforts.

It was unusual for me to put off such carnal pleasures, but I was in no mood this morning. I had to get home, clean up, and find the bottle of Laudanum before making my way to the office. Sitting on the edge of the bed, I leaned over to pick up my pants when a wave of nausea hit like a boat crashing through the raging Atlantic seas. Hands on my knees, I pushed back and sucked in several deep breaths to quell the bitterness threatening to rise.

Sitting there unmoving, I waited to see if I needed to make a quick trip to the water closet. After several minutes of silence, I was satisfied I could make it home. Damn! I have to bend over again. Last night, in my state of intoxication, I'd carelessly left my coat on the floor. Hoping not to fall flat on my face, I gradually leaned forward and picked it up.

My bedmate had left her clothes, which indicated her wealth, draped over a chair. No trollup could afford that silk and satin gown. I had chosen my bed companion well. Something glittery on her nightstand caught my eye as I glanced over my shoulder. Tempting as it was, the diamond-studded necklace would have to wait for another night.

Donning my coat, I quietly turned the brass knob and left the room, not looking back at the high-priced whore. I'll have to find out her name for a later date.

◈◈◈

Even today, the elite and monied of Boston had their seamier sides. Of course, there were no emotional attachments. That would be too confining. I was no different than any other man I knew. It was a matter of time before our wives became cold and distant after the honeymoon. It was even worse during their confinement period when a husband's needs took precedence by seeking other avenues of pleasure.

Last night had just been a pleasurable encounter of the physical kind, nothing more. I would never again conform to being the dutiful, adoring husband society expected. You could call last night's foray into lustful bliss just a 'business proposition.'

Once home and refreshed, by early afternoon, I took a hansom cab to the Boston Pinkerton office. I wasn't about to run around the country looking for my wife and sons when I could hire someone to do the dirty work for me. Besides, my absence from work and social events would garner too much suspicion at the club and around town if I left Boston. As it was, I had to make up a story that my wife had gone off to visit distant family in the south, hoping to keep the old society biddies quiet for the time being.

Meeting with the lead detective, I gave him just enough information about my 'missing' wife. Playing a Shakespearean actor, I relayed a story that I feared for my dear wife and my son's well-being. After paying the required fee, I was assured the agency would use its best detective to locate my wife. I made sure the agent's orders were clear: they were to locate Rebecca and report her location to me and I alone. The police were not to be involved.

I didn't need any unpleasant details as long as my sons were returned to me. As far as my dear wife was concerned, it would have to look like an accident the boys would witness. Of course, it would only be for legal purposes, so her estate wouldn't become tied up in court. I needed her mother's hidden money as soon as possible.

I could easily play the grieving widower for a month or two, and no one in Boston would be the wiser. After all was said and done, by sending them off to boarding school, I would ensure the boys soon forgot about their mother.

Returning to the paper, I went through my day's routine as if nothing had changed. Yet, I kept pondering the idea of hiring someone besides a Pinkerton agent to 'take care of things,' hoping my wife would never make it to Arizona. I was not too fond of the thought of traveling all that way to complete the mission myself.

⤞⤟

Nathanial "Nate" Burns

The train's rocking motion caused me to lose my concentration as the nightmare of my previous life took over. To this day, I still don't understand how my life changed so dramatically. I was satisfied working a job I loved in 2016 as a Boston police officer with a devoted family and great friends.

More importantly, I was about to marry the woman who'd captured my heart. Back then, I could never have imagined living in another place, let alone another century.

The lady across the aisle reminded me of what I'd lost and yet still yearned for. A wife and family. Five years was a long time to grieve for what once had been. But grieve, I did, almost daily.

Losing focus on what I was reading in the newspaper, I continued to glance over its edge at the raven-haired beauty sitting two aisles down from me. Her momentary glance my way had me drowning in those lustrous pools of her azure blue eyes. Dragging me under, I imagined it would be a glorious way to drown in their mysterious depths.

Could I be so lucky?

15

BOSTON, MASSACHUSETTS,

SUMMER 2016

Nathaniel

"Roxbury, Charley 106."

"Charley, 106, go ahead."

"Roxbury, Charley 106, received call of domestic in progress. Address 2348 Seaton Avenue. No known weapons. RP (reporting person) is involved and will be standing by on the front porch. White female, red dress."

"Charley 106, clear, in route."

The dispatcher's familiar voice, calm and concise, came through my car's intercom. I pictured her sitting at her desk, headset in place, eyes determinedly focused on her computer screen while her fingers furiously typed the information relayed by the frantic caller.

As police, we took an oath to serve and protect. But in the same breath, we despised domestic calls! Violence between intimate partners was dangerous and often volatile, if not deadly, for the victim and officers involved.

Having never personally experienced such behavior, I was probably naive in thinking why a victim of such violence didn't seek help before their life spiraled out of control to this point.

Frequently, the incoming caller cannot or will not provide the much-needed information that will protect an officer. Despite all the additional training we receive, responding to a domestic call is one of the most dangerous tasks a law enforcement officer can undertake.

"Charley 106, Roxbury headquarters."
"Roxbury, Charley 106, go ahead."
"Charley 106 Roxbury, I'm 10-97 (arrived)."
"Roxbury, Charley 106, was clear at 2310 hours."

Parking my patrol car out of view and south of the address in question, I saw that my backup had done the same two houses to the north. My usual area to patrol was in the 'H Block' of Roxbury. It was named such because most of the streets started with the letter H, as in Harvard and Humboldt.

Sadly, the local government was disinterested in the area, leaving some mid-nineteenth-century houses unsafe and unfit for habitation. Those that happened to be occupied were in disrepair and scattered amongst the abandoned homes taken up by the homeless and addicts.

Adequate housing in this area was almost non-existent. Here, the poverty level exceeded that in other areas, and the crime rate was rampant. Law enforcement was considered the enemy by some residents in this part of town. Still, they didn't hesitate to call us when the need arose.

With strong Scots-Irish descent, I grew up in brick-row housing on the East side of Boston. One of six children, we were considered dirt poor, but at least we had both parents who loved us. They worked two to three jobs to keep a roof over our heads. With help from our local parish, food was always on the table, and secondhand clothes were on our backs.

I was no prize when I hit my teens. As a kid, I could be a hellion, giving my parents plenty to worry about. But, after a close call on the street of hard knocks, I had to decide between being on one side of the law or the other. Thankfully, I chose a career in law enforcement, following in my father and grandfather's footsteps.

Life was a hard, uphill battle, and I was determined never to be poor again. I wanted to make a difference in the local communities of Boston.

࿇

Officers no longer went solo on domestic calls. All across the country, police departments learned this the hard way. Walking to the house in question, I noticed curious neighbors staring out their windows.

All it takes is one stray bullet!

The squeak of rusted hinges caught my attention across the street as a man with a cast on his left leg and right arm in a brace pushed open his screen door, minus the screen. Hobbling onto his small front porch, I unsnapped the leather securing my weapon and rested my right hand on the pistol's grip.

Despite his physical restraints, I couldn't turn my back on him and proceed unless I was sure he wasn't an additional threat. It was a call I alone had to make. Motioning to the man, I yelled, "Get back inside!"

Before he did as I instructed, he yelled to me in his thick Bostonian accent, pointing across the street. "I heard gunshots coming from inside that house earlier this afternoon. Didn't think much of it since those two are always fighting. And that guy's always shooting off his guns. I've called you guys before, but the same thing happens. You drag him off, but he always comes back nastier than before he left." Shrugging his shoulders, he continued, "So, I ignored it tonight."

Turning, the man limped back inside his house. For now, I was satisfied he wasn't a threat. Yet, I couldn't be certain he wouldn't come back out with his weapon and shoot the suspect himself. Not having eyes in the back of my head, I would have to trust my gut.

Knowing there were potential weapons involved only intensified the risk. An officer could never predict what and how they would be used. Clearing leather, I proceeded forward with my weapon below my line-of-sight, where I could quickly raise it to meet any threat.

It never gets easier. I'd seen too much heartache and death in my ten years on the force. You never become immune to it. Unless you're in my position, you truly couldn't understand.

The stress was grueling, and I often went home at the end of my shift drained of all energy with brain fatigue. My job put a strain on my relationship with my fiancé. She wanted me to find a safer job, but I told her no job out there was safe.

Sweat ran between my shoulder blades, and the painful thumping in my chest left the taste of fear festering in the back of my throat. Swallowing back acid, I sent a silent prayer heavenward as I approached the side of the house.

Looking up, I stared unswervingly into the eyes of the woman in the red dress. Blood trickled from her right nostril, and the pleading look in her eyes had me taking one cautious step forward. What transpired next happened too fast for me to intervene.

I watched in horror as a beefy tattooed hand shot out from the open doorway, forcefully shoving the woman over the iron porch railing. Stopping mid-stride, I watched helplessly as the silky red dress billowed up around her thighs, and she lurched backward through the air. Arms extended heavenward, her terrified screams pierced the night, followed by a sickening thud as she landed headfirst on the pavement below.

Damn it!

Suddenly, life at that moment turned in slow motion, and within seconds, I raised my gun, took aim at the perp in the open door, and fired. I expected it, but the unnerving sound of returning gunfire shattered the humid Roxbury night.

What I didn't expect was the perp had been right on target, and the intense pain at the side of my neck had me dropping to the ground.

16

BOSTON, MASSACHUSETTS,

SUMMER 2016

Nathaniel

Nathaniel! CRIED A familiar voice I hadn't heard in years.

It couldn't be. My mother's dead.

Son, I'm here. Don't be afraid.

There she was again. Even though my thoughts were fuzzy, why should I be afraid? Her memorable calloused palm, from years of hard work in the woolen mills, gently caressed my cheek. Trying hard, I leaned my head to the side, wanting to lay it on her soft breasts for comfort, as I did as a young child.

Instead, I lay on the hot, jagged pavement with my entire body numb and racked with pain. I was rapidly transforming into a lifeless skeleton. My mother's familiar honeysuckle perfume was soon replaced by the coppery scent of my blood and the sound of my ragged breathing.

More gunfire pierced the night. Pop! Pop! Pop! I jerked. In my mind, I could feel the revolver's recoil with each trigger squeeze. Who's doing all the shooting?

Someone was yelling at me. Why are they yelling? I thought I called out, "I'm right here," when a fiery-hot pain and numbness surged down both my arms. They wouldn't move, and I groaned as someone rolled me over. Whoever they were, they were applying pressure on the side of my neck.

It hurt like the knobs of hell. But it didn't last long because I was swiftly fading away to somewhere I didn't want to go. Not yet, anyway.

I recognized my partner's voice laced with panic as he continued to yell at me, "Nate! Nate, can you hear me? Hang in there, man! The paramedics are on their way!"

Somewhere in the distance, I could hear sirens blaring and more people shouting. I couldn't tell if they were yelling at me. My partner's voice once again boomed as he bellowed, "Get back! All of you, get back!"

By this time, I was cold and uncontrollably shaking. Why was I cold? Last I remember, it was still eighty degrees out despite it being night. My head spun, and the ringing in my ears became a thunderous roar.

Just let me rest a minute, and I'll be fine.

I caught bits and pieces of a hushed conversation between dispatch and my partner, the man holding my neck. The words 'shot' and 'lots of blood' were not reassuring.

Dang that hurts! I wanted to tell him to stop applying pressure to my neck, but I couldn't force out the words between my numb lips. So, I resolved myself to let those around me do what they needed to keep me alive.

How strange it was, but I could feel my body floating to a pleasantly peaceful place and, thankfully, painless. Where was I going?

I wasn't sure the paramedic's efforts were going to work. It felt like hours had passed when my mother's icy grip took my hand and pulled me to an unfamiliar place.

"Mom! Where are you taking me?"

She didn't answer. I desperately wanted to shake my head and regain focus, but the hand holding my neck wouldn't budge. The adrenaline rush normally having me on high alert no longer surged within me. I couldn't rely on that fight-or-flight instinct to get away.

I heard people mumbling to each other as they came at me from all sides, poking, prodding, and invading my body. My neck. Why are they still pushing on my neck?

Suddenly, it became painful to breathe, and that penny coppery taste, as if I had bit the inside of my mouth, gurgled from the back of my throat. I was spiraling downward like a capsized boat submerged under Boston's murky harbor.

Aw, son! What did that man do to you? Just like your father, you're leaving the world too soon.

I hadn't heard my mother's voice since she passed, and I didn't understand why I was hearing her now. It couldn't be because, no, I'm not dead. I can't be. I stuck to police procedure.

❧

Watching the surreal motions of people below, I focused on my body. How strange it was to see it from this vantage point. That's all I could call it since I had no idea where I was.

"We'll lift on the count of three. One. Two. Three."

The next thing I knew, I was off the ground and being laid on something just as uncomfortable. Jostled forward, I heard grunts and groans. I wanted to shout at them, "I'm not that heavy," but nothing came out.

Again, hands were coming at me from all directions. Raised voices calmly gave instructions above the dim ringing in my ears. As the aid unit carrying my body sped into the humid Boston night, I told myself I would survive.

I was wrong.

Why am I looking down at my body? My body rocked back and forth on the stretcher, and I was viewing the aid car dodging potholes and weaving in and out of traffic at high speed with its sirens blaring.

It was such a confined space for three people, including myself, on a stretcher. Feverishly working as a well-orchestrated team, they attached me to every piece of equipment imaginable that could fit into one unit. An oxygen mask covered my mouth and nose, EKG leads were attached to my chest, dual intravenous lines hung from both arms, and a blood pressure cuff pulsed painfully on my upper right arm, not to mention the constraining pressure bandage around my neck.

I heard someone call out loudly, "His O2 sat is dropping. I'm going to intubate."

The voices surrounding me rose in alarm. Suddenly, my head was tipped back, and my mouth pulled open with a firm grasp. What little gag reflex I had left took over.

A gag reflex. That's a good sign. Isn't it?

Oh no! I can't watch. That nasty-looking laryngoscope was eased, and I say that mildly, down my throat. I'm glad I didn't become a paramedic. But what I heard and saw from above, I didn't like. An erratic rhythm of my heart, which wasn't reassuring, played out on the tiny screen.

I cautiously looked over a paramedic's shoulder, seeing crimson cover the once-white sheet beneath me. Swearing, it hit me. That's my blood! It was a horrible thing to watch a body die. And there was nothing you could do but watch.

No longer in control, I wanted to scream, please, don't let me die. I have too much left to do. I thought of the woman I loved. Dang! I can't even remember her name. What am I going to tell her?

I won't be telling her anything. She'd receive that dreaded knock on her door telling her I was gone. I could only feel for the Captain who would be delivering the message.

Three heads turned to the monitor as someone called out, "He's in arrest. Start compressions."

The last thing I remember was the intense pulsing pain in my neck caused by each push on my chest. What little blood I had left in my body surged to my brain. It was the only organ keeping me alive at this point.

I can't watch it anymore.

17

SOMEPLACE FAR AWAY

IN ANOTHER TIME

Nathaniel

NATHAN, I HEARD my mom call, drawing me out of a daze. Her cool hand touched mine as she lovingly pulled me to her side and away from the scene below.

It's time to go, dear. There's nothing more for you to see here. You must follow me.

As the boy of my youth, I turned and obediently followed. "Where are we going?" I asked.

To a new place and time, my dear boy.

I don't remember much as we walked along a grassy path following a calm, winding creek. The landscape was unfamiliar, but the scent of pine from towering trees nearby brought me a sense of contentment.

Looking into my eyes, my mother answered, *This is the place you always wanted to go.*

As a child, I'd wanted to go many places, but my father's work schedule at the precinct didn't allow extensive travel outside of every other weekend and one week a year. And that one week off was too short to travel to the places I'd read about in my books.

My mother's misty figure stopped alongside a tiny cabin in a golden grass-covered field. It looked newly built from hand-drawn fir, bringing back memories of the Lincoln Logs I played with as a child. Outside the entrance was a crudely made bench where Mom motioned me to sit.

I did as she told me. One thing I knew for sure: I was no longer in Boston or the East Coast. But already, it felt right. Facing my mother, whom I dearly loved, I saw tears forming in her eyes. I desperately wanted to bring her into my arms and tell her everything would be alright, but she had no mortal form I could hold onto.

Son, do you understand what happened tonight?

Somewhat confused, I stared at the landscape, trying to put the pieces of tonight's events together. I knew she would give me the details, but I also knew what Mom had to say would be hard to comprehend.

"My memory is a bit foggy, but I remember being on a call in Roxbury." Taking a deep breath to relieve the tension in my neck, I inhaled the earthy scent of wild grasses and pine, wishing I could stay here forever.

That's right, son. But that call didn't end well for all involved, including you.

The silence between us seemed eternal until she added, *You were killed.*

I wanted to scream. Killed! How could that be? Alarms went off inside my head, and I started to panic. Mom had to be wrong! Rapidly running my hands over my chest, I wasn't in pain. If there's no pain, I can't be dead? Right?

Then, it hit me like a punch to the gut. Mom was right. She had been dead for five years. And here I was, sitting beside her in the middle of a lush green forest I had only dreamed of. Shaking my head, I could only hope I was hallucinating and would soon wake up in my apartment complaining about Boston's sweltering heat when I felt the soft touch of her wrinkled hand on mine.

Gently linking our fingers, that one touch brought all the good memories of my life to come flooding back. I remembered how she caressed my fevered brow as a child. Or when she gave me special hugs and patted my cheek in a way only a mother could do when I skinned my knee.

I had to keep reminding myself she was dead. I had stood at her grave when they lowered her coffin into the ground next to Dad's. It didn't matter. Right now, in this place, this time, wherever I was, her presence felt real.

Nate. Do you remember your grandfather O'Donnell?

"Of course I do. He was your father." Laughing, I added, "He was a hard man to forget with his thick Irish brogue." Turning to face her, I said, "Why do you ask me about him now? He's been dead a long time."

Looking down, Mom twisted her hands together in her lap as a long moment of silence ensued. Finally, she answered. *Your grandpa had a special gift he passed along to me.* She awaited my response.

Hesitantly, I asked, "What kind of gift?"

This will be hard for you to believe, son, and I had my doubts until tonight. This gift allows certain people of Celtic descent to save someone of their bloodline at the exact time of their death.

I remained silent. She was right. It was hard to believe. But I let her continue, hoping it would make better sense when she finished.

Until tonight, I didn't believe in it either. But as I watched you lay there dying, I had to try using this gift.

My mouth slacked open in disbelief as I responded, "I'm not sure I understand. How can you save a dead man?" My stomach twisted in a knot. "Are you telling me that you actually stopped me from dying?"

No, son, you did die. But the gift allowed me to bring you to life in another time, another place, at the exact moment your heart stopped beating in 2016.

"So what you're saying is that I died tonight in Boston? Right?

Yes, she answered, patting the top of my hand once again.

"So, where are we now?" Turning my head from side to side, I tried placing my surroundings. "This certainly isn't Boston."

No, it's not Boston, son. You're in Wyoming.

"Wyoming! O.K. So, tell me, what year is it?" Tightly closing my eyes, I was afraid of her pending answer.

It's 1875.

"It can't be. How did this happen?" Frightened, I watched as a fine mist began to form around my mother's ankles, slowly moving upwards and then surrounding her whole body.

"Mom, what's happening?" I reached for her hands, but all I could feel was frigid air, like water over dry ice. "Are you kidding me?" I rushed out before she was gone.

"What am I supposed to do in 1875?"

You'll know soon. Please remember I love you, son, and I always will.

And with that, she was gone, leaving my questions unanswered. I was a survivor, or at least I thought I was until tonight. I only hoped I would do better in 1875 than I had in 2016.

~⚬ 18 ⚬~

1880, TRAIN TRAVEL

Nathaniel

I⊤ SEEMED A lifetime ago when, in fact, it has only been five years in this century. I didn't understand why I was just now contemplating my last night in Boston. All I could think about was what I could have done differently to keep from dying.

Nothing. Absolutely nothing.

Not that I believe in fate, mind you. But it had been my fate to die that night. Since then, I'd made the most of what 1875 had to offer and slowly became content living a new life in a new century.

At least I was alive.

My focus once again turned to the captivating woman sitting on a bench across the aisle from me. I had to meet her. But how? I didn't want to seem too forward and scare her. The two boys beside her made me think she was a married woman. Or, more than likely, it was the ring on her left hand that gave it away.

Not to wish her misfortune, I could only hope she was a widow. So many scenarios played out in my mind—none of which diminished the fact I at least had to get her name. I formulated my plan. Pretending to read, I stared mindlessly at the words on the newsprint when they unexpectedly liquefied, dissolving at the bottom of the page.

Think man. You can do better than this!

⋯⋯

Rebecca

I could only imagine what my face would look like if I hadn't used the rice powder to cover the discoloration. After six days of travel, the bruising was beginning to fade, but not enough for me to go without covering the damage Elliot had caused.

I whined silently. Will we ever reach Arizona? I was complaining to myself, so at least no one had to listen. I was aching all over, dirty, tired, and hungry for more than the mystery stews we had been served at the rail stops along the way. Oh, how I longed for the luxury of the Pullman car's soft beds, overstuffed chairs, French soaps, and warm water.

Porter and Daniel's energy was relentless, always fidgeting in their seats when they weren't asleep. We had run out of ideas to keep the boys occupied, and I could tell by the look on Pearl's face that she was just as weary as I was. But, she would never complain. We still had a long way to go before reaching Arizona, and we desperately needed rest.

⋯⋯

Nathaniel

"Excuse me, Ma'am." I must have dozed off momentarily when Daniel pulled on my coat sleeve, and the unassuming male voice standing next to my seat earned my attention. Looking up, I stared a bit too intensely for a proper lady to look into the most captivating green eyes I'd ever seen.

"Ma'am. May I be of service?"

"Excuse me?" I replied, squinting my eyebrows together, not understanding what he meant.

"I'm sorry, Ma'am. He took off what I surmised was a cowboy hat. Of course, I wasn't familiar with the apparel, not seeing men in Boston wear them.

With a short bow, he added, "Let me properly introduce myself. My name is Nathaniel Burns."

"Mr. Burns," I replied, nodding my head while not taking my eyes off him. His rugged style appealed to me. Something Elliott couldn't achieve in a lifetime. From where I sat and the kink in my neck, I made him out to be well over six feet tall.

Studying him, from his reddish-blonde hair to his handsome tanned face, it was his eyes that caught my full attention, holding me captive with their golden flecks surrounding a sea of emeralds.

"Yes, Ma'am. I couldn't help but notice that your boys here have a bit of energy to burn off. If I may be so bold, I thought I could be of assistance to you and your lady's maid by keeping them entertained for a while, allowing you both to rest undisturbed."

Stuttering, I couldn't find the right words to reply. "I ah . . . That's very kind of you, sir. But I'm sorry, Mr. Burns, I don't believe we've met before. Have we?" I had to be careful. This man could be working for Elliot.

"I apologize, Ma'am. I just thought I could be of assistance. But I understand your hesitance."

Turning away and placing his hat back on his head, he touched the brim with his fingertip and returned to his seat. I found myself gawking at his backside. I couldn't help it as I watched his masculine form gracefully move away. Once seated, he smiled, nodded, and then raised his newspaper, probably dismissing our encounter.

"You're blushing, Ma'am," Pearl said, grinning while simultaneously grasping the back of Porter's coat with little effort, keeping him from running out into the aisle as he slipped out of the sleeves.

"What? I am not," I answered, touching my warm cheeks. "What are you thinking, Pearl?"

"Oh, nothing, Ma'am," she chimed, pulling Porter back into his seat by his suspenders.

"Pearl, that is not a look meaning nothing."

Taking a handkerchief out of my reticule, I dabbed at the dampness under my eyes. Of course, I wasn't crying. It was just the glow of moisture. Pearl's questioning had me ruffled. And so did those eyes across the aisle!

Leaning forward, I kinked my index finger, motioning Pearl toward me, and whispered, "Pearl, what if Elliot hired Mr. Burns to find us? What if I let him watch the boys, and we fall asleep? He could abscond with Porter and Daniel, and we'd never notice.

"You can't be sure of that, Ma'am. What if he is just a kind gentleman offering to help?"

By now, Daniel and Porter were both annoyingly swinging their legs energetically back and forth under their seats. At the same time, Pearl and I placed our hands on their knees to stop their movement. Looking up at me with long pouts, Porter and Daniel crossed their arms over their chest in what I could only describe as two young boys' sheer defiance.

Sighing, "What am I going to do with these two?" They, too, were tired, and I didn't have the heart to reprimand them. Looking at Pearl, I rolled my eyes in frustration. Maybe she was right. But could I take that chance?

Pearl recognized my quandary when she suggested, "What if Mr. Burns has the boys sit with him for a brief time? Let's say an hour. He can entertain them, and we can take turns getting some well-needed rest. I'll stay awake for thirty minutes while you sleep. Then we'll switch, making sure his offer is sincere."

"You're probably right," I replied, yawning and sitting back in my seat. "It really would be nice to have some uninterrupted rest." Now, I would have to humble myself to Mr. Burns decent side. Shoulders back, head held high, I stood, running my hands down the front of my gown in an attempt to smooth out the wrinkles. Approaching his seat, he appeared engrossed in his newspaper, or he'd chosen to feign ignorance at my presence.

Standing in the aisle to his left, I cleared my throat to garner his attention. "Mr. Burns." Upon hearing my voice, he slowly lowered his paper, holding firmly to its edges, and looked up, waiting for me to continue.

Oh! There were those eyes again. Quickly gathering my thoughts, I proceeded. "Mr. Burns. I want to apologize for my rudeness earlier. You were only being kind in offering your assistance to watch my boys. My lady's maid and dear friend's name is Pearl. We discussed your offer. Bowing my head as if to acquiesce, which I wasn't, I twisted my handkerchief between my hands.

Rushing out before I lost my nerve, "If your kind offer still stands, we would be ever so grateful to accept your help."

Was his silence an indication that his offer had expired the moment he walked away from me? Why is he just staring at me? I'd asked him a simple question. I wasn't about to beg. I would never do that again with any man.

About to return to my seat, I was resigned to the fact that sleep would be elusive this day when he spoke. "Ma'am, I would be happy to help."

I waited. There had to be more. What could Mr. Burns possibly want from me in return? Surprised as I was, he didn't impose any conditions upon me. Nor did he belittle my previous decline or go into a tirade like Elliot would have.

"Thank you, Mr. Burns. I will speak with my sons to let them know of our plan. Then we can make introductions all around."

Without warning, the train lurched forward. "Oh!" I cried out as I reached for his headrest to steady my balance. But before I knew it, I was tumbling onto Mr. Burn's lap and crushing his newspaper.

"Oh my! I'm so sorry, Mr. Burns." Frantically, I struggled to upright myself, but his hands held firm around my waist.

"Are you alright, Mrs. Ackerman?" His lips were so close to my ear, but I still couldn't tell what he'd asked. Surrounded by his alluring musky scent, I lost my ability to speak. He made me feel lightheaded—nothing like the sickening cologne my husband used.

Shaking my head, I held my breath, and it wasn't because my corset was too tight. With my eyes pinned on his piercing stare, I gave in and let myself enjoy the moment in his strong arms.

Good heavens! What's happening to me? While Mr. Burns continued to hold me close, he cleared his throat and asked again, "Are you sure you're alright, Mrs. Ackerman?"

"Yes," I replied, trying to loosen his grasp with my hands. "I'm so sorry, Mr. Burns."

Finally releasing his hold, I quickly stood up as gracefully as possible.

"That's quite alright," he replied with a mischievous grin.

Stammering, I answered, "I ah, I'll return in a moment with my sons."

Turning away, I could feel the heat of a blush moving up my neck. Awkward as it might have been, it was rather exciting being held close by such a handsome gentleman.

~☙ 19 ❧~

TRAIN TRAVEL

Rebecca

DANIEL AND PORTER were now in Mr. Burns's care. While Pearl watched over all three of them, I settled as comfortably as possible in my seat, using my reticule as a makeshift pillow. Leaning against the cold window, the warmth from my breath clouded the view outside.

Before I could look back over my shoulder at Mr. Burns and my boys, I was drifting fast asleep, dreaming of another time, another place, another life.

~☙❧~

Remembering

A crackling fire roared in the large marble hearth, bathing our Brownstone's opulent parlor in golden brilliance. Leaning my head back against the soft velvet cushion of my chair, I sighed contentedly. I was a happily married woman with a husband who loved me and two wonderful children we adored.

Drifting on a mist of uncertainty, I imagined my once happy life. All I had ever wanted was to be loved by Elliot. Sadly, tears filled my eyes, remembering I had never seen any gestures of love between my parents.

Dreaming, I smiled, hearing the sound of my son's laughter echoing throughout the house. Unexpectedly, Elliot came home early from work, eagerly greeting me in the parlor. Holding me lovingly in his arms, we barely made it out of the foyer when his body's evident reaction had us eager to head upstairs.

Alas, our time alone would have to wait. Despite being married, tongues would wag if news got out that we were having clandestine meetings in the middle of the day. It was considered socially unacceptable. And not all of the house staff could be trusted to remain silent. Their wagging tongues had a habit of talking to other household staff. That's how scandalous rumors started.

Pearl, our housekeeper, knocked on the closed parlor door, awaiting admittance. "Come in," Elliot answered, displeased that we had been interrupted.

Holding me tightly in his arms, I glanced toward Pearl and smiled.

Not wanting to stare, she lowered her head and cleared her throat before speaking. "Good evening, Sir. I trust you had a pleasant day at work."

Elliot didn't answer. He rarely responded to Pearl's questions. When he did, his answers were always terse. Why, I wasn't sure. But it didn't matter then since Elliot was head of the house and could act as he pleased. That didn't mean I approved of his behavior since I cared dearly for Pearl. I hoped she understood why I kept quiet.

Remaining at the parlor entrance, Pearl avoided eye contact while adding, "Dinner will be served in ten minutes."

"Thank you, Pearl," I answered.

Elliot looked down at me blankly. Without turning toward Pearl, he added, "We'll be there when we're ready." Taking my shoulders in his hands, I returned my attention his way. I shuddered as he captured my lips hungrily, continuing our ardent foreplay before being interrupted.

Reluctantly, I was the one to break his embrace. Hands shaking, I gently pushed back against his chest while wickedly licking my lips and staring into his steel-gray eyes. "We better not keep dinner waiting much longer. We don't want it to get cold."

Looking at the closed doors, I added, "The boys are upstairs. Pearl fed them earlier so we could dine alone." Smiling demurely, I feigned the temptress, adding, "Perhaps we can continue this after dinner with dessert?"

Turning to leave, I stopped and looked over my shoulder, pointing my finger, "Upstairs."

Elliot groaned and pulled me back into his embrace, crushing me to his chest as he whispered in my ear, "I have an appetite for something much more enticing." His warm breath on my neck sent a tingling sensation down my spine as he placed one last passionate kiss on my already swollen lips.

⌒⚬⌒

"Mrs. Ackerman. Mrs. Ackerman," Pearl whispered, gently shaking my shoulder. Why would Pearl be calling for me? She had just been serving Elliot and my dinner. Groggy, the next thing I remember was Pearl placing her warm hand on my face.

"Dear girl. You slept so soundly, I hated to wake you. But I think the boys have learned to play poker quite handily. They've had considerable practice."

"Oh, good heavens!" I hadn't thought how Mr. Burns would entertain them. No doubt he's one of those cowboys I've read about.

Sitting upright, I asked, "How long have I been sleeping?"

"Just a little over an hour. It did you good to get some rest. You look more relaxed than I've seen you in days."

"I do feel better," I replied, slowly easing myself upright. "I'll just go gather the boys, and you can get some sleep."

Approaching Mr. Burns, I could see he, Daniel, and Porter were engrossed in something within the newspaper. No cards were visible. That sneaky Pearl! Mr. Burns looked up at me, placing a finger over his lips, indicating he wanted me to wait.

Remaining quiet, I listened as Porter, with his head on Mr. Burns' shoulder, read aloud from the newspaper. My heart ached knowing how much my boys longed for the love and companionship of a father—something Elliot would never find time for. Here they were with a total stranger receiving that attention and comfort.

All three looked up at my announcement. "Boys, I believe we have taken up enough of Mr. Burns' valuable time. Please, thank him for his kindness." Making me proud, both Porter and Daniel thanked Mr. Burns, using their best boyish charm. Holding out my hand, I said, "Now, let's return to our seats. Pearl has a snack waiting for you."

At the mention of food, both boys dashed over to Pearl. I remained beside Mr. Burns, taking in his features for my lonely nights ahead, knowing we would never see each other again once we departed the train.

Suddenly, a sense of sadness overcame me. Why? After all, he was still a stranger to me. Maybe it was because his kindness toward my boys had touched my heart. No, it was more than that, but I couldn't describe or admit it at that moment.

Mr. Burns made a motion to stand. Although I wanted to remain close, I knew it wasn't proper and stepped back to allow him room.

"Mrs. Ackerman, I thoroughly enjoyed my time with your boys. They are good boys and must make their father and you very proud."

My heart skipped a beat. I loved my boys, but I couldn't tell this stranger that their father could care less about how good they were. That was something I'd keep to myself.

Mr. Burns continued, "I don't mean to scare you, but I must tell you that the next leg of your journey can be somewhat dangerous. The train from here will go through Indian territory and areas of previous train robberies. It will be important that you and Mrs. O'Callaghan be vigilant of your surroundings."

"Oh, my!" I hesitated before continuing. "I'm grateful for the warning."

My senses heightened at the thought of such trouble. "Thank you, Mr. Burns. I'll share this information with Pearl."

Mr. Burns reached out as if to take hold of my hand, then thought better of it and pulled back.

"I would hate for anything to happen to you, your boys, and Mrs. O'Callaghan."

"Mr. Burns, I appreciate your kindness in caring for my boys, even if it was for a short time. It seems you've made quite a lasting impression on them. How can I ever repay you?"

Looking down at my hands once again, I asked, "I hope they didn't cause you too much trouble?"

"No, they were well-behaved, and I enjoyed their company." Glancing down, he winked and added, "That Porter is one smart boy. He read several small articles with little help, except for the larger words."

Did Mr. Burns just wink at me? Can you imagine that? Elliot would never do such a thing. He had no sense of humor. I could hear him say, "They're sons of a newspaper magnate, after all. They better know how to read!

"I'm glad they were no bother." About to return to my seat, I added, "Again, I appreciate your kindness. I wish you well on the rest of your journey."

"Thank you, Mrs. Ackerman," he answered. "I wish the same to you, Pearl, and your boys. Please stay safe."

Despite my mind telling me this was just an infatuation, my heart told me to imprint his face and kindness deep within my memory. Obviously, Mr. Burns was a gentleman and definitely not Elliot.

20

TRAIN TRAVEL

Nathaniel

As Mrs. Ackerman turned to leave, I understood how much I wanted this raven-haired beauty to stay by my side. Was it the fragrant scent of her lily perfume that held my intrigue? Maybe it was the way she tilted her head when she gazed into my eyes or those lush pink lips that formed a perfect smile. They all drew me in. She was a lady who had my mind careening headlong off the nearest trestle.

I only heard her laugh once, and I sensed she was a woman who hadn't laughed in quite some time. But the sound of her laughter made my head spin. If only I could be the one to place a smile on her face each day and stare endlessly into those soulful eyes every morning, I would be the happiest man alive.

Did her husband know how lucky he was?

What would happen if I were to be so bold as to ask her to sit with me awhile? Would she think me too forward and never speak with me the rest of the trip? I couldn't risk it. I had to remain the perfect gentleman.

At that inopportune moment, a familiar voice from my past snuck in. *Nathanial, what are you thinking? Have you completely lost your mind? She's a married woman, after all. Be the gentleman I raised you to be.*

It had been five years since we last spoke. Though I'd longed to hear my mother's voice again, she picked the untimeliest moments to present herself.

Nathaniel now is not the time to get involved with a woman despite her alluring beauty. You have to get to Yuma. You have important business to attend to.

"I know. I know," I whispered under my breath. "You're right as usual, Mom." Biting my tongue, I nodded my head despite a strong urge to move on my desire. I would have had no trouble approaching this attractive woman in another century. Here, it was different. Mrs. Ackerman was a refined and sophisticated lady, and I wouldn't tarnish her reputation.

BOSTON, MASSACHUSETTS

Elliot

What is taking that Pinkerton agent so long? That irresponsible man must have some news about Rebecca's whereabouts by now unless he doesn't want to tell me where she is. Well, I'll show him who he's dealing with. He can't fool Elliott Ackerman.

I rang for my new valet since the previous old codger, Vernon, had left without a word. Unlike him, this new man, Sinclair, was an Englishman who had been in service in a royal household, so he declared. I wasn't sure about his story or references, but he kept to himself, which was more than I could say for Vernon. Vernon had been too overprotective of my wife.

Standing in the doorway, Sinclair asked, with a no-nonsense air of authority and regal British accent, "You called for me, Sir?"

"Yes. I want you to personally take this note to the Pinkerton Agency in town. And tell them I expect a reply today." Pausing, I added, "Better yet, have them send a response back with you."

"Yes, Sir. Is there anything else I can do for you, Sir?"

"No, that will be all," I answered, brushing him off with a wave of my hand. Stopping him, I quickly added, "Make sure you bring me their response as soon as you return. I don't care how long you have to wait for it. Just bring it to me today!"

While Sinclair was out, I packed my bags and secured them in my lavatory. I couldn't have anyone knowing that I'd recently purchased a pistol in an out-of-the-way shop in the seedier part of town. The weapon would not only protect me from the ruffians as I traveled west, but it would come in handy in handling Rebecca if she refused to return with me.

I had other plans for her future. Either way, my sons would be coming back to Boston. As soon as Sinclair returned, I was ready to leave on the next available train.

⁓✥⁓

FORT WORTH, TEXAS, 1880

Rebecca

We arrived in Fort Worth, and despite the bright sunshine, the winter air was cool and crisp. The surrounding landscape was flat as far as the eye could see. I had never experienced scenery so devoid of color yet beautiful in its own right.

I was grateful that I hadn't seen the man from the train station since we left Boston. If indeed he was following us and had been on the same train, he was doing an excellent job of keeping himself hidden. I only hoped seeing him had been my imagination running wild and Elliott hadn't employed his services.

Mr. Burns kindly assisted Pearl, the boys, and myself off the railcar. Standing on the platform, I ran my hands down the front of my gown in an attempt to rid it of two weeks' worth of dust. It was an automatic reaction and purely a futile attempt.

Looking up, I caught Mr. Burns watching me. Clearing my throat and not knowing what else to say, I expressed my thanks. "Mr. Burns, again, I can't thank you enough for your assistance the past few days. You were a great deal of help to Pearl and me." I averted his eyes and added, "You've been a perfect gentleman."

"It was my pleasure, Ma'am," he responded, tipping his hat while the sides of his mouth turned up in a grin.

I noticed he had one bag sitting at his feet and surmised he was eager to be on his way, so I added, "We won't keep you any longer. I'm sure you have business to attend to." Taking one last look into the depths of those emerald eyes, I held my breath. This was goodbye. I disliked goodbyes, so I didn't say it. It had such a finality to it as if placing a warm hand on a cold casket and saying your final farewell.

Breaking eye contact, I looked down at the dust-covered board-walk and revealed, "We'll be staying here the next two days to get some much-needed rest. The boys definitely need to run off excess energy." I was hoping to see him again before we departed Fort Worth.

"I think that is a wise idea, Mrs. Ackerman. May I offer some advice?"

"Why, of course," I answered, looking back up. After all, I didn't think he would lead us astray.

Using his hands to encompass the street, he expressed his concern for our safety. "Please don't wander about the town in the late afternoon or evenings. It's not safe. There are all kinds of nefarious characters lurking about who would not hesitate to. Well, I don't need to go into detail other than you're a beautiful woman if you don't mind me saying."

Blushing, I replied, "Thank you for your concern, Mr. Burns. I will definitely take your advice to heart." With my hand on Daniel's shoulder, I added, "We have no intention of moving about. Our only purpose for staying here is to rest."

Taking his hat off and catching me by surprise, Mr. Burns gently took hold of my fingers, leaned forward, and placed a soft kiss on the top of my gloved hand. My heart skipped a beat as a tingling sensation ran up my arm. Elliott had never been able to accomplish such an amorous sensation.

Somewhat reluctantly, I eased my hand away. Did he feel it too? Surely, he must have. Or was I being presumptuous?

"Well, I guess this is goodbye." He'd said it. That awful word I tried to avoid! "It was a pleasure to make yours, Pearl, and the boy's acquaintance. As brief as it was, meeting you made my journey much more enjoyable."

Replacing his hat on his head, what I soon learned to be a Stetson, he turned, leaving us standing on the boardwalk in front of the hotel. Frozen in place, I couldn't put one foot in front of the other as I watched Mr. Burns' tall, muscular form disappear into the dust-covered masses.

Turning to face the hotel door, I stopped and turned back for one last look. Letting out a sigh of disappointment, he was already gone.

The hotel was conveniently located next to the Texas and Pacific rail station, where a constant whirlwind of dust and debris swirled around the building. Despite the street and outside of its building being dirty, the foyer was clean and a welcome relief from the railcar's cramped seating and stagnant air.

Fort Worth was near the end of our train adventure until we reached southern New Mexico Territory. Rail lines were limited in east Texas and, for the time being, non-existent in the western part of the state.

I had a difficult choice to make. One, head to Galveston along the Texas coast and travel by steamer through the Isthmus of Panama, then up to California. Once there, we would take another train, the Southern Pacific, to Yuma. The second was to travel by stagecoach, a more direct route but riskier considering the dangers of traveling through the unforgiving desert and Indian territory. Both would add days I didn't think my brother had. Either way, I had to get to Yuma, and time was running out.

21

FORTH WORTH, TEXAS

Benjamin

I DESPERATELY NEEDED to find a room with a bath and, more importantly, a bug-free bed. Riding at the back of the train in less-than-desirable accommodations had me bone weary. I'd worn the same two sets of clothes for the past two weeks, and depending on which way the wind blew, I'd smelled odious for far too long.

Fortunately, throughout the trip, I had been able to keep myself concealed from Mrs. Ackerman. To my advantage, rarely was she without the boys and her lady's companion. It wouldn't do to have me staying in the same establishment as my assignment and risk being discovered.

Caught behind a long line of departing passengers, I watched from within the car as Mrs. Ackerman was assisted by a gentleman I didn't recognize. Such an alluring vision, she appeared comfortable taking his hand. Holding her head high, like royalty, she lifted the hem of her dress with her free hand and descended the stairs of the railcar.

Once she reached the platform, something must have told her to turn around as if she knew I was watching her. As she scanned the platform and train windows, I abruptly turned in the opposite direction. But I didn't miss the man assisting her kissing the top of her hand.

Who is he? Was this her brother, my supervisor, spoke of? I didn't think so. I was positive that Mrs. Ackerman had noticed me outside her Pullman car window in Boston, and if she saw me now, she would easily conclude I was following her. That wouldn't do if I were to make the remainder of the journey to Arizona unseen.

After acquiring lodging, I would need to find a shop where I could purchase clothing more suited for the West and less recognizable to Mrs. Ackerman. Once I departed the car, I watched from a safe distance as the gentleman walked her and her entourage through the crowd to the upscale hotel across from the train station.

Tomorrow, rising before daybreak, I'd post myself in the café across the street from her lodging, making it easy to watch her movement unseen. Watching and waiting is what I did best. I would need to find out what her next move would be. Until then, it would be a long night and an even longer day tomorrow.

෧ᢒᡒᢣ෨

Rebecca

I'd been drawn to Mr. Burns the same as a schoolgirl with her first crush. As if his leaving had taken all the air from my lungs, I struggled to make sense of my reactions. Despite Pearl and the boys being by my side, I felt so alone once he left. His presence had lent a sense of security to the last part of our trip, knowing no one would bother us as long as he was nearby.

Unexpectedly, the hair on the back of my neck stood up. Someone was watching us. Scanning the crowd and the windows of the train, I didn't see anyone I recognized or thought was suspicious. Nor did I see the man from Boston. Yet, that didn't mean he wasn't there.

Then again, any of the people moving in the mass of bodies pushing toward the stack of luggage could be working for Elliot. Feigning confidence, I turned and asked, "Pearl, please stay here with the boys while I procure a porter to carry our luggage."

Shading her eyes from the glaring sun, Pearl answered, "Of course, Mrs. Ackerman," With a hand on each of the boys' shoulders, Pearl moved them toward the protection of the building.

Locating our trunks on the loading dock, I motioned for a porter while pointing to our luggage. A large bald and bearded man saw me pointing his way and came forward with his handcart. Indicating the building, I asked, "Sir, would you be so kind as to take this luggage to the hotel over there?"

"Yes, Ma'am. I sure will," he answered, his bright smile lighting up his face. Following me across the street, he deposited our trunks just inside the hotel door, where I paid the man and thanked him for his help.

Once inside, I turned in circles and stared into the lobby's corners. I still suspected someone was watching us. Momentarily reassured, I stopped and looked about the foyer one last time, then hesitantly moved toward the reception desk.

Most assuredly, this establishment was not the Tremont House in Boston. I only hoped the rooms and linens were clean and the meals agreeable. The sign on the desk instructed patrons to 'Ring the Bell for Assistance.' I did just that and waited for someone to appear. It didn't take long for a stout, balding man to step out from the back door and stand behind the small counter.

With a greying handkerchief, he methodically cleaned first one, then the other lens of his spectacles. Placing them back on his face, he turned his attention to me. Speaking with an accent I'd never heard before, I couldn't help but stare at his lips as they formed his words in a drawn-out, exhaling breath.

"May I help ya, Ma'am?" he drawled, once again adjusting his spectacles above his nose.

"Yes. I need two adjoining rooms, please."

"Yes, Ma'am. Just so happens we have two rooms down the hall from each other," he responded, spinning the registration book around in a motion he had probably done a thousand times.

"No Sir, that won't do!" Letting out a frustrated breath of fatigue, I was close to losing my patience when I responded. "You must have misunderstood me." Using my hands to explain, I detailed my request. "I asked for two rooms beside each other with a door between their sitting areas."

Scratching the few hairs he had left on his head, he glared at me as if I were asking him for the sun, the moon, and the stars. "Ma'am, that's all we gots. Take it or leave it."

His arrogance was wearing on my last nerve, and I was too tired to argue. Before he could spin the ledger back around, Pearl placed her hand on the book and replied to the gnat of a man. "That will be fine, sir. We'll take the rooms as long as they are on the same floor."

"Yup!" he replied. Satisfied, he went straight to the financial business. "That'll be eight bits. A night! For each room!"

I looked at Pearl as she nodded her head in an attempt to keep me from further arguing with the man. I couldn't help but think what an outrageous price he was charging for this establishment.

Reaching into my reticule, I pulled out the excessive amount he'd quoted and placed it on the counter. Grabbing the coins greedily, I couldn't help but notice the brown staining on his teeth and fingertips. Oh, what have I gotten us into now?

I wanted to turn and run out the door but knew it was no good. I'd dragged Pearl and the boys on this journey, and we desperately needed to rest. Signing the register under an assumed name, I wished the stout man would hurry up and give us our keys so we could get to our rooms and clean off the dust and grime.

"Tell me," I asked. "Does this establishment have a Lady's Ordinary?"

Wrinkling up his nose as if he smelled something foul, he responded with a confused look and asked, "A lady's what?"

"A Lady's Ordinary," I calmly repeated. Did I really need to tell him that it was socially unacceptable for a lady to dine alone in public rooms of hotels where men convened? Many of the East's hotels opened women-only dining rooms referred to as a Lady's Ordinary. They were quite a pleasant area where we didn't have to listen to the incessant droning of men discussing one form or another of boring business.

Pearl leaned close to my ear and whispered while pointing to the attached dining hall. Shaking my head, I looked down at the dirt trail on the floor and was shocked to see ladies eating amongst men of all stations. Well, that solved my problem of trying to explain myself to this man.

I had a lot to learn about this place called the West.

Thank heavens our trunks had made it to our rooms ahead of us. Fortunately, the hotel was small enough for our rooms to be just three doors apart. I would have Daniel and Porter sleep with me the first night and Pearl the second. That way, each of us could get one uninterrupted night of rest.

Famished after the bland train-stop fare, we returned to the dining room after freshening up. Although it wouldn't be Pearl's delicious cooking, I hoped it would be palatable. As we entered the dining room, I searched the faces of its patrons, a habit since leaving Boston. Satisfied there was no sign of the man from the Chicago train station, I relaxed for the first time in days. Of course, this wasn't the only sleeping establishment in town, and he still could be nearby.

We hadn't been back in our rooms an hour when a thundering noise from below rattled our windows and shook the floorboards. The boys, ever ready for adventure, dashed to the window, squealing with glee at the scene below.

Coming to stand behind them, Pearl and I watched in amazement as a herd of the largest animals I'd ever seen thunderously ran down the main street. In front and behind the beasts were men on horseback yelling words we couldn't make out. Which was probably for the best, considering young ears were listening.

It truly was a remarkable scene. Better than a circus. The animals were of varying shades of beige, brown, and white. Atop their heads were long sharp horns that looked as if they could cause a great deal of pain if a person got too close.

If I thought the street was dusty before, it certainly was now. The racing animals produced swirling cones of dust, creating small tornadoes rising as high as the rooftops. Coughing, I waved my handkerchief before my face as the dust rushed through the open window. Before I could pull the boys back and shut it, we were once again covered in dust.

⚬⚬⚬

The brilliant sun shining through the once-white curtains woke me at five the following morning. Pearl, bless her heart, had insisted on having the boys stay in her room last night and I was ever so grateful.

Tonight, they would sleep in my room in order to prepare for the next leg of our journey when we would have to be up and fed before five and ready for our conveyance to leave at six. While remembering Mr. Burns' warning, we walked along the boardwalk, not venturing far from the hotel. It felt good to move about and have the unrushed opportunity to shop for necessities.

By nightfall, I felt somewhat rested yet anxious to be back on our way to Arizona. I would have kept going the day we arrived, but the boys were restless, and I feared the trip was becoming too much for Pearl, although she would never admit it.

Ready to leave with a basket full of food prepared by the kitchen staff, the four of us stood in front of the hotel, waiting for the stage to arrive. We were finally back on our way.

Rattled as I was, I'd forgotten to telegram Miss Sweeney in Yuma to let her know we were coming and give her our approximate arrival date. Well, there was no time now as the stage rounded the outskirts of town.

I prayed my brother was still alive.

~⚬ 22 ⚬~

STAGE TRAVEL

Rebecca

AS WE PUSHED through the unforgiving desert, the lurching stage hadn't missed a rock or rut in the winding trail. We weren't far outside Fort Worth when my lower back began to throb painfully. I tried easing the discomfort by changing positions, stretching, then twisting from side to side, but nothing worked, especially since we were packed into such a small space with three other strangers plus mailbags under our feet.

All of us were too busy holding onto leather straps dangling from the coach's ceiling with one hand while gripping the edge of our leather seat with the other. It took all our strength to keep seated. I couldn't believe I was thinking this, but what I wouldn't give if we could be back in the comfort of the hotel in Fort Worth.

As the horses pushed forward, the sound of straining leather and metal harnesses jangled over the stage driver's yelling. When I wasn't holding on, I tried looking out the window to catch a glimpse of the desert as it rapidly flew by.

All covered in dust from head to foot, I didn't think we would ever be clean again. The only thing endeavoring to keep the churning dust out of the inside of the coach was a square piece of fraying canvas crudely tacked over each window.

Dirt was the least of my worries. The cactus-laden landscape all looked the same, and for all I knew, the coach could have been traveling in circles. I could only pray we made it to Yuma in one piece. Better yet, alive.

❦

After days of tortuous travel, it was late afternoon when the horses slowed their pace. They must have sensed they were near the end of their journey, where a meal and a well-deserved rest awaited.

After our last stage stop, we were the only four passengers left on the coach. The farther west we went, the more my anxiety increased. I was impatient to see my brother. I'd gradually come to understand why he suddenly left five years ago. But I was still angry with him for not telling me where he had been headed.

Truthfully, at the time, I don't think he knew where he was going. All I remember is that too many people had hurt him for him to stay in Boston. Yet, I couldn't keep the thought of him dying before I reached Yuma out of my mind.

Pearl and the boys had thankfully fallen fast asleep several miles back, with Daniel's head on Pearl's lap and Porter's on mine. I hated to wake them, but they needed to be ready as we approached Yuma.

The coach driver repeatedly yelled to the horses, "Whoa, boys! Whoa!" The pounding of the creaking wheels and jangling metal stopped, after which there was a moment of silence. Listening closely, I heard the sound of rushing water, unable to imagine where it was coming from, considering we were in the middle of a desert.

While trying not to awaken the boys, I lifted the dusty canvas covering and peered out the window. I couldn't believe what I was seeing. Water! Lots of water. Actually, a river of swift-moving water.

The coach driver had to be crazy to think he could cross that churning liquid mass with this coach. We'll all drown. Panicking, I tapped the coach's ceiling several times to attract the driver's attention. Unfortunately, my action awoke Pearl and the boys, and the next thing I knew, the man was peering in the window at me from above with his head upside down.

"Yes, Ma'am. Ya'll need something," he asked with a toothless grin.

I turned my head sideways to focus on his upside-down face. At the same time, I bit the right side of my lower lip, cleared my throat, and croaked out, "Yes, Sir."

My heart painfully thudded inside my chest. Fear mounting, I pointed out the window as I struggled to get my question past my lips. "You are not thinking of crossing that river in this conveyance, are you, Sir?"

Chuckling, he pointed to a crude floating device tilting precariously to one side at the river's edge. "No, Ma'am, we're not crossing the ole' Gila in this here, coach. Well, ya all be in the coach, but we're going over it on what they call that there ferry."

Fear and lack of control were not unfamiliar to me. Powerless, I nodded, pointed toward the river's bank, and asked, "You mean to tell me we are getting on that floating thing?"

His only response was a nod.

I quickly brought my head back inside the coach as he sent a long line of tobacco juice streaming out between his brown-stained teeth. Swallowing back the bitter bile lodged in my throat, I stared out the coach's small window at an unsavory group of men standing along the water's edge.

Men in wrinkled, mismatched military uniforms stood alongside filth-covered characters draped in what appeared to be animal skins. Slapping each other on their backs, they pointed to the coach while laughing loudly at me with my head hanging out the window.

They must have heard me question the driver. Dear Lord, we're doomed!

Our driver yelled out to the group in question. "Well, ar' ya all going to just stand there scratching yer mangy backsides, or ya going te help me load this here coach?"

The men approached, tipping their hats and grinning at me with toothless smiles. My insides quivered, and I shook my head, hoping we'd survive the crossing.

The so-called ferry didn't look any safer than if we all tried to swim across. I only hoped we didn't tip over and wind up in the frigid waters because I never learned how to swim. All of us would last but a few minutes in the fridged waters, with our heavy clothing sinking us to the bottom and sweeping us under in the turbulence.

I had entrusted our safe travel to this man thus far, so I only hoped he would safely deliver us across this churning waterway. Lurching forward, I prayed, Nathan! Where are you now when I need you?

I gathered Porter and Daniel close while the groaning coach tilted from side to side. Their eyes were wide with excitement, but I couldn't let them sense my fear as I held the boys firmly in place.

The shouting between the ferry driver and those back on land, the groaning coach, and the roaring of the raging river had me pleading for our lives. I held my breath as the water surged higher and higher around us, and we drifted closer to the other shore.

I'll never understand how the horses remained so calm. But they did. They must have crossed this river several times before and obviously survived, giving me a glimmer of hope, albeit a slim one.

When we arrived on the opposite shore, Pearl continued to keep her eyes tightly closed. Sagging back against the seat, I struggled to speak. When I could finally get the words out, I said, "Pearl, you can open your eyes now. We're safely on the other side."

After all this, dear brother, you better still be alive.

~ 23 ~

ARIZONA TERRITORY, 1880

Rebecca

HOW WE MADE it to Arizona in one piece was beyond me. Surely, Elliot wouldn't travel this far. I couldn't imagine the illustrious Mr. Ackerman covered in filth and smelling as we now were.

As much as I grumbled at the soddies and their meager meals, they had been a blessing. The small adobe homes called waystations provided the stage with fresh horses and the passengers with meager meals.

A flat bread served with a spicy mixture of meat was nothing like I'd ever tasted, but sided with red beans, they added a certain flavor. Instead of turning my nose up at the fare, I ate it with gratitude but not before taking several deep breaths and praying it would stay down. Surprised as we were, the meals were filling and tasty, and our hosts were pleasant.

After eating, we had a few spare minutes where the boys could release their pent-up energy by running free around the station while Pearl and I walked about in an effort to stretch our legs. At this point in our travels, I was no longer concerned about how dirty the boys became. I only hoped hot water and a bath were awaiting us at the end of our journey.

Free from the cold and icy snow of Boston, I peered lovingly at their dust-covered faces as the white of their eyes shone brightly in the sunshine. Seemingly happy and without a care, it did my heart good to see them smile and laugh again. It had been such a long time and well worth all we'd been through.

After several hours back on the road, the stage suddenly jerked to a stop in front of a dusty two-story building with brown peeling paint. Looking out the small window, I watched swirling tunnels of dust reach skyward then make their way through the stage's small window, causing Pearl and me to cough.

"Yuma! Last stop!" yelled the driver. We had finally arrived in Yuma dusty and a bit disheveled early on Christmas Eve Day after a miserable ride on a stage. Our bodies would never feel the same again. They had been jostled through the dirt-barren countryside littered with slithering animals and strange trees with prickly needles.

All I wanted was a bath, clean clothes, and a palatable hot meal where I could identify its contents. Was that too much to ask for?

⌇⌇⌇

As we arrived at our final destination, the desert air was cool and clear, and we could finally take a deep breath. Standing on the well-worn boardwalk was a red-haired gentleman whose shoulders, I would imagine, were almost too broad to allow him passage through any door.

Stepping forward as if on cue, he opened the stage door. "Ma'am." His deep voice resonated throughout the coach in a thick Scottish accent. Extending his gloved hand, I couldn't help but notice they were almost as large as his shoulders, yet I gave no thought nor hesitation and accepted his assistance.

Bending my head down, I exited the stagecoach a bit off balance. Although I was on a stable platform, I was glad to have his firm hand to hold on to. He then extended his kindness to Pearl and my boys.

When all four of us stood near the hotel door, he announced with a slight bow, "Ma'am, Angus MacLachlan at your service."

"Mr. McLaughlan. Thank you for your kind assistance." Looking him directly in the eyes, I wouldn't show him how nervous I was. But he didn't elicit that uneasy perception I'd expected from a stranger. Was it a coincidence that he happened to be standing there when the stage arrived?

Probably, but I wouldn't let my fears get the best of me. Still, I had to be cautious that he wasn't part of Elliot's devious plan.

"It's a pleasure, Ma'am. Smiling, he pointed to the rear of the coach and asked, "I can retrieve your bags out of the boot and place them here on the walkway if you'd like."

"A boot? Whatever do you mean?" I looked down at my feet, a bit confused.

"I'm sorry, Ma'am, that's what these Westerners call the luggage stowaway," he replied, pointing to the back of the coach.

"Oh. I see." I really did have much to learn about Western ways and their strange vernacular. "Thank you again. That would be very kind of you."

"Grateful, Angus," the coach driver yelled down from his seat.

"You're welcome, Whip," Mr. McLaughlin answered.

Before I had time to take in the activity on the street, our luggage sat on the boardwalk beside us, and the stagecoach was lurching away, leaving us in a cloud of dust.

"Ma'am," Mr. McLaughlin asked, drawing my attention back to him. "Is anyone meeting you here?"

"No. We'll be staying in the hotel," I answered, looking up at the sign indicating The Palace Hotel, H. Fox, Proprietor. Swallowing the lump in my throat, I hoped we had made the right decision to travel all this way. I couldn't help but think of possibly being too late to find Caleb alive.

"Well, I'll just take your luggage inside and let you ladies take over." Picking up our two heavy trunks without effort, I opened the door for him to walk through. I was surprised he fit. He set them down near the side of the main desk as I looked around the entry.

"Thank you again, Mr. McLaughlin." I started to reach into my reticule to tip him, but he quickly reached out his hand to stop me.

"That won't be necessary, Ma'am. It was a pleasure to help you lovely ladies. If there is ever anything I can do for you while you're in town, please come by the mercantile and let me know."

I thanked him again as he proceeded to tell me that he and his wife owned the mercantile and that I was welcome to come by his establishment anytime. Tipping his hat, he moved to exit the lobby. Watching him leave, I hoped I'd just made my first friend in Yuma. Something I would definitely need if Elliot showed up.

I intended for Pearl to come to the clinic with me, but she was too exhausted to make it beyond the hotel. Acquiring a room, I ensured she was comfortably settled in before I left to look for my brother. "Pearl, you need to get some rest. I'm going to look for Caleb. I may not be able to return this evening if I find him. But I'll send word to you where I am."

Kissing her good night, Porter, Daniel, and I headed downstairs. I stopped at the clerk's desk and ordered a tub and hot water to be delivered to her room. A hot bath would help soothe the aches from weeks of travel. I only wished I wasn't in such a rush that I could take in this luxury.

Asking the clerk for directions to the doctor's office, I was grateful to learn it was only three blocks away. The sun was beginning to set behind the distant hills, and I didn't want us wandering around in an unfamiliar town after dark.

YUMA, ARIZONA TERRITORY, 1880

Rebecca

WITH MY NERVES on edge, I stood outside a white picket fence in desperate need of repair.

"Ouch! Mommy, you're hurting my hand," Porter cried, pulling away to get my attention.

"Oh, Porter. Mommy is so sorry." Caught up in what I was about to do, I had no idea how firmly I grasped his hand. I eased my hold while returning my attention to the building with the gingerbread trim.

What if the doctor gives me the news that Caleb has died? I couldn't handle that. If it were true, we would have no choice but to move on. Heaven only knew where I could hide next.

Although I hadn't seen the man from outside the train in Boston since we'd left, I had that sixth sense he had followed me here. It was just a matter of time before we came face-to-face. As I looked around the yard, I pushed open the gate and moved the boys ahead of me.

Following close behind, we walked up a path lined by dead and dying rosebushes. Standing at the bottom of the stairs, I read the sign over the porch announcing this was the clinic of Mathew Sweeney, M.D. Curious, the last name on the sign was the same as on the letter I'd received asking me to come here. Was Emily his wife?

With a sense of unease, I raised my hand to knock on the clinic door. Quickly pulling it back, I had a sickening feeling in the pit of my stomach.

You're letting your fear take over, Rebecca. Calm down. It was my mother. I was ever so happy to have her here with me now. I missed her wisdom, and she'd know what to do.

Just knock on the door and get on with it, she said.

Once again raising my hand, I knocked. There was no going back now. I would soon find out what happened to my brother. The door opened, and a rush of heat surrounded me.

⚬≼⧫≽⚬

"What can I do for you?" announced the husky voice I remember so well. "Becca!"

Hearing my nickname pass my brother's lips in a hushed whisper caused my heart to pause a beat. Caleb was alive.

Reaching out, he pulled me into his arms with a firm embrace. I had no choice but to place my head on his chest and let the tears I had been holding back minutes ago soak the front of his shirt. Alternating between hugging, laughing, and crying, I wouldn't let go. I wasn't about to lose him again.

Time stood still.

Caleb's complexion paled. With trembling hands in an effort to ensure I was real, he began running his warm fingers over my face and down my arms. All the while, my sweet boys remained silent, standing beside me on the porch.

"It's you. It's really you. I can't believe you're here. How did you know where to find me? How did you get here?"

So many questions I couldn't answer before he asked another. Pulling me inside, Porter and Daniel followed and took their seats on the couch while Caleb brought me back into his arms. I finally felt safe for the first time in weeks. No, months.

"How did you get here?" he asked again. "Oh, never mind that. What's important is that you're here." Leaning back, he whispered, "Oh, Becca, I've missed you so much."

Our arrival had stunned Caleb, who was still recovering from his wounds. The fact that he hadn't the forethought to ask me how or why I was there, minus my husband, made my lie all the easier to keep for the time being.

My questions swirled inside my head. I thought I had them all sorted out before stepping off the train, but now they were lost somewhere in the night. I was just happy to see my brother alive. There would be enough time for questions. I hadn't heard from him in five years, and I only hoped Caleb would be honest with his answers.

Now, I just wanted to make sure he was well, considering the telegram I'd received from Miss Sweeney.

⌒⊗⌒

Emily Sweeney, MD

After I finished suturing Mrs. Mueller's wound, I escorted her and her son out the back door and turned to clean the instruments when another knock sounded at the clinic's front entrance.

Calling out to the parlor, I asked, "Caleb, can you answer that for me?"

"Sure. I'll get it," came his reply.

The next thing I heard was loud crying. Thinking it was another patient needing immediate attention, I made my way to the parlor. My heart seized at seeing Caleb standing in the doorway with his arms tightly around an elegantly dressed woman who happened to be embracing him back.

Behind her were two handsome young boys I'd never seen before. Was this the infamous Anna Caleb had mentioned in his delirium while in the desert? He hadn't mentioned having sons, but there was definitely some resemblance.

Gray clouds cast an opaque haze through the open doorway, framing Caleb and the beautiful woman at its entrance. Selfishly, I thought, that embrace is only meant for me! Hands tightly clutched under my apron's fold, I put on a fake smile and gracefully made my way into the parlor.

Coming to stand next to the settee, I looked down and realized I hadn't removed my blood-stained apron. Waiting for Caleb to notice me, he drew the woman closer to his side, not removing his arm from around her shoulders. The raven-haired beauty caused a pang of jealousy to find its way into my heart. I couldn't speak, afraid I would embarrass myself if I did.

Finally, Caleb acknowledged my presence. "Oh, I forgot to tell you. Doc said you're in charge while he's gone."

"What!" My heart sank with disappointment. That's it? That's all he's going to say? This Anna, the woman who'd betrayed him, had returned, and the look on Caleb's face told me all I needed to know. I hated to admit it, but he looked happy.

I didn't think I could ever make him feel that way.

When it comes to love, our hearts are funny organs. It's only a muscle within our chest. Yet, it can sense our every emotion in a single beat by reacting to chemicals our brains produce during times of surprise, fear, or even happiness. Almost instantly, it changes its rhythm, sending a signal to our brains and allowing our bodies to react.

Well, my heart was telling me I was jealous in a way I'd never been before. A small part, a very small part of me, was happy for him, while the larger half was slowly dying inside.

Lingering in the doorway, I focused on the woman Caleb held far too fondly. Clearing my throat, I politely interrupted, "Well, Mr. Young, aren't you going to introduce me to your guest?"

"Oh! Of course. I'm sorry, Doc." Reaching for the woman's hand. "Emily, may I introduce Mrs. Rebecca Ackerman."

I recognized her name just as I extended my hand. "Why, you're Caleb's."

I didn't get to finish when Caleb quickly interjected, "Rebecca's my sister," he said, squeezing her shoulder. "Who did you think she was?"

My heart slowly returned to its normal rhythm, and then I answered, "It isn't important." *Thank heavens, this isn't Anna.*

"Becca, this is Doctor Emily Sweeney."

Rebecca extended her gloved hand, waiting for me to grasp it, but instead, I pulled her into a firm embrace. "Caleb, that's wonderful," I replied, looking over Rebecca's shoulder. Releasing my hold, I turned my attention to the boys, sitting quietly on the couch. "And who might these two handsome young gentlemen be?"

"They're my nephews," Caleb answered proudly, pointing to each boy. "This is Porter, and this is Daniel."

"It's nice to meet you both," I said, shaking their small hands.

Rebecca whispered in my ear, "Thank you, Doctor Sweeney for sending me the telegram. Seeing Caleb has been well cared for and recovering here in Yuma did my heart good. It means the world to me. I prayed all the way here that he would still be alive."

Pulling back from our embrace, she added, "I thought I would never see him again." Smiling up at her brother, I watched as she entwined her arm through his, pulling him close to her side. Caleb beamed. I hadn't seen him smile since; well, I don't think I'd ever seen him so happy.

Feeling warmth move up my neck, I silently thought, *well, maybe there were a few times.*

It was apparent that brother and sister shared a special bond. "How did you know where to find me," Caleb asked his sister again.

Nodding her head in my direction, she said, "I received a telegram from Doctor Emily. "She told me you had been gravely injured."

Caleb gave me a quizzical look, silently indicating if I had told Rebecca everything in the telegram. I sensed his question and shook my head ever so slightly from side to side to answer him no.

"We have so much to catch up on, Becca. But I must ask, did you travel all this way from Boston alone with the boys?"

"No," Rebecca answered, waving her hand in front of her face as if shooing a bug away. "No. Pearl came with us. Maybe a bit unwillingly at first," she chuckled. "But that's a story for another time, and I think I'll let Pearl tell it. I was so grateful to have her accompany us. She was a great comfort and help, especially when keeping an eight and ten-year-old occupied in the rail cars' small spaces."

"Where is she now?" I asked, looking out the door, expecting her to come up the steps.

"When we arrived, the stage stopped at the hotel, and she wanted to take a room to rest, allowing us time to be alone together. So, I ensured she was settled before I came to the clinic." Looking between Caleb and myself questioningly, I said, "I do hope the hotel is a safe place for her to stay for a few days."

"Yes, it is. I'm glad you were able to get her a room. You and the boys will stay here with Caleb and me, won't you? Of course, Pearl is welcome to stay here as well. We'll make room for all four of you."

"Thank you, Emily. That's a kind offer." Rebecca smiled as she reached for my hand. "But I'm sure Pearl will enjoy a few days alone without the boys and myself interrupting her well-deserved rest."

"I understand."

Suddenly, my stomach growled, and I excused myself to return to the kitchen to finish the meal I had started earlier in the day. "If you'll excuse me, I have some unfinished business to attend to. I'll let you and Caleb catch up.

⤳ 25 ⤳

Rebecca

AFTER FIVE YEARS of being separated, Caleb and I sat in the parlor, trying to put the missing pieces of our lives back together. I knew it wouldn't happen in one conversation, but I had so many questions I needed to ask him.

Unfortunately, we weren't allowed to continue when a knock sounded at the door. Caleb excused himself to answer. A waif who couldn't be more than fourteen years old stood at the entrance. Caleb brought her into the parlor, where I could better see her young features.

My eyes scanned this child's frail form. Her petite lips and rosy cheeks, flushed red from the cold night air, were accentuated with touches of rouge. Her wheat-colored hair was piled high on her head, held in place with a plume of feathers, and she wore layers of cream-colored gauze fabric that reached just above her knees.

Standing there shivering, the patched pale pink stockings and worn ballet slippers did little to ward off a chill. Her crystalline blue eyes were as big as saucers, and she continued gazing behind herself as if ready to run. She was so young, and I could tell she was frightened. But of what? I wasn't sure.

She had come alone, and Caleb seemed to know who she was. He urged her near the warmth of the fireplace and placed a blanket from the couch around her shoulders. What is she doing out this late at night? Won't her parents be worried?

Of course not. That was a silly question, dressed the way she was. The dear child was what they'd call a soiled dove, and my heart ached for her.

Emily came back into the parlor, and we exchanged questioning looks.

"It's Miz Abigail!" the girl blurted out between sobs. It was obvious she was frightened about something going on in the saloon. She pointed across the street and added, "Doc Sweeney sent me to fetch you, Miz Emily. He saz there's something wrong with the baby."

Placing a sheltering arm around the young girl's shoulder, Emily brought her into the safety of her arms. "It's OK, Lydia," she comforted, pushing a lock of golden hair from the girl's face. Trying to sound reassuring, "Don't you worry, we'll help Miss Abigail." Pausing before she continued, she asked, "Has the baby been born yet?"

"No, Miz," the girl answered. Dancing from one delicate foot to another, she added, "Poor Miz Abigail is screaming somethin' awful o'er there."

It was clear that Emily was needed at the saloon, and our getting to know each other would need to wait until she returned. Shutting the door to the cool night air, Emily asked if I would take care of the young girl while she went to the saloon. Of course, I'd gladly oblige while trying to allay her fears for Miss Abigail.

Emily, with Caleb close on her heels, headed down the hall. I had no idea where they were going since I had yet to leave the confines of the parlor. The next thing I knew, Caleb kissed me on the cheek as he held onto the doorknob. "I'm going to see what's happening. I'll be back soon."

Lydia anxiously said, "I'm goin' too!"

Caleb asked, "Are you sure you want to go back there, Lydia?"

"Yez, Ms. Abigail needs me."

⚜

While the boys sat on the couch, I walked down the hall searching for Emily. Upon finding her, I asked, "Is there anything I can do to help? Having delivered the boys, I may be of assistance."

"No, but thank you for offering," she replied. "I'm sure I'll be back soon. I just need to make sure that both Abigail and the baby are stable before I return."

She continued to place items into her bag that I'd never seen before when she added, "Why don't you and the boys make yourself comfortable. There's food in the kitchen that I started to prepare. You're welcome to eat it. Upstairs, there is one room open that you and the boys can take and make yourselves comfortable in. Please, don't wait up for us since I don't know how long we'll be gone. If I need your help, I'll send one of the girls over."

Before she left, she hugged me and thanked me for coming. "I can't tell you how happy I am that you're here. I'll send Caleb back as soon as I can."

⤳ 26 ⤳

Rebecca

SUDDENLY I WAS alone in a strange house. I only hoped that no other patients would come seeking medical attention until Emily or Doc Sweeney returned. Although Caleb and Emily had welcomed us into their home, a certain uneasiness settled over me. I felt as if I was invading their private space. But, considering what we'd been through the past weeks, I knew I could handle this as I walked through the house looking for our sleeping arrangements.

Our evening meal was a simple affair from what Emily had left cooling on the stove. I added eggs I'd located on the back porch to the bacon already in a skillet. Eggs were all I knew how to cook since meals had always been Pearl's responsibility.

My lack of worth in household tasks tugged at my conscience. I had been useless in running my home, and as I stood there in the empty kitchen, I chastised myself for never having learned to keep a house or cook.

We had so many servants to keep the house in Boston that Mother never needed to cook or clean. She'd been the lady who instead instructed our staff. Father would never allow her to lower her social standing by doing what he considered menial tasks. For me, as a married woman, that didn't change. My husband barely acknowledged our house staff. He made sure I had a lady's maid to help me dress and coiffe my hair in the mornings to his liking.

All that changed the day I stepped on the train in Boston. I was determined to become a self-sufficient woman my mother and Pearl would be proud of.

~⚬≶⚬~

One day had run into another, and I'd almost forgotten that tonight was Christmas Eve. Laying my fingertips over my lips, I forgot I had very few presents for the boys. This Christmas would certainly be different from Christmas's past. I only hoped they would understand and not be too disappointed.

After cleaning up from our meal, I left a light burning low on the kitchen table and took the boys up the back stairs to a small room under the staircase containing two small cots.

Opulent it wasn't. But all that mattered was we were safe, fed, clean, warm, and miles away from Elliot. Daniel and Porter had chosen this space and were excited to have their very own cubby to hide in. Looking at their angelic faces, I brushed wayward curls from their brow before kissing their flushed cheeks.

Exhausted, I went to the room I'd chosen, changed into my nightdress, and slipped under the stiff white sheets that held a fading hint of lye. The scent mattered not, for I was asleep before I could finish my prayers of thanks.

~⚬≶⚬~

Benjamin

It was late on Christmas Eve, and once again, I found myself alone on an assignment. Being a solitary man, I rarely took a day off. Mine was a lonely life, but one I chose after the war ended. Berating myself was something I'd become good at, thinking no woman would want half a man like myself.

Leaning my shoulder on a splinter-filled post adjacent to the saloon, I longed to be in a warm bed, drawing a loving woman close to my side. Shaking those thoughts off, I would be satisfied with being comfortable and sleeping off weeks of unease and aching bones.

The familiar deep throbbing pain was beginning to muddle my concentration as I rubbed my left thigh —something I couldn't afford.

Damn that war!

I had a job to finish.

Stretching my neck to ease the stiffness, at this point, I would be willing to share a stable with a horse as long as the hay was fresh.

Watching across the street, a man and a young girl came out of the clinic, walking swiftly into the unusually quiet saloon. Next, another woman I'd never seen before came out carrying a large leather case that appeared quite heavy. As she moved through the saloon's batwing doors, I heard them squeak in protest.

I waited, but no other person from the clinic appeared. I knew my assignment remained inside its warmth. Jealous, here I'd wait in the cold dark evening while watching crystal snowflakes drift from the grey sky.

⤳ 27 ⤶

Rebecca

MORNING IN UNFAMILIAR surroundings came early, especially after a restless night. I eased into my slippers, put on my wrap, and headed to the cubby. Looking down at my still-sleeping boys curled around each other, I then headed down the back stairs as a chill wrapped its icy fingers around me with each step I took.

I would have to fumble my way through lighting a fire in the stove, hoping I didn't burn the clinic down. Thankfully, Pearl had taught me how to cook the basics, and at the most, I could boil water for coffee.

Rubbing the sleep from my eyes, I made my way to the base of the stairwell and found my brother sound asleep with his head leaning over his arms on the table. He was wearing the same clothes he had on the night before. So, it was obvious that he had not been to bed.

Quietly approaching his side, I touched his shoulder and asked, "Caleb, where's Emily?"

Slow to arouse, Caleb mumbled an unclear response. Standing at his side, "I repeated my question, "Where is Emily?"

Looking up at me through sleep-deprived eyes, he responded, "She's probably upstairs sleeping. I didn't want to disturb her. That's why I stayed down here."

"I don't think she's up there, but I could be wrong. The door to your room is closed."

More alert now, I removed my hand from his shoulder as his worried look only increased my concerns. "You stay here, and I'll go back up and check." I knocked on their door and received no response. Quietly opening it, I called out her name. "Emily, are you in here?" Opening the door further, I found the bed neatly made with no signs of it having been slept in.

Heading back downstairs, I announced, "She's not up there. Where do you think she could be?" Pacing, I asked what I was afraid to admit. "Do you think there was a complication with Miss Abigail or the baby?"

With a low groan, Caleb pushed himself out of the chair, answering, "I hope not. She probably stayed at the saloon and let Doc Sweeney come home to rest." Looking about the kitchen, "Have you seen him this morning? He's usually an early riser and would have coffee on by now."

Shaking my head, I replied, "No. I haven't seen him. But I'll go back up and knock on his door." Taking the stairs to the second floor, I knocked, awaiting a response. None forthcoming, I knocked again. Still no response. Slowly, I opened the door and quietly called out his name, "Doctor Sweeney."

When he didn't answer, I thought, hang propriety of a woman entering a strange man's room. I took the liberty to open the door wider. He wasn't there, and his bed was still neatly made. My concerns intensified as I headed back downstairs, and my heart became heavy with dread. I found Caleb staring out the kitchen window into the still black of early morning.

A warning shudder passed through me as I walked to his side. "He's not there," I announced. "And I don't believe he came home last night either."

Without turning to face me, Caleb explained, "When I left Emily around two-thirty this morning, she told me she would be right behind me and asked that I have a pot of coffee made for when she returned."

Raising his hand to his cheek, he grinned. It struck me as a strange reaction, considering we couldn't locate Emily or Doc Sweeney until Caleb said softly, "She kissed me and wished me a Merry Christmas."

Turning his attention to the cold stove, he added, "I must have fallen asleep before making the coffee. Maybe Abigail or baby Holly needed her to stay?" This was the first I'd heard the baby's name. Sweet as it was, I was troubled that neither doctor had returned from the saloon.

Though Caleb and I had been separated for five years, I still could read what rambled through his mind. That wary look in his eyes told me something more than casual friendship was going on between him and Emily.

Caleb had secrets. We all do, for that matter. Maybe he and Emily both did, but now wasn't the time to delve into them. What was important was finding Emily and Doc Sweeney.

My brother's next comment confused me more as he yelled and slammed his fist on the sideboard. "Why didn't I think of that!"

"Think of what?" I asked, touching his forearm, which caused him to turn away from the window.

"Nothing!" came his sharp reply.

I knew it. The tone of his voice gave it away. His secrets ran deep as the Gila River I'd recently crossed. Despite my insides quivering, I remained calm, "Caleb, maybe you should go to the saloon and find out what is happening."

"You're right, Sis." Pushing away from the counter, he took a ragged breath, wincing and pushing his fist into the right side of his abdomen. I knew he was still in a considerable amount of pain, but his stubborn pride kept him from admitting it.

For his benefit and Emily's, I had to keep my emotions under control. Now wasn't the time to give in to the fear clenching my heart. A loud knock at the back door came before Caleb made it to his hat and coat. Cursing, he pulled the door open so hard it slipped out of his hand, hitting the wall with a resounding thud.

Standing on the back stoop was an exceptionally large and very intimidating bald man I had never seen before. Dwarfed by the size of his hands, I recognized the satchel and muddy shawl he held out to Caleb as he looked between us.

"Caleb. Ma'am." From where I stood, I could see the man was obviously trying to catch his breath while holding on to the doorjamb. With rushed speech, his words spilled out. "I just stepped outside the saloon for a smoke when I found this bag and Emily's shawl lying in the mud near the hitching post."

Caleb's color went pale as a lye-bleached sheet. Taking a shaky breath, he bent slightly forward with his left hand on the wall and winced in pain. Swiftly moving to his side, the sizable man grabbed Caleb's upper arms before my brother could collapse on the floor.

We both tried helping Caleb into a chair, but he shrugged off our hands in his stubbornness. Instead, he turned the chair around and straddled the seat, crossing his arms over the top and laying his head on his arms.

Assured that Caleb wouldn't fall, the man beside me introduced himself as Henry, the Pick and Shovel saloon's bartender. Caleb took in several deep breaths before looking up between the two of us. Kneeling beside his chair, I placed a hand on his thigh and asked, "What's going on?"

Lifting his head, Caleb stared blankly at me. Why isn't he answering? Standing abruptly, I began pacing back and forth, only to stop and look between both men. "Emily didn't strike me as a person to up and run off for no reason."

Unconsciously, I ran my hands nervously through the ties of my robe. It was out of the ordinary for me to yell, but I did so now out of exasperation. "Something terrible has happened. I know it."

Taking a deep breath, Caleb stood and walked over to where his coat hung on the wall. Instead of taking it off the hook, he drew back his right arm and with a resounding thud, slammed his clenched fist into the fading wallpaper, creating a jagged hole. Bringing back his bloodied knuckles, I screamed loud enough to wake the boys, if not the entire town.

Roaring, Caleb yelled, "She can't do this to me. Doesn't she know I love her?"

I'd never seen this side of my brother, and he was scaring me. I remember him as always being a gentleman. That was until our father took his revenge on him. Besides being shot, I had no idea what he had endured in the last five years.

Turning to the bartender, I pleaded, "Henry. Please get the Sheriff and bring him here,"

Henry looked between my brother and me. Did he expect Caleb to make a rational decision in his current state? Couldn't he see that he was in pain and filled with anguish?

"I'll be right back," he answered, dropping Emily's bag and shawl on the table. "But first, I need to make sure that Abbie and the baby are OK before I pull the Sheriff away. In the meantime, I'll get the word out through the men in the saloon that they need to gather everyone they can find to form a search party."

Looking directly at me, he added, "Don't you worry, Ma'am, we'll find Doc Emily."

"Thank you, Henry." Moving around Caleb, Henry left quietly, pulling the door closed behind him.

28

Rebecca

CHAOS HAD STRUCK less than twenty-four hours after we arrived in Yuma. With my hand on my brother's arm, I encouraged him to turn away from the wall as all thoughts of my own predicament were put aside. Younger sister or not, my brother would listen to what I had to say. "Caleb Young! You look at me right now!"

With all his weight on his hands, he raised his hanging head. "Oh God, Sis, I've lost her. She's gone back. I didn't think she would do it. I thought she was happy here with me."

Are those tears I see slipping from the corner of my brother's eyes? I've never seen him cry like he did when he was a little boy and skinned his knees. But there was no denying his emotions now.

"Caleb, you're not making any sense." Moving my hand to his shoulder, I continued, "You need to tell me what's happening. And please, tell me the truth."

Pushing off the wall, he continued to ramble nonsense while rubbing his bloodied fist. "Emily told me she needed to try. She wanted to make sure that she really died."

"Died! Caleb, what are you talking about? The sour taste in the back of my throat rose to a level I didn't think I could contain. "Please, Caleb, tell me what's going on."

"Ah Sis, you wouldn't understand." Shaking his head from side to side, he added, "I didn't at first. Maybe I still don't. But I love her!" Raising his head to the ceiling, he continued, "She's the air I breathe. I can't lose her, Sis. Not now. Not after all we've been through."

The color drained from my brother's face, and I knew he was truly in love with Emily. Not just the mindless infatuation he had five years ago with that woman who cheated on him. The love he had for Emily was something I could only dream of having someday. I was tired of fooling myself that love had existed between Elliot and me. Well, no more. That part of my life was over.

Once again, I focused on my brother, drawing myself out of my troubles. "Caleb, please come sit down and explain to me what's going on." Approaching the chairs surrounding the table, I heard soft footsteps behind us on the stairs. Eyes wide with fright, Porter and Daniel were peaking around the corner.

Daniel quietly whispered, "Momma. Why are you yelling at Uncle Caleb?" Walking to my side, he threw his tiny arms around my legs. I bent down and pulled him into a hug. Looking up at me through his innocent eyes, he asked, "Has Uncle Caleb been bad?" Porter then came to stand stoically next to his brother. Looking between Caleb and me, he asked, sounding much older than his eight young years, "Momma, father didn't find us? Did he?"

Trying to appear calm, I answered, "No, dear, your father didn't find us. "He doesn't know where we are." I couldn't lie and tell them their father would never locate us. But I only hoped and prayed he would come to his senses and leave us alone.

Looking up at their uncle, I ignored Caleb's questioning look and shook my head. That conversation was for another time. "Now, boys, it is still too early for you to be up." Turning their small bodies toward the staircase, I added, "Now, go back upstairs and try to sleep a bit longer. I'll come up before breakfast is ready."

Astonished yet pleased, without argument, my sons took to the stairs to leave their uncle and me alone. Once they were out of ear-shot, Caleb yelled, "I have to go find her." Guarding his abdomen, he walked back to the wall rack to retrieve his coat.

Begrudgingly, I helped him slip his arms into the obstinate sleeves. I was close enough to see the fine beads of sweat forming on his brow, but arguing with him at this point would be futile. I knew he shouldn't be riding in his condition, but it was clear he wouldn't be deterred from finding the woman he loved.

"Caleb, please come sit down before you fall," I asked, indicating the kitchen chair. "At the least, wait until Henry comes back with the Sheriff. Besides, Emily left no clues as to which direction she went, and you'd only be wandering around out there in the dark, alone."

I was anxious and needed something to do. Going to the stove, I added ground beans to the coffee pot. Then, touching the kettle on the back of the cooktop, I deemed it hot enough and poured the boiling liquid into the pot. I knew when things were sorted out, we would all need a few cups.

The back door creaked open just as Caleb was about to argue with me. A tall, gray-haired, weary-looking gentleman carrying a black leather bag in his left hand walked in. On its front, in gold lettering, was the name 'Mathew Sweeney, MD.'

So, this was the elder Dr. Sweeney, Emily, and Caleb had spoken of. His thick and wavy silver hair touched the edge of his collar, making him look handsome and refined in a rustic sort of way. After placing his hat and coat on a vacant hook, he turned to face us. "Mornin'. Is tat fresh coffee I be smellin'?" Pulling spectacles out of his front shirt pocket and placing them on his nose, he scanned the room.

"Yes. Yes, it is," I quickly replied. "I'll get you a cup." Anything to keep busy and avoid the oncoming conversation, I hurried to the stove.

"And who might this lovely lass be?" he asked Caleb.

"I'm sorry, Doc, this is my sister, Rebecca, Rebecca Ackerman. She came on the stage yesterday while you were at the saloon. She's come all the way from Boston with her sons."

I turned back from the stove and nodded my greeting to the older gentleman. "It's nice to meet you, Doctor."

"It's Mathew. Please call me Mathew or just Doc. Which er' ye be comfortable using. We don't stand on formality here."

"All right, Doc," I replied, nodding my head with the coffee pot in hand.

Warily, Caleb looked at the doctor. "Emily sent her a telegram telling her I wasn't well."

"Not well, ye say! Is that what you'd be calling shot full of holes?"

Gasping, I almost dropped the pot. I couldn't believe what the doctor had just revealed. Had Caleb been shot more than once? Slowly, the heat rose from my neck to my face. I wanted to scream at my brother for lying to me once again. But there were more important matters to attend to.

Looking between Caleb and myself, Doc asked, "Where's my beautiful granddaughter tis fine mornin'?"

Caleb and I turned at the same time to stare at the Doc. I was glad the boys were back upstairs because this is where the conversation's pleasantries ended, and the words between the doctor and my brother would have burned any man, woman, or child's ears.

29

Rebecca

I COULD ONLY make out every other word or two as Doc's Irish brogue became heavier the angrier he became. He and Caleb were yelling so loudly I didn't think either man knew what the other was saying.

Edged on by Doc's bellowing, Caleb shoved his way toward the door. "Get out of my way, old man. I'm going after Emily."

Well, I'd finally had enough of these two men's infuriating banter, so it was my time to give them a piece of my mind. Placing my hands on my hips, I raised my voice and yelled, "Caleb Young! That is no way to speak to your elder." Sounding more like our mother, I stomped my foot and added, "You apologize this instant."

Looking between the two men, I lowered my voice, "Both of you apologize! Now! This conversation is accomplishing nothing, so shake hands and get out there and find Emily."

By the time I finished admonishing both men, my insides were trembling. Standing there, I watched as the adult schoolboys finally shook hands and apologized to each other.

While arguing about how they would rescue Emily, the pounding of horse's hooves drew our attention to the back porch. Caleb opened the back door with Doc and me trailing close behind. Standing side by side, we were caught off guard as we stepped onto the cramped back overhang.

Before us on horseback were twenty scruffy and sleepy-eyed men. With lanterns held high in one hand and shotguns in the other, they looked as if they had been dragged from their warm beds, which, indeed, they had.

I couldn't have been more grateful at the sight before us as I sighed with relief. Henry had kept his word.

"Sheriff," Caleb acknowledged as he scanned the group and stepped to the edge of the stairs.

My brother nodded his head in Henry's direction as a gesture of thanks for gathering these men together.

"Mr. Young, Henry here tells me tat little lady of yours hast gone missing. Care to tell me vhat you know."

Caleb quickly relayed all he knew, from when Emily met him downstairs in the saloon after delivering his and Abigail's daughter to when he left alone at three in the morning to return to the clinic. "So, you see, sheriff, I have no idea where Emily could have gone."

Judging from Caleb's tone, I knew he intentionally omitted details from his story. Again, I sensed my brother kept secrets from a lot of people. Doc moved to Caleb's side, placed a hand on his shoulder, and lightly squeezed without saying a word. Caleb didn't need to turn around. He only nodded.

That simple act, unnoticed by the men, told me Doc shared the same secrets as my brother. But for the life of me, I couldn't figure out what they were hiding.

Sidestepping and snorting clouds of billowing white steam, I didn't need to be an expert horsewoman to know the horses were anxious to be on their way. As the men who rode them, they, too, had been pulled away from the warmth of their bedding.

There was a light dusting of snow on the ground, and it was getting colder by the minute. I was anxious to return to the kitchen's warmth. Pulling the wool shawl tight around my shoulders, I looked up at the December full moon shining brightly in the sky, grateful for the men before me.

I made to move back into the shadows of the porch when my eyes locked on one man in particular. He's here! Could it really be him? The man from the train I couldn't get out of my thoughts.

The sight of him caused my heart to beat in a long-forgotten rhythm. Instantly, I became a besotted schoolgirl and placed a hand over my heart while attempting to swallow the lump that had taken up space in my throat.

It seemed a lifetime had passed since we parted in Fort Worth. As innocent as it was, I prayed silently, hoping Mr. Burns wouldn't say anything to give our previous encounter away. On the train, he had been the perfect gentleman, refined in speech and manner and impeccably dressed.

Of course, being handsome beyond words, he immediately caught my eye. But tonight. Well, I had no words to describe how I felt at seeing him again dressed as a cowboy.

Shaking my head, I thought, a cowboy, of all things. What happened to his tailored suit and starched white shirt? I had only read about cowboys in the dime novels I kept hidden from Elliot. Looking confident and comfortable upon his horse, this new look suited him well.

I desperately tried calming my nerves before anyone noticed and tried refocusing my attention on his magnificent and powerful mount. But I knew my efforts would be for naught. Mr. Burns was sitting astride a black stallion on the outskirts of the posse. I didn't think I would ever see him again after exiting the train in Fort Worth.

The sheriff's voice drew me back to the present. "Ma'am, Doc, Caleb," the sheriff addressed each of us, pointing toward the man on the stallion. "Tis here ist Nathaniel Burns. He owns te Burnside Mine up in the hills outside of town. I tink he'll be of some help with our search since he's familiar wit the area."

The sheriff had paused in his introductions while Caleb silently assessed Mr. Burns. Then he added, "Caleb, I believe you've met te rest of te men when ya ver here in town last."

Wincing, my brother carefully descended the stairs and thanked the men for coming. Then he extended his hand to Mr. Burns. Motioning for me to step forward, he began introducing me to the men when he must have noticed that Mr. Burns continued to look in my direction.

"Mr. Burns," my brother said. "I believe you know Doc Sweeney, but let me introduce you to my sister, Mrs. Rebecca Ackerman."

Touching his fingers to the brim of his Stetson, he responded, "It's a pleasure to make your acquaintance, Mrs. Ackerman." Saying no more, he turned his attention toward the men in the posse.

My chest tightened, and I found myself unable to breathe in remembering Mr. Burns's dazzling smile. But it was gone. His expression instantly changed, and his smile turned solemn when Caleb introduced me as Mrs. It was like watching a shooting star swiftly fade from the night sky.

Once I persuaded my legs to move, I shuffled back into the shadows provided by the porch overhang until I hit the siding with my back. There, I leaned my head against the cold boards, hoping to cool the fever Mr. Burns had once again ignited within me.

Unfortunately, my retreat wasn't far enough. And yet, hidden in the darkness, he elicited a visceral response that weakened my resolve. How could I let this happen after all I'd been through with Elliot? I couldn't. It was that simple. Or so I thought.

Did he, or anyone else for that matter, notice the intensity of how I watched him? If they did, I cared little at this point. I was veiled within obscurity and could stare as long as I wanted. My eyes roamed from the top of his head down his sculpted torso, stopping at the tight denim, hugging his powerful thighs.

With a hitch in my breath, I had difficulty swallowing while imagining how comfortably his thighs squeezed his saddle. Certainly, his wool suit hadn't done his physique justice or previously drawn this intense a response from me.

Rebecca. What are you thinking? Came that familiar voice.

I whispered, "Not now, Mother!" I thought I had been dreaming when I heard her voice on the train. Obviously, I hadn't.

Thinking back to our brief time on the train, I remembered Mr. Burns' magnetic energy. Shaking my head from side to side, I had to stop thinking this way. After all, I was a married woman, and I didn't really know this man. For all I knew, he could be just like Elliot once his respectable façade faded away.

My heart pounded wildly in my chest, knowing it would do me no good to start something I couldn't finish or shouldn't even start. I held my thoughts in check, but my heart was another matter. It was slowly being cut in two, knowing Mr. Burns and I could never be together.

⌘

I could finally admit Elliott was a vile man whom I was desperately trying to escape. I wanted him forever out of our lives, and I didn't care how it came about.

Not prone to violence, I would protect my sons no matter the cost. Forgive me, but I couldn't help but think death would be too good for Elliot. After all the pain he put us through, he needed to suffer just as much, if not more. Without remorse, I couldn't believe I was thinking those horrible thoughts.

Letting out a long-held breath, I was forever grateful Mr. Burns didn't admit our past meeting.

Stiffly, Caleb made his way back up the steps. Grasping my upper arms gently, he said, "I love you, Sis, but I need to find Emily." Kissing me on the cheek, I admonished him to be careful before he turned and made his way back down the stairs to his horse, River.

Glancing one last time at Mr. Burns, he turned his horse to follow the rest of the posse. Compelled to watch, I stood firm until the light from the men's lanterns gradually faded into winter's first blush of morning when I caught Mr. Burns glance over his shoulder, taking one final look my way.

Once the men were gone, an eerie silence surrounded the clinic. No one could predict what my brother and the men would be facing. But I feared for them and sent a silent prayer heavenward to keep them all safe and bring Emily back alive.

$\backsim$ 30 $\backsim$

Rebecca

THE COLD NIGHT air leached deep into my bones when a light touch on my arm had me turning. "Tis too cold te stand out here any longer. Ye must be half frozen. Come in and have a cuppa tea wit me."

Something in the back of my mind told me to stand there until the last hint of lantern light had faded. But Doc was holding the back door open, and I didn't want all the heat to escape from the kitchen's warmth.

"You're right. It is extremely chilly out here." Walking through the door, I welcomed the radiating warmth coming from the wood stove.

"Can I make you a cuppa tea, my dear.? Or would you prefer coffee?"

"Thank you. A cup of tea sounds wonderful," I replied, clasping my hands firmly on the table. Taking a chill, I asked, "Doctor, do you think it will snow more tonight?" I was concerned the cold and potential snow would hamper the efforts of the posse, let alone poor Emily.

I knew it was small talk, but I needed to keep my thoughts off my brother's condition and one particular stranger. Sitting at the table with me, Doc looked up and answered, "No. It might snow in te higher hills, but I don't tink we'll get more down here. Te dusting we had earlier today was unusual. I can remember only one other time since I've been here when it snowed in te lowlands."

Taking off his glasses, he pinched the bridge of his nose before adding, "It's much different here than back in Boston. I must say that I don't miss te snow. Me ol' rheumatism doesn't care for it."

"I don't miss it either," I replied. "Although, I have fond memories of Caleb and I playing in the snow as youngsters." Smiling, I couldn't help thinking of better times. "Mother and Mr. Edwards, our butler, used to take us sledding on the hills behind our home."

A cold breeze circled the room from a crack in the window pane, causing me to pull my shawl tighter around my shoulders before continuing. "Mother always made sure we had fun when it snowed. The cook would have hot chocolate waiting when we came in, wet and chilled to the bone. Those were good times."

Looking about the room, it seemed too quiet. Porter and Daniel must still be sleeping. Pointing to the stairs, "If you don't mind, I'm going up to check on the boys. I won't be long."

"Go right ahead, dear. Take yer time. It will be a bit before te water boils."

Walking up the stairs, I wondered what would happen if the posse couldn't find Emily. Or, if they did and she wasn't alive. I couldn't think that way. She had to be alive. Caleb needed her. He'd obviously found a woman he loved beyond measure and could make a new life with.

Opening the bedroom door just a crack, hoping the hinges wouldn't creek, I peeked in on my boys. Both were curled on their sides, still fast asleep. I had been concerned that their little foray into the kitchen earlier when they heard their uncle and me arguing would prevent them from falling back asleep. Thankfully, I'd been wrong.

Heading back downstairs, I could smell the fragrant tea calling me to come sit and relax. Doc was back at the table with an intricately flowered teapot and a matching cream and sugar set.

Sitting down, I smiled faintly and asked, "Would you like me to pour?"

"Yes, Dear. That would be nice," he replied, holding out a chipped cup that looked well-used with tea stains circling the bottom. "My Ma used to make my Da a pot o' tea whene'r he'd come in from the cold."

His thoughts looked to be wandering back in time as he paused, then added, "He'd come in from a day's work in the fields coated in mud and give my Ma a big hug and kiss." Chuckling, "Ma didn't mind that Da was dirty and covered in cow dung. Her heart seemed to swell with love each time Da looked at her. Those are good memories."

Sipping his tea, he asked, "What about you?"

"What about me?" I countered, lowering my eyes. I wasn't ready to be questioned about my life.

"Tell me about ye Ma and Da. Did yer Da ever go sledding with ye and Caleb?" he asked, squinting over the rim of his cup.

"Oh no!" I answered, shaking my head with bitter memories of my father. "Father never had time for Caleb and me. He was always too busy with work," I added sadly. "But Mr. Edwards, our valet, was always there for us. He was such a dear man and more a father figure to Caleb and me."

"I'm sorry te hear tat. What did he do for a living?" he asked, placing his glasses back on his face.

"He was a lawyer." My answer was short. I had no intention of delving into our sordid family history. Turning my attention back to the doctor, I asked, "Do you have family here in Yuma?"

Clearing his throat before answering, I felt I'd hit on a painful subject. "Aye. My wife died many years ago." Smiling, he continued, "I have a daughter, though." Looking up at me through tear-filled eyes, he added, "I believe she'd be about yer age now." He pushed himself away from the table and added, "She lives in New York."

Doc's expression turned to sadness as he looked down at his crepe-skinned hands and continued. "She wasn't pleased when I came out West, and I'm sorry te say that I haven't seen her in years."

I watched as he walked toward the stairs. "I barely receive letters from her. My sister took over her care after my wife died, and I'd decided to come here. Regrettably, my sister died a few years back."

"I'm so sorry to hear that." I twisted my hands on the table and added, "I didn't mean to bring up painful memories." Trying to lighten the conversation, I asked, "Maybe you should write to her and ask her to come for a visit."

With his hand on the railing, his steps hesitated and replied, "Perhaps yer right. I'll give it some thought."

Bringing up his daughter had obviously upset him, and I wouldn't mention her again.

"Are ye coming up te bed? It's bound te be a long night, and I don't tink that Caleb and te posse will be back anytime soon. Maybe not until tomorrow, if then."

Holding up my cup, I answered, "No. I think I'll sit here for a while and enjoy my tea. It's been a long time since I've been able to sit in quiet. You go on up. I'll lock the door and be fine down here alone."

Looking around the kitchen, the warmth from the stove surrounded me with a peacefulness I hadn't experienced in a long time. As the doctor made his way slowly up the stairs, I asked, "Do you mind peeking in on the boys? They should still be asleep."

"Of course, me, dear. You stay there and relax. You've had a long trip. I'll call you if they need you."

"Thank you."

Once I was alone, my mood turned sour as Elliot invaded my thoughts. It was almost like having him here in the room with me. I couldn't be naïve in thinking the two thousand miles separating Boston from Yuma could possibly keep us safe. Just the thought of him finding us sent my stomach rolling.

Nevertheless, I had to remain vigilant. He had the means to find us. My only hope was he had forgotten all about us and remained occupied by one of his Mistresses.

The sounds of the house creaking in the cold pulled me back to reality. Looking down, my hands shook, and the cup rattled on its saucer. Elliot had that effect on me. Angry at myself for letting him creep in once again, I turned my thoughts to one man—a man I desperately wanted to know better.

Please be safe, Nathaniel, I silently whispered.

Rebecca

I WAS ASHAMED I hadn't seen Pearl since I dropped her off at the hotel the day we arrived in Yuma. We'd missed Christmas altogether, and she was probably worried sick, wondering what happened to us. Thankfully, neither Porter nor Daniel asked where their Christmas presents were. Truthfully, I had yet to retrieve them from my luggage.

Once dressed, the boys and I made our way to the hotel. Checking in with the desk clerk, he pointed me toward the dining room. There, seated alone at a table, was Pearl. "Pearl!" I called out excitedly. Unexpectedly, Porter and Daniel flew past me, running straight into Pearl's arms.

"Oh, Mrs. Ackerman. I've been so worried. Where have you been all this time?"

I placed my hands on her arms and answered, "Pearl. Please forgive me. And you need to stop addressing me as Mrs. Ackerman. I much prefer you call me Rebecca. After all we've been through, we are more family than an employer and housekeeper." Winking, I added, "So, I think we can dispense with the Boston formalities."

139

Turning serious, I added, "You must understand that I think of you like a mother. You protected me from father, and now." I couldn't finish as unshed tears formed in the corner of my eyes. Brushing them away with a gloved hand, I glanced down at the dusty floor.

In her nurturing way, Pearl pulled me into a loving embrace, surrounding me with the peace I longed for. With her fingers under my chin, she tilted my head up to look at her. "Now, Rebecca, none of this crying. We have lots to talk about. So, tell me, what are we going to do next?"

"Pearl, I'm too tired and confused even to think straight, let alone make plans. So much has happened since leaving you here and seeing my brother. He's well, for the most part," I said, drawing Porter and Daniel close to my side.

Dear Pearl once again led the direction with her strong Irish confidence. "Well, the first thing we are going to do is sit down and have breakfast."

Putting on a smile, I replied, "I'm starved." Looking down at the boys, I asked, "How about you, my darlings?" Porter and Daniel answered by excitedly nodding their heads and clapping. Straightening my back, I thought as long as I had Pearl and my brother at my side, I was confident that I could handle whatever life threw my way in this desolate landscape—even Elliot.

Sitting across from Pearl, I leaned forward. Under my breath, to keep my message from young ears, I whispered, "Pearl. I haven't told Caleb or anyone else that I've left Elliot. I believe it is safer that way for now." I went on to explain the events of the past forty-eight hours and that we were all anxiously awaiting Caleb's return, hopefully with Emily by his side.

Breakfast was a delicious feast of pancakes covered in freshly churned butter, fried eggs, and crisp bacon. I was about to put a piece of pancake in my mouth when I turned to look across the street. Dropping my fork, it clattered on my plate. The man I'd seen looking up at me from the Chicago train station's platform stood across the street in front of the sheriff's office.

I whispered in shock, "Good heavens, what is he doing here?"

Pearl, catching my faint murmur, followed the direction of my stare. "What is it, Rebecca? You look like you've seen a ghost."

So the boys wouldn't hear, she leaned in and whispered, "Is Elliott here?"

Without taking my eyes off the man, I answered, "No. No, it's that man I told you about from the train station in Chicago." Pointing in his direction, I added, "See. That's him over there."

"Yes. I remember you telling me about him. But I didn't catch a glimpse of him back then," Pearl answered. "Now that he's turned around, I can't see his face. Do you think he's following us?" she asked, putting her hand on my forearm.

Biting the corner of my lip, I turned to face Pearl, shaking my head. "It's silly, really. He can't be following us. It's just a coincidence he's here." Turning back to face the window, I watched as he made his way into the sheriff's office.

My appetite now gone, a sense of dread settled in the pit of my stomach. Once breakfast was complete, I convinced Pearl to pack her bags and return to the clinic with us. Not that I didn't feel safe at the clinic, but I wanted her with me in case we needed to make a quick exit out of town.

I was a bit nervous since I hadn't asked Doc about bringing her back, but I was almost certain he would love having an Irish lass to reminisce with.

⚜

Benjamin

I'd been staying at one of the local boarding houses for the past two nights. It wasn't the best of accommodations, but I hadn't planned on staying long enough to warrant finding someplace more comfortable.

Traveling from Boston via train and then horseback had been long and arduous. My leg was aching from days on end of travel with little rest. Reaching down, I rubbed my fingers deep into my left thigh, hoping for some relief. Unfortunately, it didn't come. I paid dearly for the price of my job and past war.

Somehow, thanks to a young and boastful surgeon, I came out of The War Between the States alive, and gratefully, my leg remained attached to the rest of my body despite a life-threatening injury.

During the bloody battle that had taken my childhood friend, I could have lost my leg from the shrapnel that had driven deep into the muscle and bone. While floating in and out of consciousness, I remember the doctor telling me he wouldn't make any guarantees that I would survive, let alone ever walk again. Yet, in the end, he saved me.

To this day, I remember lying on the blood-soaked battlefield, waiting to exhale my last breath into the cold earth while screams of the dying surrounded me. At one point, I sensed my life rapidly draining into the field. I didn't want to die that day. But if it were to be, I prayed death would come quickly, stop the excruciating pain, and forever block out the screams.

But it didn't; the screams just became louder and louder until I thought I would go mad. Lucidly, I remembered a white, low-lying mist of smoke from the cannons surrounding the battlefield that even a ray of sunlight couldn't penetrate. God help me, but I would have ended my torment if I could have only reached my pistol.

Why did we fight wars created by a few angry men who never touched a foot on a battlefield? It didn't make sense. Nothing about wars did!

When I made it to the field hospital, the moans of the dying intensified. Closer and closer, their tortuous screams closed in around me. Bound by the demon of impending death, I shook uncontrollably. I couldn't escape it, yet grateful when the black hole of unconsciousness from the laudanum overpowered me, taking me under to a dark and dangerous place.

When I awoke in a foul-smelling room, I remember turning my head to the side only to see row upon row of cots filled with bloodied and dying men. It was a horrible scene, and I remember it perfectly to this day. The masses of bandaged heads and stumps where arms and legs used to be and eyes forever blind to the world was a testament to how war changes lives forever.

There would be no going back for these men, including myself. How could anyone survive this den of death? But I had to! At that moment, the only thoughts running through my mind were surviving and getting out of that hell and back to my family.

I couldn't take much more. Even in a laudanum stupor, there was little relief from the pain as I lay in filth. The gagging and retching from the demon drug kept me awake. I tried fighting it, but it was to no avail. So, I prayed for death to take me out of this nightmare.

Since then, night after night, drenched in sweat, I longed for the abyss that laudanum produced. It was torture, but I had to resist its pull. Suffering fits of agonizing nightmares, all I could see were bloodied apparitions walking on the once fertile ground turned into a bloody battlefield.

The Army doctor told me I was one of the lucky ones. After surviving weeks of fevers, near-death experiences, and the smell of chloroform mixed with rotting flesh, was I really that lucky?

Slowly recovering from that dismal death trap of the Army hospital, I decided never to depend on anyone else ever again. Besides, what woman would want a damaged man like me? Coming from the South, I had been in Connecticut, finishing my training as an engineer when the war broke out. My beliefs aligned with the North, so I enlisted in the Union Army.

Post-war, I returned to my home in Williamsburg, Virginia, hoping to reunite with my family. But the homestead and family were either dead or gone. I had no one left to care about. When I wasn't spat on or cursed at, I spent my days wandering the streets, searching high and low for a job while trying to hide the fact that I had served the North.

My pronounced limp was a definite deterrent, and news traveled fast that I was an ex-Union officer in a Confederate state. Animosities ran high with people from my youth. It was ridiculous having gone back there. I don't know why I did. In the long run, there was no reason for me to stay. And I'd been smart enough to leave while I still could and not endure a battle of a different kind.

My perseverance held out. Wandering northward, I fortunately signed on with the Pinkertons. Grateful to the Agency for accepting half a man, I held my head high and made my way into a line of expert detectives.

Now, I was in the desert town of Yuma, a dirty, dusty city on the edge of the Colorado River, following a woman without a nefarious history other than an angry husband wanting her back. I was anxious to complete my mission and return to Boston, where genteel civilization dwelled.

⤛ 32 ⤜

Benjamin

MAKING MY WAY into a crudely constructed building, nothing resembling the Pinkerton offices in Boston, I took my hat off, nodded, and introduced myself to the town's sheriff, Anders Johannson. "Sir, it's a pleasure to meet you."

The sheriff was an imposing man of well over six feet as he stood to shake my hand. Sitting down in his chair, it groaned as it accepted his large frame. I chuckled to myself, looking at him behind a desk that seemed child-sized compared to his build and thinking it must have been built for a smaller predecessor.

Motioning to the seat across from his desk, I accepted his invitation to sit. But before I did, I took one quick glance back across the street at The Palace Hotel, where earlier, I'd watched Mrs. Ackerman and her boys enter. Knowing she was there, I felt it was time to tell the sheriff what I was about.

"Vell son, vat is it ya'd need to discuss?"

Not missing his Scandinavian accent, I replied, "Sir, I'm a Pinkerton detective here on business." I watched his eyes scrutinize

145

my frame with curiosity. He'd obviously noticed my pronounced limp. It was not something I could hide. I wondered, did he think I wasn't capable of doing my job as an agent?

"Ve haven't had a Pinkerton here in town for quite a while. So, vat brings ya this way?"

Leaning forward, elbows on my knees, I looked up and answered, "I'm looking for a woman that just arrived here in Yuma with her sons and lady's maid. From what I can tell so far, she doesn't seem to be a threat, but my instructions were to follow her from Boston to her final destination and report her whereabouts back to my supervisor. Since I'm a stranger here, I just wanted to report to you so you wouldn't wonder why I'm hanging around looking suspicious."

Leaning his arms on the desk, I noted his muscles strain within the sleeves of his shirt. He was definitely a man I did not want to cross. "I appreciate tat. Do ya have a description of te lady? I may be able to help out."

"No, that won't be necessary. I've seen her and where she's staying. Now, it's just a matter of informing my supervisor. So, if you wouldn't mind pointing me in the direction of the telegraph office, I can take care of that and leave town."

Pointing to his left with his thumb, he replied, "Sure ting. It's the next block over near the livery. Ya can't miss it. Charlie Stanhope ist the telegraph operator. Tell him I sent ya over."

Standing, I held my hand out over the desk as the sheriff's firm grasp caused my fingers to tingle. I thanked him for his help and headed to the door.

With my hand on the door handle, he stopped me and said, "Agent Reynolds, yust, so you know, I don't need any trouble in my town."

"I understand, sheriff. Once I've informed my supervisor where my assignment is and had a few days' rest, I should be on my way." Pulling the door open, I added, "Thanks again for your help."

"Son," the sheriff added as he came around to stand in front of his desk.

Stopping, I turned back to face him without letting go of the handle.

With a serious expression, he mentioned, "If ya ever tink of leaving the agency and settling down, ve could sure use a goot man here in Yuma. The town ist growing, and I can't be everywhere. Besides, I vill be leaving office soon, so give it some thought."

Grinning, I replied, "Thanks, sheriff. I sure will." After his first look at me limping into his office, I was more than surprised at the sheriff's offer. I figured I would be the last person he would propose a job to. I guess I was wrong.

After years of traveling on assignments from coast to coast in not the most pleasant surroundings, with often time unpleasant outcomes, his offer sounded inviting. I had been thinking of leaving the agency within the next two years. Maybe I should think of doing it sooner when the opportunity presents itself. I would give it some thought before returning to Boston.

Heading out into the bright desert sun, I secured my beat-up hat in place while scanning the busy street from east to west. Although I had been in the sheriff's office a short time, I was sure Mrs. Ackerman and her entourage had already left the hotel. I was wrong again.

Standing in the shade of the boardwalk's overhang, I kept close to the stucco building and picked up a copy of the Arizona Sentinel that someone had left on the nearby bench. I pretended to read it in hopes of concealing myself.

That one look we'd shared back in Boston had lasted long enough to generate enough uneasiness while allowing her to commit my features and obvious limp to memory. I knew this to be so because as I walked lamely away from below her train window, I turned one last time to see her eyes boring into my back and my features into her memory.

I could get used to this relaxed attire as I changed from the tailored suit I wore in Boston to comfortable denim and well-worn boots. I stood before the jail long enough to see Mrs. Ackerman, her sons, and lady's maid wander through the Palace Hotel's main doors, stopping only to speak with one of the hotel porters.

I noted that both she and her maid were carrying small portmanteaus. Were they leaving already? I didn't think so, but I continued to watch where they headed. Pushing off the outer wall of the sheriff's office, I followed along on the opposite side of the street. Enough wagon traffic and people walking along the boardwalk kept me from being recognized.

Soon, they stopped in front of a white picket fence needing a great deal of repair. According to the name over the porch, it was a clinic. Opening the gate, all four proceeded up the steps and walked directly inside without knocking. I found that strange. Was this where they were now going to stay?

⋯⋯

Lately, my leg had been giving me a lot of grief, and I felt this was a good time to give it a rest. I found a quiet place to sit, out of view, to watch for any further activity from Mrs. Ackerman. After two hours of observing with nothing to lend suspicion, I headed to the Western Union Telegraph office at the other end of town. Out of habit and pain, I rubbed my left thigh again to ease the numbness and tingling, then steeled myself for a long walk.

I was greeted by Charlie, the telegraph operator, who pointed to a small shelf by a window that contained writing material. Taking a piece of paper and a stub of a pencil, I wrote the following note.

26 Dec
A. Chamberlain
Pinkerton Agency Boston
Subject located Yuma, A.T.
B. Reynolds

Satisfied with my note, I paid the operator two bits, an outrageous price, and informed him I was staying at the Colorado Hotel on Gila Street. He conveyed that as soon as he had a response, he would send a courier to the hotel with the reply.

Tipping my fingers to the brim of my hat, I exited the building into a cloud of dust from a wagon rolling by. Brushing my hands down the front of my vest, I stood looking at the burgeoning crowd forming on the street as the noon hour approached.

Until I was informed otherwise, I was still obligated by the agency to watch and report any changes on my subject. Fortunately, my room had a bird's eye view of the clinic where Mrs. Ackerman and her entourage had entered earlier.

It was nearing noon, and I'd skipped breakfast when my stomach noisily growled, telling me it was time to eat. Stopping at the local café, the yeasty aroma of freshly baked bread and roasted meat overpowered my senses. Purchasing a thick slice of butter-slathered bread and a serving of juicy roast beef with all the trimmings, I returned to my room to continue my surveillance.

It would prove to be another long day. My eyelids grew heavy after a delicious meal, and soon, my head dropped to my chest. When I awoke, the sun was drifting behind the buildings along the main street, and the sky was darkening.

It was obvious I desperately needed a good night's sleep. Probably against my better judgment, I dismissed further surveillance to lay down, fully clothed. I knew I was taking a chance, but I only hoped Mrs. Ackerman wouldn't be making any serious move to leave at this hour of the day. Besides, the next stage wasn't scheduled to leave until tomorrow morning.

ᐳ 33 ᐸ

Rebecca

HAD IT REALLY been forty-eight hours since Emily went missing?

Clothes torn and covered in dirt, Caleb and the posse finally returned to the clinic in the early morning darkness. Slowly dismounting, Caleb carefully reached up to lift Emily from his horse. I watched as they tenderly held each other close.

His pale features had me worried. Beneath the dirt, beads of sweat had turned into dry rivulets crusted on Caleb's brow. Refusing help and not pausing to speak to Doc or me, they held on to each other while staggering up the back steps.

My prayers had been answered. Emily was alive, albeit bloodied and bruised. Though it was evident in her eyes, she didn't offer any information on what she had endured over the past two days. I could only imagine.

Her physical wounds would heal, but it was her emotional state that I worried about. I knew all too well about such matters.

Without drawing attention to myself, I tried making out the form of Mr. Burns within the group of men. All I saw was his riderless horse as a sense of panic set in, wondering what could have happened to him.

Deep breath, Emily. He's there somewhere, or maybe he chose to leave the posse and not come back to face me. But why would someone have his horse?

Turning my attention back to Caleb and Emily, I followed them into the warmth of the kitchen. Quickly, I pulled out two chairs from around the table and motioned for them to sit. Taking two warm blankets from in front of the stove, I wrapped them around their hunched shoulders.

Behind me, I heard a loud commotion and the Doc calling out, "Come in, come in." Turning toward the door, I watched the Doc roll up his sleeves while pointing toward the surgical suite.

"Take him to te back room. Careful now," he added, watching as those carrying a limp form moved past him. Despite trying to be watchful, the men happened to graze the tight doorway with the man's legs, thus eliciting Doc's wrath.

"Watch out fer his leg. Take it easy, will ya men! Ye don't need to cause him any more harm."

My heart sank. I recognized the lifeless form. The four men moving past me carried a bloodied and unconscious Nathaniel.

Rebecca, it would be best if you remained calm, came my mother's reassuring voice.

"I'm trying, mother," I whispered. "Can you make sure he doesn't die?"

You know that's out of my hands, dear. I know how you feel about Mr. Burns; though I don't approve, I wouldn't want him to die.

Eyes closed, Nathaniel's head hung back over one man's arm and rolled from side to side as he was jostled down the narrow hallway. I quickly scanned his limp form from his head to his dirt-covered boots, and my eyes settled on his bloody leg. It didn't look good.

Following the Doc's directions, the men headed down the hall into the surgical suite. I could just make out the shallow rise and fall of Nathaniel's chest as I silently prayed, *Please don't let him die.*

Torn between staying with Emily and Caleb, I decided to leave them alone and followed behind the Doc. I tried convincing myself that I had no emotional ties to Nathaniel other than he had been a perfect gentleman on the train.

But I had to admit there was an immediate connection between us on the first day we met, where he had ignited a spark inside my numb heart.

Regrettably, it was a spark I couldn't allow to catch flame. Despite that, I needed to be there for Nathaniel as he had been there for me.

Ever since I left Boston, I knew I would never return to Elliott, so who was I fooling? I cared deeply for Nathaniel. The least I could do was assist Doc Sweeney with his surgery.

Standing on one side of the raised bed on which the men had placed Nathaniel, I stared at his still form and asked, "Is he dead?"

"Not yet," Doc replied calmly.

Not yet! What does he mean by that? My eyes widen in disbelief. Doc knew he had shocked me.

"I'm sorry, dear. But I can't give ye false hope. Wounds such as tis can be life-threatening, especially when large blood vessels are involved."

Without looking up, he returned to examining the wound when he added, "I'm sorry, but I can't have you in here. I was hoping Emily could help, but she is in no condition to assist me."

Surprising myself, I assuredly declared, "I can do it!

"Ye can? Are ye sure now?" he asked, finally looking up. "Have ye ever assisted with surgery before? Because if not, I won't have ye fainting on me!" In another breath, the Doc added, "If ye do, I'll just leave you on te floor until I'm done."

Standing up straight, I replied, somewhat confidently, "No, Sir. I've never assisted before, but . . ." I paused, then continued, "I don't become squeamish at the sight of blood. And in all my life, I've never fainted."

Now wasn't the time to tell him there had been many instances when I thought I would. Now wasn't the same as caring for my boy's bloodied knees. When in reality, Pearl had been the one to take care of them.

"Alright," Doc replied. "Let's get ye man fixed up." My man! What made him say that? But I didn't take the time to question him.

⚜ 34 ⚜

Rebecca

EXHAUSTED AFTER HOURS spent in the surgical suite treating Nathaniel, Doc and I returned to the kitchen. I stood at the sink, washing the remaining blood off my hands, then turned and leaned against the counter to stretch my back. It ached from standing in one place for so long and holding what Doc called a retractor. It was a nasty-looking device that held Nathaniel's bloodied tissue apart while the Doc inspected the wound, aligned the bone, and performed the final suturing.

Doc had been patient with me, and I learned a great deal assisting him. I actually surprised myself at how calm I remained throughout the surgery. When Doc wasn't deep in thought, he had pointed out the various tissues, muscles, tendons, and vessels and the names of his crude-looking instruments.

After Nathaniel's surgery, I was encouraged by the prospect of helping him and Emily in other surgeries if and when the need arose. Maybe this was another reason I was here.

Caleb and Emily were in a whispered conversation when they saw Doc and I walk into the kitchen. Still looking pale, Caleb stood to ask, "How is Nate? Is he going to lose his leg?

The strain showed on Doc's aging face as he dried his hands with a tattered towel and answered, "No, I don't believe so. But te next twenty-four hours will tell te tale. Tis lucky you got him here when ye did. He's lost a lot of blood and will take some time te heal, but I hope he'll make a full recovery."

Pulling Emily up to his side with his arm firmly around her waist, Caleb released a shaky breath of relief and replied, "That's good. I'm grateful for his help in finding Emily. He put himself in harm's way and was willing to give his life to save us both."

Glancing lovingly at Emily, he announced, "It's been a long two days, and we're both weary. Emily and I desperately need to clean up and get some rest. We're heading upstairs."

"Together?" Doc questioned, looking between the two.

"Yes, together. Emily has agreed to be my wife, and I'm never letting her out of my sight again. And that starts right now," Caleb answered, pointing a finger at the floor. With a stern expression, he asked, "Do you have a problem with that, Doc?"

Not uttering his reply, Doc only shook his head.

Anyone could tell that Caleb and Emily were deeply in love. Doc needn't worry. Caleb would be a faithful husband and take good care of his granddaughter.

Sighing, I could only dream of sharing that kind of love. I had come from a life where a woman followed a strict set of societal rules decreed mostly by men. Our father was one of those old-schooled men who had carefully chosen Elliott as my husband.

Naively, I had done as I was told and married into wealth. Well, no more. My father was dead, and Elliott was thousands of miles away. This was the West, not Boston, and it was time I lived by my own set of rules.

Placing my hand on Doc's forearm to ease his mind, we watched as Caleb led Emily up the back stairs to their room. As they walked away, I realized life is filled with what-ifs—such unsettling questions.

What if Caleb never found Emily?

What if he had and she was dead?

What if I never left Boston?

What if Elliott had killed me?

What if he finds us?

A chill passed through me at my last thought. I was mentally and physically drained, that I became lightheaded and needed the back of a chair to steady myself. Finally, I had to leave the room.

"Are ye alright, dear," Doc asked.

"Yes, thank you. I'm fine. I'm just tired." Pointing my finger down the hall, I replied, "I think I'll go sit with Mr. Burns for a while just in case he wakes up."

"That's a good idea. Call if ye need me. I'll send word te the sheriff te have a few men help move Mr. Burns to a more comfortable bed."

"Thank you, Doc. I'll sit with him until they arrive."

⚬⚭⚬

Returning to the surgical suite, I stood quietly over Nathaniel, who lay there so deathly still. If it weren't for his chest's shallow rise and fall, I would have thought. No! I couldn't think like that. Nathaniel had to live. Selfishly, I needed him.

Two days ago, this man had looked so regal upon his black stallion. His face, now pale from blood loss, was covered in two days' growth of a light red beard infused with a touch of gray. Despite all he'd been through, he was still handsome.

Pulling up the blanket just enough to check the bandage on his leg, I heard that familiar voice questioning me, *Rebecca, what are you doing?*

"I'm just going to check his dressing. Why do you ask, Mother?"

As a lady, do you think you should be doing that? I mean, that doesn't seem proper.

"Mother, I'm not in Boston anymore, and what you deem proper doesn't seem to matter here."

I see.

"Do you really, Mother?"

I'm sorry for doubting your intentions. I'll leave you be.

Relieved my mother had left me alone, I continued with my observations and noted a moderate amount of red oozing that contrasted against the white dressing. Examining it further, I was satisfied it wasn't enough to call for the doctor, so I replaced the bed covers.

Remembering the heated blush as his masculine form stood over me on the train, my eyes roamed the length of his now frail and vulnerable body when a light groan brought me out of my drifting thoughts. His breathing had increased, and his brows were tightly furrowed. I could only surmise that Nathaniel was in a great deal of pain.

Hesitantly, I reached out and passed my palm over his stubbled cheek when a lock of golden red hair fell over his right eye. Gently pushing it back, my fingers lingered in his thick curls longer than was appropriate.

A tingling sensation moved up my arm, and within seconds, his features relaxed. I couldn't help myself. I barely knew him, yet I was dangerously attracted to this man.

Of course, I knew my mother would soon be making more comments. And, yes, there she was.

Remember Rebecca. You are a married woman.

"How could I forget when you're here to remind me."

Rebecca, please don't take that tone with me.

"I'm sorry, Mother, but you must understand I'll never return to Elliot or Boston. I plan on making a life here in Yuma with Caleb and Emily." Looking down at Nathaniel, I added, "And hopefully with a man who truly cares about me and my boys."

Forgive me, but it would be best if you didn't give Elliot anything to hold over you regarding legal action if it comes to that.

"Of course, you're right. I'll be careful, Mother." With that, she was gone.

⁓❦⁓

Unsettled, I rearranged the clean instruments and took stock of the medications behind the glass-faced cabinet. Finally, too tired to do more, I checked on Nathaniel once again before I settled in the rocker.

Doc had said he tried cleaning all the dirt and wood fragments from Nathaniel's wound as best he could. According to him, the surgery had gone well, but the risk of infection would always loom nearby until Nathaniel was fully healed.

I was concerned when I saw Nathaniel's brow glistening with beads of sweat. I wiped them with a cool, damp cloth, praying that the deadly fever Doc Sweeney spoke of wasn't setting in. Nathaniel was becoming restless and mumbling things I didn't understand.

Placing my hand on his shoulder, I tried calming him down and reassure him he was safe, but he continued moaning with each agitated move he made.

Doc had instructed me to administer the correct measure of laudanum if Nathaniel's pain became unbearable. Turning away, I went to the glass door cabinet, which held the cleaned instruments, dressings, and the dark brown bottle I needed.

Shaking my head, I read the label and the bottle's contents, knowing it was a physical pain reliever for some but also a ghostly demon for others. Grateful, I had never needed the drug myself, yet I knew Elliott had taken to using it all too frequently for his headaches.

Shaking off those memories, I opened the bottle and poured the reddish-brown liquid into a teaspoon. Holding it under my nose, I inhaled its sharp odor. It smelled of tar, tobacco, a hint of pepper, and coffee. Most medicines, such as this, weren't made for their scent or taste.

Satisfied I had the correct dose, I touched Mr. Burns on the shoulder. Slowly opening his eyes, he seemed to look through me, not at me. "Mr. Burns. I have some medication to help ease your pain. Can you raise your head to swallow?"

"Rebecca?" he groaned out in a gravelly voice.

Surprised by his familiarity with using my first name, "Yes," was all I managed to say. "Let me help you sit up." Carefully holding the spoon in one hand, I positioned my other behind his shoulders. He was a large man, and my back protested from the strain. It took only a second for him to swallow while his face wrinkled up in disgust at the bitter liquid.

In a soft voice, while lowering his shoulders to the pillow, I said, "I'm sorry about the taste. What's important is that it should only take a few minutes before it helps ease your pain."

"Water. I need some water," he choked out.

"Of course." Reaching for the glass on the nightstand, I missed, tipping its contents onto the floor. Flustered, I grabbed a rag hanging on a nearby hook and mopped up the liquid before refilling the glass.

Coughing, he closed his eyes briefly, then stared directly at me, asking, "Where am I?"

"You're in Doc Sweeney's clinic." I straightened his sheets for distraction, only stopping long enough to ask, "Do you remember what happened to you?"

"I remember an explosion." Unexpectedly, he grabbed my wrist and rushed out, "Emily. Caleb. Where are they?"

Gently removing his hand from my wrist, I answered, "Mr. Burns, you need to remain calm."

Nathaniel attempted to sit up, but failing, he rushed out, "Tell me, are they alright?" Falling back onto his pillow, he looked about the room and added hastily, "I need to see them."

Rubbing his hands over his face, he continued, "God, what a mess I've made."

"They're both fine, Mr. Burns," I answered, reassuring him with my hand on his shoulder. "They're upstairs getting some much-needed rest, which you should be doing. The laudanum should start working soon. Please close your eyes, and I'll leave you to sleep. You can ring the bell on the nightstand if you should need anything."

35

Rebecca

I turned to leave and felt a light tug on the cuff of my sleeve. "Please, don't go," Nathaniel slurred as the effects of the laudanum were rapidly taking hold. With a pleading look, he added, "I don't want to die alone."

"Please, Mr. Burns, don't talk like that," I said, trying to alleviate his fear. "You are not going to die. Doc Sweeney said your surgery went well, and you should be fine in a week or two." I wouldn't tell him the risk of an infection could potentially take his life. Adding to his worry, it would do his recovery no good,

Despite my words of reassurance, I could see the fear lingering in his eyes as he held me in his stare. I wondered what happened in his past to make him so fearful like this. Patting the top of his hand that held my sleeve, I acquiesced. "Alright, I'll sit here until you fall asleep."

"Thank you," he replied, giving my arm a weak squeeze.

Though the night air was cool, I opened the window just a bit, allowing a fresh light breeze to flow through, hoping it cleared the room of its tell-tale medicinal odors. As I looked out the window at the velvety black sky with its brilliant white moon, I silently sent a prayer heavenward that Nathaniel would recover.

Moving a well-used rocker close to his bed, I made myself comfortable and pulled a patchwork quilt over my lap. As hard as I tried, the tension in my shoulders wouldn't relax. Drawing in a deep cleansing breath, I leaned my head back and closed my eyes while setting the chair in motion.

As if natural, I lay my hand close to Nathaniel's. I told myself I was doing this for no other reason than that if Nathaniel needed me during the night, he knew that I kept my word.

Unexpectedly, his hand firmly grasped mine, causing me to stop rocking. The heat from our connection made me think we had entwined our hands like this a thousand times before. I wouldn't pull away. It felt right to have his hand in mine.

Awakening sometime in the early morning hours with a stiff neck, I leaned forward and stretched my back. Looking over at Nathaniel, who was still asleep, with a more relaxed look to his features, I watched his chest rise and fall in a reassuring rhythm.

My stomach gurgled when I remembered the last time I ate was early yesterday afternoon. Leaving the room quietly so as not to wake Nathaniel, I made my way down the hallway to the kitchen. Sniffing and twitching my nose, I inhaled the fragrant aroma of freshly brewed coffee, wondering who was downstairs.

Caleb stood barefoot at the stove alone, in denim, minus a shirt, with his healing wounds evident on his shoulder and abdomen. Despite him being my brother, he was quite a handsome site to behold. Emily was a lucky woman. Absent from the room, she must have remained upstairs.

Caleb turned as he heard me come up behind him. Going to his side, I placed my hand on his forearm, leaned up on my tiptoes, and gave him a sisterly kiss on his cheek. Unexpectedly, in return, he enfolded me in his arms, telling me, "I love you, Sis, and I'm so glad you're here. I've missed you, Becca."

Looking up, I knew his expression was genuine, and I happily replied, "Caleb, you have no idea how glad I am to be here. I've missed you too." Gently squeezing his hand, I asked, "Is Emily still upstairs?"

"Yes, I told her to stay in bed as long as she liked. She's been through a lot in the past few days."

"You both have been through so much. I can't imagine what you went through. Is she, I mean, did the men?" I couldn't get the uncomfortable question past my lips.

As if reading my mind, Caleb answered. "No. She told me they tried, but she fought them off tooth and nail." He choked up and ultimately couldn't finish what he wanted to say as tears formed in the corner of his eyes.

"It's fine, Caleb. You don't have to say anymore. I'm just grateful Emily is home safe with people who love her and will help her recover." Leaning back, I could hear in the somber tone of his voice he was still in a great deal of pain when I asked, "How are you feeling, Caleb? Riding didn't open your wounds. Did it?"

"No, I just ache more than usual. Emily looked at my wounds last night and told me I was healing fine. Although, she was a bit annoyed that I rode too soon and such a long distance. She made me promise her that I would get more rest."

"You are such a fibber, Caleb Young," I teased in a sisterly way. "You hurt more than you let on. But I'm glad that Emily is watching out for you."

"Why, Rebecca Young, I've never heard you call me a liar."

"I didn't say, liar. I said, fibber."

"Isn't that one and the same?" he asked with a teasing grin.

"Oh, let's not quibble over a silly word."

"I'm only teasing you, Sis. It feels so good to be able to do that again."

I smiled up at him as my tone turned serious. "Caleb, as you well know, life is too short. From now on, your sister will speak the truth as she sees fit." Stepping back and holding my head high, I continued, "No longer can Father or Elliot control my actions or opinions, nor will any man ever again." Lightening the mood, I smiled and winked, then added, "I'm a woman of the West now!"

"That's the spunky sister I remember! I'm glad to see you're finally standing up for yourself."

"Yes. So am I.

Hesitating, I'd hoped to avoid this conversation a bit longer, but now was as good a time as any. Not that it was going to be easy, mind you, but since Caleb and I were alone, I hoped we wouldn't have any interruptions.

Clearing my throat, I proceeded. "Caleb, we need to talk."

"O.K.," he replied, stepping back while still holding my hands. "But I get the sense I won't like what you're about to say."

"You're probably right," I answered, shrugging my shoulders. "I need to tell you about Boston and Elliot, and I must do it while we're alone."

"Are you alright, sis?" Caleb asked, squeezing my hands tightly. I saw concern written all over his face as he moved his hands to my forearms.

I could only imagine his reaction when I told him what had transpired between Elliott and me. "I'm fine now that I'm here and you're alive." Turning to sit at the table, I added, "You have no idea the torment I went through while traveling here, thinking you might have died before I could arrive. I couldn't bear it if that happened."

"It's O.K., Sis, we're together now." Moving toward the stove, Caleb added, "Let me get us some coffee, and we can talk."

I would need the coffee's strength to fortify my resolve and get me through what I was about to tell him. Before he placed a cup in my hand, my fingers fidgeted noisily on the top of the table, making Caleb look back over at me.

Handing me a steaming mug, he eased himself into the chair and asked, "Alright, what is it you need to tell me?"

Biting my lower lip, I inhaled deeply and then explained about Elliott and our volatile relationship. The hardest part was telling my brother what Elliot had done to me the night before I left Boston.

I watched Caleb's jaw tighten and a vein in his left temple pulse. Turning his eyes downward, he examined his fists as they clenched and unclenched. I waited for his barrage of anger to unfold, only imagining the years away from Boston had hardened him.

Slamming both fists on the table, he swore and abruptly stood towering over me. In doing so, his chair fell back onto the planked floor with an earsplitting thud that would wake the rest of the house. Eyes wide, I half expected to see flames shoot out of his mouth, resembling a fiery dragon in one of my son's books.

Responding in an abrasive tone, "If I ever see that man again, I'll kill him!"

Reaching for his hands, I pleaded, "No! Caleb. You mustn't. You have to promise me you won't do anything so rash. You have Emily to think about now. I'll obtain a divorce and be rid of Elliot." Looking up into his smoldering eyes, I added, "Surely, a divorce would be granted based on his abuse alone."

Wringing the handkerchief in my hands, I wasn't so sure. Divorce was not easy for a woman to obtain. "You can help me, can't you?"

"Sis, I'll do anything for you. But you must understand, I haven't practiced law since leaving Boston five years ago."

My heart sank at his words. Who will I get to help me? He must have read my thoughts when he said, "I'll help you, but I need to telegram a former colleague to see what I have to do to become reinstated in Boston. And I'm not sure about it here in Yuma. I'll have to get in touch with the jurisdictional judge."

Placing my arms around my brother's waist, he pulled me close enough to rest his chin on the top of my head. I began to cry, feeling safe for the first time in months. This is how Emily found us as she came down the back stairs rubbing the sleep out of her eyes.

Rebecca

LOOKING BETWEEN CALEB and me, Emily asked, "Rebecca, why are you crying? Is everything OK?" Rushing to our side, "It's not Nate. He didn't?"

I didn't give her a chance to finish her question before jumping in. "No! No! Nate, I mean, Mr. Burns is fine. Doc Sweeney is watching for signs of infection." Averting eye contact, I continued, "Caleb and I were just talking about why I'm here."

"Well, that's obvious. Isn't it? I invited you here. Or should I say, I implored you to come,"

"Yes, you sent me the telegram about Caleb's injury, but there's another reason why I'm here." I watched her expression turn to one of confusion.

"I'm not sure I'm following you," Emily said, coming to stand next to Caleb. Caleb placed an arm around her shoulder as I tried shaking off the somber mood. Then I suggested, "Let's have breakfast first, then we can all talk."

Looking at the stairs, I informed them, "Pearl is now here with us. She'll watch the boys so we can talk in private. There are no secrets between her and me. She already knows what I'm about to tell you."

After eating, I retold my story while Emily listened without interrupting. But there was no denying that her facial features gave her emotions away. As she remained patiently seated and I continued, I watched as her eyes became round as saucers, and her face progressed through various stages of confusion, sadness, and then fury.

I gave her credit for remaining silent and letting me finish. If she had interrupted, I don't think I could have completed what I had to say. Without thinking, I blurted out, "I'm sorry, but I didn't know where else to turn. The day I received your telegram was the day I knew I had an excuse to leave Boston for good. I finally felt as if we were free to start a new life with my brother."

By the time I finished, I was exhausted and realized it was still early morning. Taking Emily's hands in mine, I added, "Dear Emily, you are a blessing in my life." She smiled and pulled me into a hug. More tears threatened, but I willed myself not to cry again. I had a new life and a new family— finally, something to be happy about.

"Now, if you'll excuse me, I'll leave you two alone. I'm going upstairs to check on the boys and Pearl. I'll be down later."

～ﮨﮨﮨ～

Emily

After Rebecca left the room, I pulled on Caleb's shirt sleeve to get his attention and asked, "What are we going to do?"

With a confused look, he asked, "What do you mean?"

Grabbing Caleb's hands, I expressed my concerns. "Rebecca, Pearl, and the boys can stay here as long as they want, but what if Elliott finds out where they are? What if he comes looking for her? We can't hide them forever." Snapping my fingers, I added, "That's it. We'll find them a safe place to hide. I don't want anything happening to them."

"Whoa! Slow down, Doc. Let's not get ahead of ourselves. You, of all people, understand how I feel about Elliot."

I watched Caleb's expression change at the mention of his brother-in-law's name. Eyes smoldering with loathing and something I couldn't decipher, I knew he would do anything within his power to protect his sister.

Caleb snarled, "If he comes here with the intent of harming Becca or my nephews, he's a dead man."

Placing my hand over his, "Let's hope it won't come to that, and he has sense enough to leave Rebecca and the boys alone. Rebecca impressed me as a brave woman traveling all this way with Pearl and her boys with no male escort."

Caleb gave me a look I knew all too well. "I know, I know. I'm the last person to be talking about traveling alone. Like I've told you before, I did it all the time in 2019. But, we had no problems carrying protection."

I learned fast how different it was for women in 1880. Women now, other than the rare few, didn't carry protection of any kind. And terrible things often happened to them while traveling alone. I, for one, was grateful Rebecca was here now, and we would help her however we could.

Although an abusive partner may seem affectionate and appreciative at times, they rarely were able to think things through reasonably, and the pattern of abusive behavior ultimately came to the forefront. All they wanted was to exert their power and control over their intimate partner. Unfortunately, with all that Rebecca told us about her husband's abusive behavior, I couldn't convince myself that Elliott would have enough brains to stay away.

⁓⚬⁓

I flinched as Caleb drew me into his embrace. I knew he would never hurt me, but the touch of a man, no matter how much I loved him, triggered flashbacks of the mine where Vermin had tried raping me.

Vermin was dead, along with his deaf and mute brother, Stubbs, and I knew neither of them could hurt me ever again. But from past experiences dealing with abused women in Seattle, Caleb would have to give me time and space to ease my anxiety and fears.

I could only imagine what Rebecca was going through.

Caleb asked with a hurtful expression, "Did I do something wrong?" Slowly pushing back from his embrace, I saw the fear growing in his eyes.

The past few days had taken a toll on both of us, and I wondered if he were afraid I would never allow him to touch me again. Of course not! "Caleb. You know I love you. Don't you?"

"I'm not so sure," he replied, looking defeated. "You didn't answer my question. Did I do something wrong?" he asked again.

"Please, just give me some time. You must understand what I've been through in the past seventy-two hours." I continued standing before him while rubbing my hands up and down my cold arms. "As a man, you can't possibly comprehend what Vermin tried to do to me. It's every woman's nightmare." I took a deep breath and added, "Maybe I should feel sorry for saying this, but I'm not. I'm glad Vermin's dead."

"Em, Just because I'm not a woman doesn't mean I don't understand what you're trying to say. And no, you don't need to feel sorry for what happened to Vermin. He got what he deserved. I'm just sorry that his brother had to die along with him. Stubbs did a brave thing by saving you."

"I know. That's the only thing I regret. I wish I could have saved him." "Emily, you're a great doctor, but as painful as it is, you can't save everybody."

I allowed him to pull me back into his arms when he added, "I would never do anything to hurt you. I love you now and always will.

"I understand, Caleb. It's just."

"Em, I'll give you all the time you need. Please, don't shut me out. Or worse, leave me."

"I won't ever leave you." That's all I could manage to say for the time being. I loved this man and felt the love he had in his heart for me. His warm embrace made me feel safe and secure. That he would be patient with me was all I needed to hear.

37

Rebecca

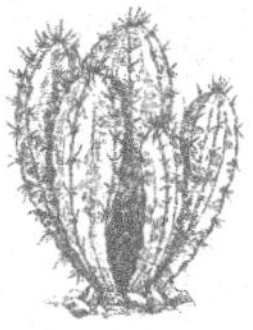

I KNOCKED ON the bedroom door that the boys now shared with Pearl. They had missed her the two days she was at the hotel and had been eager to leave their cubby. I found her sitting in the rocker next to the only window in the room. Placing my finger over my lips, I indicated that we should remain quiet to avoid waking the boys.

Kneeling beside her, I spoke in a low voice and told her about what had transpired since she arrived at the clinic. I told her Caleb and Emily were home safe and now resting in the room down the hall from us.

Pearl took my cold fingers in her warm hands and said, "You look so tired, dear. Why don't you lie down next to the boys and rest."

"I'll be fine, Pearl. I'm just glad that we're all together again." Rubbing my fingers over my forehead, I added, "I don't know what I would have done if Caleb hadn't been alive."

Patting my hands and using her comforting voice, Pearl responded, "Now, dear, you don't have to worry about that anymore. He's here, and he's alive."

Squeezing her hands, I answered, "Yes. You're right. All I need to do now is concentrate on finding us a home and planning our future here in Yuma. First, I'll need to find a job since I have little money left to keep us going for too much longer."

"A job! What er' do you expect to do? Rebecca, I don't mean to be condescending, but you're a sophisticated lady who's never had to work outside the home before." Patting my hands, she quickly added, "I still have some money put aside that we can use."

"My sweet Pearl, I can't take your money, and what little I was able to bring with us won't last forever. The boys and I can't live off the charity of my brother and Doctor Sweeney forever. Genteel or not, I can work serving in one of the restaurants. Or possibly cleaning at the hotel."

"Dear girl, we'll think of something. But for now, I have enough funds to keep us going for several months." Winking, she added, "I had a good employer that paid me well."

"Oh, you cheeky lady." I'd heard Pearl use that term many times and felt it suited her now. "That's why I love you."

"Our first order of business should be to find a place where the four of us won't live in one small room."

"You're right," I answered, hugging Pearl. "I'll have to ask Caleb where we can locate a safe place to rent."

I hesitated before asking, but Pearl would find out sooner than later. "Pearl, you remember Mr. Burns from the train?"

"Why yes. He's that handsome young man who watched over Porter and Daniel for a time so we could get some rest." Curiously looking at me, she continued, "Why do you bring him up now? Have you seen him here in Yuma?"

"Yes, I've seen him. He was part of the posse that went out with the sheriff and Caleb to find Emily."

Pearl's voice squeaked when she asked, "Well, what did he say when he saw you?"

"Nothing. He didn't say anything. Besides, I didn't want to give away to the others we had met before. Pearl, it's all so complicated."

Standing, I walked to stand at the bed where the boys slept. "I believe I saw him before he noticed me." Turning, I faced Pearl and continued. "What caught my eye first was a stately black stallion and a man wearing clothing I'd seen most men in town wear, including Caleb. The only reason I knew it was him was when he looked straight at me. I recognized his emerald eyes."

"That's wonderful," Pearl said until she saw the look on my face that indicated I was worried. "It's not wonderful? But why? What's going on, Rebecca?"

"Caleb, Emily, and the posse came back this morning."

"I heard the commotion downstairs but didn't want to interrupt." Standing, Pearl placed her hands on my arms and asked, "What are you not telling me? Did something awful happen to Mr. Burns?

"Yes and no."

"Well, which is it, girl? There's no need to be mysterious with me at this point."

Pearl knew I had feelings for Mr. Burns. But she also knew I would never act on them. I stepped back, taking her hands in mine, and continued. "Mr. Burns was seriously injured in an explosion while rescuing Emily. His leg." I didn't get a chance to finish when she surmised he'd lost his leg.

"Oh, good heavens. The doctor had to amputate. That poor man."

"No. No Pearl. That's not what I meant. Doctor Sweeney did have to perform surgery, but he saved his leg. And I helped."

"Oh, I'm so thankful he didn't lose his leg. Wait! What did you say? You helped the doctor perform surgery? But Rebecca, you can't stand the sight of blood. Even when the boys skin their knees, I have to take care of them. How did you ever manage to help him in surgery?"

"Since Emily was in no condition to help. Doc Sweeney would have had to do the surgery alone, which would have been difficult, or I would have to volunteer my services to help. Really, I wasn't thinking straight at the time. But I did it. And Pearl, you would have been proud of me. I didn't faint."

Placing her arms around me, "I am proud of you, Rebecca. You've come a long way since leaving Boston. You're going to do fine here in Yuma!

∽ 38 ∾

Rebecca

THREE WEEKS HAD passed since Emily was found alive, and Nathaniel had been injured. His physical wounds had healed, but once he left the clinic to complete his recovery at his ranch, he became distant, staying away from town and all those who cared about him.

Nathaniel was constantly on my mind, but thankfully, Emily kept me busy helping her plan her wedding to my brother. So, I didn't have time to pursue his reasoning for remaining absent. At first, I thought he didn't want to speak with me. That was the excuse I used. But as the days wore on, I wasn't so sure, and I didn't know how to approach him for answers.

For the most part, Emily remained closed off from sharing what had transpired while being held captive. She had put on a brave front since returning, and I knew it wasn't my place to pry, but I worried about her well-being.

On the other hand, Caleb was Caleb, the stoic brother I remembered so well. Still, he hadn't told me how and why he'd been shot. It seemed we all had muddied pasts, but what was more important before confessions were revealed was that we allowed ourselves the time to heal.

The good news was that Caleb had heard back from the Boston Bar and had been reinstated to practice law in Massachusetts. From what he told me, Arizona was still a Territory and didn't have a formal bar association, so he was free to set up his law practice in Yuma.

As the town grew, a never-ending stream of sick or injured patients came through the clinic doors. Doc Sweeney was grateful that his granddaughter was gradually getting back into practicing medicine and seemed happiest when she was treating patients.

Pearl, I, and the boys settled comfortably into a small two-bedroom casita conveniently located behind the clinic that Doc had previously used for storage. Besides being a mother, I finally felt useful when I helped the doctors during the day while Pearl stayed with the boys. I tried not to think of Elliot, but in the back of my mind, I always wondered where he was and what he was planning. The last thing I wanted to do was put my family and newly found friends at risk, so I remained vigilant in my comings and goings.

<hr />

Elliot

Finally, I heard back from the Pinkerton Agency. I knew I said I would never go wandering off to the West to find her, but I couldn't leave Rebecca's departure, so to speak, to a stranger. So, I left Boston the following day, taking the train as far west as possible.

It was unimaginable what possessed my wife to leave the civilized comforts I provided for her to travel to the brutally hot and uncivilized West. I knew it was to locate her brother, but I felt he wasn't worth the time and energy it would take her to find him.

He never approved of our marriage, and I was glad when he suddenly left Boston without warning or leaving a trail. Regardless of Caleb's former fiancé cheating on him, he'd left a lucrative career and a woman whose compelling charms captivated every man she'd ever met, including me. I would have overlooked her misgivings for her beauty and the physical comforts she nimbly provided.

Caleb was such a foolish man, and he deserved whatever misfortune became of him.

"Damn!" This noisy, miserable train is giving me a headache. Taking the brown bottle I was never without out from inside my vest pocket, I took a swig, careful not to waste a drop. Closing my eyes, I leaned against the smelly sweat-infused cushion, and soon, the throbbing on the right side of my head eased, and I drifted into a state of euphoria, a place where I could tolerate this insufferable journey.

It seemed hours had passed when I awoke with a stiff neck and shoulder muscles painfully tight from my head's awkward position. Lips held in a tight line, I whispered under my breath, "When I get my hands on that woman, I'll kill her!"

Had I spoken aloud? Looking about the car, I needed to ensure no one had heard me. I couldn't have that. Clamping my eyes shut, I clenched my fists into tight balls where my nails painfully dug into my palms. I was so angry with Rebecca that I envisioned my hands squeezing around her delicate neck. It was one way for me to obtain my revenge.

My selfish wife was putting me through hell, and I wouldn't allow her to do it ever again. If I had my way, it would soon be over.

"Fort Worth!" yelled the conductor as he walked past me down the aisle. It was enough that I had to travel with total strangers, but there were no Pullman cars on this leg of my journey. The lack of comfort and amenities was utterly degrading for a man of my stature. I didn't think I would ever be the same.

I would be more than grateful once I stepped off this wretched fire-breathing contraption and onto stable ground. Longing for a drink and covered in dust with a parched throat, I ran my tongue over the roof of my mouth. I would first find the nearest bar, drink the pain away, and find a clean bed and a willing woman.

ᥟ 39 ᥠ

Nathaniel

IT WAS SIX o'clock in the morning, late for a rancher to rise, but since the accident, I hadn't been able to keep up with my chores around the ranch, let alone the mine. I was grateful I had capable ranch hands to help out.

I didn't need to worry about the mine. It had been closed since the day before Christmas. I always tried to give the men a few days off to be with their families during the holiday. Not many mine owners I knew did. But I treated my men with the respect they deserved since they put their lives on the line for me by working daily in the damp darkness beneath the earth.

This wasn't the same mine Caleb and I had been in when the explosion occurred while searching for Emily. Since the holidays were long over, I needed to open. I had buyers waiting for the silver and miners who needed their pay.

Since discarding the crutches, I could now walk using a cane and came out onto the porch each chance I had. It was a place where I could let my mind wander and enjoy the desert air. Not being able to ride

175

Silver Star put a crimp in many of my plans. Truthfully, I was becoming grumpy and impatient, and my ranch hands had no trouble telling me so.

It wasn't that I didn't want to go into town to see friends, but I couldn't find the nerve to be close to Rebecca. The worst part was being unable to act on my feelings for her, and it was driving me crazy.

An inviting aroma and the creaking of the screen door behind me alerted me that Enedina, my housekeeper and cook, had come out with a cup of her delicious Mexican brew.

"Buenos dias, Señor." Smiling, she handed me a steaming mug, and I inhaled the aromatic nuttiness with a hint of chocolate. There was no better coffee. Not in my previous life could Starbucks compare to this.

"Gracias, Enedina, this smells wonderful, as usual." Grasping the mug with both hands, I nodded my approval and took a tentative sip of the hot liquid as I made my way to the porch railing.

"Eres bienvenido, Señor."

"I'll be in shortly." Enedina always waited for me to take the first sip before returning inside. My stomach growled, and my mouth watered, eager to taste her breakfast of huevos rancheros. She fed me too well. That's why I needed to hurry up and recover so I could work off her delicious meals.

As it happened every cloudless morning, I stood facing the ranch's eastern yard and watched the rising sun illuminate the sky in hues of yellow and purple as it crested the hills. Here was the perfect place, and I was grateful to have been given a second chance at life. I'd come to love it here. It was a world farthest from anything I knew in Boston in 2016, and I couldn't ever imagine going back.

After last night's rain, I inhaled the Pinon Pine's earthy scent surrounding the ranch. The only thing missing was the woman I'd fallen in love with, standing by my side.

My leg began to throb, and I realized I'd been standing on my feet too long. Sitting down in one of the porch rockers helped ease the pain and took the weight and pressure off my leg.

I looked out over the dirt-filled yard as I set the rocker in motion. Biting the inside of my cheek, I shrugged off the sense of melancholy, knowing the woman I cared deeply for was out of my reach. But was it wrong to want her beside me to enjoy this beauty and life here on the ranch?

It had been weeks since I left town to come home and recover. Under the doting and watchful eye of Enedina, I was in bed for seventy-two hours before I thought I would go mad.

Bless her, but she still followed me around like a mother hen, often chastising me in Spanish because I wasn't getting enough rest. Oh, and let me tell you, when I turned my crutches in for a cane, it was a scene I cared not to repeat with Enedina.

Some of her words I understood, but definitely, her actions and facial expressions told me all I needed to know. Yesterday's conversation in her broken English was a prime example of her mothering.

With her hand on her hips, she declared, "Señor Burns, you must go back to bed. Your leg is not healed."

Whining my reply like a two-year-old, I said, "Enedina, I'm fine. You're smothering me. Stop fussing so."

She admonished me while shaking her head and wagging her finger, "Well, someone has to watch over you, Señor!" Placing her hands on her hips, she smiled, adding in Spanish, "Necesitas una esposa, Señor."

"E-n-e-d-i-n-a," I responded, dragging out her name teasingly. "I comprehended perfectly what you just said."

"Humph!" She mumbled something else in Spanish that I was probably better off not grasping its meaning.

She and her husband had been with me since I came to Yuma and acquired the ranch. I considered them family, the only ones I had in this century. I didn't know what I would do without either of them. I understood her now loud and clear. She was only looking out for me, and she was right as usual. But I had too many chores around the ranch and mine that needed my direct attention.

Pain or no pain, I wasn't used to lying in bed helpless and being doted on, and four long weeks had given me enough time to think about the beautiful brunette who lingered in my thoughts both day and night. With Enedina trying to get me to go back to bed, I chuckled at thinking of lying in bed all day with Rebecca by my side.

I was running out of supplies, and the ranch hands were too busy to take time out to go to town. Since Enedina's husband was busy, she offered to drive me in the wagon. But I had my pride after all and didn't want to be seen coming into town with my housekeeper driving. I wouldn't be able to live down the haranguing from my ranch hands.

Doc Sweeney had wanted me to come by the clinic after being home a week, but I couldn't bring myself to go back to town with the possibility of running into Rebecca.

My leg healed, albeit stiff in places, and I no longer had an excuse to sequester myself on the ranch. It was time I faced Rebecca. Maybe then I would be able to lay aside my feelings for her.

~ 40 ~

Nathaniel

IT WAS NO use denying the love I had for Rebecca. But before I could let my heart become more deeply involved than it already was, it was imperative to know if I had the slightest chance with her. I hoped Caleb could tell me if I did. If not, and as hard as it would be, I would somehow swallow my pride and step aside. It would be one of the toughest things I'd ever done since meeting her on the train that day.

I found myself smiling as I recalled that exact moment. Inhaling deeply, I imagined her lily perfume filling my senses and turning my world upside down. And the way those wayward wisps of raven hair tumbled freely from under her hat had made me want to run the unbound tendrils through my fingers.

I only wished she was here, now, beside me. Unknowingly, she had captured my heart in one fleeting beat. I needed to know if she was still a happily married woman and only here for a short visit without her husband.

My mind raced with all sorts of scenarios, none of them in my favor. I had this funny feeling there was more to Mrs. Ackerman than

179

she let on. Something was deeply troubling her. On the train, her steel blue eyes were always darting about the rail car and out the window as if she knew she was being followed. If she and her boys were in trouble and needed protection, I wanted to be the one to provide it.

Driving the wagon into town, I stopped first at Caleb's new law office to see how he was doing. I had an ulterior motive for going there. I wanted to find out more about his sister, Rebecca. I couldn't help it; she had been in my thoughts both day and night since coming home.

I silently groaned while stiffly stepping down out of the wagon. I probably needed to rest up more, but there was too much for me to do on the ranch to spend my time lying around. I looked up at the new sign, 'Caleb Young, Attorney at Law. It was good to know that Caleb was now in business and away from his previous life as a gambler. Emily, his fiancé, was definitely good for him.

Standing in the open door, I removed my hat and waited for Caleb to look up from the papers he had strewn across his desk. He was so engrossed in his work that he had yet to notice me standing there. So, I cleared my throat to garner his attention.

"Nathan, I didn't see you standing there. Please come in," he asked, with a wave of his hand. "How are you doing?"

Rising from his overstuffed leather seat, he pulled a chair forward for me to sit in. We shook hands, and then he indicated with one hand, "Please, sit down. I'm sorry. I meant to get out to the ranch, but opening the office has taken up most of my time. Plus, there's Emily and the wedding plans. I know those aren't good excuses, so please forgive me."

Sitting back down, he added, "You're looking well. How is the leg doing?"

I lied when I said, "I'm doing fine. Thanks for asking." I tried focusing on our conversation and not the throbbing running down my leg. "And you don't need to apologize. I know you've been busy. The boys at the ranch have kept me up to date on what's happening here in town."

Sitting across from Caleb's large desk, I rolled the brim of my hat around in my hands and kept our conversation short. I wanted to ask him about his sister but lost the courage and continued with small talk. "How's the law practice going?"

"Well, I've only been open one week, and already I have four clients. Nothing major, mind you, but each case helps. I hope in time the business will grow as the town does."

"How is Emily doing? Is she back working with her grandfather?"

"Yes, she is. She's happy to be keeping herself busy. But I do worry about her. She doesn't talk about what happened to her up at the mine, and I'm afraid she's keeping her fears bottled up inside."

"Give her time, Caleb. She went through a lot before we caught up with her." Not one to be giving advice, I dropped my eyes to the floor and added, "She'll talk when she's ready." To lighten the conversation, I changed the subject. "Is she happy about your upcoming nuptials?"

"I hope she is. I know I certainly am. She and my sister have been busy making plans when they're not working in the clinic." Pausing, Caleb placed his elbows on the desk and leaned forward before adding, "You know, Nate, I didn't think I would ever say this, but I can't wait to make her my wife. I love her. She completes me, and I can't think of any other woman I would rather spend the rest of my life with than Emily. I guess you could say I've loved her since she leaned over me up in the hills, trying to save my life. I don't think I could go on breathing without her beside me."

"Wow! You do have it bad," I chuckled. "Did you say that your sister is helping out at the clinic?"

"Yes, she is. Both Mathew and Emily are grateful to have her there."

"Doing what, may I ask?" This was one way of finding out how Rebecca was doing without being too obvious. It sounded as if she planned to stick around Yuma. I could only hope so. Maybe my luck was about to change.

"She's assisting with exams and procedures and helping keep the clinic organized. She's even helped out with some surgeries. I was surprised to hear that, since she can't stand the sight of blood. But she seems to be happy. Pearl takes care of the boys during the day while she's at the clinic. You know, Porter started school a week ago. I'm not sure he's thrilled about it, but you know how boys are about school?"

"That's great. I'm glad to hear everyone's doing so well." I wanted to ask more but didn't dare. "Well, I came into town to get some supplies for Enedina, so I better head on over to the mercantile and see if MacLachlan has my order ready." Placing my hat back on my head, I started to leave when the office door burst open, and a boy looking no older than eight with his blond hair sticking straight up and his face covered in dust rushed in. At first, I didn't recognize him, but it was Joey, who worked odd jobs around town.

Leaning over in the entry, with his hands on his knees, he struggled to catch his breath. "Mr. Young! Mr. Young!" he rushed out. Eyes round as saucers, he added, "Come quick! There's been a shooting at the Prickly Pear Saloon."

"Slow down, Joey," Caleb said, laying his hands on the boy's shoulders. "Did you tell the Sheriff first?"

"I went to his office, but he wasn't there."

"It's OK, Joey. You did the right thing by coming here. Now, I want you to go over to Mrs. Ackerman's house and stay with Pearl. The boys will be in school, where you should be, may I remind you." Squeezing his shoulder, Caleb turned him towards the open door. "We'll talk about that later. For now, I don't want you going back to the saloon. You hear me?"

"Yes, sir. Please, just hurry."

After Joey left, Caleb pulled his revolver out of the top drawer of his desk and checked to see that it was loaded. I pulled mine out of its holster and did the same. Then, we quickly headed to the Prickly Pear.

The Prickly Pear was known for being one of the seedier establishments in town. Whereas the Pick and Shovel, now owned by Henry Calhoun, who didn't put up with any shenanigans, was an establishment recognized for being a bit more civilized with a less rowdy group of patrons.

Once there, we were told by a couple of the old-timers there had been a fight over one of the soiled doves, and shots had been fired.

"Caleb, look," I called out, pointing to a spot on the floor near the back door. Walking to the red stain, I gingerly knelt to see if it was fresh blood, and sure enough, it was. The men we spoke with told us it was a stranger they'd never seen before who had done the shooting.

Opening the saloon's back door, Caleb and I followed the trail of blood staining the dirt. "I don't like where this is taking us, Nate."

"Neither do I," I replied. "But I'm sure both Emily and Rebecca are fine." I only prayed I was right. The trail of blood led us right to the back porch of the clinic. My gut twisted in knots, and by the looks of Caleb, I knew he wasn't faring any better.

Near the back step were unmistakable splatters of fresh blood. Looking up from the crimson stain, I sighed in relief at seeing Anders already speaking with Rebecca near the open door. Seeing her unharmed, the muscles in my shoulders immediately relaxed. Still breathing heavily, Caleb rushed past me, only stopping to receive nonverbal directions from his sister. I knew he was anxious to find Emily.

YUMA, ARIZONA TERRITORY

Elliot

I WAS PARCHED and craving liquid sustenance the minute I stepped off the stage in Yuma. Watered down as the liquor had been in Fort Worth, I didn't care what they served in this town as long as it numbed the throbbing in my head.

It had been hell traveling from Fort Worth in stagecoaches seated next to stinking bodies and the odor of dried leather and wet horses wafting through the windows. Never before having experienced such repugnance, the stench was too much to endure. I spent much of my time with a handkerchief over my mouth and nose, holding back my gag reflex. But endure it, I did. And Rebecca would pay dearly for putting me through this.

What the West called waystations had been nothing short of dirt hovels serving what I called pig slop for meals. Never would I go through that again. I'd move heaven and earth to find another way to return to Boston and civilization.

After spending the night alone in one of Yuma's questionably finest hotels, I'd been on my way to meet the Pinkerton agent. The less I had to roam around this town, the better. Thankfully, he had done all the leg work and had located Emily in this Godforsaken place.

Opening my pocket watch, I saw that I had two hours to spare, so I detoured to a saloon closest to the hotel. As I entered through the batwing doors, my eyes scanned the darkened room. The mirror on the wall behind the bar was murky at best, eliciting wavy reflections of sweat-stained shirts standing side by side while leaning on a stained wooden bar.

From the ceiling hung two glass chandeliers, the establishment's failed attempt at class, covered with a thick film of cigarette smoke and dust. On the warm plank floor was a thin layer of sawdust used to catch what patrons missed at placing into the spittoons stationed at each end of the bar or the dung clinging to their boots they dragged in from outside.

What was Rebecca thinking about giving up her life of luxury for this hovel of a town? I felt dirty just walking through its doors. It was a seedy place filled with men in all stages of drunkenness and scantily dressed women.

Smiling to myself, I found the expendable whores to be one conciliation to this trip to use for one purpose only, the purpose that now held my interest. I longed for the smooth distilled spirits found in Boston as I made my way to the bar and ordered what this saloon called whiskey. The fiery liquid's taste was a back-woods molasses concoction mixed with what smelled like turpentine. Despite this, I choked it down.

If I wanted to keep my headaches at bay, I would have to settle for the Laudanum because this so-called liquor wouldn't ease the pain. Coughing with as much dignity as I could muster, I spit the remaining bitter solvent into a spittoon conveniently located at the end of the bar. I would certainly never perform such a disgusting act in Boston. However, it seemed natural here, considering the bucket was half full.

But I wouldn't stoop so low as wiping my mouth with the back of my hand as I'd seen so many of these classless men do.

Pulling a white linen handkerchief from my vest pocket, I wiped the remnants from my lips. Turning around, I leaned back on the bar, catching the eye of a Rubenesque scarlet dove who would take care of my immediate needs until meeting with Mr. Reynolds, the Pinkerton agent. The only good thing about this place was the low price I would pay for their desert whores.

Grabbing the strumpet's arm, I pulled her across the floor and through throngs of stuporous drunks. "Hey! Mister, you're hurting me," she yelled, shrugging her shoulders as she tried pulling from my grasp. Holding firm, I wasn't about to let my nymph du prairie get away from me. But a fight broke out between cowhands behind us before we could reach the stairs.

Screams from the other whores could be heard above the men's vulgarities, while the cracking sound of chairs and breaking bottles sent the room into a frenzy. Moving quickly through the smoky haze toward the stairs, I was about to place my boot on the bottom rung when a large, beefy hand painfully gripped my shoulder, spinning me around. Before I had time to think, I twisted, drew my pistol, and fired.

The man must have anticipated his fate and quickly jumped out of range, sending my shot aimlessly flying into the room. Unfazed, I watched a bullet, possibly mine, pierce the shoulder of a black woman standing off to the side of the bar. As she dropped to the floor, I caught her shocked look of disbelief and pain.

Turning away from the chaotic scene, I cared not if the woman belonged to anyone, so I grabbed my whore by her wrist and pulled her up the stairs. After all, I'd paid for her and would exact my money's worth.

Kicking a random door open, I flung her into the empty room, where she landed giggling on the squeaking bed. If she knew I'd been the one to shoot the woman, she didn't dare mention it. She was a smart one, alright. Teasingly, she removed her sheer robe and tattered stockings, leaving little to a man's imagination. I was certain I'd enjoy our little foray into cardinal pleasures.

Once satisfied, I left my sleeping prairie tumbleweed under the rumpled sheets and exited the seedy room. I stood at the hall railing, looking down while tightening my belt, straightening my tie, and ensuring my pistol was tucked safely within my vest pocket.

Gazing below, it was business as usual. I couldn't locate the whore I apparently shot. It was as if nothing had ever happened. Gone were the signs of a recent fight due to the task of an older man busily righting chairs and sweeping up glass.

In a failed attempt, someone had worked hard to scrub the blood from the wall where the woman had slid to the floor. Ignoring those standing at the bar, I strode out to an overcast day, glad to be out of this hole, and headed to my prearranged meeting place at the livery. Another distasteful location.

The smell of horse manure, urine, and wet hay permeated the air to the point of making me gag once again. I knew that taking a deep breath would only worsen the nausea. So I quickly proceeded inside, hoping to get our meeting over as quickly as possible.

"Mr. Ackerman." I heard my name called out from deep within the stable's darkness.

"Who's asking?" I replied, not moving. I kept my hand firmly around my pistol.

"You requested this meeting, Mr. Ackerman. My name is Reynolds. I'm with the Pinkerton Agency."

His voice came from behind a stall, but I still couldn't see him. "Come out where I can see you, Mr. Reynolds!"

"I'd rather not."

"Damn it man! I said come out!" His insubordination infuriated me. I was used to getting my way when I made business demands.

"Either we continue as is, or this conversation is over," he answered.

His voice remained calm. More so than mine. I wanted the information he possessed about my wife. So, blowing out a breath, I gave in. "Fine! Have it your way! What information do you have for me?"

I kept my hand fixed on the pistol in my pocket. My sole purpose for this meeting was to find Rebecca, not be involved in a shootout I knew I would lose.

"I found the woman you're looking for." A long silence followed.

"Well man, tell me where she is. I've already paid your supervisor. Now give me the information, and this meeting can be over." The throbbing in my right temple increased, as did the pressure behind my eyes. One of my headaches was about to undermine my plans, the collective odors of this retched place being its cause. Reaching into my vest pocket, I pulled out the brown bottle filled with the elixir I craved and took a long swig.

"Mrs. Ackerman is staying at Doctor Sweeney's home."

"Where is that?" I demanded. Damn it! Why wouldn't he get to the point and stop playing games with me? I wanted to shoot the man based solely on his dragging out my misery.

"At the north end of town. In a small white casita. You can't miss it. His name is hanging on a shingle above the porch."

"Is she there now?" I waited for his response, but silence ensued. I knew he had left me standing in the darkness, our conversation over. Such an infuriating man! If he were in my employ, I'd fire him.

Turning, I heard a moist squish under my right foot. Lifting my foot, I realized I'd just stepped in a pile of fresh horse dung. Swearing out loud, I cursed the day I married Rebecca.

⤳ 42 ⤴

Rebecca

SITTING IN THE warmth of the kitchen, Emily and I were enjoying each other's company while having our morning coffee and discussing her upcoming wedding to my brother.

"Emily, when did you first realize you were in love with Caleb?"

Pausing, she replied, "I can't say it was the first time I saw him. I had been through what you'd call a harrowing experience. But that's for another discussion," she said, waving her hand in the air. "When I found your brother outside that dilapidated cabin, it was dark, and I couldn't see his facial features. I couldn't tell if he was young, old, handsome, or ugly."

Taking a sip of coffee, she looked at me over the rim of her mug and smiled. She must have seen the questioning look on my face, so she clarified using her hands expressively. "I mean, Caleb had a beard covering most of his face, and he was lying in the dirt."

Then, Emily's expression turned serious as she continued. "But to answer your question, I had just done crude surgery on your brother using his hunting knife to remove a bullet from his abdomen. I feared

189

for his life, and as a doctor, I worried an infection would take hold and put him through the most agonizing death I had no control over."

Grasping my hands, Emily added, "Rebecca, you need to know I tried my best to make your brother as comfortable as possible. At the time, I didn't have the strength to move him, and he was in so much pain I made the difficult decision to leave your brother lying in the dirt."

"That's where we spent our first night together. It broke my heart that I couldn't make him more comfortable, especially if he were going to die. As the night grew colder, I covered us both with a filthy quilt left behind by the cabin's previous occupants."

"Then your brother surprised me. I think it was with his last bit of energy when he squeezed my hand and pulled it over his heart, asking me not to leave him." Tears started forming in the corner of my eyes when Emily relayed to me. "He told me he didn't want to die alone."

I couldn't even begin to imagine what my brother and Emily had gone through. Like me, unshed tears were filling the corners of Emily's eyes as a profound silence hung between us. I placed my hand over hers and urged her to continue. Dabbing her tears with a napkin, she said, "I think that was when I fell in love with your brother."

Finishing her coffee, she added, "It's silly, I know. We had only known each other for less than a few hours. But something in my heart told me this man would mean more to me than life itself, and I would do anything within my power to save him."

"Oh!" was all the response I could get out as tears rolled down my cheeks. Emily quickly changed the subject in an attempt to lighten the mood.

"Rebecca, we only have less than two days before I marry your brother."

"Yes. And I'm so excited for you. That's why we need to finish your veil. But I sense there is something else you want to ask me."

"Yes, there is." Emily hesitated before proceeding, "Do you approve of me marrying your brother?"

Shocked that she felt she needed to ask, I quickly responded, "Of course I am. I've never been happier for Caleb that he has finally found someone to love and care for him. And it's no secret, Emily, that Caleb loves you more than life itself. I can see it in his eyes when he thinks you're not looking at him. He will always be faithful to you." Grasping her hands in mine, I added, "I wish you both only happiness with many years ahead. And, of course, it wouldn't hurt if you soon made me an aunt."

Laughing, we stood to hug each other before returning to the task of finishing the hem on Emily's veil. It was to be a simple wedding in the church where Anders and Abigail Johannson had married less than two weeks before.

Tomorrow morning, the two of us and a few of the townswomen would spend our time decorating the church and setting the tables for the dinner reception.

⚜

Emily

WE HAD JUST been laughing and hugging each other, but since we were alone, I had to ask the burning question that had been in the back of my mind since Rebecca told us about leaving Boston. "Rebecca. Can we talk openly?"

"Of course, but I thought that is what we were doing. What is it you want to talk about?"

Never being one to beat around the bush, I was direct and to the point. "What are you holding back from telling Caleb and I? I know what you told us about Elliot's recent behavior, but I think there's more to your story."

"What makes you think that?" she answered somewhat evasively while focusing on my veil.

"Please don't blame Caleb, but he felt it necessary to tell me about Elliot and how your father arranged your marriage to him." Rolling my eyes, I added, "I can't even imagine my parents doing that to me."

Rebecca's head snapped up, eyes wide open, and a stunned expression on her face. I knew I had probably pushed my limit. If the following silence indicated how Rebecca felt about Caleb disclosing her secret, I feared she would collect her boys and Pearl and leave town on the next stage.

I sat in silence, hands clasped on the table, waiting. Rebecca would have made a great poker player with her silence and granite pose. I couldn't stand it any longer, "Rebecca, you have to appreciate that Caleb told me in strictest confidence so I could help you if the time arose. He didn't tell me to betray your trust."

Sitting firmly in her seat, the veil we had been working on now long forgotten, she finally spoke. "It's hard to admit that I was naive and allowed my father to arrange a marriage for me. My mother was furious, but she was afraid to admit such to my father."

Head held high, she took a deep breath and continued. "Elliot is not the man I married ten years ago. For a time, he was a kind husband. I may have even come to love him back then. But truthfully, I didn't expect much from him in the beginning since it was more of a business arrangement between my father and Elliot. But I took our vows seriously. You have to understand I wanted our marriage to work, at least for the sake of our sons."

I reached for her hands and said, "Rebecca, I'm here to help you however I can. You're my family now, and this family takes care of each other." I watched as Rebecca's rigid body slowly relaxed back into her chair.

"Yes. I feel so lucky to be a part of this new family. But that is not the way it was after our mother died. Our father was not capable of loving." Turning to face me for the first time since I asked the difficult question, she added, "Did Caleb ever tell you we believed our father sent our mother to an early grave?"

I could only nod my response before Rebecca continued.

"She loved Caleb and me both very much and kept us safe from our father. Caleb and I never forgave him for how he treated our mother. When he pushed me into marrying Elliot, I truly felt my life was over. But as the ever-dutiful daughter, I put on a bright exterior and thought I could make the marriage work."

"No matter how much mother pleaded with him, he would never change his mind. Nothing seemed to matter anymore except his money. When Caleb was there, I had him to lean on. But when he left, and I never heard from him again, I lost all sense of purpose and hope. I struggled through my days the same as the rhythm of a broken clock."

"Then, once Porter and Daniel came along, my life had new meaning. I was a mother, and they became my whole world. I would do anything to protect them. That's why I decided I could no longer tolerate Elliot's deadly tirades the night before I left Boston."

Avoiding my eyes, she added, "That night was his first to be physically abusive. So, come morning, I took what little I had saved up, and with the help of the household staff, who were more family to me, I left and not once have regretted my decision."

"Well. I'm glad you're here now." Letting go of a breath I didn't realize I'd been holding, I added, "You made a brave choice to leave your husband, and I'm sure you saved yourself and your boys from a great deal of pain. Not many women would do what you did."

Squeezing my hands firmly, Rebecca became tearful once again. "Emily, I almost died that night. He would have eventually killed me and possibly the boys if I hadn't left. He's a sick man, and I hope to never set eyes on him again."

I patted the top of her hands, hoping I wasn't speaking too frankly, but then again, I'd already said quite enough. "Caleb will protect you to the ends of the earth and do all in his power to get you a divorce. It shouldn't be hard with the abuse he's put you all through. And I'm sure that Pearl will be a reliable witness."

Watching, Rebecca shook her head and whispered, "Emily, you don't understand what that man is capable of. I fear he'll find us, and I couldn't stand the thought of someone I care about being hurt or possibly killed because of me."

"Now, Rebecca, don't think like that. You're here now and can stay as long as you need. We'll do whatever we can to protect you and the boys.

Rebecca

WORKING IN SILENCE for the next hour, a loud pounding at the back door had us both jumping in our seats. Emily and I looked at each other. Was she reading my mind thinking it was Elliot? The knocks became more persistent, even sounding desperate.

Please, God, don't let it be Elliot!

Emily motioned me to stand away from the door's view as she headed in its direction. I was just as stubborn as she, if not more so, and of course, I wouldn't let her answer the door alone. Giving me that 'I told you look,' she held me back with an outstretched arm behind her. Her act of protectiveness overwhelmed me with gratitude, considering what we had just been discussing.

Carefully peering through the break in the door's curtain, we stared at a frightfully thin colored woman leaning against the porch frame, clutching her left arm to her chest with blood seeping through her fingers. Beside her stood a young child crying and pulling on her tattered brown dress.

Emily quickly opened the door and asked, "Rebecca, help me get her inside." Bending in obvious pain, the woman whispered, "I cans't go in there. It's not right!"

"Nonsense," I replied. "Emily is a doctor, and she can help you. We both will." I had to quell my anger when I noticed the long strikes of raised scarring along the right side of her neck. It was obvious she, too, had been beaten sometime in her past.

"I shouldna comz here," the woman painfully added, trying to stand up straight.

"You came to the right place," I said with compassion.

Emily added, "Mrs. Ackerman and I will take care of you and your son."

Looking down at her wide brown eyes filled with fright, I could only imagine how desperate she had been to risk coming to the clinic. The Arizona Territory was not a slave state, so, whether right or wrong, I could only assume she had been brought here by her enslaver sometime after the Civil War.

Emily and I worked together to help the woman walk. I held her right arm while Emily held her up around her waist. "Can you walk?" Emily asked.

"I think's I can," she replied through a clenched jaw. Beads of sweat glistened on her forehead and ran down the sides of her face. Her whimpering broke my heart with each step she took, showing strength to remain upright and make it to the exam room despite her injury.

The small boy continued to desperately hold on to the thin fabric of his mother's dirt-brown dress. I was afraid it would tear if he pulled too hard. But neither Emily nor I could take our hold off the woman for fear she would crumple to the floor. Walking slowly down the hall, the boy sniffed several times and followed behind as his tiny feet shuffled, trying to keep up.

We paused at the entry to the surgical suite to catch our breath. Soon, we had our patient lying on the stretcher where Emily could begin a more thorough exam. The young woman shook from head to toe, and what few teeth she had fiercely chattered.

Emily whispered in my ear, "Rebecca, she's lost a lot of blood, and I'm afraid she is going into shock. I need to stop the bleeding quickly."

"Colt. I'z so cold't."

With her body shaking and faint voice, I had to lean in close to hear what she was saying. I made out that she was telling us she was cold. Of course, she was. With the thin fabric of her dress, blood loss, and the cool temperature outside, she was lucky to be alive.

When I knew Emily had things under control, I retrieved the warm blanket from in front of the kitchen stove. "Here now, this should take the chill off," I said, covering her frail form.

In a soft, reassuring voice, Emily told her, "I'm going to look at your shoulder. I will need to cut the fabric away, but we will find you another dress to wear."

"I cans't take no charity! It's not right!"

Fear shone in the woman's dark eyes when she looked up between Emily and me. I touched her shoulder reassuringly and said, "It's alright. What's more important right now is getting you feeling better. We can worry about the dress later."

Before surgery, Emily and I had tried coaxing the small boy from under the table. Each time we did, he only scooted farther away from us. So, we thought it best to let him be since he was causing no harm and returned our focus to his mother.

While Emily cut away the thin fabric, performed her exam, and cleansed the wound, I prepared the instruments for surgery. I'd learned so much in the short time I'd been assisting in the clinic, and working here beside the doctors allowed me to learn a great deal. It gave my life a new purpose, as did being a mother. "Everything is ready for you, Doctor."

While we were all in the clinic, I addressed Emily and her grandfather as 'Doctor' to provide the air of professionalism they were both due. Pulling the instrument table up next to Emily's side, I stepped to the head of the surgical bed, ready to administer the ether as instructed. Holding the mask up for our patient to see, I spoke to her in a calm tone. "I'm going to place this over your nose and mouth. It

will have a sweet smell that will help you sleep and feel no pain while
Dr. Sweeney takes care of your shoulder."

With the mesh cone in place, I counted the drops of the overwhelming pungent liquid out loud. "One. Two. Three. Four." I watched
carefully as the drops slowly left the glass chamber, becoming absorbed
into the cotton fabric encased in the mesh. The woman's eyes, wide
with fright, began to flutter and, within seconds, peacefully closed.
"She's asleep, Doctor."

Emily worked with a refined skill borne of years of practice. First,
she enlarged the wound's entry with a scalpel. No longer needing to
hold the ether mask, I assisted Emily by holding small retractors and
gently applying tension at the wound's edge to make visibility easier.

Blood oozed from the site at a constant rate, and I had difficulty
keeping the opening dry with gauze as Emily deftly tied off the tiny
vessels with a suture to control the bleeding. Using long curved forceps, Emily carefully probed the wound. Finally locating the cartridge,
she removed it with the bullet extractor and dropped it with a clang
into the metal kidney-shaped basin.

Satisfied there was no further bleeding, she closed the site with
a suture and allowed me to apply a dressing. The small boy had sat
quietly and unmoving under the table the entire time.

Surgery complete, Emily held up the bullet between the teeth of
the forceps. Shaking our heads in unison, we wondered out loud
who would want to harm this young woman and potentially leave
a boy motherless.

While the woman remained asleep from the lasting effects of the
ether, it allowed me the opportunity to retrieve two more blankets—
one for our patient, the other for the small boy.

I was in the corner of the surgical suite cleaning the instruments
when Emily brought in a bowl of leftover stew. Sitting on the floor
under the table, she began feeding our little waif.

I watched as Emily spoke softly to the boy, who only stared back
with dark brown eyes rimmed with fear. Smiling, I couldn't help but
think Emily would make a wonderful mother someday.

Our waif tugged at my heartstrings, making me think of Porter and Daniel and how fortunate they were despite their father. Even with our gentle coaxing, the boy still wouldn't come out from under the table. I couldn't blame him. He had probably witnessed atrocities no child his age should ever see in his short life.

I didn't think he would allow me to pick him up, so I folded a large quilt and placed it on the floor under the stretcher. With hand motions, Emily indicated it was for him to sleep on. There was no acknowledgment of understanding, but I hoped he would sense our meaning at some point and crawl under the blanket's warmth.

⚴ 44 ⚵

Rebecca

WHILE I WAS standing at the sink pumping water, Doc Mathew rushed through the back door, letting it hit the wall with a thud. Startled, I dropped the kettle into the sink and splashed water onto the floor.

"What's going on here?" he blurted out. "Where did all tat blood on ta porch come from? Are ye all right, girlie? Where's me granddaughter?"

I couldn't get a word in, so I let him finish with his rapid succession of questions before I tried to answer. Finally falling silent, the Doc stood there looking at me as if I had two heads.

"Well, girlie, are ye going to answer me?" he yelled.

"I was trying to, but you wouldn't let me get a word in. Now that you've finished asking all your questions, I can." Turning back to the sink, I began refilling the kettle.

"Piff," he blew out between pursed lips. "Will ya tell me already?"

Raising my hand, I answered, "Emily is fine." Tipping my head to the side, indicating down the hall, I added, "She's in the back room with our patient. We were in the middle of wedding preparations when there was a knock at the door. We found our patient leaning against the door frame, bleeding from a gunshot wound to her left shoulder, and a small boy clinging to her.?"

"Oh. Who ist the woman?" he asked, sounding a bit apologetic. "Do I know her? Is she alright? I mean our patient," he added, rubbing the back of his neck. "Does Emily need my help?"

I knew I was being a bit sarcastic, but I couldn't help it when I began answering his many questions. "First, our patient didn't give us her name. Of course, we didn't ask in all the commotion since we were in a hurry to get her back to the surgical suite and stop her bleeding. And yes, thankfully, she seems to be doing OK. Secondly, no, Emily doesn't need your help at this time. Our patient is still too sleepy for us to move her to the recovery room. Maybe this is something you can help us with later?" Lightening the conversation, I asked, "I'm going to make lunch. Are you hungry?"

"Thank ye. Yes, I'm famished. But first, I need a cup of tat strong coffee ye be brewing."

"I thought you would be a tea drinker coming from Ireland."

"I was. But once I arrived here in te West, it was coffee or whiskey, and I wouldn't take to te bottle. Although, I'm not against taking a nip now and then."

"Ah ha!" I said, knowing full well I'd seen him and Caleb take that 'nip' he'd just described. "Well, as soon as the coffee is done, I'll bring you a cup. You go ahead down to Emily and see how she's doing. She'll fill you in on all the details."

Without responding, he headed down the hall to the surgical suite. In the meantime, I gathered meat from last evening's dinner from the cold storage and bread and butter from the larder. It would be a simple meal I'd serve until Pearl came over later in the day to assist with dinner preparations.

Once alone, I started preparing our midday meal when there was another knock on the door. I concluded that this clinic could be busy at all times of day and night. "Come in," I called out over my shoulder.

Dang! I need to be more careful. It could be Elliot. I held my breath as the back door opened slowly. After hearing its creaking hinges, I remembered I'd forgotten to tell Caleb that the door needed oiling. I'll have to ask the Doc where the oil can is and do it myself. Caleb was too busy now with his law practice to help with simple household repairs.

Wiping my hands on my apron, I turned to see Anders Johannson standing in the doorway. Relief swept over me, and I smiled at seeing the sheriff. "Good morning, Sheriff. What can I do for you?

Taking off his hat, he addressed me in his thick Swedish accent, "Ma'am. I understand ya have someone here who's been shot. How ist she doing? Ist she up ta talking vit me?"

"I'm not sure. I'll go ask Dr. Emily." Curious, I paused before heading to the surgical suite and asked, "Sheriff, who told you we had a patient here?"

"One of ta boys in the saloon, let me know." Looking toward the stove, he asked, "Ist tat coffee I smell?"

"Yes, it is," I replied, pointing to the pot. "Please help yourself. Clean mugs are in the cupboard to the right of the sink. Why don't you have a seat in the parlor, and I'll be back in a minute."

Heading down the hall, I met Dr. Sweeney coming out of the surgical suite with the boy at his side, clutching his hand. "Goodness. How did you manage this?" I asked, indicating the boy with a nod.

Patting the boy on his shoulder, the Doc answered, "Wit te mention of more food, including cookies, he seemed eager ta follow me,"

"Wonderful. Maybe after dinner, we can get him bathed and find him some new clothes. I'm sure Daniel's will fit with some minor alterations. I've made sandwiches. They're on the counter waiting, and fresh milk is in the cold storage."

"Did I hear a knock on the door?" Doc asked, pointing down the hall.

"Yes. The sheriff is here. I asked him to wait in the parlor. He wants to ask our patient questions if she's up to it."

"She's still sleeping at te moment. Emily will come out soon and speak with Anders."

We returned to the kitchen to find the sheriff standing at the open door with a mug of steaming coffee in his hand.

"Sheriff, do you mind closing the door, please? I don't want to let out all the warmth from the stove."

"Rebecca tells me you want ta speak with our patient," Doc asked. "She's sleeping at te moment. Emily should be out shortly and can talk wit you. Or, if you wouldn't mind, I can send word over te your office when te patient awakens."

"Don't bother Doc Emily now. I can speak vit her later. I have men in te saloon I can talk vit before I speak vit your patient. Tanks again, Doc," he answered, holding the mug up. "Tanks for te coffee, Mrs. Ackerman."

"You're welcome, sheriff." Smiling, I asked, "Would you care to stay for dinner?"

"Thank ya, but no. I better be getting back to ta saloon and start asking questions." Smiling, he added, "And I'm sure my Abigail vill be waiting dinner for me, and I vouldn't vant to disappoint her."

"Maybe another time then when Abigail and Holly can come with you. Oh, and Sheriff, please call me Rebecca. Mrs. Ackerman is too formal."

"I don't tink tats proper."

Smiling, I replied, "It's fine, sheriff." As he turned toward the door, I stopped him with a question, whispering so the boy didn't hear me. "Sheriff, did you find out what happened to our patient?"

Turning away from the boy, he replied in a calm voice, "From vhat I understand, Nathaniel vas in Caleb's office when Joey came running in saying there vas trouble in the Prickly Pear Saloon, and shots had been fired. Vhat I need to know is vhere your patient vas at the time of ta shooting. A stray bullet could have hit her, or maybe it vas intentional. Sorry, Ma'am, but her being colored and all."

Holding my hand up, I stopped him from further comments. "I understand. It sickens me. Her skin color shouldn't matter. The war is long over, and she's a free woman here in Arizona. It's just awful. She didn't deserve this," I added, shaking my head. "Thank you, sheriff. She will be well cared for here. I'm just grateful Joey and the young boy wasn't hurt."

"I am, too, Ma'am. I'm glad tat your patient ist going to survive. I'll find out who did tis," he said, nodding. It was getting a bit crowded in the tiny kitchen when Caleb came through the door, breathing heavily with Joey and Nathaniel trailing close on his heels. I pointed down the hall, indicating where Emily was, and without a word, Caleb moved past the sheriff and me.

Joey, always the bright-eyed and ready-to-please lad, looked slightly taken back upon seeing the colored boy standing next to Doc Sweeney when I asked, "Joey, this is our guest. His mother is with Doctor Emily. Can you kindly show him where to wash up before dinner?"

"Yes, Ma'am," Joey eagerly nodded while reaching out to take his hand. "Come on," he said to the boy. "I'll show you where we can wash up."

Before moving, the boy looked up at Doc Sweeney as if questioning his safety. "It's OK, son. You go ahead wit Joey, and when you've washed up, we'll have someting ta eat."

Almost forgetting that Nathaniel had been standing in the open door all this time, I remained in the middle of the kitchen. Turning to face him, neither of us spoke. How childish we were as we stood there, not speaking, only staring at each other. He hadn't been to town in weeks since he went home to recover from his injuries.

Doc Sweeney must have recognized the tension between Nathaniel and me when he interrupted the silence, pointed over his shoulder, and said, "I'll just be going back ta check on Emily and our patient."

"Fine, Doc," I responded, not looking his way.

Why now? What was Nathaniel here for? I hated to admit it, but I was happy to see him. In his absence, I'd thought of him daily and wondered what had kept him away. Yet, I couldn't help but wonder if he had a special woman at his ranch who cared for him in more ways than one.

Was he hiding something? It did no good for me to make assumptions that would only confuse me. My love for him had grown with each passing day, and I knew these thoughts were shameful being a married woman. But I wouldn't deny what I was feeling.

Still not speaking, we continued to stand and stare. He had to be here for some other reason than seeing me. We were adults, for heaven's sake. Why were we both at a loss for words? Should I tell him how I felt? No, now wasn't the time to reveal that I thought of no one else but him.

45

Nathaniel

I DON'T KNOW how she did it, but Rebecca was more beautiful each time I saw her. I recalled the exact moment we met on the train. I'd been a besotted fool the minute I'd glimpsed her over the top of my newspaper.

Slowly inhaling, I imagined her lily perfume filling my senses and turning my world upside down. The way those wayward wisps of raven hair had tumbled freely from under her hat had made me want to run the shiny, unbound tendrils through my fingers.

Shaking off my reminiscing, I knew I couldn't take much more of not knowing if I had an inkling of a chance with her before my heart would shatter to pieces. It was no use denying my love.

I just stood there staring at her like a love-struck fool. Why couldn't I tell Rebecca how I felt? But before I could let my heart become more involved than it already was, it was imperative to know if I had the slightest chance at capturing her heart. I'd hoped her brother Caleb could tell me if I did. But our conversation earlier today had been cut short when Joey came rushing into his office with news of a shooting at the Prickly Pear.

Now, what was I going to do? Should I take Caleb aside when he comes back into the kitchen? If I did, would Rebecca be suspicious? Of course, I could tell her we were only going to talk business. That's it! I'll do it!

Standing here, I felt this invisible rope pulling Rebecca and me together, where I could feel her soft curves leaning into my firm body and her feather-like touch on my face. Then, without a moment's notice, the rope snapped, and we fell fathoms apart. Was this a premonition?

Swearing silently, maybe I should just give up and go back to being a lonely rancher in the middle of the desert. As hard as it would be, I would somehow swallow my pride and step aside.

Nathaniel! You've got cold feet. Stop you're moaning over this woman and tell her how you feel. You'll never know her feelings until you declare yours.

"Mom, I don't think I should," I whispered.

What in heaven's name is happening? I hadn't heard from my mother since the day she took me away from Boston. This whole love thing was making me delusional.

Son, you're not delusional. You're in love.

Mom was right. I had to stop second-guessing myself. I wanted Rebecca in my life forever. She'd unknowingly captured my heart in one fleeting beat. Even though she was still a married woman and was only here for a short visit without her husband, I had to tell her how I felt. If her feelings were not the same for me, I would walk away. No more questions asked.

But, I would always have this feeling there was more to Mrs. Ackerman than she let on. I couldn't put my finger on it, but something deeply troubled her. On the train, I remembered her steel-blue eyes darting about the rail car and out the window as if she knew she was being followed.

If she and her boys were in trouble and needed protection, I wanted to be the one to provide it.

Rebecca and I had been so caught up in a staring game that we both forgot the sheriff was still standing in the kitchen when he interrupted, "Tank you for the coffee, Mrs. Ackerman. Let me know vhen your patient ist ready ta talk."

"Oh! I will, sheriff," Rebecca replied.

I moved to the side to let the sheriff pass as Joey tugged on the arm of my coat, helping me find my voice. Thankfully, Rebecca spoke first. She must have known how nervous I'd been.

"Good afternoon, Mr. Burns."

I stuttered, "Good afternoon, Mrs. Ackerman. I'm glad to see you are well."

"I'm fine, thank you. How are you feeling?" she asked, pointing to my leg.

Small talk was all I could handle at this point. It had been too long since I was in her presence. Unconsciously rubbing my thigh, I answered, "My leg is healing nicely. Just some aching now and then if I sit in the saddle too long."

"I'm glad to hear that. I mean that you're feeling better. You gave us all quite a scare, you know."

Rebecca stood in the middle of the kitchen, nervously folding and unfolding the towel in her hands when she said, "Please, have a seat. Would you care for some coffee," she asked, pointing to the pot on the stove.

"Thank you. I sure could use a cup." I nodded, took off my hat, and hung it on an empty peg near the back door. Tensely, I wiped my sweaty palms down the side of my pant legs.

She'd seen my nervous gesture and added, "There's fresh water in the basin there if you wish to freshen up."

Out of the corner of my eye, I could see Joey and a young black boy looking back and forth between us with bewildered looks. I was about to say something when we were interrupted by the elder Doc Sweeney coming back into the kitchen.

"I need ta go check on te Thompson's new babe. I won't be gone long. Will ye please let Emily know where I've gone?"

"Yes. Of course I will, Doctor," Rebecca replied, nodding. "I'll keep your dinner warm on the back of the stove in case you come in late."

"Thank ye kindly," Doc answered.

Once he left, I quickly spoke in case we were interrupted again. "Mrs. Ackerman." Her radiant smile and bewitching eyes pierced my heart. Before she could react, I proceeded, "Mrs. Ackerman, is there someplace private where we can talk? Uninterrupted."

Not looking up, she answered, in a whisper I could barely hear, "Yes." She seemed to hesitate before pointing in the direction of the parlor. Stepping away from the stove, she proceeded down the hall without saying more.

Acting as a dutiful child, I followed, leaving Joey and the young boy in the kitchen staring after us. I remained standing until Rebecca took her position on the settee. Wanting to keep some distance between us, I then took the chair closest to the fireplace. What was I thinking? I was already too warm as I ran my fingers around the inside of my collar. I certainly didn't need the radiating heat from its glowing embers.

Gathering my nerve, I sat in silence for a few heartbeats when I finally worked up the nerve to speak. My voice croaked, "Mrs. Ackerman, I'm so glad we have this opportunity to be alone." I feigned a cough and cleared my throat. What had I just implied? Hurriedly backtracking, I swiftly added, "What I mean is that we have time to speak without being interrupted."

"I understand, Mr. Burns," Rebecca replied, sitting primly in her seat. Her lips pulled up to one side, and I wondered if she was smiling.

Oh, how I loved this woman. Once my tongue felt free of its nervous constraints, there was no stopping me. "Mrs. Ackerman, I know we've only spoken once before on the train, but I will always remember our first meeting fondly." Pausing, I waited for her to respond and break the awkwardness of the conversation.

"Mr. Burns, that is kind of you to say. I, too, enjoyed our encounter on the train, and again, I can't thank you enough for your kindness in helping Pearl and me with my boys. They have spoken of nothing else since we arrived here. You've endeared yourself to them."

Bowing my head at her compliment, I said, "Porter and Daniel are special boys, and I enjoyed what little time we had together. With your permission, and of course, their father's, I hope to spend more time with them while you visit your brother."

Out of nervousness, I rambled on. "They're welcome at the ranch anytime. And I could teach them to ride. They would have so much space to run wild in." I quickly added when I saw the concerned look on her face, "Of course, they would be supervised by me or one of my ranch hands. And Enedina would love to have two young ones around the house."

⤶⤷

Nate, slow down. You ramble when you're nervous.

"I know, Mom. But I don't want her to leave Yuma."

My darling son. You have to remember that Rebecca is a married woman.

How can I forget?

⤶⤷

"I believe they would enjoy that." I watched as she turned her gaze toward the fire before adding matter-of-factly, "Their father isn't here, and you have to understand that I can't allow them to become too attached since we will be leaving soon."

I had my answer, and it was what I feared. Rebecca was leaving.

"I understand, Mrs. Ackerman."

The chasm in my heart opened wider at her admission to leaving. I would never be able to make her part of my life. I knew it. She would be returning home now that her brother had recovered.

Biting the corner of my lip, I had to ask. "Why are you leaving so soon? Won't you be staying for the wedding?"

"Yes. Of course, we'll stay for the wedding, and then we plan on taking the train to California. Looking down, she stammered before adding, "It's time we moved on."

I knew by the tone of her voice she was afraid of something. Once Caleb's wedding to Emily ended, she would be gone and out of my life forever. Staring into the fire, I saw her mind warring about what she wanted to really tell me.

"Yes, we can't stay here forever. I can't impose on Emily and Doctor Sweeney any longer. He has been so kind to let us stay in the casita behind the clinic. Pearl and the boys have enjoyed being here, as have I, and it will be hard to leave."

"Then stay." I shocked myself, having no idea what possessed me to ask.

46

Nathaniel

"Mr. Burns, we hardly know each other. One chance encounter does not make us. Well, it's difficult to explain, and I don't want to create something we both know can never be."

I leaned forward, placing my elbows on my knees, looked down at the fraying carpet, and replied, "How can you be so sure." Shaking my head from side to side, I added, "I'm sorry. I don't mean to be forward, but I'm not good at these things."

Dear God, please help me. How do I tell Rebecca I've fallen in love with her even after one chance encounter on the train? My mind can't rationally explain it, but my heart tells me it's possible. All I know is life is too short not to confess what my heart is feeling. I have to make her understand even if there is a chance of losing her.

Her words brought me out of a deep, confused state when she said, "Not good at what, Mr. Burns?"

I forgot my question. So, speaking directly from my heart, I stared at the face I'd come to love. "I'm not good at telling someone I care deeply for them."

In the silence that ensued, I heard the sharp intake of her breath. "Mr. Burns, this is highly improper. I'm a married woman."

"But are you happy?" Oh boy, I'm messing this up. Looking back into the flames, I asked, "If you're happy, why are you here alone, without your husband?"

I'd done it. As my Nana would say, I'd opened a can of worms. I didn't believe Rebecca. Yes, she was married. But happily, I didn't believe it one bit. I could see it in her eyes now and when we were on the train. She was afraid of something.

"Mr. Burns, I think you've said quite enough. I need to go check on Emily."

"Please don't let my forwardness ruin our friendship. I've been on the ranch too long and may have forgotten proper etiquette."

If I talked like I was back on the force in Boston, she would surely think I was vulgar. Rebecca started to rise from the settee when I quickly reached out. I had to keep her from leaving before I finished explaining myself. "Mrs. Ackerman, please don't leave."

Standing rigid, I could see the wheels in her head turning. Should I go, or should I sit and continue to listen? Grateful, she sat. Folding her hands in her lap, she waited for me to continue. She was more lovely than I remembered.

In the room's dull lamplight, the heat from the fire had her cheeks blushing, making her skin glow luminescent. All I wanted to do was hold her in my arms and smell the sweet scent of lilies. "I'm sorry if I offended you. That was not my intention. I just wanted to speak with you." *And hold you in my arms.*

Rebecca remained seated but on the edge of the settee as if ready to bolt at my next question. The muscles in my chest tightened as I stood beside the mantel. I didn't think I could proceed, but I had to. I couldn't leave tonight without telling her how I felt. "Mrs. Ackerman, may I call you Rebecca?"

"Mr. Burns, I'm not sure that is a good idea."

"I understand." One hurtle stumbled over. Now on to the next. "Mrs. Ackerman, I have to know, are you happy in your marriage?"

Standing abruptly, she boldly responded, "Mr. Burns, that's quite enough with your questions. You have no right to ask me that?

Why am I making such a mess of this? She's going to hate me by the time I'm done. "I'm sorry, Rebecca. But it's important I know."

Now I've done it. I just called her by her first name when she asked me not to. She said it wasn't a good idea, but it just slipped out. I next expected to feel the burn as she slapped my face. But she didn't, so I took that as a good sign.

Standing there, we stared at each other for the longest time, neither daring to speak. Under her spell, I was praying Rebecca would say something, anything.

Enough with this silence. "Rebecca."

"Mr. Burns, I told you not to use my first name." She turned to leave. I had to stop her. The palms of my hands were sweaty, and my chest felt as if a tight band was squeezing the air from my lungs. I didn't know if I could finish when a burst of resolve pushed me ahead. "Wait, Rebecca," I grasped her wrist to keep her from leaving. "Let me finish, and then, if you want, you can tell me you never want to see me again."

Clearing my throat, I started, "Rebecca, the moment I saw you on the train, I recognized that my heart was telling me I had to have you in my life. It sounds ridiculous, I know, but approaching you that day was the most difficult thing I'd ever done. I've never been that bold with any woman before. But I couldn't let you leave the train without speaking to you."

Surprised, Rebecca didn't run from the room, so I continued. "When I saw you standing on the porch Christmas Eve next to Caleb and Doc, I was speechless for the first time in my life, yet ecstatic with the luck of seeing you again." Bowing my head, I added, "But when your brother introduced you as Mrs. Ackerman, my world crumbled. I couldn't speak. So, I didn't. I just rode off, letting you go while holding the memories of our chance encounter close to my heart."

Changing the conversation to a more serious tone, "Rebecca, you need to know that when I was lying in the mine thinking I was going to die, you were all I thought about, and the missed opportunity I'd have at making you a part of my life."

I pasted on a smile and cautiously continued, "Rebecca, you have to know that prayer and thinking of you while I lay there kept me alive."

Rebecca walked around the parlor's center table. Once again, I thought she was about to leave the room without saying a word, but I was wrong. Instead, she came to stand directly in front of me. Close, so close. The heat radiating from her body sent my senses scrambling for clarity. I tried concentrating on anything but the vision before me.

Could I be so lucky? Had Rebecca accepted my presence and questioning? Looking up at me, she smiled and then asked, "Mr. Burns. May I call you Nathaniel? Oh, is that a sly grin I see gracing that charming face of yours?"

"Now you're just making fun of me, Mrs. Ackerman. Please don't. I don't think I could handle that." It was my turn to want to leave.

"No, Nathaniel, I wouldn't dream of doing such a thing. But you need to understand I am married, and it's best we end our friendship on a neutral note for now. We have much to discuss, but here and now isn't the right time or place."

What suddenly changed her mind? But I wasn't sure this would end well for either of us. But I can't stop now. She was finally willing to talk with me. "All right. Mrs. Ackerman, may I be so bold to ask you to join me for dinner tomorrow night, followed by a stroll around the square when we can speak freely?"

Shaking her head, she replied, "I know I shouldn't. I don't want the townspeople to think poorly of your reputation seeing you with a married woman. You know how people gossip. But it would be nice," she added, lowering her eyes where I could see her dark lashes flutter the tops of her pale cheeks.

"You let me worry about what the townspeople think of me," I replied. "I know it was bold of me to ask, and I'm the one who should be worrying about your reputation. But does that mean you will join me?"

"Yes, I will join you for dinner, Nathaniel."

I left the clinic with hope in my heart for the first time in. I couldn't remember when. I smiled. She'd called me Nathaniel. I knew I was playing with fire and might wind up in hell, put there by her brother or absent husband. Right now, it all seemed worth it.

47

Rebecca

GOOD HEAVENS, WHAT have I done? I'd become infatuated with a stranger I'd only known for a few short weeks. Standing alone in the clinic's parlor after Mr. Burns had excused himself, I felt a burst of excitement work its way into my heart, along with a bit of angst.

I didn't understand why it was socially acceptable for Elliot, as a married man, to dally with his mistresses while the whole town of Boston knew. Yet, I couldn't have a friendly meal in a public place with a male acquaintance.

Recently, I've come to understand that I don't think I ever had any true romantic sensitivities for Elliot. I'd been playing the part of society's expectation of a dutiful wife, which had cost my sons and me dearly. I had been going through the motions, thinking I could make the marriage work. But who was I kidding? I longed to be treated as a lady and no longer cared what people would think. I was going to enjoy myself for the first time in years.

Rebecca dear. What are you going to do?

"Mother, I'm so glad you're here. I need to speak with you. I've just done something crazy, but I don't care. If Father or Elliot were

216

here, they'd have me put away in an asylum for the remainder of my days. Either that or Elliot would kill me and save himself the trouble."

Well, neither of them is here, so you don't need to worry about that now.

"Accepting Nathaniel's dinner invitation may seem reckless, but it also feels wonderful and freeing. Is that wrong?"

Remember, you are still a married woman. But I also understand that you'll never return to Elliot or Boston. I want you to be happy, and Mr. Burns seems like such a nice man. But you have to be careful. I don't trust that husband of yours.

"Are you angry with me?"

Of course not. Your happiness and that of my grandsons is more important. So, I say enjoy yourself. For what you've been through, you deserve some happiness.

"Mother, can you tell me if Elliot is coming here?"

My dear, I cannot see his actions since he is not of our blood. Although he's your husband, I never trusted him and thought your father was wrong for making you marry him. But I was just his wife, and he never listened to what I thought.

Leaving the warmth of the parlor, I returned to the kitchen when Emily asked, "Rebecca, are you all right? Your face is flushed. Did something happen between you and Nate?"

Patting her hand, I answered, "No, Emily, I'm fine." Smiling, I left my answer at that.

∽◦≫◦∾

Nathaniel

I nervously fidgeted with my tie, adjusting it repeatedly as I stood at the front door of the white-washed casita. The flowers I held in my sweaty hands would be crushed beyond recognition if Rebecca didn't open the door soon.

Click. Thank heavens! I stood there with my mouth gaping like a fish out of water, gasping for its last breath. I'm sure I looked ridiculous as all the air rushed out from my lungs in a whoosh. Despite the night air holding a chill, I suddenly felt hot as I stared at the vision in the doorway. The lamplight shining from behind cast Rebecca in a celestial glow. She was so beautiful. I tried to speak, but no words came out.

Blushing, thankfully, Rebecca broke the silence, "Mr. Burns, how nice to see you again."

Without speaking, I extended the flowers, and our hands touched, sending a shock wave of emotions straight to my heart. Rebecca would be mine if only for a few short hours.

Finding my voice was the least of my concerns. Toeing the dirt on the doorstep and nodding my head, I said, "You may want to have Mrs. O'Callaghan put these in a vase."

"Yes, of course. Please wait here. I'll be just a minute."

Turning away, I watched her gown sway from side to side, accentuating her full, round hips as she glided across the floor. I couldn't hear what she said to Pearl, but I took the opportunity of Rebecca's absence to quiet my nerves. I couldn't wait to get her alone, if only in the restaurant, so that we could talk freely. I hoped she didn't care what people would say seeing us together.

Nathaniel

MY DINNER WITH Rebecca had gone better than I could have hoped for. We'd enjoyed a simple meal with pleasant conversation, followed by a short stroll through town. I'm sure it was nothing as fancy as the lavish affairs she attended in Boston, but she didn't seem to mind.

Not wanting the night to end, I nervously asked, "Do you enjoy being in Yuma with your brother and Emily?"

Looking up at me, she answered, "It's taking some getting used to the desert, but I find it more pleasant than Boston's cold and snowy winters. It is quite a change, but I think it suits us. And everyone here has been so nice. Even Pearl is enjoying herself. Truthfully, I think she's sweet on Doc Sweeney. They seem to have a lot in common regarding Ireland."

"That's wonderful," I said, staring into her eyes, lost in those deep blue pools. I had to keep her in Yuma.

"I'm just so thankful that Caleb is doing so well and he's going to settle down."

"Yes, he and Emily seem so happy together. I only wish them well. What about Porter and Daniel? Are they settling in?"

"Oh yes. They're doing fine. They think it's one big adventure. But I do worry about how they will take having to leave again."

There was something she wasn't telling me. Why did she have to leave? I needed to find out. But I wouldn't push her. It was too early in our relationship if you could call it a relationship. She probably thought of what we shared as a passing friendship. One she would soon forget once she returned to Boston.

We continued up and down the boardwalk. I didn't want to take her home just yet. I enjoyed having Rebecca close to my side. As we continued, her boldness surprised me when she placed her delicate hand through my arm and took that moment to smile at me. It was my undoing.

In return, I took a chance and settled my hand over hers, gently squeezing it to keep it in place. I was grateful she didn't pull away. Her every breath and the gentle sway of her body next to mine seemed so natural that I didn't want the night to end, so I kept our conversation going.

"How is the lady from the saloon doing? Has her son started speaking yet?"

"Oh, Miss Baptiste is doing much better. Emily offered Clarice a job helping out in the clinic. She will start as I did by washing the instruments, keeping the clinic rooms tidy, and keeping supplies in order. Emily is hoping at some point, she will be able to lend a hand in the surgeries. She's a bright woman and a hard worker."

Turning to me, we stopped walking when she added, "Oh, and Doc Sweeney offered her and her son to stay in one of the rooms above the clinic until other accommodations could be found. None of us want her to go back to that saloon. That's no place for her or her son."

With a more serious look, she added, "Unfortunately, Gabriel has not spoken a word yet. It's not that we don't think he can't speak. It's just that I'm sure he's still frightened over witnessing what happened to his mother."

"That's understandable," I responded. "I can't imagine the horrors he's witnessed in his short young life. Give him time."

❦

Heaven help me, but I hadn't felt guilty about escorting a married woman to dinner. If our feelings for each other grew, as I hoped they would, I would eventually have to tell her about myself. Hiding my previous life from a century ago from so many people, how would I begin to explain it to her? And when I did, would she think me crazy?

I believe Rebecca enjoyed our time together tonight just as much as I had. I was grateful she had been honest with me about being married, but it didn't diminish how I felt about her. Still, I couldn't help but wonder where her husband was and what made her come to Yuma without him. As of now, I didn't think it was my place to ask. I would need to be patient. In time, I hoped she would be comfortable enough to fill me in.

Our evening concluded, and I escorted her to her home behind the clinic. Gently turning her to face me, I said, "Rebecca, thank you for the wonderful evening. I hope you will allow me to escort you to dinner again sometime?" Holding my breath in anticipation of her answer, I linked our hands together. I didn't want to let her go.

"I would like that, Nathaniel."

Standing in the darkness, she surprised me by placing the softest of kisses on my cheek before turning and slipping quietly inside. As the door closed between us, I placed my hand on my cheek where her soft kiss lingered, hoping to keep the feeling from vanishing into the cool night air.

Lightheaded, I stood unmoving like a lovestruck fool and continued staring at the closed door, hoping she would come back out. I knew waiting for two days to see her again at Emily and Caleb's wedding would be torture.

❦

Could it happen so fast? Was I really falling in love with Rebecca?

Could what happen so fast, Nathaniel?

"Mother, what are you doing here?"

I'm watching out for your well-being, son. You know you're playing with fire, don't you?

"Yes. I do. But why does it feel so right? She's all I think about. I've never felt this way, not even when I was engaged in 2016."

Oh my!

"Oh my, what?"

It's because you're in love with her.

"I guess I am. But why does it have to be so complicated?"

Son, that's what love does.

⁓ↃᏬↄ⁓

Mom had a way of popping up at the most inopportune times. But I valued her wisdom and only wished we could see each other in person again. What I wouldn't give to have her arms around me and hug me as she did when I was a child.

Being late in the evening and after our long walk, I knew my leg wouldn't hold up with the long ride back to the ranch. So, I headed back to town, where I had arranged to stay the night at one of the local respectable boarding houses.

~ 49 ~

Rebecca

SOMEHOW, I SENSED Nathaniel remained standing on the other side of the door. Leaning against the solid wood, I ran my hands up and down my arms to ward off the evening's chill. Smiling to myself, I felt happy without any burdening guilt. Still, in the back of my mind, that little voice, or should I say my mother's voice, reminded me I was playing a risky game.

But it wasn't a game. These emotions I felt were real.

Once again, my mother came through loud and clear. *What are you thinking girl?*

Before I could answer her, I heard Pearl's calling my name. "Rebecca."

Turning to face her standing in the hallway, I asked, "Pearl, what are you doing up so late?"

Holding up a kerosene lamp and dressed in her nightgown and robe, she stood there straight-faced. Normally, I could read her expressions, but this time, I was at a loss for what was going on in her mind.

"I heard the door open and wanted to make sure it wasn't that husband of yours."

After all this time, I didn't think Elliot would come looking for us. "Hopefully, he's keeping company with one of his lady friends."

"You mean one of his whores," she replied with a disgusted look on her face.

I laughed. "Pearl! I've never heard you use that word before. But you're most certainly correct!"

"Well, at the mention of his name, it gets my Irish up, and I don't have to worry what he would think of my behavior anymore." Switching the lamp to her left hand, she reached out. "Now, come get ready for bed and tell me all about your evening with Mr. Burns."

⟿⟾

Elliot

Wiping the condensation from the cold windowpane, I watched from the darkness of my hotel room as my wife was being escorted down the boardwalk by a man I'd never seen before. "Well, it didn't take that harlot long to find someone to cozy up with."

From how she clung to the stranger's arm and the smile she graced him with, it was obvious that she was enjoying herself. I knew all too well those crystalline blue eyes he was looking into, but I never remembered her looking at me in such a way.

Out of anger and jealousy, I shook my fist heavenward and yelled, "Damn him! If it's the last thing I do, I'll see you both in hell."

Seeing them together made my blood boil. With the heat rising from the base of my neck, up and across my face, I contemplated their punishment as the veins in my right temple pounded out a precarious rhythm, a sure sign of an impending headache. Hoping to ward off its debilitating effects, I pulled the coveted brown bottle from my vest pocket and took a generous swig, hoping relief would come soon.

Once I lost sight of the adoring couple, I turned away from the cold air seeping in from under the window casement. Pacing in slow motion, I looked down at my leaden feet. My medicine was quickly taking effect, and I had difficulty putting one foot in front of the other to add to the faded carpet's worn lines.

Calm yourself, Elliot. Remember what that quack told you to do. Slowly breathe in. Breathe out. Repeat. You can't go off half-crazed. Taking in a ragged breath, I tented my fingers under my chin to quell the rising anger, something I frequently did at work.

Rebecca can't know I'm in town. Not yet. As of late, when thinking of my wife, calmness left my body, and anger prevailed. I wanted this over with now! I cursed, "Damn you, Rebecca! You won't get away with this. Never again will you make a fool out of me!"

Lightheaded, I sank onto the chaise as the familiar drowsiness took hold, and my headache began to ease. If I didn't make a move soon to undress and get into bed, I would never make it across the room without passing out on the floor. More important than going to bed, I had to formulate a plan that my darling wife would soon regret her leaving me and coming to this God-forsaken place.

⌘

Awakening in the late morning, I found myself still on the chaise in yesterday's clothing but a bit more rumpled. I was alone. No woman warmed my bed—something I wasn't accustomed to of late. But I needed a clear head to carry out my plan for my wife and her lover.

By noon, I'd completed my ablutions and headed downstairs for coffee and a bite to eat. I wanted to be at the saloon by three to get a feel for its sordid customers. Finding the right man to carry out my plan was paramount to its success since I was hoping to be out of this town within three days and heading back to the civility of Boston.

As luck would have it, I located just the right person. Not used to negotiating with lowlife, we came to an agreement that would ultimately cost me. Of course, I could turn any negotiation to my benefit, and I'd have no regrets. A disposable witness was exactly what I needed.

⤳ 50 ⤳

Emily and Caleb

I COULDN'T CONTAIN my excitement. Screeching, "I'm getting married!"

Cozying up next to Caleb, he cocooned us together by pulling the covers over us as we comfortably lazed in the warm winter's sun coming in through the window.

I couldn't believe our wedding was only two days away. My love for this man lying next to me was stronger than ever. When I thought back on what we had endured over the past month, it amazed me that we were still together, let alone alive.

Leaning over, I whispered in his ear, "Caleb, are you awake?"

"I am now," he teased, drawing me into his embrace and nibbling on my ear.

"Stop it," I said, pushing him back. "As much as I'd like to continue, we don't have time for this. We have a lot to discuss."

I saw the worried look in his eyes when he replied, "Oh! You're serious, aren't you?" Pushing up on one elbow, he asked, "You haven't changed your mind about getting married, have you?"

"Of course not, silly." I heard the air rush out of his lungs in relief as I added, "You're too crazy and short-tempered to wish you on any other woman."

In his serious, lawyer-like voice, he replied, "Oh really! If that's how you feel, we can cancel the wedding right here, right now!" Shrugging his shoulders, he added, "I can easily find another woman who will have me."

"Good luck with that, cowboy," I answered, patting his bare chest. Grabbing the covers, I sat up and leaned back against the head-board. "We need to talk about the house."

"What house?" he asked in all seriousness.

"This house. It's getting too crowded. We won't have any privacy with my grandfather, you, I, Clarice, and Gabriel." Whining, I added, "I want you all to myself. And I want my own house."

"That sounds perfect to me. As much as I love everyone, it has been a bit cramped around here lately. Thank heavens Rebecca, the boys, and Pearl are in the casita, or it would be really overcrowded. We'd each have to pick an exam room to sleep in." Smiling cheekily, he added, "And believe me, from my experience, those cots downstairs are far from comfortable. Plus, it only accommodates one person," he added, teasingly shifting his eyebrows up and down.

"Well, I'm here to inform you that the modern-day version of those stretchers has not improved. They are still the most uncomfortable thing to lie on."

Easing the tension, we both had a good laugh.

"In all seriousness, Caleb, we need to make other arrangements before the wedding." Wondering how to approach the subject, I blurted out, "I've been looking around town at vacant houses."

"Of course you have," he said, pulling me closer.

I ignored his remark and proceeded. "I found one on the outskirts of town. It's only about a ten-minute ride from here. Both of us can be at our offices in no time at all. The best part is, it has five bedrooms."

"Five bedrooms! What do we need with five bedrooms?"

I gave him my best "Really" look before it dawned on him what I meant.

"So, you plan on filling the house with little crawlers?"

Slapping him lightly on his good shoulder, I replied, "Don't call our future children 'crawlers. You make them sound like worms!"

Catching my hand, he pulled me in for a kiss, a very long kiss. I think he was hoping for more, and he made it hard for me to resist, but I still had some things to discuss. Groaning in frustration at the arousing sensations he elicited, I again pulled back to his dismay.

"We have one more thing we need to talk about."

"Ok. Then can we please kiss some more?" he asked, pulling me tighter into his arms.

"Yes, we can kiss some more," I teasingly groaned.

His grin told me I'd made Caleb an extremely happy man with my surrender. So, I rushed out, catching him off guard, "We need to talk about Joey."

"Joey. What about Joey? Is he alright?"

"Joey is fine. Well, maybe," I answered.

"E-m-i-l-y," he drawled out.

Avoiding eye contact, I proceeded with my thoughts. "I don't think Joey should be wandering around town doing odd jobs, not having a family, or attending school. He's still too young and smart to be left on his own. I'm afraid he will eventually get into trouble."

"I understand, Em. He's a good kid," Caleb replied.

"That's it. Joey's just a kid and needs a loving family and stable home life." I was hoping Caleb was getting where my conversation was going. But so far, he didn't seem to be catching on. I think he had other 'things' on his mind. Men!

"What are you thinking, Doc?" he asked, sitting up on the edge of the bed with his face away from me. That was never a good sign in my experience with him.

I cautiously answered, "I want Joey to come live with us. I want us to be his family."

Caleb lowered his head and rested his elbows on his knees. I waited. I'd found that not interrupting Caleb when he was deep in thought was best for the both of us, but his silence was killing me. Once again, I felt as if I'd pushed him too far. Now, he certainly would have second thoughts about marrying this crazy time-traveling woman.

Finally, he spoke. "I've been thinking the same thing."

"You have!" To say the least, I was surprised. My insides were bubbling with joy, but I wouldn't show it. Not yet, anyhow.

"Yes. Ever since Clarice was shot, the thought of Joey possibly being killed made my heart ache." Turning to face me, he added, "Don't get me wrong, I'm sorry that it was Clarice, and she had to endure the horrors of that day. But Joey is so young, with his whole life ahead of him. I don't think I could forgive myself if it had been him that was shot." "

"Caleb, you couldn't have known what was going to happen that day. It's not your fault." Taking his hand in mine, "Let's just focus on giving Joey a family who dearly wants him. Of course, he'll have plenty of sisters to watch over in the future." I couldn't help but chuckle at the mention of him possibly being a father to daughters.

Puffing out his chest, "You mean Joey will have brothers," he said confidently.

"Don't be silly. We have no say in whether we have boys or girls. That's up to God." Teasingly, I added, "But we will have girls."

"Well, a man can hope, can't he? Having a daughter as beautiful as her mother would make me more than nervous. I'd never let her leave the house until she was thirty. If then!"

Taking his hands in mine, I added insult to injury by saying, "I don't think that would go over well with your daughter, nor me."

"So it's settled then? We'll ask Joey to join our family. Of course, he would stay with Rebecca and the boys until after our honeymoon."

It was my turn to raise my eyebrows and laugh. "So, it's settled! Now, all we have to do is tell Joey." Snuggling back into his arms, I said, Now, about that kiss, Mr. Young."

Wow. I'd fallen in love with a real cowboy and was getting married with a ready-made family all within two months—no wonder I walked around with my head in the clouds half the time. Life couldn't be better.

Rebecca

CALEB AND EMILY'S wedding day had finally arrived.

Standing in the antechamber to the sanctuary, I pinned the veil we had worked hours on in Emily's hair. She looked elegant in an ivory lace and satin gown made by one of the local seamstresses. Dazzling opalescent beads trimmed the neckline, and cascading rows of tiny crystals flowed down both arms and throughout the folds of the gown. The crystals must have cost a fortune and been hard to acquire at such short notice. But for Caleb, no expense was too much for his bride.

Lace made by one of the town's Scandinavian ladies captured the bodice, causing Emily to glow from the top of her head down to her satin slippers. Her great-grandfather, Doctor Sweeney, awaited excitedly outside the door to escort her down the aisle.

Holding my arms open in awe, I said, "Emily, you're stunning. Glowing, for that matter. My brother is a lucky man to be marrying such a beautiful woman." Leaning in close, I carefully placed my arms around her shoulders and whispered, "Thank you for saving him."

Emily spoke softly, "I'm just glad you are here to share in our special day, and I can finally call you my sister."

"Me too," I replied, pulling back and wiping away tears with a linen handkerchief I had tucked inconspicuously in my sleeve for such a need. "Are you ready?"

"Yes, most definitely," Emily replied, beaming.

I placed a desert bouquet in her hands that the church ladies had arranged, consisting of winter poppies, lupines, and owl clover. "Alright, my sister, your husband-to-be is waiting." Opening the door to her awaiting grandfather, I happily said, Let's get you two married."

I was just as anxious as Emily as I gazed down the aisle at the man I was falling in love with, standing beside my brother. It was a forbidden love no one could know about. But I had a feeling that Caleb and Emily knew well that my affection for Nathaniel went deeper than friendship.

Emily had graciously included my sons Porter and Daniel in the wedding. They acted as ring bearers, each with a ring sewn to the top of a small white satin pillow. I couldn't help but think that they both had grown since coming to Yuma and looked so handsome in their freshly pressed suits. I was proud of them both.

As Emily accepted her grandfather's arm, my sons and I walked past them, making our way to the front of the church before Emily began the walk that would change her life forever. Every pew was full of well-wishers who had impacted the lives of both Emily and Caleb over the short time they had been in this small community outside of Yuma.

Nodding my head in her direction, the organist began playing the old pump organ, and I started my slow walk down the aisle while staring at the man who stood as Caleb's best man. Nathaniel Burns was more handsome than I remembered. There he stood, tall and stately, better than any man of the Boston elite, in a black suit coat and a white shirt complemented by a black string tie and polished black boots. At the sight of him, my heart skipped a beat. He caught me watching him and winked, which caused me to stop mid-isle until Daniel tugged on my hand, bringing me out of my daydream.

Oh, how I wished Nathaniel and I were the ones exchanging our vows today. With that thought, my smile slowly faded, knowing it could never be. But I wanted him to be more than just my friend. Unfortunately, there was still the matter of me being a married woman. I hadn't lied to Nathaniel; he knew I was married. Yet, our interest in each other was becoming complicated. I was caught up in a deadly charade and falling in love for the first time in my life.

Mrs. Mueller began playing the traditional wedding march when a hush fell over the sanctuary, giving the cue for all to stand and face the back of the church. I was already in place at the front of the altar and on the opposite side of Caleb as we awaited Emily's appearance.

⤞⋯⤝

Emily

I didn't think this day would ever come. In the blink of an eye, I had died, been transported to another place and time, and fallen in love with a man who had been dead for over a hundred years before me. But here I was in 1881, holding on to my great-grandfather's arm, ready to walk down the aisle on my wedding day.

Unbelievably, I was a woman from 2019 marrying a man in 1881 who had lived his whole life in the nineteenth century. We had defied the odds of death and separate centuries to prove our love could survive.

I had once been angry and fiercely determined to return to the twenty-first century. I didn't think I would ever come to understand the Celtic gift my grandfather had used to give me renewed life here in 1881 as I lay dying in modern-day Seattle. He called it a gift his Irish ancestors had passed down through generations, giving certain family members the ability to give a dying blood relative the gift of life again, albeit in another century. But my love for Caleb had won out in the end, and now I couldn't think of ever leaving him. He would be my whole world 'till my last breath.

I wasn't nervous, just anxious as the organ began to play. I was ready to have the ceremony over and finally be Mrs. Caleb Young.

My dearest Emily, you look positively radiant, whispered the familiar voice I hadn't heard in several weeks.

I asked in a hushed tone, *"Gran, is that you?"* I couldn't have my grandfather hearing me and thinking I was losing it on my wedding day.

Yes, dear. I won't miss your special day. Caleb looks nervous the way he's fidgeting with his tie, not to mention handsome standing up there next to that nice man. Nathaniel, isn't that his name?

Smiling, I nodded my head as if my deceased grandmother could hear it rattle.

I'll be here if you need me for anything.

"Thank you, Gran. I'm so glad you came. It makes me feel that a part of home is with me." *Remember, I'll always be here for you. Now, go marry that handsome man!*

Caleb

Son, you look so handsome, came that calm voice I lovingly remembered.

"Mom! What are you doing here?" I whispered under my breath, or so I thought. I guess I hadn't when Nathaniel turned to me with a questioning look on his face. Startled that my mother was once again speaking to me from the beyond, I was thrilled she was at my wedding.

Ignoring Nathaniel, I turned back to face the full sanctuary when my mother spoke again. *I am so happy, Emily, and you are finally getting married. Your wandering days are finally over after lusting for every pretty girl since finishing school.*

"Mom! Stop embarrassing me. How can you bring that up of all times on my wedding day?"

Ignoring my question, she instead answered, *Emily is a wonderful woman. Better than that other woman who betrayed you.*

"Mom, please don't speak ill of the dead despite what she did." Nathaniel once again gave me a questioning look. He must have thought I was crazy or just plain crazy in love.

I'm sorry, dear. That wasn't kind of me. I'll not bring her up again. Changing the subject, she added, *Your sister looks stunning. But why does she look so unhappy? I thought she was pleased to be here with you. You know I want her to be happy now that she's away from that awful husband of hers. He's done terrible things I won't mention now. I don't want to dampen your happy day. I love you, son.*

"I love you too, Mom.

WEDDING DAY

Emily

I WAS FLOATING on air and barely remembered saying "I do" when Caleb pulled me into his arms and pressed his lips against mine in a kiss like no other. He hadn't even waited for the pastor to tell him, "You can now kiss your bride." I held tightly to his shoulders as he deepened the kiss, bringing us together as one.

Whoops and hollers went out around the sanctuary before Caleb broke away. Grinning, he whispered in my ear the plans he had for our honeymoon night. Blushing, I felt a wave of heat surge up my neck. But when he whispered he would love me till his last breath, I knew we were meant to spend the rest of our lives together as husband and wife.

We were still embracing when several gunshots resonated through the church. I thought it might be townspeople celebrating our union. But when Caleb pushed me behind him, I knew it wasn't what I'd hoped.

Reaching for their guns, Caleb and Nathaniel forgot they had been placed securely in the pastor's office for the ceremony, as well as all the guests. There wasn't time to get them as the Chapel doors burst open, and in stumbled an intoxicated man brandishing a gun and pointing it directly at the front of the church.

Panic set in as I followed his line of aim. Good heavens, he was pointing directly at my sister-in-law, Rebecca, who had since gone pale at seeing the man. Caleb started toward his sister, but I held him back as the gunman's direction switched to my husband. Gritting his teeth, Caleb firmly called out, "What do you want, Elliot?"

So this was Rebecca's husband. Now I understood why she was here in Yuma alone. Daniel and Porter stood frozen in place with fear written all over their tiny faces while looking at their mother for directions.

Out of the corner of my eye, Rebecca dropped her bouquet to the floor and took one unsteady step forward while holding her right hand out to stay her boys. "Stay here," she instructed with a tremor in her voice, not looking down. "Elliot, what are you doing here?"

Sneering, Elliott answered, "Well, well, well, if it isn't my dear sweet wife. I'm here to take back what's mine. You and my sons are coming back home with me. I'm taking you from this filthy backward town."

"Go sit down with Pearl," I heard Rebecca whisper to Porter and Daniel before answering Elliot. Thank heaven she was sending them out of harm's way.

Proudly holding her ground, Rebecca said, "I'm not going anywhere with you. The boys and I no longer have a home in Boston. You destroyed that long ago."

Nathaniel leaned forward, "Please Rebecca, don't say anymore."

With a snicker, Elliot slurred, "If it isn't the cowboy my wife has been lusting over."

"Damn you!" Nathaniel growled.

Starting to take a step forward, I called for him to stop, "Nate, don't do it. That's what he wants. He's drunk and just trying to edge you on."

Thankfully, he listened. But my husband was another story. Grabbing Caleb's arm, I felt his muscles tense under my restraint.

"Don't provoke him Caleb. Please try and remain calm for Rebecca's sake and mine."

Caleb nodded, but I could see the tension in his shoulders remained, and I feared for his life. I wouldn't let go. It would mean certain death if he made the mistake of charging his brother-in-law, and I didn't want to become a widow on my wedding day.

"She's not going anywhere," Caleb disdainfully yelled. While keeping Elliott's attention on himself, Nathaniel cautiously moved behind us in an attempt to get to Rebecca's side. He was trying to push her back when Elliot caught his movement.

Speaking hatefully, Elliot was hell-bent on degrading his wife in front of all the attendees. "My darling wayward wife, it didn't take you long to find a lover. Such an adoring couple you make," he said, waving his gun in the air. "But not for long," he added.

Nathaniel yelled at Elliot to put the gun down. "Ackerman, she's not going anywhere with you. Just think of your boys and what this is doing to them."

Weaving from side to side in the aisle, Elliot suddenly lurched toward the front of the church while screaming a response and pointing his gun at various people sitting frozen in the pews.

"May I remind you all that I'm the one holding the gun here! If Rebecca doesn't return with me, you can't have her either."

With a catch in his voice, Nathaniel replied, "Don't be stupid man. You don't wanna do this."

At the front of the church, I caught movement behind Elliot. Quietly rising from the pew, Henry, the owner of the Pick and Shovel saloon, was making his way towards the aisle. I wanted to scream and tell him to stop, but I only managed to vigorously shake my head, trying to gain his attention in hopes of deterring him. But he didn't see me.

Being of formidable size and force, Henry lunged at Elliot from behind. At that same time, Nathaniel made a move to step in front of Rebecca, but sadly, he was too late. Elliott had already fired his pistol, with the bullet hitting true and striking Rebecca in the side of her abdomen.

At the resounding pop, Rebecca looked down; seeing blood, she grabbed her side and let out a sickening scream of pain that echoed off the Chapel walls. Collapsing, she fell back into Nathaniel's arms.

Chaos ensued as Henry Calhoun jumped Elliott from behind, crushing the pew flowers in his wake. Anders Johansson, on the opposite side of the aisle, with his wife and daughter, rushed to Henry's aid to keep Elliot down under their hold. Elliott's attempts to free himself were futile. With their combed weight, they held him firm to the floor while successfully removing the gun from his possession.

Screaming women quickly gathered their children and rushed them out the chapel's front door while the remaining men hurried to the pastor's office to retrieve their guns.

Caleb and I aided Rebecca. Quickly examining the entry room, I staved off the bleeding with the hem of my wedding gown, hoping the bullet didn't hit any vital organs.

Nathaniel was frantic, repeating her name over and over while running his shaking hand over her face. "Rebecca. Rebecca, don't you dare die on me, you hear me." Pushing back a damp lock of her hair, he added, "I love you, Rebecca. I love you. Did you hear me?"

Despite Rebecca remaining unconscious, I spoke to her as if she could hear me. "Rebecca, I know this pressure hurts, but I need to slow the bleeding down."

The hem of my gown, now crimson with her blood, would eventually be thrown in the burn barrel after the seamstress removed the crystals. After today, I wouldn't keep such a reminder of my wedding.

Without removing my hand from Rebecca's abdomen, I turned to Nathaniel and squeezed his forearm to get his attention. "Nate. Look at me. Rebecca's going to be fine."

Why did I say that? I knew better. I couldn't make those guarantees, but it was all I could think of at the moment. With those words out in the open, I saw the tension in Nathaniel's face change to one of anguish. "We need to get her to the clinic so Doc Sweeney and I can examine her."

Caleb began to ease his arms under his sister when Nathaniel pushed his hands away and reverently lifted Rebecca into his arms.

Caleb and I had to double-time our steps to keep up with Nathaniel's pace as he raced for the exit, ignoring Henry, Anders, and Elliot, who were still on the floor. The aisle cleared akin to the parting of the Red Sea, allowing us to hastily make our way out the door and down the street to the clinic.

Emily

"Hurry, Nate, Bring Rebecca in here," I called out, motioning with my hand while holding the door to the surgical suite open with the other. Nathaniel moved past me and gently placed Rebecca on the operating table.

I didn't take the time to change out of my bloodied wedding dress but instead slipped on one of my clean surgical aprons. Seeing Rebecca lying there helpless was difficult since, normally, she would be the one assisting us in surgery.

I called out for Clarice, who had remained at the clinic during the wedding in case of an emergency. Coming through the door, she abruptly stopped at the entrance when she saw who our patient was. Laying a hand on her chest, she cried out, "Lord have mercy. What's happened to Mizz Rebecca?"

Ignoring her question, I motioned for her to come into the room. "Clarice, we need your help. You've watched Doctor Sweeney, and I do surgeries before."

"Yez, Ma'am," she replied, nodding her head.

"And you know the instruments."

"Yez, Ma'am, I do."

"Now, I need you to do something important for Miss Rebecca. I need you to administer the ether for us. Do you think you can do that?"

At the mention of asking her to assist in this task, her face turned momentarily pale. Then, straightening her back, she moved to the head of the table and replied, "Youz all tell me what to do, and I'll help ya."

Letting out a sigh of relief, I instructed Clarice on how to administer the ether. But first, I asked, "Please wash your hands, then bring me the bottle of ether and the mask we use."

With confidence I'd never seen before, Clarice did as requested, and at a moment's notice, she had turned from a frightened helper to a woman of self-assurance that I would be proud to work with any day.

❧

We kept a large kettle of water heating on the stove at all times. Memories of my first day in the clinic had me shuttering. When Caleb required surgery, the surgical table had held spots of dry crusted blood, the sheets were stained brown, and the instruments were, well, need I say, disgustingly dirty. But I couldn't blame my grandfather. He had been without assistance and was the only one caring for all the residents in this part of town.

Thankfully, that was no longer the case. With my knowledge of contamination and the spread of disease, my great-grandfather now understood that such would lead to infection, sepsis, and a horrible death. At my recommendation, he had eliminated using bromine to treat wounds, knowing it would damage the surrounding healthy tissue.

❧

Now filled with clean water, it was my grandfather's turn at the basin. Since I arrived in Yuma, he had learned much from my teachings, or should I say, lectures on the spread of disease by examining patients and doing surgery with unwashed hands.

We now made sure to boil our instruments in water and then lay them out on bleached cloths. Although the autoclave had recently been invented in 1879, it wasn't a luxury we couldn't afford at this time.

Eyeing Nathaniel warily, Doc asked, "Nathaniel, you and Caleb need to wait outside in te parlor. One of us will come te get ya when we're done."

Maintaining a calm tone, Nathaniel replied, "Sorry Doc, but I'm not going anywhere. I'm staying right here with Rebecca."

Caleb left the room as Nate gave me a pleading look as if asking me to back him up. "Nathaniel, I have to agree with Doc. Caleb will stay with you, and I promise we'll come get you when you can sit with Rebecca." The defeated look on his face broke my heart, but the Doc was right. We couldn't watch him and take care of Rebecca at the same time.

Nathaniel broke the silence by adding, "Listen, Docs, I've seen much worse in my lifetime, and blood doesn't make me squeamish. I promise I won't be fainting on you. So, that's a no to me leaving the room."

I didn't argue. Instead, I stepped away from the table to wash Rebecca's blood from my hands in clean water. Her wound was already contaminated, but I didn't need to add any more bacteria. I prayed in the end, she wouldn't develop sepsis.

Although Rebecca remained unconscious, she let out the occasional moan. She would require the ether to keep her sedated and pain-free during the surgery. I instructed Clarice to place the wire mask over Rebecca's nose and mouth and told her how to hold the bottle to limit the number of drops that came out. More importantly, I instructed her not to get close to the wire mask and inhale the ether, or she would be on the floor in no time, and we couldn't have that happen. I needed her assistance.

I began to count the drops flowing from the bottle. One. Two. Three. Four. A deep sigh escaped Rebecca's mouth, indicating the ether had taken her into a deep sleep, and she would feel no pain while we performed the surgery.

Not wasting any more time arguing with Nathaniel, modesty went out the window as I began removing Rebecca's gown in his presence. She would understand.

While I was away from the table, my grandfather had cleansed the wound with the water expressly used for this purpose. I ignored Nathaniel for the next hour as my grandfather allowed me to take the lead in Rebecca's surgery.

She had a penetrating wound just above her left hip where the bullet entered but failed to exit, which made me concerned about the damage it had done internally and possibly to her kidney.

Until I examined further, it was a mystery if the bullet had taken a straight route or wandered within her abdominal cavity. Enlarging the entry wound with a scalpel, I tied off any oozing vessels with suture before I could locate the top edge of the bullet and extract it with forceps.

Upon further examination, Rebecca was lucky the bullet had remained clear of her kidney. Closing the wound, my grandfather applied a thick cotton pressure dressing to keep the oozing to a minimum. Now, the waiting began to see if Rebecca would develop any signs of an infection.

Surgery complete, Rebecca's skin was cool to the touch, probably from the loss of blood and her exposure to the cool air while dressed only in thin cotton linens. Clarice placed a blanket warmed by the kitchen stove over her body as I watched Rebecca's shallow, steady breathing, reassured that we had done all we could for now.

Now came the hardest part: waiting for her to recover.

⌒⚭⌒

Nathaniel

When Doc Sweeney turned away from the table, I leaned in close to Emily and whispered, "Please don't let her die."

Before Emily could respond, I added, "Can't you start an I.V. and give her some antibiotics?"

Damn! Why did I say that? My words were out before I realized what I had said.

Emily stared at me with a puzzled expression on her face. She probably thought I was crazy when she pointed a bloodied finger at me and said, "You and I, Sir, need to talk after I'm finished here."

That was enough to put me on edge until the time came. What was I going to tell her? Obviously, the truth. But when I did, she would only think I'd gone off the deep end. I wouldn't blame her, but until then, I would sit by the woman I'd come to love and pray she survived.

~ 54 ~

Benjamin Reynolds

UPON HEARING GUNSHOTS, I grabbed my holster off the bedpost and ran out of my hotel room. Rushing downstairs as fast as my leg would allow, I passed the registration desk, where the clerk was staring outside wide-eyed in fright.

Pushing the main door open, I stopped and scanned the street, wondering which direction the shots had come from. Momentarily standing on the boardwalk, I saw several men running toward the church, where I knew there was a wedding being held between one of the doctors and the town's new lawyer.

As I got closer to the church, Sheriff Anders Johannson and Henry Calhoun were dragging a man down the church steps. Approaching to lend a hand, I could see the man being dragged was dressed in a wrinkled yet expensively tailored suit and reeked of alcohol.

"Good heavens! It was him. Ackerman. The man who'd hired the Pinkerton Agency to find his wife and the man I spoke with in the stable. I was glad he hadn't seen my face that day. What had he done?

"Get him out of my sight!" the sheriff yelled, thrusting the man in my direction. Throwing the cell keys in the air, I watched them

246

slowly arc above me before catching them in my right hand. As I did, the sheriff turned and swiftly returned to the church.

Since the man's hands were cuffed behind him, I grabbed his upper arm and tugged him forward. As I did so, I saw Ander's wife, Abigail, rush out the door with their crying infant in her arms and two frightened boys by her side. I recognized the boys from the train. They were Mrs. Ackerman's sons. But where was she?

I looked around for their mother, concern growing when I didn't locate her. Anders walked up to his wife, pulled her into a firm hug, and buried his face in the side of her neck. I knew then something serious had happened within the church's consecrated walls.

Nodding my head sideways toward the church entrance, I asked, "Henry, what happened in there? Where is Mrs. Ackerman?" The man in my grasp slurred, "I shot the whore! She's dead!"

Shocked, I stared at Henry. She couldn't be dead. My knees weakened. What have I done? As Ackerman struggled to be free, I wrenched his arm forward, not caring if I dislocated his shoulder.

He screamed in pain. "You'll pay for this," he ground out. I caught a whiff of his breath, smelling not only of alcohol but oil of cloves that brought back memories of my time in the war. It had been a long time since I smelled the demon laudanum and remembered how it ruined many of its victims' lives, including mine. Soldiers may have survived the bloody battles only to be left to fight a more powerful, unrelenting war. A war I had thankfully won.

"Henry, what is he talking about?" We continued to pull our prisoner through the dusty street toward the jail when he answered, "He came in the church yelling something about getting his wife and sons back. When she didn't budge, he shot her. Right there in front of the whole church." Henry slapped our prisoner hard on the back of his head, adding, "You'll hang for this, you scum."

I felt no remorse as I jerked Ackerman forward. I needed to vent my anger toward this devil. It was either that or shoot him. And I was tempted. He deserved no better.

The man stumbled in the middle of the road. It was Henry who pulled him up, forcing him to continue walking. "I'll tell you more once we lock this devil up," Henry answered. I nodded, stepped up on the boardwalk, and unlocked the jail's door.

Henry kept a firm grasp on Ackerman while I opened an empty cell. Then Henry, not so gently, shoved our prisoner forward, causing the rotund man to land hard on the metal cot, making the springs groan under his weight.

I was more than happy to lock the door and throw the key away. But because of my training, I knew this alleged killer deserved a trial. Tapping the gun in my holster, my instructions to him were minimal, "Keep your mouth shut, or you'll deal with me. The privy pot is under the cot. And don't expect it to be emptied each time you use it. You get to smell your own stench. Oh, and by the way, I hope you've eaten today since your next meal won't be until morning."

"Why you son-of-a." He couldn't finish as he choked on his spittle. "I'm not staying in this stinking hole!" he yelled. "I've paid for a room at the hotel. And my bags are there."

"The minute you shot your wife, you lost the opportunity to stay in the comfort of the hotel. You'll be lucky if you see the light of another day when you're found guilty. Just to be nice," I added, snickering, "I'll have your things brought over to the jail. But that doesn't mean you'll be able to have them in the cell with you. It's just to vacate the room so they can rent it out again."

I placed the cell keys in my pocket and added, "You'll go up in front of the Territorial Judge when he arrives next week. In the meantime, make yourself comfortable and enjoy your new accommodations."

Chuckling to myself, I hoped he would try to escape and allow me the opportunity to shoot him, saving the judge a trip. I joined Henry in the sheriff's outer office, where he was pouring himself a cup of coffee from the pot resting on the stove.

Shaking his head, he said, "I should have taken him down sooner, and none of this would have happened. It's all my fault."

Leaning against the large oak desk, I stretched my aching shoulder muscles from dragging our jail guest across the street. Looking at Henry, I needed answers. "What do you mean it's all your fault? Do you know something about that man?" Pointing toward the back cell, I didn't let on that I had met Ackerman before and had been sent here as a Pinkerton Agent to track down his wife.

"From what I heard in the church, he's Mrs. Ackerman's husband. I guess he came here to take his wife and sons back to Boston but changed his mind and decided to kill her instead." Taking a swig of coffee, he added, "What kind of man does that to a woman he's supposed to love?"

Rubbing the stubble on my chin, I answered, "Henry, I'm sure you already know there are a lot of sick people in this world, and I've run across many of them in my line of business."

"What is your line of business?" Henry asked.

"It's a long story, Henry. Someday, when we don't have ears listening," I said, nodding in the direction of the cell, I'll tell you all about it."

That seemed to satisfy the big man as I stood away from the desk. I already knew his answer, but still I asked, "Henry, will you be O.K. here alone? I have some business to attend to."

"Sure, I'll be fine," he answered, pointing his thumb over his shoulder at the occupied cell. "He'll be no problem. Besides, if he tries anything funny, I'll just shoot him."

"It seems we both harbor the same thoughts." Slapping his shoulder and chuckling, I said, "You're a good man, Henry Calhoun."

The heat of vehemence sat like buckshot in the pit of my stomach, making me believe this was something I'd created. I needed to get to the clinic to find out more. Walking out the door, I was more than happy to leave our prisoner to the mercy of Henry Calhoun.

55

Benjamin

AS I APPROACHED the clinic, several townspeople stood outside the picket fence with worried looks masking their features. Excusing my way through the crowd, I knocked lightly at the clinic door, where Sheriff Johannson greeted me.

"Ben, what are you doing here?" he asked, looking behind me with concern written all over his face. "Where's our prisoner?"

"Don't worry, sheriff. He's locked up, and Henry's with him. I've come to see how Mrs. Ackerman is doing. Any news on her condition?

"Yes, but come in first." Entering the warmth of the parlor, I removed my hat and nodded a greeting to Mrs. Johannson and little Holly. My stomach clenched with worry regarding Mrs. Ackerman's condition as I turned my attention back to the sheriff.

Anders motioned me to the side of the room before speaking. "Mrs. Ackerman vill recover. Dr. Sweeney and Dr. Young are vith her now, as is Nathaniel. Ve vas told that te bullet missed her vital organs, whatever tat means, and tey expect her to have a full recovery."

Letting out a sigh of relief, I said, "That's good to hear." Hesitating, I needed to tell the sheriff my part in this potentially fatal incident. But was now the right time? Really, I didn't think any time would be right.

So, placing my hand on his upper right arm, I asked, sheriff, is there some place where we can talk privately? I think my actions may have played a part in Mrs. Ackerman being shot." If looks could kill, I would have been dead on the spot.

His nostrils flared and his lips were in a thin line; before I knew what was happening, the sheriff had grabbed my coat sleeve and dragged me down the hall. Shoving me into the kitchen, he slammed the door shut behind us and seized my coat lapels. Angrily, he pushed me up against the back of the door.

"Whoa, Sheriff!" What the heck do you think you're doing?" I grabbed his hands and wrenched them off my coat. Straightening my shirt, I stepped away from the door and the sheriff.

"Vell man, vhat do you have to say for yourself?" His face had been so close to mine that I couldn't help but focus on his flinty glare and the vein rapidly pulsing at his left temple. I knew this conversation wouldn't go well, but there was no way I could have predicted the sheriff's reaction.

My chance of becoming a deputy in this town grew slimmer by the minute. Pointing to a vacant chair, I said, "It's a long story, sheriff. And I think we better sit down to discuss it."

I could see he was barely holding his annoyance with me in check when he answered, "I do my best tinking standing up. So, hurry up and tell me vhats on your mind."

I didn't sit but took a deep breath and began telling Anders what had transpired from Boston until today.

⁓⚬⚬⁓

"So you see, sheriff, in all innocence, once I notified my Pinkerton supervisor, I'm sure he contacted Mr. Ackerman to let him know where his wife was so he could come for her. There was no way we could have known what his plans were." Pacing the small kitchen, I continued, "Mr. Ackerman gave us the impression his wife had been taken against her will, and my orders were to follow her but not intervene."

Rolling my shoulders to ease the mounting tension, I continued. "Mr. Ackerman had this planned all along. He was never the grieving husband. It's now obvious Rebecca was running from him, and I feel guilty for playing a part in his game. I'm just glad she's going to recover."

I turned to the sheriff and added, "I don't understand why she didn't tell her brother or you so you could try and protect her."

"She never told me. But she could have told her brother. I'll have to speak with Caleb."

Walking to the door, he paused, "Stay here, and I'll have Caleb come to talk with you." After encountering the sheriff, I hoped I was prepared to face Rebecca's brother and live to see another day.

⚜

Not the happy groom from hours earlier, Caleb entered the kitchen, not saying a word, just looking somber as if he'd been dragged through a knothole. Without speaking, he headed to the stove and picked up a clean mug from the sideboard and the pot of stale coffee. Placing his left hand on the metal, he shook his head and set the pot back on the stove.

I knew he was stalling for time. My palms began to sweat as I watched his calculated moves. Taking his time, as if he'd done the same thing many times before, he grabbed the metal poker from the back of the stove and moved the barely glowing embers forward in the firebox, hoping to ignite a new flame.

He then placed the pot over the heating burner and stood with his back to me for a long time. When is he going to say something? But, I thought it best to remain silent on the opposite side of the room where it was safer.

Finally, holding the pot up in my direction, he asked, "Can I pour you some?"

"Ah, no thanks." I didn't need to add to my already jittery nerves. What I had to tell him he wouldn't like, and I imagined myself getting beaten by the new groom.

"So, according to Anders you have something you wanted to tell me." Turning to face me, Caleb leaned back on the counter, a good launching place for him to come at me. I remained standing on the opposite side of the table, not that it would keep me safe, and answered, "Yes, I do."

"So, just spit it out."

"Right," I replied, digging the toe of my boot into a hole in the plank floor. Pausing, I organized my thoughts to lessen the blow to Caleb since I would be the unlucky recipient of his fury. "I believe I'm why Mr. Ackerman is here in Yuma."

"What did you just say?" He shouted before pushing off the counter, remaining firm in his stance.

Holding my hands up to stay his attack, I continued. "To start with, I'm a Pinkerton agent from Boston. Mr. Ackerman hired the agency I work for to find and follow his wife."

"Damn him!" Caleb yelled, slamming his coffee cup down on the table. What little was left spilled over the rim and onto the floor.

I rushed out, hoping to save myself from Caleb's rage. "You should know Mr. Ackerman lied to my supervisor when he hired us. He told us his wife had been taken against her will. But what I didn't understand was how he knew she was on a certain train when he asked for an agent to follow her. He also told us we were not to approach her or try to detain her. So, I didn't. When I arrived here, I wired my supervisor in Boston to tell him I had located your sister and where she was staying."

"So, if I understand you right, you led this murdering bastard to my sister!"

The strain and anger on Caleb's face were enough to have me standing straighter, ready to take a well-deserved punch. "I'm truly sorry, Caleb. If I'd known what type of man he was or what his plans were for your sister, I would have never told my supervisor where she was. Let alone taken the job."

I lowered my head and added, "Rebecca getting shot is all my fault. I don't think I can live with myself if she dies."

Caleb blurted out, "She's not going to die. You hear me!"

His next words, a bit calmer, surprised me. "Ben, it's not your fault. It's that madman's. You had no reason to believe he was deceiving the agency." Sticking both hands into his pockets and hunching his shoulders forward, he added, "I knew Rebecca came here to escape Elliot's madness. He had beaten her the night before she left Boston with the boys and Pearl."

Kicking the leg of a chair, I couldn't contain my rage. "Why that stinking son of a . . . I'll kill him myself."

"No. No, you won't, Ben. We can't be above the law. I have to plan his demise carefully."

"I like your way of thinking, Caleb, but whatever do you mean? Are you going to kill him yourself?"

"No, I won't. Elliot will go before the Territorial Judge next week and hopefully spend the rest of his life in Yuma's Territorial Prison. Although truthfully, I hope the judge sentences him to hang for what he did to my sister. If not, life in prison will take its toll on Elliot, and as arrogant as he is, some cellmate will take care of him for us.

56

Nathaniel

MY HANDS WERE still covered with Rebecca's blood, and my heart ached with such deep grief at the thought of losing her. I prayed to God she wouldn't die.

But was I presumptuous in thinking we had a life ahead of us now that her husband would spend the rest of his days in prison? Truthfully, I wanted to see him hang for what he'd done, but that was too good for that miserable man.

Watching Emily move about the surgical suite with ease as if she had done it hundreds of times before, I would be forever grateful to her and doc Sweeney for saving Rebecca's life. Every move Emily made was calculated and with purpose. She had a skill beyond this century.

Making my way across the room to the empty basin, I filled it with clean, lukewarm water from the pitcher. Washing my hands with a sliver of soap, I watched as the water turned red with Rebecca's blood. In a hate-filled trance, I found myself squeezing my hands tightly together, envisioning they were around Elliott's neck. With each breath I took, I wanted to end his miserable life with my bare hands. If it were up to me, I would see him hang.

Emily came to stand beside me while I dried my hands on a clean towel. Pointing her index finger in my direction, her authoritative look had me thinking I was about to face a disciplinary board with my former Police Academy Commander.

"Come with me, Nate. We have some things we need to discuss."

I knew protesting would do me no good. It was time for me to fess up, so to speak, and tell her who I really was. I knew I had given myself away with my inquiry into antibiotics and intravenous infusions, and I surmise that Emily knew more about me than she let on.

Rebecca was still sleeping, so this was Emily's opportunity to interrogate me. I followed the new bride down the hall to the kitchen. Emily opened the door and stopped before entering when she saw her husband and Ben occupying it. "Gentlemen, if you two are finished here, I need to have the room so Nate and I can talk."

Fatigue showed on Caleb's face as he asked if Rebecca was okay.

"Yes, she's fine. She's sleeping right now. If you would like to sit with her, you can. But please don't wake her up."

Turning, Caleb placed the empty coffee cup on the counter, took Ben by the shoulder, and left the room, but not before kissing his wife. I was jealous. I wanted what Caleb and Emily had with Rebecca. But I didn't have the right. I had already caused Rebecca enough grief by pursuing her as a married woman. Now look where she was—lying in the backroom, shot by a madman who happened to be her husband.

Running a hand through my hair, I stood in the doorway, waiting for Emily's next command. Pointing to a chair, she directed, "Nate, have a seat." Then, turning to the stove, she lifted the pot and asked if I wanted a cup of coffee. I nervously squeezed my hands and answered no thanks, but do you think Doc has anything stronger? I sure could use it about now."

"I believe he does. Let me check." Emily left the room and returned with a large bottle of amber liquid. Turning the label toward me, I saw it was one of the saloon's finer whiskeys. Thank heavens, it was the real thing. It was probably from Henry's private stash he kept for special customers. Luckily, Doc must have been one of his favorites.

Not that I frequented the place, but I heard from one of the ladies at the salon that before she was kidnapped, Emily once had a craving for beer and whiskey chasers. Setting two shot glasses on the table before me, she poured the fine-smelling potion to the rim.

As a gentleman, I waited for her to take her glass. Doing so, I grabbed mine and raised it in salute. "Sláinte."

"So an Irish toast it is. I would have thought that with the last name of Burns, you would be Scottish."

"Oh, I am with a rogue Irish relative here and there. My grand-parents were Scots. Before that, I'm not quite sure; I never had time to ask my mom.

"Well, drink up, and let's talk."

Holding the glass to her lips, I watched as she took the shot in one swallow. Unlike Emily, I held the smooth whiskey in my mouth, swirled it around with my tongue, then allowed the liquid heat to slowly glide down my throat, warming me from the inside out.

After the second shot, I felt the tension in my shoulders release, only to find it returned when Emily began her questioning. Trying to stall the inevitable, I held up my hand to halt her. "Wait Doc, don't you want to get out of your wedding dress and clean up first ?"

"No I'm fine, thank you. This shouldn't take too long, Nate. I won't beat around the bush with flowery questions. I'll get right to the point."

I bet you will.

"Tell me about your experience with intravenous fluids and antibiotics." Without allowing me to answer, Emily continued. "I'll allow your IV question to pass since its use has been attempted since the Middle Ages, but your antibiotic knowledge is another story. I think I'm safe saying that they won't be discovered until 1909 when doctor Paul Ehrlich discovered a treatment for syphilis, and Dr. and Alexander Fleming discovered penicillin in 1928. But I'm sure you don't need a history lesson. Knowing all that, I believe you have some truths about yourself that need telling, at least to me."

"Wow, Doc, that's a lot to take in." Not meeting her gaze, it was time to tell Emily my story, after which I would ask her to tell me hers.

Seeing Emily perform Rebecca's surgery today with such precision, I suspected she wasn't from the 19th century either. She was too advanced in her knowledge and skills. Taking a deep breath, I began. "I first met Rebecca on the train before I arrived in Fort Worth. She captured my interest and heart the minute she glanced my way. It was all new to me, and I couldn't explain it to you if I tried."

Patting at the air, she commented, "That's all nice, Nate, but go back to before the train ride, before you met Rebecca, and before you came to be in Yuma."

Drawing my hands into hers, she asked, "I believe you need to help me understand who you really are."

"Alright, Doc, but you probably won't believe me. As a matter of fact, I have a hard time believing it myself. I reached for the bottle of whiskey to provide some extra fortification but decided against it. I needed to keep a clear head. "Are you ready to hear what I have to tell you?"

"Yes, I think we share more in common than either of us has ever realized."

Nathaniel

I KNEW EMILY had to be from a more sophisticated time than the 1880s. Once I was finished telling her my story, I would persuade her to let me in on her secrets. Wasting no time, I filled her in on my former life.

"I'm from Boston, 2016!" While waiting for her astonished response, Emily just patted my hand, encouraging me to continue.

"At the time, I was a police officer in one of the highest crime-ridden areas of Boston." I paused again. Did she want me to continue? Sitting there with a grin on her face, of course she did.

"I was out on a domestic call."

"Oh, those are the scariest," Rebecca interjected.

"Yes, they are. It seemed hours for the following to transpire when, in actuality, it took only seconds. Anyway, long story short, I remember it was a humid summer night after a ninety-degree-plus day. While walking closer to the house in question, I prayed that things would go well. But the next thing I knew, a man was shoving a woman over a porch railing, causing her to land headfirst on the cement below.

"Then, determinedly, the perp turned toward me with a gun in his outstretched hand. We both fired our weapons at the same time. I must have hit him because I remember seeing him fall back through the open doorway with blood covering the middle of his chest."

"Unfortunately, his shot hit me at the same time." Placing my hand on the side of my neck as if it had happened yesterday, I continued, pointing a finger indicating my carotid artery.

This was going to be the difficult part for me to recall to Emily. "Instantly, I felt this intense burning pain here, then the warmth of my blood running through my fingers. The next thing I remember, I was lying face down on the hot cement, with people yelling all around me, "Hang on, Nate. The paramedics are on their way." Then, my partner was applying pressure to my neck. I remembered his actions only intensified the pain.

"Out of nowhere, my deceased mother spoke to me." Shaking my head, "It was all a blur after that. My mother had taken my hand, and the sounds of the Roxbury night had been silenced. I couldn't believe what I saw when I opened my eyes."

"I was alive, yet I was no longer in Boston, no longer in 2016."

"Can you believe it? I'd been dropped into Wyoming of 1878."

Sitting across from me, I watched and waited for Emily's incredulous response. I could tell she was formulating what question to ask next, but I didn't give her a chance to speak.

"So you see, Doc, I died that night in 2016, and my mother gave me a choice. It was either give up and stay dead or begin life over."

"What I didn't understand then, and still don't today, is that my Ma told me she was giving me a gift to live again, just not with her and not in 2016. She claimed she could give me a second chance at life because of some Celtic gift."

Emily remained silent, allowing me to continue. "After Wyoming, I made my way to Montana and its copper fields. When I'd saved enough money, I came to Arizona and purchased the mine here in

Yuma. In a stroke of luck, I met Rebecca on my way back from a business meeting with potential investors in Chicago."

Emily finally asked, "Have you heard from your mother since?"

"No. After that night, I never heard from her again."

"Does anyone else know what you just told me?"

"No! Are you kidding?" Looking down at my calloused hands twisting on the tabletop, I added, "I didn't risk telling anyone for fear they would think I'm mad and want to send me to an asylum."

"Well, the only people who know about me are Caleb and my grandfather since he was the one who saved me when I died in Seattle in 2019. Does Rebecca know?"

"Good heavens, no. I'd lose her for sure with such a story."

"You're going to have to tell her at some point if your relationship goes any further."

"I know, Doc. That's the part that scares me. It will have to be at the right time.

"You'll find a way, Nate, if you truly love Rebecca."

I was sure this wasn't how Emily expected to spend her wedding night talking to a deranged man. But she stood, walked around the table, and began telling me her story.

"I was an Emergency Room physician in one of Seattle's top medical centers. One night, a young man with a gun was able to gain entrance to the ER waiting room. I was in the physician's control center when I heard screaming from the front entrance. I thought it was my job to protect our patients, so I made my way out into the chaos."

"Like you, long story short, the next thing I knew, the young man panicked and fired his gun when he glimpsed me coming up beside him." It happened so fast I don't think the man knew what he had done until a guard ended his life."

"I had made a rash decision, thinking I was infallible. Well, I soon found out I wasn't."

Emily rubbed her sternum when she added, pointing to her chest, "He shot me here. Though my team worked for hours to save my life, it was in vain. That's the first time I met my grandfather."

"Of course, he'd been dead for close to one hundred years. To tell you the truth, having an old man with a thick Irish brogue take your hand one minute, then leave you alone in a desolate desert the next, was more than frightening."

"Of course, I was angry at first. Having been dumped in the desert hills with literally nothing to my name and trying to save a man I'd never seen before without modern-day medicines and the tools of 2019 was frightening."

"I had no choice. I quickly learned to make do with what I had and draw on my medical training to accommodate me in the present. But that doesn't mean I didn't want to return to Seattle. After pleading with my grandfather, I realized it wasn't possible. So, I made a new life here and fell in love with Caleb."

"Well, I, for one, am thankful for your advanced skills as a physician and for saving Rebecca."

I felt the relief of having someone to tell my story to. It relieved, not so much a burden I'd carried for the past three years, but being able to share my story with someone who understood took some of the strain away.

"So, where do we go from here? Are you going to tell Caleb and your grandfather about me?"

"I think we can leave Caleb out of this for now. He's still trying to understand that I come from another place and time. But if you're willing, my grandfather may be of some help. We can ask him to tell us more about Celtic legends and gifts. What do you think?"

"That would be great. I'm at the point where I need to understand more about this gift and how I came to be in 1878."

Pausing, I added, "Emily, how I feel about Rebecca is evident to you and, with my luck, probably the whole town. We've only known each other a short time, but I've come to love her." I held up my hand to stave off her question. "I know, I know, she's a married woman, and it's not right, but I can't help myself. I've fallen in love with her, and I never meant to cause her harm. But she can't stay married to that madman!"

"Trust me, Nate, she won't. Caleb will do whatever it takes to obtain a divorce from Elliot. Besides, I'm almost certain after the judge hears from Rebecca, Pearl, and Caleb, not to mention half the town who witnessed his attempt at murdering her, Elliot will be put away for a very long time."

"I hope you're right about that. If not, I may have to take matters into my own hands."

"Nate, don't go doing anything stupid. Think of your future with Rebecca and the boys.

ᥱᦂ 58 ᥱᦂ

Nathaniel

STANDING ON A hill just outside of town filled with ancient Saguaro cactus, I gazed at the gathering of thick gray clouds hovering low over the western hills. It was a fitting day to start Elliot Ackerman's attempted murder trial.

Thankfully, Rebecca had survived, but I had constant reminders rattling around in my head of that dreadful day when I'd almost lost Rebecca. Thankfully, she survived and was recovering at the casita she shared with her boys while remaining under the watchful eye of both Pearl and Doc Emily.

Once she returned home from her stay at the clinic, I headed back to the ranch to distance myself from prying eyes and the whispering of the old-town biddies until her husband's trial was over.

It wouldn't bode well for her to be seen with me just yet, if ever again. I had already caused her enough hardship, and the last time we chatted while she was still in the clinic had been a strained conversation. She didn't blame me for Elliot's assumptions about her having an affair with me, but I could tell by our conversation that it remained in the back of her mind.

Each day I'd been away from her was torture. I couldn't help it. I wanted her in my life. Trying to keep my thoughts clear, I threw myself into my work for what little good it did me. I saw her face and enchanting smile wherever I looked.

Each morning, I was up before sunrise and rode out to check on my herd or up to the mine. My ranch hands and the miners kept their distance, knowing I was on edge with the upcoming trial. Returning to the ranch late in the morning, I was met by Enedina standing on the porch.

"Señor Nate, a message came for you while you were gone. That nice young boy from town, Joey, delivered it."

"Who's it from, Enedina?" I asked while dismounting from Silver Star.

"I did not read it, Señor. It is not my place," she answered, pulling the missive out of her apron pocket.

Taking it from her aging hand, I unfolded the paper as she continued to stand on the porch, looking down at me. I read and re-read the note to ensure I understood the request. It was a handwritten note from Rebecca asking me to come see her at the casita before the trial began later today.

Looking up into Enedina's chocolate brown eyes, my sneaky friend knew who it was from because of the way she smiled at me.

"You go see Mizz Rebecca. She's a good woman for you, Señor."

I had to remind her, "Enedina, Miss Rebecca is a married woman, and I've already caused her enough pain."

Shaking her head, she said, "You no cause her pain. How you say? Her malvado husband tried to kill her. You go to her and talk, Si."

"No. I don't think that's a good idea, Enedina," I replied, with one foot on the bottom stair.

"Mizz Rebecca is going to need a good man," she declared, pointing and shaking her arthritic finger at me.

"I still don't think it's a good idea. I can't cause her and her family any more grief."

Enedina gave me that mothering look she was so good at. It was one that would make you feel guilty and confess your sins, whether you were right or wrong.

I leaned in close and said, "Alright, I'll go speak with her. Does that make you happy?"

"Si Señor," she answered, smiling. "You go now," she replied with a shooing motion of her apron.

"Enedina, I'm hungry. I haven't eaten this morning. Can't I at least have breakfast?"

"You come inside, and I'll cook you breakfast. After that, you clean up and ride to Mizz Rebecca's. That nice man, her brother, Mr. Young, he take care of everything. He send her husband away for a long time. It all be okay for you and Mizz Rebecca."

Was it some Mexican folklore that told her so? I hoped she was right. I answered, not looking at Enedina's face, "Yes, everything be okay." I wasn't as sure as Enedina that all would be fine. But I could remain hopeful.

It was a ten-mile ride into town, and in hopes of remaining unseen, I kept to the back roads the closer I came to civilization. As I rode toward the casita, hoping to stay out of sight, I could tell from the noise coming down the alleyways that the town was filled with people buzzing about the beginning of the trial.

So many people crowded the streets that the church became a makeshift courtroom. Normally, the schoolhouse was used, but it was too small to hold those who wanted to attend. I only hoped the Lord didn't mind that His house had been taken over for such a grim task.

Tying Silver Star to the post in front of the casita, I pulled my hat down over my forehead to hide my face. It was futile to keep myself incognito since anyone who knew my horse would know it was me.

I feared Rebecca would tell me she was leaving Yuma and returning to New England. Feeling as if my string tie was strangling me, my hands shook as I nervously ran a finger around the inside of my collar, not knowing what to expect once I walked through the casita's door.

Moving down the gravel path, I nervously found myself standing at the red-painted door. My hand poised to knock, I took a deep breath, readying myself for the conversation ahead. Before I had the opportunity, Pearl opened the door.

"Good afternoon, Mrs. O'Callaghan." I exhaled and took off my hat, then ran my hand through my hair. By greeting me, she'd given me a few minutes of reprieve before having to speak with Rebecca.

"Good afternoon, Mr. Burns. Please, won't you come in? We've been expecting you."

"Thank you, Ma'am," I answered, following her through the door.

"I take it you received Mrs. Ackerman's note that she wished to speak with you?

"Yes, Ma'am. How is she doing?"

"She's doing fine. She's been waiting for your arrival." Extending her hand, she asked, "May I take your hat?"

Handing her my hat, she hung it on a hook in the hallway, then turned to add, "Rebecca is in the parlor with the boys. Why don't you go on in."

Pearl must have read my hesitation to go in on my own, so she led the way. Still having a pale pallor to her features, Rebecca looked more beautiful than ever. I didn't want to interrupt since she was deep in conversation with her sons. So, I paused at the entrance, watching the familial scene, wishing I was a part of it. It was evident in the boys' eyes how much they loved their mother.

Clearing my throat, "Good morning, Mrs. Ackerman. You asked to speak with me?"

Putting an arm around each boy, she asked of them, "Boys, why don't you go to the kitchen with Pearl so Mr. Burns and I can talk."

"Can't we stay?" whined Porter.

"Maybe another time," Rebecca replied, hugging each of them. "Now run along and find Pearl."

As the boys passed me in the doorway, each of them spoke. "Good morning, Mr. Burns."

"Good morning, boys. I won't keep your mother long."

Smiling, they started down the hallway when I called out, "Save me one of Pearl's biscuits."

"We will," they yelled back.

Nathaniel

MY FEET WERE frozen to the floor, and my brain wouldn't allow me to form the words I desperately wanted to say. Finally working up the courage, all I could ask was, "Mrs. Ackerman, how are you feeling?"

Looking up at me and smiling, I was drawn to the ethereal glow radiating around Rebecca as she answered. "I'm doing well, thank you. Pearl and Emily have been taking good care of me, and I'm almost back to my normal self."

"I'm glad to hear that." With my hands in my front pockets, I squirmed in place. I was more nervous than if I was going on a first date at sixteen.

With her right hand, Rebecca motioned me forward, "Please, come in and have a seat in the chair. I don't think we'll be interrupted, and we have important matters to discuss."

Hesitating, I slowly made my way to the chair across from her. Sitting on its edge, I remained poised, ready to flee if needed. "Mrs. Ackerman, I don't think it was a good idea for me to come here this morning. I don't want to cause you any more harm than I already have."

"Nonsense, Nathaniel. And please stop calling me Mrs. Ackerman. That's a name I'd rather no longer use. I'm a grown woman who can speak with anyone I choose. Let the wagging tongues of this town say what they want."

Sitting up straighter, she added, "And you didn't cause me any harm. It was all my husband's doing, and he will finally be punished for it. I only hope that I never have to see him again and my brother can handle the legal issues to provide me a divorce."

"That's kind of you to say, Mrs. Ackerman. I mean Rebecca. I'm sure Caleb will do all he can for you. But what is it you wished to speak to me about?"

"The trial is making me nervous enough, and what I'm about to say will only add to that. So, I'm requesting that you please refrain from asking any questions until I'm finished.

"I'll try," was all I could promise. All I could think of was she was about to banish me from ever seeing her again, and I didn't think I could take it.

"You may be called as a witness. And if the judge asks you about our relationship, you don't have to hold back any information or lie. Please, tell him the truth because I'm not afraid of Elliot anymore or what the townspeople may say about you and me. We did nothing wrong, and we each deserve to be happy."

Considering what she'd endured, her bravery didn't surprise me. It only made me love her more. "I won't lie, Rebecca. I have nothing to hide. It was an innocent dinner. I just want you and the boys to be happy and safe."

"Oh, we'll be safe, and I plan on making sure we are happy for the first time in our lives. With a pleading look, she added, "I'm so tired of dancing around the subject, so can we please stop with the formalities? You must know that I care a great deal for you, Nathaniel. And it goes well beyond friendship.

Wow! Talk about getting right to the point. Rebecca had changed since I last saw her in the clinic. I was proud of her, and I couldn't help but smile at the inner strength she'd found. I wanted to take her in my arms and tell her that nothing would ever come between us again and that I wanted her to be with me until my last day.

But the timing was off. We had to get through the trial first and then her divorce. I wish I had my hat so I could have something to do with my hands. They were sweating something fierce. I wiped them down my pant legs before responding. "Rebecca, I've had feelings for you since we met back on the train. But I knew then you were a married woman because you wore a wedding band."

Standing, I nervously paced back and forth in front of her before continuing. "I can't keep doing this. Unless you're divorced, I won't sully your name and that of your family any longer."

Her eyes showed a questioning look. "Whatever are you talking about, Nathaniel?"

Suddenly, I found myself sitting next to Rebecca on the settee and taking her hands in mine. Lowering my head, I couldn't look into her eyes when I added, "There are things about me that you would never believe. I'm not the man you think I am. I have a past."

Grasping my hands firmly, she responded, "We all have a past, Nathaniel. Some that we're proud of, others not so. It shouldn't make us care any less for each other. Maybe some things are better left in our past."

Lifting my head, I stared into the sparkling eyes I wanted to look at every day for the rest of my life. Acting on a crazy impulse and without consideration for who might be looking, I grasped Rebecca's shoulders and pulled her toward me for a kiss neither of us would ever forget.

Mercifully, she didn't pull away, and the kiss went on forever as if it were our last day on earth. Rebecca was bold in her response, and her passion was evident as she moved closer, and our bodies meld together in a heated bond. Both of us became lost in our hunger for each other, so we didn't hear Pearl clear her throat at the entrance to the parlor.

"Ahem. Ahem. Excuse me, but I hate to interrupt this lovely scene, but Rebecca, it's time to get ready."

Quickly pulling away from each other, I saw the smile on Pearl's face as she winked her approval. "Mrs. O'Callaghan, please, you have to understand how I feel about Rebecca. I mean her no further harm." Taking a deep breath, I finally felt free to declare, "I love her."

Arms crossed over her chest, and staring at me over her spectacles, I was ready to be taken apart by this spunky Irishwoman.

"Nathaniel Burns, stop saying you've caused Rebecca harm. You have no idea what she's endured at the hands of her revolting husband." Looking at Rebecca, Pearl added, "I'm sorry, dear if I spoke out of turn."

"Pearl, you should know by now that you can always speak freely around us. We have nothing to hide from each other. And I'm sure Nathaniel feels the same way.

"Of course I do," I answered.

"Nathaniel, you don't have to tell me how you feel. Every time your name is mentioned, Rebecca's eyes light up. And just looking at the two of you together just now, you obviously feel the same. It's written all over your faces, and I couldn't be happier for the two of you."

Rebecca smiled while I let out a breath I'd held since we stopped kissing. "Mrs. O'Callaghan, you scared the life out of me. I thought you were going to banish me from the casita and never be able to see Rebecca again."

"Nonsense, Nathaniel. But you understand this, young man, you both have to remain vigilant in not seeing or speaking to each other until the trial is over and Mr. Ackerman is put away. I don't want anything to mislead the judge's decision."

Pausing, she added, "And, if I ever find out you've broken Rebecca's heart or laid a hand on her or the boys, you will have the wrath of this Irish woman to deal with."

With her smile gone and a firm stance in the doorway, she added, "Do you understand what I'm saying."

"Yes, Ma'am." Rebecca and I replied in unison.

Standing, I bent to give Rebecca a light kiss on her cheek. "As hard as it will be, you won't see me until the trial ends. That doesn't mean I won't be in the courtroom or nearby. I just won't be visible to the judge. We won't speak, and we can't acknowledge each other."

Grasping my hand firmly, Rebecca expressed her understanding, "I'm glad you will be there to lend your silent support." Pulling me in closer for a parting kiss, she whispered in my ear, sending chills down my spine, "I love you, Nathaniel Burns. No matter what happens, never forget that."

For only Rebecca to hear, with my lips close to hers, I whispered, "I love you, Becca, more than you'll ever know." All I wanted to do at that moment was forget the trial, wrap her in my arms, and hold her close, never letting her go.

As excited as I was, I couldn't feel my feet touching the floor. I floated to the hallway, where Pearl was waiting to hand me my hat. Taking it without thought, I gently kissed her on the cheek and nodded my head in Rebecca's direction. "Pearl, take care of her for me. She's my life."

Placing her hand over my heart, Pearl responded, "I will. You're just what she and the boys need. A man who truly loves them."

I walked out the door, heart lighter, knowing Rebecca felt the same about me as I did her. And the most important woman in Rebecca's life, Pearl, approved.

⚈ 60 ⚈

Nathaniel

AFTER LEAVING THE casita, I had two hours until I had to be at the church when the trial would start. Although I rarely took a nip, today was the day I desperately needed a drink. But I didn't want to risk visiting Henry's Pick and Shovel saloon. If I were to be seen there, too many men would start asking questions. More importantly, I didn't want to take a chance at having liquor on my breath during the trial.

I needed solitude to clear my head and think things over about my future with Rebecca and the boys. The best place for me to do that was to ride back up to the nearby hills. The clouds still covered the sun, and thunder rattled the distant skies, indicating a rainstorm would soon besiege the valley, making my earlier assessment wrong. I only hoped it would hold off until the end of the day.

I tied Silver Star to a low-hanging branch of a mesquite tree and sat on a rock overlooking the town below. It was hard to comprehend how my life had changed from being a police officer in 2016 to a mine and ranch owner in 1891.

Snickering, I thought I'd been in love once, but what I had with Rebecca was more than an infatuation. We shared a passion for each other and her sons. Before she came into my life, I had accepted that I was going to spend my remaining days alone with only Enedina, my ranch hands, and ornery cattle as my family. But fate had put me on that train, bringing Rebecca and me together, and after today, I would let nothing keep us apart.

⚜

Rebecca

My side burned, and I still walked stiffly, so holding on to Caleb's arm made me feel secure in my steps. His closeness lent me a sense of confidence and safety as we slowly made our way into the courtroom.

My breath hitched at seeing the number of people filling the room, causing me to hesitate at the entrance. Emily, who stood behind us, placed a reassuring hand on my back and whispered close to my ear, "You're going to do just fine. Caleb and I are here for you. And so is Nate."

Eyes wide, I searched the room, looking for the one person who would silently help me make it through the day. I found him sitting alone at the back of the courtroom, trying to remain inconspicuous amongst the throngs of people.

I didn't blame him, but I desperately wanted him to sit next to me, to feel his gentle hand on my arm, and to have his courage seep deep into my soul. But we both knew that wouldn't bode well with the judge or the jurors.

The jurors, all men, made me feel uneasy. I wondered if any of them had beaten their wives and gotten away with it. It wasn't right. Women weren't allowed as jurors. Shaking my head in disgust, I questioned, yet knew the answer, what did any of these men know about abusive husbands from a woman's perspective? None of them!

As I walked by, the men looked at me as if they had already judged me guilty despite the fact that I was the one having been shot. If my fate was in their hands, I felt doomed. On the other hand, I might be able to set a precedent that wife-beating or attempted murder was against the law, as it should be.

Caleb urged me forward toward the table reserved for us. I shivered and pulled my shawl tighter over my shoulders. Across the aisle, Elliot sat with his hands shackled in front of him. A single heavy chain running through a large metal loop secured to the table and shackles on his ankles were all that kept him away from me.

A small balding man, dressed impeccably, whom I assumed was his lawyer, sat next to him. Elliot looked more disheveled than I'd ever seen him before. He'd lost weight, making his clothes hang from his once muscular frame. Good! I didn't feel one bit sorry for him. He deserved all the anguish and pain he was enduring.

I hoped he understood what he had put me and the boys through. But I had my doubts. "Are you ready?" my brother asked, patting my hand wrapped through his arm.

"Yes," I replied, smiling up at him. My insides quaked at what was about to take place, but I oozed false bravado and said, "Let's get this over with."

⁓⧉⁓

My mouth was as dry as the desert sand in the hills behind the makeshift courtroom. A sure sign of nerves, I kept licking my lips for moisture. Emily, realizing my need, handed me a glass of water.

She was the first witness called by Elliot's attorney to recount the events from her wedding day. I admired her calm demeanor during her questioning and hoped I could do the same when called to testify.

Emily was a savvy woman and wouldn't be tricked by Elliot's attorney, who had an annoying habit of rewording the same questions he'd previously asked. His tricks didn't work with Emily, and they wouldn't work with me! Remaining composed with her head held high, she persevered in her testimony.

My heart ached for ruining her and my brother's wedding. It was supposed to be one they would remember all their remaining days. Oh, they would remember it all right, but not for the reasons they should. Elliot would forever taint those memories.

Caleb and Elliot's attorney called and questioned witnesses from that fateful day. I had been hopeful this would all have been over in one day, but as luck would have it, it wasn't. When five o'clock came, the judge called for a recess until the following morning. I slept fitfully, if at all, that night.

⌒⨯⌒

It was time for my resolve to be tested. Today, I would recount my life with Elliot, his abuse, and the day he shot me.

With a sinister snare, Elliot's attorney faced me and called my name. Oh, how I wanted to give him a piece of my mind for even representing Elliot. He had no idea what I'd been through at the hands of his client. Well, he was about to find out.

Caleb assisted me to the witness stand and then returned to his seat. The judge swore me in, and Elliot's attorney began attempting to tear my reputation apart. Caleb had prepared me for such questions, and though I was filled with doubt and fear, I held firm to my answers.

"Mrs. Ackerman, please state your full name and where you now reside."

With my hands tightly clasped in my lap, I replied to Elliot's attorney, "My name is Rebecca Young Ackerman. I am residing in a casita behind Dr. Mathew Sweeney's medical clinic with my two sons and Mrs. Pearl O'Callaghan."

"I see. And where did you previously reside?"

You know darn well! "I resided in Boston with your client, Mr. Ackerman."

Elliot's attorney continued questioning me while slowly walking ever so annoyingly back and forth in front of the witness chair as if trying to make me more nervous. Unfortunately, it was working, but I wouldn't let it show. "

"If you please, Mrs. Ackerman, tell the courtroom how you came to stay in the casita."

"When I arrived in town, I went to Dr. Sweeney's clinic searching for my brother. He had been gravely injured not long before, and I wanted to know his condition."

"I see. So you just happened to arrive at Dr. Sweeney's doorstep without providing him any warning."

"Yes. We, I mean my two boys and friend, Mrs. Pearl O'Callaghan, had just arrived on the stage, and I wanted to see my brother straight away. It had been a long time since we'd seen each other."

"I see."

Why did he keep saying that? The man obviously couldn't see a fly if it landed on him.

"So, how did you know where your brother was staying?"

"Before leaving Boston, I received a telegram from Emily Sweeney telling me my brother had been gravely injured and asking me to come to Yuma as soon as possible. At the time, I didn't know she was a doctor."

"How did she know where you lived?"

"You will have to ask Dr. Emily Sweeney that question." I glanced at my brother as he nodded his approval of my answer.

Rebecca

"So, you just packed up and brought your boys and Mrs. O'Callaghan across two thousand miles without telling your husband?"

"That's correct." I became nauseous with my insides quivering. I knew where his line of questioning was heading. Thankfully, Caleb had prepared me for such, but it still didn't help.

"Don't you think that's a bit odd? I mean, not to tell your loving husband where you were going?"

"No!" Caleb had instructed me to answer Elliot's attorney's questions with minimal responses, although I knew what Elliot's attorney was digging for.

"No? Mrs. Ackerman wouldn't any dutiful wife tell her husband where she was going and ask his permission to travel such distance unaccompanied."

I ignored the part of asking permission and responded with, "I wasn't unaccompanied, Sir. Mrs. O'Callaghan was with us."

"Now, now, Mrs. Ackerman. Don't be so elusive. You understand my meaning."

"No Sir I don't. You'll need to be more specific with your question."

Loud boos from the men and women in the courtroom came out of nowhere. I couldn't determine if they were intended for me or Elliot's attorney. Bang! Unexpectedly, the loud rap of the Judge's gavel on his desk made me jump in my seat. For the first time today, I felt faint as intense heat traveled up my neck to the top of my head. I could only imagine how red my face was.

Rebecca, take a deep breath, dear. You're doing fine. Don't let this little weasel rile you.

I was relieved to hear my mother's welcoming words. I was becoming irritated with this little man, and it was just what he wanted. Taking a deep breath, I calmed myself to his onslaught of questions. I tried not to look Elliot's way, but it was hard not to. Each time I did, his lips curled in a sneer, and his devil eyes bore into my confidence.

When I left him in Boston, I had promised myself that I would never again let him intimidate me. And now wasn't the time to give in. So, I was ready to answer any questions his attorney asked.

"Mrs. Ackerman, what type of marriage did you and your husband have?"

"Whatever do you mean, Sir?"

"Let me rephrase my question so you can understand it better."

Why, you beady-eyed little man! You're the perfect attorney to represent Elliot, and I know what you want me to say.

"Did you love your husband?"

"At one time, I thought I did." I heard several intakes of breaths within the room. Just wait, I thought. Wait until I tell the court what kind of a husband Elliot really was. His questions continued.

"You thought you did? It sounds as if you no longer love your husband."

"That's correct, Sir." This time, I was the one to stare down Elliot. Being shackled to the table, he couldn't hurt me now. If he tried, any of the men in the courtroom who despised him, which there were several, would be glad to shoot him.

"Did he not provide a home for you and your sons? Clothe you? Provide nourishment? An allowance?"

"My dowry did all that, Sir."

"You mean to tell the court that your husband didn't support you? And need I remind you, you are under oath to tell the truth."

"At the beginning of our marriage, he supported us with an allowance. However, I used the supplement from my dowry to cover most of the household expenses. His earnings from the paper went to his out-of-home ventures."

"Do you have proof of this, Mrs. Ackerman?"

"What proof I have remains in Boston."

"So you have nothing to present to the court today to say that Mr. Ackerman did not, in fact, support you monetarily."

"No, Sir, I don't."

"Do you and Mr. Ackerman have children?"

"Yes, two boys."

"Are they here with you now?"

"No, they are being cared for back at the casita."

"Do you know what outside ventures your husband's money went to?"

"You will have to ask your client, Mr. Ackerman, that." After throwing his question back at him, the gnat of a man cleared his throat. I'd caught him off guard. He must have thought I was a helpless woman. Well, he was wrong. I was stronger than I looked.

Droning on and on, he continued, "Did you allow your husband his conjugal rights?"

My brother bolted out of his seat for the first time since the trial started and yelled, "Objection, your Honor! Mr. Finch is trying to demean my client's character."

At the same time Caleb objected, I looked out at the courtroom, seeing women shaking their heads behind handkerchiefs held over their mouths. I still couldn't tell if they were on my side or not.

Raising a hand before the Judge could reprimand him and disallow the question, Elliot's attorney replied sarcastically, "I withdraw my question, your Honor."

Despite the windows being open, the air within the courtroom had become stagnant, my side was hurting something fierce, and the nausea threatened to rise. I searched for Nate in the room, but he was no longer where he'd originally sat. My head was reeling. I wanted this all to be over so we could be together. *Lord, please help me get through this day.*

"Now, Mrs. Ackerman, your husband told me just yesterday that he still loves you and wants you and his sons to return home to Boston with him."

I wanted to laugh out loud at Beady-Eye's question but held back when someone, I couldn't tell who yelled from the back of the courtroom, "That's a lie!" It was a female voice I didn't recognize, but I was grateful for their supportive outburst.

Bang! The Judge slammed his gavel on the desk with authority. I didn't jump this time. After the first, I'd been ready for it. I didn't respond right off to Beady Eye since he hadn't asked a question; he'd only made an off-hand comment. But I couldn't help myself, so I finally replied, "Really, Mr. Finch? I find that hard to believe since Mr. Ackerman has a vile way of showing his love by shooting me!"

At my reply, the courtroom erupted in shouting that had my ears ringing.

Bang! The courtroom quieted, and I closed my eyes again, wondering if the yelling was a good sign in my favor or not. I could barely hear Mr. Finch when he said, "No further questions, your Honor."

⚜

"Mr. Young, would you care to question your client?" the Judge asked. Despite our relationship, I was thankful the Judge had allowed Caleb to represent me.

"Yes, your Honor," my brother replied. "But I have a witness I want to call to the stand before I question Mrs. Ackerman. But before I do, your Honor, I can see that my client is in great discomfort from being shot by her husband. So, if the court would allow, I would like to request a short break."

Beady-Eye stood and called out, "Allegedly shot, your Honor. And Mr. Young is stalling."

Bang! Went the Judge's gavel. At this point, I think the courtroom expected it every time Beady-Eye opened his mouth.

"Sit down, Mr. Finch," the Judge glared. Turning to my brother, he replied, "Request granted, Mr. Young. Mrs. Ackerman, you may step down."

Turning to the courtroom, the Judge announced a recess and for all to return promptly at one o'clock.

⁓⁓⁓

Caleb gave me a hand down from the witness box and quickly led me out the back door, closely followed by Emily. The courtroom had become so stuffy, and stepping outside with the fresh air on my face felt wonderful. In the short time I'd been here, I'd come to love the scent and sounds of the desert, and I took this time to enjoy them.

Pearl approached me, holding out a cup of water, and I savored its freshness. Taking my hands in hers, Pearl asked, "How are you holding up, dear?"

Squeezing her hands tightly, I replied, "I'm tired, and I want this to all be over with. But I'll get through it. How are our boys?"

"The boys are fine. Don't you worry about them? Clarice is taking good care of them." Turning to Caleb, Pearl asked, "Will you need to call the boys and me as witnesses?"

"I'm not sure, Pearl. I'm hoping to keep the boys out of this. But it may be necessary to do so," he answered, running a hand gently down Pearl's arm.

"I understand. We'll be in the casita if you need us."

"Thank you," Caleb replied.

"Pearl," I called out before she turned to leave. "Thank you for taking care of our boys." "Of course, my dear. I always will."

Once again, I searched the crowd outside the church, trying to locate Nathaniel, but he was still nowhere to be seen. In my heart, I felt he was near but wisely keeping himself hidden from prying eyes.

⤳ 62 ⤳

Rebecca

THE CHURCH BELL rang, indicating we needed to return to the courtroom. Once everyone was seated, the judge demanded silence and instructed Caleb to call his witness to the stand.

"Your Honor, I call Mr. Saratoga Coupeville to the stand."

I garnered Caleb's attention with a questioning look as he stood over me. For such an unusual first name, I had never heard Caleb mention this man before. With all the loud whispering behind me, I'm sure the onlookers were just as curious about what part this man played in the trial.

The front door to the church slowly opened, and in walked a man who appeared to be one of the town's less prominent citizens. Yet, he was clean-shaven with a few apparent nicks on his face, making me think this was his first shave in a long time.

His hair was slicked back with pomade, and he wore a wrinkled brown suit that looked to be two sizes too large for him. With his hat in his hand and head held high, he walked down the middle aisle as if proud to play a part in the trial.

Behind me, the whispers became louder as someone shouted, "Why, I almost didn't recognize him. That's Tipsy, the town drunk." I groaned inwardly at what my brother was thinking by calling the town drunk to the stand.

Bang! Bang! Slamming his gavel several times on his desk, the judge yelled out to the room, "Order! I'll have order in my courtroom, or I'll have you all thrown out!"

Before Caleb made his way toward the witness box, he made sure the whispering in the room had died down, after which Mr. Coupeville was sworn to tell the truth. Caleb began his questioning. Closing my eyes, I inclined my face heavenward and whispered a silent prayer, hoping my brother knew what he was doing.

"Sir, will you please tell the court your full name and where you reside."

"My name's Coupeville. Saratoga Thadeus Coupeville. But most people around here call me Tipsy. I live in the shack behind the stables."

"Thank you, Mr. Coupeville."

"You can call me Tipsy."

The courtroom broke out into laughter at the mention of his nickname. Bang! Once again, the judge was slamming his gavel, reminding everyone that he demanded silence. He'd done it often enough during the trial that the sound no longer had those in attendance flinch. But I had to wonder just how many gavels the man went through in a year.

"Thank you, Sir," Caleb said. "But for the purpose of this court, I will refer to you by your Christian name, Mr. Coupeville."

"That's fine with me," Tipsy replied, taking a brown-tattered handkerchief from his breast pocket and wiping his nose.

"Mr. Coupeville, please tell the court where you were during the day Miss Clarice Baptiste was shot in the Prickly Pear Saloon?"

"Objection, your Honor," Beady-Eye yelled out. "What does this line of questioning have to do with my client?"

Looking over the top of his glasses at my brother, the judge asked, "Mr. Young, I hope you have a good explanation for this line of questioning."

"I do, your Honor," Caleb answered. The judge allowed, leaned back in his squeaking chair, and said with a wave of his hand, "Then proceed."

Caleb instructed, "Please answer my question, Mr. Coupeville."

"I already forgot whatz you asked."

"That's fine. Mr. Coupevill. Please tell the court where you were during the day when Miss Clarice Baptiste was shot in the Prickly Pear Saloon."

"I was there in the saloon. But I never knew her name. She always kept to herself," he replied, looking out into the crowd as if he was trying to locate the woman in question. "Like I said, I was in the Prickly having my usual." Tipsy pointed to a woman in the center of the courtroom, grinning, "You can ask Millie or' there. She was sitting on my lap until the shooting started."

At the mention of Miss Millie's name, I turned to see the lady in question, lips red with rouge, dressed in a revealing low-cut satin dress, waving her gloved hand at Mr. Coupeville. All I could think, Caleb had lost his mind. But he was my brother.

"Mr. Coupeville, can you please tell the court what you saw before the shooting started."

"Sure enough. Millie was sitting on my lap. She was, ah, well, never mind. Anyways, this fancy pants man comes walking in as if he owned the place. I'd ne'er seen him before in the Prickly. Anyways, he walks right up to the bar, orders a drink, and grabs himself one of the girls.

He was none too gentle about it, either. But I wasn't giving my Millie up," he added, nodding his head matter of factly as if to make his point.

"Is that man in the courtroom today?" Caleb asked.

"Sure is. That's him or' there," Tipsy replied, pointing at Elliot.

"Thank you, Mr. Coupeville. Let the record show that Mr. Coupeville has identified the defendant, Mr. Elliot Ackerman. "Now, can you please tell the court where Ms. Baptiste was at the same time?"

"Who's Mizz Baptiste?"

I groaned, thinking this questioning was getting us nowhere.

"She is the lady who was shot in the saloon."

"Oh, I knowz who she is. She the one that was standing at the end of the bar, near the stairs to heaven," he answered, grinning.

✦

I wanted to slap that grin off Tipsy's face. Caleb better hurry up, or I would take matters into my own hands. Caleb was making me dizzy, walking back and forth, back and forth in front of the judge, while questioning Mr. Coupeville.

"Will you please tell the court what happened next?"

"Yea. All of a sudden, a fight broke out between some local cowhands. I stood up and pulled Millie to safety at the back wall. Bottles and chairs were flying through the air, and I had a good view to watch it all."

"Where was Mr. Ackerman during this time?"

"I sawz him grab his girls' hand and head fer the stairs. Just as he did, a cowhand grabbed him on the shoulder. I'd ne'er seen him before either. Anyway, that man or' there turned and came up with his pistol."

"Which man was that Mr. Coupeville?" my brother asked for clarification.

Pointing to Elliot, he said, "That man there. I su'pected he was going to shoot the man when the cowhand swung a punch. That's when Mr. Ackerman's gun hand flew to his right and fired."

"Then what happened."

"My Millie screamed and pointed to the black woman, I mean Mizz Baptiste. Her white dress was covered in blood. Then I sawz her drop to the floor."

"How many gunshots did you hear?"

"Only one, I think." Tipsy yelled into the courtroom, "Ain't that right, Millie dear? Seems right strange though, with all the commotion going on. I guess them cowhands was having more fun using their fists than their guns."

63

Rebecca

I TURNED JUST in time to see Millie nod her head in agreement with Mr. Coupeville as a woman I'd never seen before patted Millie's shoulder from behind. Caleb then continued his questioning.

"Mr. Coupeville, did you see who fired that shot?"

Without hesitation, Tipsy pointed his finger at Elliot, replying, "It was that man or' there."

Elliot's face turned beet red, and his fists strained to free himself from his binding chains. For Mr. Coupeville's sake, I hoped Elliot was put behind bars for life.

"Mr. Coupeville, please tell us what happened next."

"That there man pulled his girl up the stairs, not once looking back to see if Mizz Baptiste needed help. I don't think he cared if she lived or died." Looking directly at Elliot, he added, "A person's gotta have a cold heart to do that."

"Did you and Millie try to help Miss Baptiste?"

"We tried, but by the time we were across the room without getting hit, she was gone."

Behind me, I heard a woman yell out. "It wazz me he shot!"

"Ma'am, I'll have you sit down," the judge called out. "There'll be no outbursts in my courtroom."

When I turned around, Clarice stood surprisingly in the open doorway, pointing to her shoulder. I smiled and mouthed, "Thank you," for her courage in coming here today. Catching my eye and holding her head high, she nodded.

Leaning back over my shoulder, I asked Emily who was watching the boys since Clarice was supposed to be at the casita with them. She reassured me that Mrs. Mueller, a former patient of hers, was caring for them. I knew Emily wouldn't leave the boys in just anyone's care. Satisfied, I relaxed back in my seat.

Despite the judge's warning, Clarice continued to speak. "Yer Honor, Doc Emily, and Mizz Rebecca took good cares of me, or I woulda died. Mizz Rebecca iz good people."

"Thank you, Ma'am. Now, please sit down," the judge asked calmly.

Clarice looked around the courtroom for a place to sit, but no one made a move to accommodate her. Amidst loud whispers and intakes of shocked breaths, Emily, bless her heart, stood up and motioned for Clarice to join her at the front of the courtroom, after which Caleb continued his questioning.

"Mr. Coupeville, did you stay at the bar the rest of the night?"

"I shurz did. Millie and I waz just doin some courtin' that night."

"Were you upstairs with Miss Millie all night?"

"Nah, Millie stayed right by my side while I'z played poker with the boys."

"So you never left the bar or saw Mr. Ackerman leave his room that night?"

"No, siree. I shurz didn't. He was upstairs being entertained."

"Thank you, Mr. Coupeville. I have no further questions, Your Honor."

The judge leaned over to Mr. Coupeville. I couldn't hear what either of them was saying when Tipsy burst out, "I don't lie, Sir. My Momma, may she rest in peace, would whoop my behind 'ifin I lied."

"Good," replied the judge. "Mr. Finch, do you wish to cross-examine the witness?"

"Yes, your Honor, I would," Finch replied as he approached Tipsy.

"Mr. Coupeville, would you say you spend a fair amount of time in the Prickly Pear Saloon?"

"If'n I know what yer mean'n, I'd say, yez, every day."

"About how much time would you say you spend there?"

"Well, I don't rightly know. I don't time myself," he answered, garnering chuckles from the courtroom. All the judge had to do was raise his gavel, and the room quieted.

"Do you drink, Mr. Coupeville?"

"Course I do! Any red-blooded cowpoke does," he replied, snorting.

I had an inkling where Mr. Finch's questioning was going. He was trying to discredit Mr. Coupeville as a witness based on his drinking habits.

"Can you tell the court how much you drink?"

"I don't count."

"Well, Mr. Coupeville, can you say you have one drink, two drinks, or possibly three each time you are there."

My brother quickly stood and pointed to Beady Eye. "Objection, your Honor. Mr. Finch is trying to discredit the witness."

"Overruled. I will allow the questioning to continue," the judge replied. Mr. Coupeville looked to my brother for answers, but there was nothing Caleb could do to help him out.

"Please answer my question, Mr. Coupeville." It was Finch's turn to pace before the judge and witness. At this point, my nerves were frazzled.

"Fine, Mr. Coupeville, if you can't remember how many drinks you have in an evening, how can you remember what happened to Miss Baptiste that night in the Prickly Pear?" Finch swiftly raised his hand to stop Mr. Coupeville from answering, then added, "You don't need to answer that, Sir."

He may not have wanted Mr. Coupeville to answer, but he'd placed the idea into the jury's minds—very clever of Beady-Eye.

"Tell me, Mr. Coupeville, have you ever been drunk?" Turning to face the court, he added, "If you can't answer that question, I can always ask any member of the courtroom here today. I'm sure someone would be happy to bear witness to your drinking habits."

"Yez, I'z been drunk." Without hesitation, Mr. Coupeville turned to the judge, adding, "Your Honor, that night I was as sober as an ole' muley cow! I'd had me two drinks before the ruckus started, but I swear on my dearly departed mother's grave I was stone-cold sober that night, as I am today."

"Thank you, Mr. Coupeville," the judge replied, "Just answer Mr. Finch's questions."

"I have no further questions for Mr. Coupeville, your Honor."

"Mr. Coupeville, you may step down," the judge directed. Mr. Coupeville nodded as he walked past Caleb and me. Grateful, I attempted a smile of thanks, but it didn't seem enough.

Rebecca

I WASN'T READY to take the stand again, but at least this time, Caleb would be the one questioning me.

The judge pronounced from behind his desk, "Mrs. Ackerman, may I remind you that you are still under oath of the court,"

"Yes, your Honor," I replied before sitting on the hard chair. Then, my brother started with his questioning.

"Mrs. Ackerman, when did you first meet your husband?"

"It would have been in the Spring of 1871."

"Can you tell the court how you met?"

"My father arranged it. We met at a party my parents held at our home."

"How old were you at the time?"

"I had just turned eighteen."

"And, how old was Mr. Ackerman?"

"Objection, your Honor! What does Mr. Ackerman's age have to do with any of this?" yelled Beady-Eye.

"Sit down, Mr. Finch. I will allow the question," the judge replied. Frustrated, Elliot's attorney huffed as he sat down.

"Go on, Mr. Young," the judge urged.

"Thank you, your Honor," Caleb replied, then turned to me. "Can you tell the court how old Mr. Ackerman was?"

"He was thirty-three."

"Was your mother alive at the time?"

"Yes, sir, she was."

"When did Mr. Ackerman begin courting you?"

"My father arranged our first meeting shortly after introducing us. I'd say it was within a week."

"Just a week? How many meetings did you have with Mr. Ackerman before you married?"

"I believe it was two, possibly three."

"Before Mr. Ackerman proposed?"

"Objection, counsel is leading the witness."

"Sit down, Mr. Finch. You're beginning to get on my nerves," the judge said.

"But, your Honor," whined Mr. Finch.

"No buts. Sit down," pointing his finger at Beady-Eye.

"Mrs. Ackerman, you may answer Mr. Young's question."

"Yes, sir." Regaining my trend of thought, I proceeded, "My marriage was an arrangement between my father and Mr. Ackerman. At the time, I knew many girls my age whose parents had arranged the same type of marriage, and my father told me it would benefit his business and our standing in Boston society. As a barely eighteen-year-old girl, who was I to argue with my father."

"Did you ever have the opportunity to be courted by other men your age?"

"Oh, no, sir. Father turned away any boy who asked to court me. He told me I needed to marry into wealth."

"I see. Where you ever in love with Mr. Ackerman?"

"Being so young at the time, I thought I was. But actually, I believe I was caught up in the fantasy of being in love and having a household with children of my own. At the beginning of our marriage, I believed Mr. Ackerman when he promised to love me and keep me happy."

I was anxious for Caleb to get to the point of his questioning. The questions where I could reveal what a monster Elliot really was.

"So, Mrs. Ackerman, when did your marriage change?" Caleb sent me a gentle smile of encouragement. He made me feel confident I could answer his question truthfully.

"It was about a year ago," I paused, unsure how to proceed.

"Go on. Please tell the court what transpired since then."

"At first, Mr. Ackerman started staying out late one or two times a week, telling me he had business to attend to. Of course, he never discussed business with me, always telling me it wasn't my concern as a woman.

"Initially, I didn't pay much attention to it because I was caring for our sons. But then he began staying out nightly and even on Saturdays and Sundays."

"That's a lie," Elliot burst out, standing up as much as his binding chains allowed.

Bang! The judge slammed his gavel several times on his desk and yelled at Mr. Finch. "Mr. Finch, you will contain your client."

Mr. Finch stood and placed a hand on Elliot's shoulder, pulling him down, which he immediately shrugged off while plopping back into his chair. The look he gave me was pure evil. I expected flames to shoot directly at me.

Once calm was restored, Caleb continued to question me. "Did Mr. Ackerman tell you what he was doing when he stayed out late?"

"Oh no. I only asked once, and he yelled at me so that he frightened our boys and the household staff. I didn't ask again after that."

"Did he strike you that time?"

"No, not that time."

"But were you afraid he would strike you?"

"Yes. I was. Especially the nights he came home smelling of liquor."

"Did Mr. Ackerman drink while he was at home?"

"Occasionally."

"What do you mean when you say 'occasionally'?

"Before he changed, he would come home from work and have one or two drinks before dinner and a glass or two of wine with our meal."

"Thank you, Mrs. Ackerman."

Clutching a pencil in his hand, Caleb began to pace in front of me without saying a word. I could see the muscles in his face tighten, and his lips form a straight line when I nodded my understanding for him to proceed.

"Mrs. Ackerman, I apologize beforehand since my next few questions may be difficult for you to relive the recent events."

"Please, if you will, describe to the court the events of the night before you, your boys, and Pearl left Boston."

It was my time to be strong and describe in detail the information needed to put Elliot away for life. I looked around the courtroom for Nathaniel but couldn't locate him in the crowded room. So, clearing my throat, I began to relate to the court that horrible night.

It all seemed so long ago, but I relayed the events of when Elliot arrived home to when Pearl, the boys, and I boarded the train. I left nothing out except the part about meeting Nate. I couldn't get him involved unless asked by the court.

⌒⚭⌒

"I was sitting in front of the fireplace, in the parlor, alone as I had been each evening for the past month. The hall clock had just chimed midnight when the front door crashed open. I heard glass shatter across the entryway when Elliot yelled for me. Arriving in the vestibule, he was standing unsteady and disheveled, leaning with his palms on the foyer table."

I paused, gathering my thoughts before continuing. Looking at Caleb and then the judge, he instructed, "Go on, Mrs. Ackerman. Please tell the court what happened next."

Holding my head high, I resumed my testimony. "Elliot told me I was his to do with as he wished. That it was his husbandly right, then, he called me a harlot." Lowering my head, I held back the tears that threatened to fall. I wouldn't show Elliot any weakness.

"I stood on the opposite side of the table and told him he was drunk and needed to go upstairs to sleep it off. Before I knew it, he heaved his briefcase at the vase on the table, sending it shattering to the floor. When I tried grabbing it before it fell, Elliot violently slapped me across the face, not once but twice."

Holding my hands out palms up, I said, "I fell to the floor, cutting my hands on the glass shards from the vase. But when I tried escaping up the stairs to my room, he grabbed the hem of my gown, trying to pull me back. Mercifully, I was able to pull free, run to my room, and lock the door. I then dragged my dresser in front of the door and listened to his screams and pounding in his attempt to gain entry."

I took another deep breath before I continued. "He gave up either from fatigue or his drunken stupor."

Beady-Eye jumped up, yelling, "Speculation, your Honor. My client denies being drunk that evening."

"Oh, sit down, man. I've had enough of your interruptions," the judge snapped. "Please continue with your questioning, Mr. Young."

"Mrs. Ackerman, what happened after you locked yourself in your room?"

"I looked for a way to escape, but my room was on the second floor. Climbing out the window wasn't an option unless I wanted to die in the fall. And I knew I couldn't leave my boys to his fury. Then, I must have dozed off because the next thing I knew, Mrs. O'Callaghan was knocking on my door."

"It took days for the bruising on my face to disappear and the body pain to ease."

"Thank you, Mrs. Ackerman." Turning to the judge, Caleb added, "Your Honor, I have no further questions for Mrs. Ackerman."

There, I'd done it. I was exhausted, but I truthfully told the court and judge about the evil Elliot had inflicted upon me in Boston. It was late afternoon, and I thought this should be all over. But it wasn't.

"I have a few more questions for Mrs. Ackerman, your Honor," Mr. Finch boldly requested. "Denied," the judge curtly answered.

❦ 65 ❧

Rebecca

LOOKING BETWEEN CALEB and Mr. Finch, the judge asked, "Do either of you have any other witnesses to call?" I didn't understand why Finch wasn't putting Elliot on the stand. I surmised, which is always dangerous to do that he was afraid his client would go off on a rampage and harm his case more than he already had.

Caleb was the first to speak. "I do, your Honor. I call Doctor Emily Young to the stand."

Keeping a straight face, my brother asked his new wife, "Doctor Young, can you tell the court what happened on the day of your wedding when Mr. Ackerman entered the church?"

"Yes. You, I, Nathanial Burns, and Rebecca Ackerman were all standing in front of the altar. Just about here," she added, pointing to a fading blood stain that remained on the hardwood floor. "We had just been pronounced man and wife when shots were heard outside the church's doors. I think we all thought it was revelers celebrating.

298

The next thing we knew, Mr. Ackerman came in brandishing a gun."

"Dr. Young, at the time, were you acquainted with Mr. Ackerman?"

"No. Absolutely not. I'd never met the man before."

"Please continue, Doctor," Caleb encouraged his wife without emotion.

"At the request of the Pastor, the men's guns had been secured in the back room of the church before the ceremony began, leaving us defenseless to Mr. Ackerman's attack. So we had no way to protect ourselves."

"I see. Then what happened?"

"Mr. Ackerman made his way down the aisle, all the while pointing his gun directly at his wife, Rebecca Ackerman. The scary part was Porter and Daniel, their sons, were witnesses to their father's actions. It was horrible! They saw their father shoot their mother."

Gasps filled the courtroom. I'm sure the judge heard them as well. Good. Now he'll understand the heartless man Elliot really is. I don't know if Caleb recognized his wife's struggle to catch her breath, but she needed to slow her breathing down, or she would start hyperventilating. I understood how she felt when she glanced my way, and I tried giving her a hint by placing my hand over my chest as an incentive and taking in several slow, deep breaths.

"Go on, Doctor."

"I remember you asking Mr. Ackerman what he wanted as you moved toward your sister. But I stopped you."

Caleb asked, "Why did you stop me?"

I silently prayed, *Do not cry, Emily.* Now's not the time.

With her head bowed, Emily replied to Caleb's question. I'm sure she didn't want the spectators to see the tears forming in her eyes, but she bravely continued, "I didn't want you killed and make me a widow on our wedding day."

"Was Mr. Ackerman drunk when he entered the church?"

"He was definitely unsteady on his feet and slurring his words, so yes, I believe he was under the influence of too much liquor."

"Doctor Young, can you explain to the courtroom what you mean by 'under the influence?'"

"Yes, it means Mr. Ackerman was suffering impairment, to the degree, of his ability to safely perform any activity in question as a result of the use of alcohol."

I pulled my chin back, squinted my eyes, and tilted my head to the side as I looked at Emily. She must have seen the confused look on my face and that of the judge and jurors when she quickly added, "In other words, Mr. Ackerman had drunk too much liquor and wasn't able to control his actions."

"Thank you, Doctor Young, for your clarification."

⚬ঞৎ⚬

Emily

An unknown male voice yelled from the back, "What does a woman know about drinking!"

I wanted to laugh. This man obviously had not heard about my foray into drunkenness at the Pick and Shovel saloon last year.

"I will not have those kind of outbursts in my courtroom. The judge called out, "Mr. Reynolds, remove that man now."

I was impressed with the judge's action, and I had to give him credit for that. This world differed from 2019, when judges were too lenient with disobedience in the courtroom.

After the momentary outburst, I continued, "Mr. Ackerman said he wanted to take what was his back to Boston, meaning his wife and sons. He started yelling and calling his wife and Mr. Burns lovers while verbally degrading her.

You and Mr. Burns tried encouraging him to put down his gun. And before Henry Calhoun, with the help of the sheriff, could wrestle him to the ground, he'd shot his wife."

"Can you tell the courtroom what happened after that?"

Why does Caleb want me to keep going over this? I knew, but I was just frustrated and wanted this nightmare to be over, and Elliot remanded to prison for the rest of his life. Forgive me, Lord; life in prison was too good for him. We all want to see him hang for what he did to Rebecca.

"Once Mr. Ackerman was restrained, all of us at the altar rendered aid to Rebecca and took her to the clinic where Dr. Mathew Sweeney met us.

"Can you tell us where on her body was Mrs. Ackerman shot?"

"She was shot in the abdomen and lost a considerable amount of blood. She is fortunate to be alive and sitting in the courtroom today."

"Thank you, Doctor Young. I have no further questions, Your Honor."

"Mr. Finch, do you wish to question the witness."

During my testimony, Beady-Eye had been in a heated conversation with Elliot. What they spoke about was anyone's guess. But we would soon find out.

"Mr. Finch, I will ask you one more time. Do you wish to question the witness?"

"No, Your Honor."

Mr. Finch's response was suicide for Elliot. He probably knew there was nothing further he could do in his client's defense. From the witness chair, I watched the stunned looks on Caleb and Rebecca's faces. All I wanted to do was rejoice. Could this really be coming to an end?

The judge instructed, "Doctor Young, you may step down."

"Yes, your Honor." I made my way to my seat behind Caleb and Rebecca without saying a word to either of them.

ᥱ 66 ᥲ

Rebecca

BANG! CATCHING EVERYONE off guard, the judge slammed his gavel on the desk and announced, "I've heard enough."

Silence fell over the makeshift courtroom as we sat stone-still waiting for the judge's declaration. Looking toward Caleb, I hoped he could make sense of the judge's behavior, but all he did was shake his head, seeming to be just as confused as I was.

Emily leaned over the railing, tapping Caleb on his shoulder, and whispered in his ear, "What just happened?"

"I don't know, but I'm going to find out. Stay here with Rebecca."

"Your Honor, may I approach the bench," Caleb asked.

"Yes. Both you and Mr. Finch come with me," he demanded. Before he stood to leave, the judge spoke to the courtroom, "Court is in recess until after lunch."

"Hey! What about me!" Elliot yelled while pulling on his chains.

"You, sir, will be taken back to jail by Agent Reynolds."

Emily came around to sit beside me in Caleb's vacant chair as we waited for the room to clear. I didn't want to face any questions from

302

those in attendance. So we waited. And after a few minutes, Emily suggested, "Let's go out the back door." Taking my hand, she led me toward the back of the courtroom.

Thankfully, Anders Johannson was standing there with the door open. "Come on, ladies, let's get ya back te the clinic."

I was grateful for his presence since one look from him was all that would be needed to thwart onlookers from heading us off. I knew Elliot was going back to jail because Ben Reynolds, the Pinkerton Agent, had handcuffed Elliot before I left the room. I didn't bother to acknowledge my husband. As far as I was concerned, he no longer existed.

Once inside the clinic, I was greeted by my boys and Pearl. Exhausted, I sat on the parlor couch and gathered Porter and Daniel into my arms. They were safe, which was more important than what was happening with Caleb, Beady Eye, and the judge.

⌒⌒⌒

Nathaniel

My nerves were on edge as I wiped the sweat dripping down the sides of my face with the back of my hand. I wanted to be with Rebecca but knew I couldn't, so I merged toward the exit with the rest of the crowd leaving the courtroom. The best I could do was send Rebecca silent messages that I was proud of her and loved her no matter what the judge decided.

⌒⌒⌒

Caleb

Mr. Finch and I stood before the judge in what must have been the Pastor's antechamber. The religious relics that had been carefully stored on the room's wooden shelves during the trial seemed out of place as we stood there in semi-darkness.

The judge was a good head shorter than me and stood eye to eye with Finch. His bulging waistline reminded me of my father, a man who never missed a meal. His bushy eyebrows rose irritably every time he used his authoritarian voice. He didn't scare me. I was concerned about my sister's future and wanted to see her husband sent to Hell.

"Sir, may I ask what is going on?"

"No, you may not, Mr. Young! My decision is final. Having you both here is only a courtesy meeting."

Mr. Finch and I looked at each other and then back at the judge.

"Sir, I must say that this is highly unusual. I'm sure Mr. Finch is just as confused as I am."

In what could only be described as a mocking manner, the judge replied, "Well, let me enlighten you both. I just pronounced that my decision is final. And there is no room for discussion."

"Then why bring us here," Finch asked.

The judge ignored his question. He occupied the only chair in the windowless room, leaving Finch and me to stand staring down at him. Clearing his throat, the judge looked over at Elliot's attorney and said, "Mr. Finch, I understand you were assigned Mr. Ackerman as a client. If not, I'd say you had chosen unwisely."

Leaning back in the chair and tenting his fingers under his chin, he said, "You both may be surprised to learn that I've done my own investigating regarding this case and have telegrams from Mr. Ackerman's business and social associates along with Boston's legal authorities."

"I was not surprised to find that Mr. Ackerman is not the upstanding man you may believe him to be. He has been involved in some unscrupulous business dealings and hurt many people in Boston. I also found out, not surprisingly, that the legal authorities there have had him under investigation for several months."

I snorted as Finch repeatedly adjusted his tie and rubbed the back of his neck before he spoke. "Sir, I request to see the telegrams you received. My client's life is on the line."

The judge bellowed, "Your client should have thought of his life before he attempted to murder his wife. This court was to learn if Mr. Ackerman, indeed, meant to cause his wife harm, and I have my answer."

"As I said, I have all the information I need to declare my verdict. My judgment is final and will be announced to the court this afternoon. Until then, I think you both should review the events of this case."

With that, the judge stood, adjusted his pants over his rotund waist, and exited the room through the back door. Finch started to argue that the judge could not cut him off from further questioning and that he would send a telegram to the governor.

I reminded Finch that he had been given the opportunity to cross-examine Doctor Young or put his client on the stand, but he'd declined. I wouldn't fall for Finch's tactics. Turning away from him, I, too, walked out the back door.

Instead of going to the clinic, I returned to my office to review my legal resources to see if I had missed anything critical with the case. I couldn't let Elliot go free and hoped the judge felt the same.

67

Caleb

AGENT REYNOLDS CALLED out, "Court is back in session."

Elliot was once again handcuffed to the thick iron ring bolted into the center of the table with Mr. Finch on one side of him and the agent on the other.

Rebecca and I sat in our usual seats. Holding her hand, we both waited for the Judge to pronounce his final decision. My stomach was in knots since I had no idea what he was about to declare, but I couldn't fathom that his verdict would be in Elliot's favor.

The Judge commanded, looking at each individual, "Mr. Ackerman, Mr. Finch, please stand. You too Mrs. Ackerman and Mr. Young.

Elliot wasn't able to stand up straight with his hands shackled to the table, but that didn't seem to make much difference. From his position, he stared at me, and I felt as though I was looking into the soul of the devil. If the devil even had a soul. I'd seen those eyes before when I stared down the cheating gambler at the Pick and Shovel Saloon last year. Those were memories I'd just as soon forget.

306

Shifting in his chair, the Judge stated, "The court will hear my decision in this case."

"Your Honor," Mr. Finch called out, shuffling papers on his desk. "This is most unusual. I must demand that we wait for an answer from the Territorial Governor or, at the very least, the jury. I sent the governor a telegram this morning, telling him of your most unorthodox behavior in this case."

OK, I'm no judge, but I think Finch just dug his hole to China a bit deeper with his demands. With eyes that were cold and hard, the Judge responded, "Mr. Finch, do you think it wise to bother the Governor with this small-town trial?"

I could tell by the Judge's ruddy complexion he was becoming more annoyed each time Beady-Eye opened his mouth. Far be it from me to interject. I'll just let Finch keep digging that hole if that would help put Elliot away.

"Mr. Finch, I can hold you in contempt if you keep pushing me. And I'm sure you know there is nothing I would like better to do."

"Your Honor," Finch called out, pointing to Elliot. "You must appreciate the fact that my client's life is at stake. You can't go making rash decisions without the jury's opinion."

Oh boy! Finch just put the final nail in Elliot's coffin. I would enjoy watching the Judge and Beady-Eye banter if this weren't my sister's trial. In a refined yet sarcastic tone, the Judge replied,

"As you so heartily spoke earlier about your client's life, need I remind you that I don't need to hear it again. I do believe, Mr. Finch, this is my courtroom, and I alone can disperse a verdict if I see fit. As such, I have dismissed the jury from making the final decision for Mr. Ackerman. And since your client was the sole purpose of this trial, I have all the evidence I need to proceed. I am sure we all, including yourself, would like to go home to our families."

Turning his direction my way, the Judge asked, "Mr. Young, perhaps you have something to add to this conversation?" Caught off guard and engrossed in the Judge and Mr. Finch's conversation, I stammered to answer, "No Sir, your Honor." I knew better than to get on this man's disagreeable side. I would doubtless need his services in granting Rebecca a divorce when all this was over.

"A wise choice, Mr. Young. A very wise choice!" the Judge replied. Looking out over the courtroom, the Judge reminded everyone this was a court of law, and they were to remain in their seats during his verdict.

"I want to thank the jurors for their time. You are all dismissed," the Judge announced. Facing Elliot, the Judge became somber. "Mr. Ackerman, despite your declared standing in Boston's society, I'm not the least bit impressed. All the money you profess to have, which I understand little is left, cannot change the outcome of my verdict. You can't buy your way out of this one."

I watched Elliot's reaction to the Judge's comments. Being a man with a cold heart, he stared at the Judge as if willing him to drop dead on the spot. My shoulders tensed in anticipation of what the Judge was about to declare, praying it would go in my sister's favor.

I believe the Judge had a bit of showman in him and enjoyed his position by putting everyone on edge. Pausing, he looked out over his courtroom. A courtroom that waited in silence for him to speak. "I find the facts presented over the past few days undeniable. You, Mr. Ackerman, are a wife-beater, adulterer, and attempted murderer. None of which should be allowed to roam the face of this earth freely. The authorities in Boston may want to take up the opportunity to try you over their findings of your illegal business dealings. But, here you are in my court, and I get to lay down your sentence.

As a Judge of the Arizona Territory, I, therefore, find you guilty of the crimes presented and sentence you to the Yuma Territorial Prison for the remainder of your days."

"Why, you son of a . . . "Elliot screamed while pulling up his hands and rattling the chains confining him in place. "You'll wish you'd never met me."

"Are you threatening me, Mr. Ackerman?" the Judge asked, pointing his gavel at Elliot. "If I could add more years to your sentence,

I would. But you, Sir, unlike a cat with nine lives, are the unlucky recipient of having only one life. The sentence stands.

Bang! "Life in prison."

Bang! Agent Reynolds, take Mr. Ackerman back to the jail while he awaits transport to prison."

Elliot screamed a litany of obscenities at the Judge as Agent Reynolds unlocked his chains. "You won't get away with this. I'll make sure your life is a living Hell!"

"Get him out of my sight." With one final slam of his gavel, the Judge roared, "Court is dismissed."

Rebecca fell into my arms as a free woman. Elliot would never again cause her or the boys harm.

"Caleb, please take me home."

᭗ 68 ᭜

Nathaniel

I REMAINED TUCKED in a far corner of the courtroom, away from curious eyes, until the judge rendered his verdict. As far as I was concerned, sending Elliot to prison for the remainder of his life was not enough. Heaven forgive me, but I wanted to see that man hanging from the gallows so he could never hurt Rebecca or the boys again.

I took this time to slip out the side door into the fresh air and began walking. In a daze, I couldn't tell you where I was headed. All I thought about was Rebecca was now free from that madman. But to my misfortune, she remained a married woman.

I loved her, and I always would, no matter what happened next. All sorts of scenarios played out in my head. Could Caleb get her a divorce? Would she ever be free to marry again? Would she even want to? I was driving myself crazy when I realized I was standing in front of the clinic's white picket fence.

I couldn't tell you how long I stood there frozen in place when I heard the clinic door open, and Dr. Sweeney came out onto the porch with his black bag in hand.

He stopped when he saw me. "Well, son, are ye going to keep standing there, or are ye going to come in?"

"I don't know, Sir," I replied perplexingly.

"Well, make up yer mind. I haven't got all day. I have te go visit the widow Ainsley. She's been a bit under the weather of late."

"Yes, Sir. I guess I'll come in," I answered, making my way through the gate.

"Good. Go on in. Rebecca, Emily, and Caleb should return from te court shortly. I hear it was good news."

"Yes, Sir, it was." I stood at the bottom of the stairs, looking up at the Doc, "Do you think it's a good idea that I'm seen with Rebecca?"

Giving me a quizzical look, he asked, "Why not? You didn't shoot her. Did you?"

"Of course not," I yelled. "I would never do anything to hurt Rebecca."

"Listen, son. You strike me as a good man. A man who cares a great deal for Rebecca and her boys. Am I correct?"

"Yes, Sir," I answered, lowering my head.

"In tat case, there is nothing wrong with you two being seen together. Let Caleb worry about what te do next in making her free from her marriage vows. In the meantime, be a proper gentleman and see to it that she and te boys are happy. Now, go inside and have a chat with that remarkable lady. I'm sure she'll be glad te see ye."

I wasn't so sure about that.

Surprised, Pearl greeted me at the clinic's door, then called over my shoulder to Doc as he made his way to the gate, "Mathew, try to make it back in time for dinner."

Doc didn't answer but raised his hand and waved it above his head in reply. Have I missed something here? When did Pearl start calling Doc, Mathew?

"Nate. How nice it is to see you. Did you just come from the court-room?"

Taking off my hat, I answered, "Yes. I left out the side door once the judge rendered his verdict. I didn't want Rebecca to see me there."

Pearl took hold of my arm, bringing me into the parlor before asking, "Why ever not? She's been enquiring about you ever since the trial began. She must have seen you there at some point."

"I didn't think it was wise for her and me to be seen together during the trial. I didn't want to give the wrong impression to the judge."

Nodding her head, she answered, "I understand."

Reluctantly, I followed her into the small parlor off the clinic's hallway. Standing there nervously, I rocked back and forth on my heels on the worn carpet.

Pearl must have noticed how nervous I was when she asked, "Here, let me take your hat. I'll just hang it near the coat tree," pointing to a hook near the front door. "Have a seat. I was just making some tea for when they all returned. Would you care for some?"

"No, Ma'am. Thank you," I replied. Unaccustomed to drinking tea, I could sure use a shot of the whiskey Doc kept hidden around here somewhere.

"Nate, you don't have to stand on my account. Please, have a seat and make yourself comfortable. I'm sure they'll be here shortly."

"Miss Pearl, where are the boys?"

"They're tucked safely at the casita with Mrs. Mueller. Don't you worry, she won't let any harm come to them."

I was so nervous my stomach was doing flip-flops in anticipation of seeing Rebecca again. I'll never know what made me wind up here at the clinic, but it was better to get this over with sooner than later. When I heard the back door open, I tried preparing myself for what lay ahead. I heard muffled voices coming from down the hall. What are they saying? Heaving a sigh of relief, Caleb was the first to enter the parlor.

"Hey, Nate," extending his hand, "I didn't expect to see you here?"

It's funny, but it seems no one expected to see me today.

Standing, I shook his hand and answered, "I wasn't planning on coming. I just found myself walking aimlessly and ended up at the clinic gate. When Doc saw me standing outside, he encouraged me to come in."

"Well, I'm glad he did."

He must have noticed my uneasiness when he asked, "Pearl is making tea for the ladies, but I'm sure you're not into tea drinking. Am I right?"

"No, I'm not."

"Neither am I," Caleb said, scrunching up his nose. "How about something a tad stronger?"

"Yes, please!"

Chuckling at my eager response, Caleb slapped me on the shoulder and added, "I'll just get us a couple of glasses and a bottle of Doc's special stash he keeps around for 'medicinal' purposes. He gets it from Henry, who orders it from California. No offense to Henry, but it sure beats the gut-wrenching so-called liquor they serve to the regulars at the Prickly Pear."

Pouring the liquid gold into each glass, I inhaled its sweet caramel scent. By its clarity alone, I didn't think it was laced with turpentine like some whiskies around here were. Although, at this point, I wouldn't care if it was. I needed something to calm my nerves and swallowed the pale ambrosia in one swig.

Hearing female voices coming down the hallway, I braced myself for Rebecca's entrance. Her arm was wrapped through Emily's as they rounded the corner to the parlor. My breath caught. It was as if I hadn't seen her in months.

Her cheeks once again had the light pink coloring from the first time we met instead of the ghostly pale complexion I remembered after she was shot. The deep worry lines between her brows worn during the trial were gone. It was quite the transformation, and it was good to see her looking healthy once again.

Rebecca greeted me formally, "Mr. Burns. How nice of you to come."

There they go again, not expecting me. And what's with the Mr. Burns? Clearing my throat, I replied, "I hadn't planned on being here. I just seemed to wander over after I left the courtroom."

"Well, I'm grateful you are here," Rebecca replied, smiling.

That smile would be my undoing. "Thank you, Ma'am. How are the boys?" I asked, changing the subject.

"They're fine. As a matter of fact, they are outside playing with Joey and Gabriel."

"That's good.

This small talk was getting me nowhere. I really shouldn't be here.

"I wanted to congratulate you on a successful trial. But I really should be going and let you rest. I'm sure the trial has taken a toll on all of you." Turning to retrieve my hat, I felt a hand gently grasp my forearm.

"Don't go, Nathaniel," Rebecca whispered.

"Yes. Please stay, Nathaniel," Emily added. "Caleb and I will be in the kitchen if you two should need anything."

"We will?" Caleb asked, looking confused. "But we haven't finished our drinks," he added, holding up his glass.

Emily cut him off by tugging his sleeve and adding, "Yes, we will," she replied with a 'come-with-me-now and don't ask questions' look. "Don't worry, we'll watch out for the boys."

Taking Caleb by the hand, Emily walked him down the hall, adding over her shoulder, "Take all the time you need."

Bless her. I watched as my brother dutifully followed his wife down the hallway, then added, "Oh yes. Take all the time you need," Caleb concurred. Whispering to Emily, I heard him ask, "Why can't we listen?"

Emily didn't reply but pulled harder on Caleb's shirt sleeve. Sweet Emily. She really has Caleb wrapped around her little finger, and he has no clue.

69

Rebecca

STANDING IN THE clinic's tiny parlor, Nathaniel's rich scent of leather and sweetgrass surrounds me with the calm I need. I could finally admit to myself that during the trial, I'd missed him more than I should have.

Was it foolish of me? Probably. But here and now, I wanted him to take me in his arms and tell me he loved me until our last day, that everything would be alright, and that there would be nothing to keep us apart ever again.

Somehow, I knew he'd remained close by during the trial, but we both knew it would have been a mistake to have the judge see us together and risk Elliot going free. But now, it still wasn't possible to be seen in public. I was a married woman.

If Caleb could get me a divorce, and that was a big if, how long would it take? Weeks? Months? Maybe even years. Knowing that I couldn't make Nathaniel wait. He deserved to be happy and live a life free from the constraints still binding me to a dreadful marriage.

But how do I bring myself to tell him that we could no longer be together? That he needed to move on and find a woman who could make him happy. My heart was breaking, but I needed to get it over with quickly.

"Nathaniel, let's sit down. I'd rather not be standing. The trial took a lot out of me."

"Of course," was his only response. The gentleman he was, he waited for me to sit. *Please, Lord, help me get through this*. "I'm glad the trial is over, and Elliot is on his way to prison," I imparted, looking down at my hands as I twisted them in my lap. "I'm not sorry that he's going away for the rest of his life. He deserves it for what he did to me and my boys."

"I'm glad, too," he declared, nodding and taking my hands in his, lifting them to his lips. "He won't be able to cause you or the boys pain ever again."

I tried to resist, but it was futile. My mind told me this was not how I planned our conversation to start. I pulled back, making him release my hands. "Nathaniel, we have to be serious about this."

"Serious about what? I thought I was being serious. You know how I feel about you. What's going on, Rebecca? Have I done something wrong?"

This is harder than I thought. "Nathaniel, please let me say what I have to before you interrupt me. It's for the best."

"The best for who?"

"Nathaniel, please just let me finish." I tried calming my nerves by looking down at the floral print on the carpet. Maybe if I focus on one flower without looking at Nathaniel, I can get through this.

"Nathaniel, we can't see each other." There, I'd said it, and my heart shattered into a million tiny pieces. And at my declaration, Nathaniel abruptly stood and moved to the cold fireplace. Turning to face me, I noticed his face had turned crimson.

"You can't mean that, Rebecca. You're talking nonsense. Of course, we can see each other. Now that Elliot is out of the picture, Caleb can surely obtain you a divorce."

"It's not that simple. It could take months, maybe years, before that happens. I can't have you waiting for me forever. What if Caleb can't get me a divorce? You have no idea how the courts in Boston work. And I won't keep you waiting! I can't."

⌒⧜⌒

Nathaniel

I knew all too well how slow the wheels of justice turned, especially in Boston. Between the centuries that separated us, nothing seemed to have changed regarding the law. But it was I who held a secret from Rebecca that could destroy our fragile relationship. In the back of my mind, I couldn't help but wonder if she were afraid I'd turn out the same as Elliot, loathing and abusing her.

I crossed the small room, kneeled beside her, and said, "Rebecca, you must know I'll wait however long it takes." Once again, I took her hands in mine and said, "We can make this work. I love you and the boys. I want us to be a family."

"Nathaniel, please, don't make this harder than it already is. I want nothing but the best for you, and being with me won't make that possible. You have to move on."

So unlike her, she sniffed and rubbed the tears from her eyes with the back of her hand and added, "That's all I can say. Now please leave."

"No. I won't leave. You don't mean what you're saying. It's the stress from the trial talking. Rebecca, you're not making any sense." Pulling her into my arms, I could feel her heart beating rapidly against my chest as she began to cry. She leaned her head against my shoulder for a brief moment, where I caught the scent of lilies that had drawn me to her the first time we met on the train.

How could I let this woman go? I can't. We're meant to be together. I couldn't tell you how long I held Rebecca in my arms and let her cry, but it felt right to hold her near my heart. I wanted her like this for the rest of my life. I wanted to be the one she turned to in the good and difficult times. When we parted, my shirt was soaked with her tears, and we still hadn't settled the burning issue of being together.

$$\backsim\!\!\infty\!\!\backsim$$

Caleb

I leaned my ear against the kitchen door and said to Emily in a low voice, "I can't hear what they're talking about."

"Come away from the door, Caleb. If they want us to know what they're talking about, I'm sure they'll tell us."

"Shush!" I said, waving my hand at Emily. "I think I hear Rebecca crying."

"What! Emily jumped out of her chair and joined me at the door. We didn't dare open it because it had a telltale squeak when you did.

"If Nate hurts my sister, I'll hang him from the livery rafters."

"Hush," Emily said, slapping my forearm. "You will do no such thing. Although, I had my days when you made me so mad I wanted to hang you from the rafters."

"What? You did not! Caleb fused.

"Yes, I did. You were just lucky I couldn't find a rafter high enough or a rope short enough, I answered, giggling. Don't you know they're in love?"

"Did we really act like that?" Caleb asked.

"Worse," I replied.

70

Rebecca

TODAY WAS THE day Elliot was being sent to prison, yet my mind remained unsettled. Although, I did feel somewhat reassured knowing that the former sheriff, Anders Johannson, was escorting the prisoner wagon out of town, and if need be, he wouldn't hesitate to shoot Elliot.

I wanted to trust that my husband would remain behind bars for the rest of his life, but there was a niggling bit of doubt that had me nervous.

I was alone with my thoughts for the first time in days. My conversation with Nathaniel still haunted me. Had I done the right thing by telling him we shouldn't be together? It hurt me to admit that my heart would always regret that I'd pushed him away.

Sitting alone in the tiny parlor of our casita, I could hear the laughter of Porter and Daniel as they played outside with Joey and Clarice's son, Gabriel. For them, life seemed to have gone on without a care in the world, and it did my heart good to hear the joy in their voices.

Ever since our lives had been turned upside down, I wanted so desperately to move on and finally enjoy a new life without Elliot and, sadly, without Nathaniel. Nate will always remain in my heart.

I think I fell in love with him the moment we first met on the train. He elicited emotions from me that I had never felt with Elliot. I only wish I had seen my husband for the evil man he was before it all came to this disastrous end.

Remaining *just friends* with the man I'd come to love was difficult beyond belief. My heart ached at the thought of never being able to be with Nathaniel. My only hope was that Caleb could secure me a divorce, freeing me from my marriage vows. By then, it would be too late for Nathaniel and I. I had pushed him away to find another woman to love, and my life had since become a jumble of regrets.

The judge who presided over Elliot's trial was to leave town in two days, and Caleb had promised to do his best to convince him to grant me a divorce before he left. I hoped it wouldn't take the months or years I feared. In the meantime, I couldn't encourage Nathaniel. I was still married. Though it was hard, it wouldn't be fair to either of us. I had permitted him to move on. Probably the biggest mistake of my life next to marrying Elliot.

Pearl was in the kitchen cooking, something I had no desire to do at this time despite her encouragement. The unfamiliar aromas wafting through the house were intoxicating. She had become friends with a local Mexican woman who ran a small restaurant in town with her family.

Surprised, Pearl was learning to speak Spanish, and at night, as we sat around the table during dinner, she would teach us what she learned. When she wasn't busy with the boys, her friend and she shared their family recipes. But Pearl wasn't quite sure her Irish stew made the same impression on her Hispanic friend's family as the Mexican meals did on us.

Happily, I'd seen her and Doc Sweeney sitting in the parlor chatting away on two occasions. Their Irish accents were so thick when the two got together that I could only distinguish a few words between them. I was glad Pearl had Doc to reminisce with and hoped it would lead to something more lasting.

Both the boys and I had come to enjoy the spicey beef, tortilla, and rice dishes Pearl learned to make. And between the traditional meals that Clarice cooked, we were all fed extremely well.

It was good to have the trial over and see my boys settling into a routine in their new home. I loved the casita style despite it being small when you added sharing with Clarice and Gabriel to our family of four. But I wouldn't have it any other way.

The sounds of laughter resonating throughout the house were healing for all our souls. Walking into the kitchen sometime later, I found all the boys sitting at the table waiting to be fed.

'Well, I see you boys haven't missed a meal lately."

"No, Ma'am," Joey piped up, laughing. "Pearl's cooking is the best. Sorry, Miss Clarice," he added, turning her way. Beaming, "I haven't eaten this good in my whole life."

Pearl chuckled, "You're just saying that Joey, so I'll give you seconds on dessert,"

"Yes, Ma'am," Gabriel chimed in, clapping his hands.

It was good to hear Gabriel finally speak. He had remained silent for so long, but once he found his voice, there was no stopping him.

"No, really," added Daniel. "Pearl is the best cook. She always gives us dessert."

"Alright, boys. Behave yourselves, or you won't get any dessert," Pearl teased.

Covering their mouths, all four boys giggled softly and nudged each other, knowing Pearl would always feed them whether they were good or misbehaving.

"Gentleman. May I join you for dinner this evening," I asked formally.

"Oh yes, Momma!" Porter answered, smiling. "This is just like Boston when father was away, and we all sat in Pearl's kitchen together. Those were fun times."

In a heartbeat, Porter and Daniel's faces turned from one of joy to sadness, remembering those happy times. I could only surmise what their little minds were thinking. Joey stood and placed an arm around Daniel in his sweet innocence and said, "It's OK, Daniel. Your father can't hurt you anymore."

It was a gift to have Joey as part of the family. Soon, he would be living with his new parents, Caleb and Emily, but I would miss his presence at the table. "It's OK, boys," I added. "Your father won't be coming back. It's just us from now on," I said, pointing around the table to everyone.

"Are you sure, Momma?" Porter asked.

"What makes you ask that?" I'd always taught them not to hold back their fears or questions, but this surprised me.

"I'm just afraid he'll get out and come back for us and make us go back to Boston. I don't want to go back. I like it here. And I don't want him to hurt you again, Momma."

Looking at his brother, he added, "Daniel and I have already decided we're running away if father comes back."

I patted his hands, "Oh, sweetie. Your father is locked away and can't hurt us anymore. And there will be none of this talk of running away. You hear me?"

In unison, my boys answered somewhat contritely, "Yes, Momma."

I couldn't share my doubts with them. What if Elliot does get out? What would we do? I can't have any more tragedy set upon this family. Putting on a smile, I continued. "Enough talk of your father. Let's enjoy Pearl's wonderful meal before it gets cold."

Looking up at Pearl, she nodded while placing full plates of food on the table. I couldn't help but wonder if she shared the same doubts I had. For me, until Elliot was in the ground, I would never stop looking over my shoulder as long as he was alive. But there was nothing I could do. The judge had made his final decision.

We were well into our delicious meal when Daniel garnered my attention. "Momma."

"Yes, dear," I responded, looking up from my plate.

"Are we ever going to see Mr. Burns again?"

Good heavens. Where did that question come from? Leave it to a child's innocence to speak his mind.

"Well, I'm not sure," I replied, wiping my mouth with my napkin. "Why do you ask?"

"I like him. A lot! I wish he could be our father," he answered matter-of-factly, not missing a bite while he shoveled in a spoonful of food.

I was at a loss for how to answer Daniel when Porter quickly interjected, "Hush, Daniel. We weren't going to ask Momma just yet."

"Ask Momma what," I said, looking between my boys. Then, smiling sheepishly, I placed my palms on the table. "OK. What have you two boys been up to? And you better tell me the truth."

I heard Pearl chuckle as I sent her a 'help me out here' look when all she did was shrug her shoulders. Oh! Sometimes, that woman frustrated me to no end when she sided with the boys.

The little devils. They're up to something. I knew it. But I gave them my answer, "That is between Mr. Burns and your Momma. And not for discussion at the dinner table."

So there, Pearl! I turned to her, smiled, and enjoyed my small victory.

71

The Boys

SITTING HUDDLED TOGETHER behind the casita, Porter led the conversation, "Guys, Daniel and I heard Momma tell Mr. Nate that she couldn't see him anymore. I don't understand why, but we have to do something to get them together now that Father is gone."

"I heard them say something called di-vor-ce," Daniel stuttered.

"What is that, Joey?" Daniel asked.

"How should I know!" he answered.

"Well, we have to do something soon because school starts in two days. Any ideas?" asked Porter.

Joey groaned. "Why does school matter? I don't need no schoolin'. That's for sissies."

Porter growled, "Are you calling me a sissie?

"Ah, you know what I mean. I have better things to do. I have a new Ma and Pa, and they won't make me go to school."

"Yes, they will," Porter said. Besides, your Ma and Pa want you to get educated. And Pearl will make sure you're there every day, even if she has to drag you by your ear."

"All right! All right! I'll go. Now, let's get back to planning.

⤶⤷

Porter

Sitting in the dirt, shoulder to shoulder behind the casita in the early morning sun, all four of us were deep in thought when Joey chimed in.

"Here's what we're going to do!"

"Shush," Porter whispered, holding his index finger over his lips. "Keep your voice down, Joey. Do you want Ma and Pearl to hear us?"

Three pairs of curious eyes turned Joey's way. "What are we going to do?" Daniel asked in his childish grammar.

"Give me a minute, and I'll tell ya."

Just as he'd seen the adults do, Joey placed his fingers under his chin as if deep in thought. "Listen up. Here's my plan. When Mrs. Ackerman and Pearl are asleep, we sneak out and head to Mr. Burns's ranch. No one will see that we're gone."

"How can you be so sure?" Porter asked.

"Because!"

"Because what?"

"Just because! Now be quiet," Joey answered.

Using his hands animatedly to describe his plan, everyone listened silently to Joey. "Once there, we'll make our way into the barn and stay there until daylight. When Mr. Burns comes out of the house in the morning, we rush him."

Daniel had remained silent this whole time when he added his two cents worth. "Are we going to kidnap him? I'z can sneak in the house in the dark, and no one will see me 'cauz I'm little."

"Why would you want to sneak into the house?" Joey asked. "Don't we want to do this quietly? Besides Daniel, you make an awful lot of noise when you walk." "

I doez not!"

"Well, we'll figure something out when we get to the barn. I say we do it tonight. Do we all agree."

Three heads nodded in agreement.

"I wanna help," Gabriel spoke up.

"Gabriel, you need to stay home and distract our mommas and Pearl in case they get up in the middle of the night," answered Porter.

Bright-eyed, Gabriel puffed out his tiny chest and replied, "Is that impotent?" "

It's very important," said Porter.

I-m-p-o-r-t-a-n-t, silly. Not impotent," Joey said. Turning to Porter, he added, "See, I don't need no schoolin'. I can spell."

"That's what I said. Impotent,"

"Whatever!" chuckled Joey and Porter.

Porter placed his hand on Gabriel's shoulder and answered, "Yes. It's very important, Gabriel. Can you do that for us? Remember, Daniel and I want Mr. Burns as our new father."

"I do it!" Gabriel replied with a broad smile.

"Good. After our Momma's and Pearl are asleep, Joey, Daniel, and I will meet behind the casita. It's the easiest since we all live in the same house. Gabriel, do you think you can get some food from the kitchen without Miss Clarice, I mean your Momma, catching you? 'Cause we'll get hungry during the night for sure.

Each one nodded their heads in unison to Porter's instructions. "Now, let's go back in the house and act like nothing happened."

⟡

Later that night, Porter and Daniel were standing behind the casita when a yawning Joey slowly made his way out the back door with a bulging pillowcase in his hand.

"Is that full of food?" Porter whispered.

"Yeah," he answered, shrugging his shoulders. "Gabriel filled the bag and handed it to me before he went back to bed. I didn't ask him what was in it."

"Did he leave any food in the house? If not, Pearl and Miss Clarise will be mighty angry when we get back."

"Like I said, I didn't ask him what was in it," Joey replied a bit sarcastically.

"Alright, you don't need to get angry with me."'

"I'm not! Now, are we leaving, or are you going to keep harping on me?"

"Let's go," Porter instructed. "It's too far to walk to the ranch, and we need to be there right after midnight. So we'll have to borrow Doc Sweeney's horse."

⌘

Heading toward the livery, Joey suddenly stopped in the middle of the street. "Ah, guys," calling attention to himself. "We don't need to go to Mr. Nate's ranch."

"What are you talking about? That's the only way we can talk with him," answered Porter.

Pointing toward the Pick and Shovel saloon, Joey said, "I don't think Mr. Nate will be home any time soon."

"Why?" asked Porter.

"Because, silly, his horse is over there in front of the saloon."

Porter followed Joey's direction. "Wow. I've never seen Mr. Nate go into the saloon before. Have you?" he asked, turning to Daniel. Daniel kept quiet except to shake his head no.

"Well, I guess that solves our problem of taking a horse from the stable without permission," Joey added.

"We weren't stealing it. We were going to leave a note for Doc," interjected Porter.

⌘

"Momma won't let Daniel and I go in the saloon. We'll have to wait here until Mr. Burns comes out."

Porter quickly offered, "I'll go. I go in there all the time when I'm running errands and cleaning the spittoons. That way, you won't get in trouble with your Ma."

Porter asked, "What are you going to tell Mr. Nate when you see him?"

"I hadn't thought that far ahead. What do ya want me to say?"

"Tell him Ma is feeling poorly and ask for him to come to the casita."

Porter pulled Joey and Daniel in close, "O.K. listen. I have an idea."

"I sure hope this plan works," Joey said, facing Daniel with a doubtful look.

"It will," replied Porter. "Daniel and I will head back home and be ready when you bring Mr. Nate back."

"Alright, Porter. But I have a bad feeling we're all going to be in time-out for the rest of our lives. If it does go wrong, it will be all your fault, Porter Ackerman!"

72

Joey

I DIDN'T KNOW what I'd gotten myself into. Since I'd been in the saloon many times before, no one paid me any mind as I walked through the swinging doors. It was late at night, and only one table in the back of the room was full of cowboys playing poker. Mr. Chauncey was in the corner playing the same old music on his off-key piano while several of the ladies sat around the room.

Away from the door, at the farthest end of the bar, was Mr. Nate—a very unusual sight, for sure. I'd never seen him in here before. I couldn't tell if he had been drinking, but by the way he was leaning both elbows on the bar, I was suspicious.

With one foot on the brass rail running close to the floor, he held up an empty glass to Henry as if he wanted a refill. I'd seen too many men in various stages of drunkenness in this place, so from what I could tell, Mr. Nate appeared to be close to being pretty liquored up.

Henry Calhoun, the owner, and bartender, stood on the opposite side of the bar, directly in front of Mr. Nate, wiping the bartop with a rag. I watched as he leaned forward, mumbled something, and patted Mr. Nate on the shoulder. I figured now was as good a time as any to make my move.

Taking a deep breath, I ran toward the end of the bar, yelling, "Mr. Nate! Mr. Nate! Come quick! Miss Rebecca needs you right away. She's in a big hurt." I hated lying, but I needed to get him to come with me. I knew I was going to catch it good when Ma and Pa found out what I'd done.

Mr. Nate swung his left hand at me as if swatting a fly and almost fell off his stool. I pleaded, "Mr. Nate. You have to come. Now!" This time, I pulled on his sleeve so hard it tore at the elbow.

"Go away, Joey. Leave me alone!" He didn't notice I'd torn his shirt, so he must have been mad about something else. Slurring, he slammed his empty glass on the bar and yelled, "Henry, Give me another."

Turning to me, he added, "Mrs. Ackerman doesn't need me. She never wants to see me again. So go tell the sheriff," he added, pointing in the direction of the swinging doors.

"Joey, what do you need Mr. Nate for?" asked Mr. Calhoun.

I tilted my head toward Mr. Nate, not saying a word, hoping Mr. Calhoun would understand and help me out, "Please, Mr. Nate. Miss Rebecca is hurt. You need to come. Now! She's asking for you."

I can already feel the burning on my backside.

Leaning over the bar, Mr. Calhoun said, "Nate, maybe it's best if you go see what's wrong with Rebecca. It could be serious," after which he turned to me and winked.

"Thank you, Henry," I mouthed.

Turning my direction and swaying in his seat, Mr. Nate looked down at me as Mr. Calhoun reached across the bar and grabbed his arm to steady him. I quickly stepped back. I didn't need Mr. Nate toppling over on me.

"I told you she doesn't want to see me. Now go away!" Grabbing his bottle, he headed toward an empty table in the saloon's darkest corner, probably hoping I would disappear. But I wouldn't give up.

"No! No!" I blurted out. "You're wrong. She's asking for you!"

How much more did I have to say to make Mr. Nate understand? Porter and Daniel would be mad if I failed to bring Mr. Nate to their house.

"Why isn't she here telling me how much she needs me?" he slurred, taking another drink, this time directly from the bottle.

When I grow up, I'm never going to fall in love, especially if it's as complicated as this. "Mr. Nate, you have to listen. You don't want Miss Rebecca to leave, do you?" All I could think was I needed him to move out of that chair.

"Of course not. But she told me she can do whatever she pleases and never wants to be attached to another man as long as she lives."

Why is he telling me this? I don't understand what he's talking about. This love stuff is crazy. I don't know why I got involved with this plan.

"And you believed her?"

Looking utterly dejected, Mr. Nate replied, "Of course, I believed her. What woman would want to live on a dusty cactus-ridden ranch in the middle of nowhere with me?"

Henry stopped drying a glass and blurted out, "Oh, for heaven's sake, Nate. Help the boy out here and get off your butt and go on over to the casita and see what Miss Rebecca wants,"

If I didn't think he'd mind, I'd hug Mr. Calhoun.

"Alright, I'll go," he replied, holding up two fingers, then changing to one to make his point. "But only to help Joey out."

Mr. Nate stood in one spot for several minutes, testing himself to see that he wouldn't fall flat on his face like I'd seen men do here before. I was thankful for that because he was too big for me to drag to the casita on my own.

"Do you need some help, Mr. Nate?" I asked, hoping he wouldn't say yes.

"No, I'm fine, son," he answered, patting my shoulder. "Just give me a minute to get my bearings. You go ahead. I'll follow you."

I didn't want to seem too eager as I headed for the door, but I knew that Porter and Daniel were anxiously awaiting our arrival.

I wasn't so sure about Mrs. Ackerman, though. I worried how she would react to seeing Mr. Nate so drunk, standing at her door in the middle of the night.

"Are you coming, Mr. Nate?" I asked, glancing over my shoulder.

"Don't rush me, Joey," he mumbled.

⤎⚬⤏

Finally, we stood at the front door to the casita. I looked up at Mr. Nate in the darkness. His face looked white as one of the sheets Miss Clarice hung on the clothesline. So, I took the initiative to knock. I didn't think he had the nerve to find the door anytime soon.

Knocking twice, I took off running around the casita toward the back door when Mr. Nate yelled out, "Hey Joey, where ya going?"

Making it inside the back door as quietly as possible, I was met by Porter and Daniel, who had been waiting for me in the kitchen.

"What took you so long," Porter asked.

I whispered, "It wasn't easy to get him here. He's drunk and standing at the front door now, waiting for your Momma to answer."

We knew better than to get caught watching what would happen next. So we made our way to our room and climbed into our beds just as we heard the front door latch click open.

Ἅ 73 Ἆ

Rebecca

"GOOD HEAVENS, WHO could be pounding on the door at this late hour? Before heading into the parlor, I retrieved my derringer hidden between Pearl's quilts in the hall cabinet. Checking the chamber, I cautiously cocked the hammer back. Even though he should be in prison, I was wary and would be ready if it happened to be Elliot.

While holding the gun at waist level, I cautiously released the bolt and slowly opened the door. My heart jumped in my chest at seeing Nathaniel standing there. I quickly released the hammer and held the derringer down at my side so Nathaniel wouldn't see it.

"Mr. Burns, what in the devil are you doing here at this hour? I could have shot you, you stupid man."

Eyes wide at seeing the gun in my hand, he swayed in front of me and said, "So, I'z made you mad enough to make you want to shootz me?"

"Don't be foolish," I said, grabbing his forearm to steady him and pulling him inside. I couldn't have him waking up the house,

333

let alone the whole town. Sniffing, I waved my hand in front of my nose, "Whew! You've been drinking, Mr. Burns! You smell like the backstreet saloon."

"I'zz had one little drink," he slurred, leaning against the entry wall for obvious support. Even in his current state of drunkenness, he was the most handsome man I'd ever seen. I wanted to throw myself in his arms, but I'm sure we would both land on the floor. Instead, I led him to the couch.

Leaning close to my face, he said, "Yourz so beautiful."

Even in his state of drunkenness, I blushed as he added, "You know, it's not nize to call Henry's saloon, what-di-ya-say, street back."

"It's backstreet," I replied, having received another whiff of alcohol. "Now, come in and sit before you fall down."

"Whatz you call it?" he slurred.

"Oh, never mind, Nathaniel. You sir, have had more than one drink." Guiding him into the parlor as if he were one of my boys, I instructed, "Sit down and keep quiet while I make you some coffee."

"Just like a wife. Nag, nag, nag."

I called out from the hall as I walked to the kitchen, "I heard that, Mr. Burns. And need I remind you, I'm not your wife." *I only wish I was.*

Nathaniel yelled back, "I'm glad youz heard me." Yelling louder, "Will you marry me, Rebecca?"

"Oh, for heaven's sake," I said out loud while feigning hearing loss, and replied, "I can't hear you, Nathaniel. Give me a few minutes, and I'll be right back." *Of course, I'll marry you, you foolish man.*

⚬⚭⚬

Rebecca, what are you going to do with that poor love-struck man?

Standing at the stove with the coffee pot in hand, I jumped at hearing my mother's voice. "Momma, you startled me. What are you doing here? We haven't spoken since the train. And then I thought my imagination was playing tricks on me because of all the stress. But you're really here talking to me."

I'm here. But as much as I wish differently, you still can't see me.
"I know. I wish I could."
Now tell me why you are keeping Mr. Burns in the dark. From what I can tell, he's a wonderful man who is clearly in love with you and the boys. Don't you want to be happy for once in your life?
"Of course I do. But how can I make Nathaniel think we can be a happy family with Elliot still alive, albeit in prison? You seem to forget that I'm still a married woman."
Details, my dear. Those are just silly details. Are you in love with Mr. Burns?
"More than you'll ever know. I can't get him out of my mind. But I hurt him by driving him away. Besides, what would people think? I can't bring shame onto the family."
Oh, piffle, as Mrs. Young would say. We often talk about you, Caleb, and Emily. We both think they make such a happy couple. They are so in love.
"Momma, we were talking about Nathaniel and me. And whatever made you change your mind about Nathaniel and I."
Oh yes! Well, all I can tell you is not to worry about what other people think. Concentrate on you, Nathaniel, and the boys. Go ahead and make yourselves happy for once in your life. To answer you're last question, I finally understood that Nathaniel is the only one who can make you happy, and he is sincere in his love for you.
"So, how do I get him back?"
Oh, you'll think of something, dear. Right now, he's very vulnerable, so proceed with caution and act with your heart, dear.
"Thank you, Momma. I will. I love you. Please, come back and talk with me again."
Oh, I will. I'm never far away.
"That's a scary thought."
I heard that, Rebecca!
I swear I could hear Momma chuckle.

⌘

Returning to the parlor with a coffee cup in hand, I found Nathaniel lying on the divan, legs hanging over, sound asleep and snoring loudly.

"So much for sobering you up, Mr. Burns, and sending you home."

I took the afghan from the back of the chair nearest the fireplace and laid it over him. He was so tall it didn't quite fit, but I made sure to cover his arms and chest. Picking up his long legs, I placed them, boots and all, on the cushions. I wasn't about to struggle to get his boots off, not in his condition.

I stood over him, staring at his peaceful face. Leaning forward, I pushed a lock of his honeyed red hair back off his forehead, then kissed him on the cheek. I watched as his lips turned up in a slight smile, though he remained asleep. I knew then in my heart that I would love this man until my last day.

Once I was sure he wouldn't fall off the divan, I headed back down the hall to bed. Whatever had brought him to the casita this night would have to wait until morning.

Nathaniel

SLOWLY OPENING ONE eye, then the other, I groaned in pain. "Oh, my aching head." Pounding like a hammer on the livery's anvil, I vigorously rubbed both hands over my eyes until they hurt.

For a moment, I had no idea where I was. On the table in front of me was a cup of coffee. I didn't care that it was cold. Caffeine was all I needed to ease the aching behind my eyes, so I drank the cup in three gulps as I tried throwing off the afghan someone had placed over me. It was tangled in the toes of my boots, and I didn't want to tear it. Successful, after several attempts, I sat up woozy and glanced at my surroundings, recognizing it as the casita's parlor.

What am I doing here? I must have had one too many drinks last night because all I remember is Joey coming into the saloon and telling me that Rebecca was hurt and needed me. My eyes darted back and forth as I searched the room. Dear God, where is Rebecca?

I jumped up, which wasn't the smartest thing to do in my condition. I reached into thin air to steady myself, made my way to grab the back of a chair, and bellowed, "Rebecca, where are you?"

The next thing I heard were rapid footsteps coming down the hall and Rebecca calling out, "Mr. Burns, keep your voice down. It's too early, and I won't have you waking the entire house."

She looked breathtaking, with her cheeks flushed pink and her hair tussled about her face. Standing there in a gossamer robe that left little to the imagination, I couldn't turn away if she demanded it. I had dreamed of waking up to this vision every morning for the rest of my life. How could she deny me this?

Catching me staring, Becca hastily pulled the robe tight around her waist and crossed her arms over her chest, giving me a pleasing view of her ample breasts. I groaned and held my breath as she tied the sash ends around her full hips. Luckily for me, Rebecca had no idea what she was doing.

"Nathaniel, what's all your bellowing about?"

I didn't move as her voice drew me back to her face.

"Are you all right? You're looking a bit flushed," she added. Pointing to the divan, "Maybe you better sit back down."

I rushed out, "Becca, I came here last night because I thought something horrible had happened to you, and I couldn't live with myself if that were true." Holding my open arms toward her, she didn't move. Disappointed, I dropped them to my sides and continued, "Joey came to tell me that you'd been hurt and were asking for me."

My head was still fuzzy, but I knew that Joey finding me at the saloon was no coincidence, and he hadn't planned this all on his own.

Placing her hands on her hips, Rebecca looked at me suspiciously and asked, "You say Joey came to get you in the saloon last night? What was he doing in the saloon? I told him not to go there ever again."

"Yes." Suddenly, it hit me, but I needed to finish my story. "He dragged me out of the saloon and over here to the casita, then left me standing at the front door where you found me."

Oh, boys, are you in such big trouble!

Turning away from me, Rebecca yelled as only an angry mother could, "Boys! Come out here this instant!"

I was glad I wasn't one of her sons right now.

So much for not waking the entire house. Rebecca's yelling was going to wake up the entire town. Four sets of eyes stared at us from the hallway. Suddenly, they seemed so small and innocent, standing there together. I'm sure they knew what was about to happen next.

Lips pressed in a straight line, Rebecca turned her questions to the boys. "Porter. Joey. Explain yourselves."

Though Daniel and Gabriel stood beside them, I'm sure Rebecca felt they were too young to be a part of last evening's charade. I was glad not to be on the receiving end of their mother's anger.

"Yes, Ma'am," answered Porter.

Daniel and Gabriel hung back behind the older boys. Probably hoping Rebecca wouldn't notice them. I'd do the same thing if I were in their position. I was interested in hearing their explanation.

"What have you boys done?" Quickly adding, "And don't tell me any fibs."

Porter and Joey looked as if they were being taken to the woodshed. Yet I doubted Porter knew what that was like. Joey, on the other hand, probably knew well enough.

Looking down at the floor, Porter answered, "Momma, we were only trying to help."

Tilting her head to the side, she asked, "What made you think I needed help?"

"Daniel and I heard you talking to Mr. Nate the other day." Looking up with sadness in his eyes, Porter added, "You said you never wanted to see Mr. Burns again. And we want him to be our father now."

Sucking in a breath of surprise, Becca looked up at me with sadness in her eyes. It was obvious that little ears had overheard our private conversation. *Man, what a mess I've created.* What Porter said hit me head-on. I couldn't say a thing, but my heart swelled with gratitude and love for these boys. They wanted me to be their father!

"Come here, boys." Rebecca opened her arms to all four, and they willingly obeyed, moving close to her side. Leaning down to the innocent faces, she comforted them and said, "Listen to me. What Mr. Burns and I were talking about was a private adult conversation. Do you understand that?"

Four heads nodded in unison, but I doubt they understood its meaning. I let Rebecca continue. I, too, was interested in hearing how she would explain herself and our previous conversation.

"It's complicated."

It's complicated! Is that all you can say? You better keep explaining, Becca, because I'm trying to understand all this myself.

"Why is it complicated," Porter asked.

Good question, Porter. Let's hear how your mother explains this.

"Because it is," Rebecca replied.

Now, that's a typical answer from a mother. How is it women are so good at skirting around answering important questions? Well, it's not a good answer for me.

Placing her finger under Daniel's chin, she tilted his head up to her and continued, "Sometimes adults have difficult conversations they regret afterward. It doesn't mean that we're angry with each other." Drawing the boys closer, she added, "I want Mr. Burns to be a part of our life just as much as you do. But it takes time for these things to work out."

I suddenly sobered as I listened to Rebecca say she wanted me to be a part of their lives. Finally! I had hope.

"Now, I want all four of you to return to bed. It's still too early to be up."

I watched as each boy kissed Rebecca on the cheek when Daniel spoke up. "Momma, are you going to scold Mr. Nate?"

I had to hold back a chuckle, so I turned my head toward the divan until I was under control. I wouldn't undermine what Rebecca told her boys.

"No, Daniel, I'm not going to scold Mr. Nate," Rebecca answered, tousling his hair.

"Good night, Mr. Nate," Daniel said.

"Good night, son," I replied. It seemed so natural to call him son that I wanted to be able to do that for the remainder of his days. If only his mother agreed.

Turning her attention back to me, Rebecca announced, "It seems, Nathaniel, that you and I need to talk.

❦ 75 ❦

Nathaniel

THE AIR IN the parlor suddenly felt heavy and stifling after the boys returned to their beds. The walls began to close in around me, so I took a deep breath as Becca silently stood before me. Was I going to like where this conversation was headed?

I was a good foot and a half taller than Rebecca, which allowed me to look down into her hypnotic eyes. Those pools of blue had me drowning and dreaming of all the things I wanted to do to her. I didn't care. I wanted her in my bed and wake up next to her every morning until my last day.

What would she say if I told her what I was thinking? Would she turn and run? She must have read my mind when her boldness surprised me. I took a tentative step back when she moved one foot closer, giving me a sultry look that melted my resolve.

My heart felt as if it would spontaneously ignite as the palms of her warm hands reached through the opening of my sleep-rumpled shirt and detonated a spark I'd never experienced before.

Is this really happening? I let out a low groan at her tender touch while the muscles of my chest rippled under her soft fingertips.

Was this vixen my Becca? She obviously wasn't going to play fair. Sucking in a deep breath, I reluctantly grasped her hands firmly between mine and pulled them away. It was with great effort I managed to squeak out, "Becca, be careful. You're playing with fire here!"

"Um-hum," was her answer as she placed one hand around my neck and pulled my head down to meet her lips. I was at her mercy. What she wanted, I was willing to give. All thoughts of taking my time went out the window as her moist, demanding lips pulled me deeper into desperation.

I lost control and met her passion for passion.

My hands went around her waist of their own volition, pulling her as close as our bodies allowed. I'd never felt anything so magical. I didn't want her to stop. Grasping a handful of hair, I drew her head back to deepen the kiss while the flashes of color sparking behind my closed eyelids had me reeling. Was I dreaming? If I was, I never wanted to wake up. I finally had the woman I loved in my arms, and she'd come to me willingly.

❦

"Momma!" At the sound of Daniel's voice, we quickly pulled apart. Leaning our foreheads together, we tried catching our breath. Thankfully, his sweet voice had come from down the hall and not in the doorway to the parlor.

"I'll be right there, dear," Rebecca called out. Patting my chest, she stood back, straightening her robe.

Becca left as quickly as she'd come to me. Left standing in the parlor alone and deflated, I couldn't help but ask myself, what just happened? I paced the worn carpet, rubbing my chest where her hand had burned her touch into my soul. Holding onto that feeling, I shook my head and tried to figure out what to do next.

Running my hand through my hair, I mumbled nonsensically to the empty room. That's when I heard the front door open.

"Mr. Burns, I didn't expect to find ye here.".

"And yet, here I am, Doc," I retorted with a lopsided grin.

Smiling, the Doc said, "Ah, ye look a bit flushed. Are ye sick?"

"No, sir. But thanks for asking."

"Well, I be looking for Miss Clarice to help me in te clinic. I have an emergency tat just came in, and it seems tat Caleb and my granddaughter are busy at te moment."

So was I before you came in!

"I can tell her that she's needed at the clinic."

"Thank ye. Tat would be helpful."

No, thank you, Daniel. You helped your mother, and I dodge a bullet.

Miss Clarice headed to the clinic, after which Rebecca returned to the parlor without the boys. Speaking from the doorway, "Nathaniel, I'm sorry for my behavior earlier. I can't imagine what got into me."

"Please," I pleaded, "There's no need to apologize, Becca. I was just as much to blame," I replied, looking down at my boots. "But I'm not sorry for what happened. I've wanted to kiss you like that for a long time." Looking into her eyes, I said, "What we did wasn't wrong."

"Then you're not sorry? she asked, stepping further into the room.

"No. Why should I be? I love you with all my heart. And from what I gather," I added with a chuckle, "I think you feel the same way." I held my breath before asking, "Am I right?"

"Yes, Nathaniel, I do love you." Stepping closer, she added, "I've been so crazy to deny my love for you. I'm just sorry I put you through that torment."

"Truth be told, it was hell. I don't think I could have gone on much longer without you and the boys in my life." Chuckling, I added, "Enedina was right."

"What about?" Becca asked with a furrowed brow.

"You're good for me," I replied, smiling.

"I like Enedina's way of thinking. I'm sure we'll get along just fine."

I wanted to run out of the casita, shouting at the top of my lungs that Rebecca Young loved me. But for now, I was satisfied that only the two of us knew.

"Now, Mr. Burns," Rebecca said so formally, "I think you better head home and get cleaned up. Tell Enedina I will be out to meet her soon and bring Pearl and Clarice with me."

With that, she gave me a peck on the cheek, handed me my hat, and turned me toward the front door. I don't think my feet touched the ground as I walked toward the stable. I would count down the hours until I returned.

Rebecca

My heart felt lighter than it had in years. For the first time in my life, I was truly in love. I couldn't wait to tell my boys and Pearl. I would be ever thankful for my mother visiting me and telling me she approved of Nathaniel and that I deserved happiness.

76

Rebecca

RUSHING DOWN THE hall to the kitchen, I found Pearl sitting at the table with paper and a pen in hand. I couldn't wait to tell her about Nathaniel and me. "Pearl, may I interrupt you for a minute?"

"Of course," she replied, looking up smiling. "Can I make us a cup-a-tea?"

"No, that won't be necessary. I don't think I can sit still right now," I replied, moving from one foot to another.

"What is it?" she asked. "You seem a bit nervous. Is everything alright?"

"Oh yes. It's more than alright." I couldn't contain my happiness any longer. "Nathaniel and I have come to an agreement."

"Whatever do you mean? What type of agreement?" Pearl's eyebrows furrowed with concern, and I could only imagine what was going through her mind.

"Nathaniel loves me," I announced, laughing nervously.

"I knew it. That's wonderful," Pearl responded, standing and bringing me into her arms. "I knew you would work things out." Pausing, "Have you told Daniel and Porter yet?"

Stepping back from our embrace, I replied, "No. I wanted you to be the first to know."

My heart suddenly skipped a beat when I added, "I hope they will be as excited as I am."

"Oh, I'm sure they will be. They told me they think of Mr. Burns as their real father now." Patting my hand, "They've seen too much of your suffering at the hands of Elliot. It's time they make good memories by being loved and nurtured."

I was hoping you would be happy for us." Pulling her back into my arms, I continued, "Pearl, you must stay with us no matter what happens or where we live. I won't let you leave. You've been a mother to me since my own mother died, and the boys love you so much."

"Now, don't get me crying. We'll have time to talk about that later."

I knew she didn't want to cry, so she quickly changed the subject.

"I really must go into town and pick up supplies from McLaughlin's Mercantile. Why don't you come with me? Since Clarice is here, I'll ask her to watch over the boys while we're gone. Then you can tell me all about your talk with Mr. Burns."

"Alright. That sounds like a good idea since I have a dress that's ready to be picked up in town. I'll tell Clarice and the boys I'm going out." I turned to get my hat and reticule when I had a thought and stopped to face Pearl. "Pearl, I believe I'll stop at Sheriff Reynold's office. I have something I need to discuss with him."

Most of the townspeople already respected him for his work. And since taking over from Anders Johannson, he'd been a busy man, so I hoped I could catch him in his office.

"I think that's a wise idea," Pearl said. "It's time you two spoke about his part in Elliot finding you. I believe he didn't think it would turn out the way it did, and I'm sure there has been a lot of guilt he's been carrying since Elliot shot you."

"Yes. I want the sheriff to understand that I hold no hard feelings toward him and that he was only doing his job."

"I'm sure he will be glad to hear that. I'll finish my list and meet you in the parlor in a few minutes."

"I'll be ready," I replied. As I went down the hall to my room, thinking about how to broach the conversation with Sheriff Reynolds, my mind kept wandering to Nathaniel. I walked on air every time I was near him.

⌘

Pearl and I walked in animated conversation toward the center of town before we parted midway, with her going to the mercantile and me going toward the sheriff's office. We planned on meeting at the café in an hour to have tea.

The door to the sheriff's office was open, so I called out from the entrance, "Sheriff Reynolds, may I come in?"

The new sheriff was standing near the stove with a coffee pot in his hand. He turned when he heard his name called. Setting the cup and pot down, he answered, "Mrs. Ackerman, What a pleasant surprise. I didn't expect to see you here. Please come in and have a seat," he said, pointing to a chair in front of his desk. "You're looking well?"

"I'm doing very well, thank you." I sat across from him nervously, folding my hands in my lap, wondering how to begin this awkward conversation.

The sheriff sat behind his small desk and leaned his arms on its top. "I hope this is just a friendly visit and there is nothing of concern you need my help with. Either way, I'm glad to see you finally up and about and looking well."

"Thank you, Sheriff," I answered with a tentative smile while slightly nodding. "I appreciate your concern."

"Mrs. Ackerman, I think we can dispense with the formalities, so please, call me Ben."

Fidgeting, I ran my gloved hands down my skirt, wondering how to begin. Just get it out, Rebecca. He's probably just as nervous as you are. "Sheriff, I mean, Ben, I came here this morning to apologize."

"Apologize for what?" he asked in a concerned tone. "You've done nothing wrong that I can think of."

Bowing my head, I said, "Well, you see, I have a confession to make."

He responded with a bit of levity, probably hoping to break the tension that hung between us. "Mrs. Ackerman, I'm not a priest and don't accept those types of confessions."

Flustered, I replied, "Oh! I don't mean that, sheriff." I could feel warm beads of sweat forming on my brow and could only hope they remained hidden under my hat. "What I mean is, I knew you were following me once I saw you standing on the train platform in Chicago. Don't ask me how I knew." Shrugging my shoulders, I added, "Just call it a woman's intuition."

"I see," he answered, neither denying nor admitting his actions.

Despite not wanting to, his response allowed me the opportunity to continue. "When I saw you here in Yuma, I knew you were indeed following me. I was frantic. I didn't want to confront you because I was afraid you worked directly for Elliot, and he'd sent you to kill me."

The sheriff's eyes widened in surprise, but he remained silent. By this time, my mouth was as dry as if I'd swallowed a cup of desert sand, and I hoped the sheriff didn't see my hands shaking in my lap.

"When I heard around town, you were a Pinkerton Agent, well, that confirmed my suspicions."

I looked around the office at the posters on the wall, the warm stove toward the back of the room, and the row of rifles standing neatly in a case. This place suited him, and he wore the badge of his office proudly.

"So," I continued, "Through the town's chatty grapevine, I understand you stepped down from your job with the Pinkertons when you found out what my husband was about.

Eyes lowered, the sheriff regarded the top of his desk while responding pleadingly. "Mrs. Ackerman. Please understand that I would never have taken the assignment if I had known what your husband had planned to do to you. I've regretted it ever since and blame myself for him shooting you."

"Benjamin. May I call you by your given name?"

"Yes, by all means, please do."

"Benjamin, there is nothing for you to regret. You didn't make Elliot shoot me."

"That's true." The tone of his voice deepened as he added, "But if I had been there in the church, I could have prevented it from happening. As the law, the pastor would have let me keep my gun."

Shaking my head from side to side, I replied, "You don't know that. We have to let this go. It could have been some innocent bystander if it wasn't me." Pausing, I added, "How a madman's mind works is a mystery best left alone. And Elliot is a madman who is out for revenge. I was always his target. I'm just glad that the trial is over, and he's now in jail for the rest of his life."

Standing, I made to move around the sheriff's desk when Benjamin abruptly stood, causing his chair to hit the wall. Face to face, I added, "I think we need to move on from the past events since we will be living in the same town. I hold no ill toward you and want us to be friends. And since you hold Nathaniel and my brother in high regard, I wish to do the same."

"Thank you, Mrs. Ackerman."

"Please, from now on, call me Rebecca. Using formal names amongst friends is not necessary."

"Alright. Thank you, Rebecca. Please don't hesitate to ask if there is anything I can do for you."

I held out my hand, and Benjamin took it firmly, adding, "I'm sure this has been very difficult for you and your family. I hope that better days are ahead."

"As I hope they are for you, too, Benjamin. Please, always be safe in your job."

It may not have been appropriate, but I took a chance and leaned in to hug the sheriff, which he graciously accepted. This was when Nathaniel walked into the sheriff's office.

∾ॐॐ∾

Nathaniel

I stood quietly in the open door and watched my future wife and sheriff holding each other close. "Ahem. Ahem." When they heard my voice behind them, Rebecca and Ben quickly released each other.

Teasingly, I asked, "Well, now. What do we have here, Sheriff? Are you trying to steal my girl?"

"Don't be silly, Nathaniel," Rebecca answered, straightening her hat. "Benjamin and I were just discussing an issue concerning us. I'm sure you understand."

"Nate, I'm sorry." Flustered, Ben added, "It isn't what you think. You have to believe me."

"Don't be silly, man. Rebecca only has eyes for me. Right, dear?"

"Of course, dear." Men! When they're jealous, they are worse than women. "Now, if you'll excuse me, gentleman, I have some shopping to do before I head back to the casita." Walking past Nathaniel, I winked at him and added, "Now, you boys, be nice to each other. I don't want to hear any gunfire coming from the sheriff's office after I leave."

I heard both men laughing when they probably thought I was out of earshot. It was good to be around people that cared about each other. And, I was happy that Nathaniel, too, held no grudges against Ben. It was time for all of us to heal and move forward with our lives.

∾ॐॐ∾

Benjamin

"Whew," I said, falsy wiping my brow. "Rebecca had me scared there for a minute. I thought she'd come to shoot me."

"Whatever gave you that crazy idea, Ben."

Chuckling, I placed my hands in my back pockets and said, "Well, I heard it through that crazy grapevine that she almost shot you the other night."

"Ah, about that. I'd had one too many drinks at Henry's and probably should have stayed away from the casita until I'd sobered up."

We both laughed and then sat down with our cups of coffee.

"In all seriousness, Nate, Rebecca may be a force to reckon with, but she wouldn't hurt a fly."

"So you say, Nate. But after all the grief I caused her by bringing her husband here, I wouldn't blame her if she did shoot me."

"Ben, you didn't bring Elliot here. He came on his own. You were just doing your job. And if your supervisors didn't know his plans, how could you be expected to figure them out?"

"You're right. But I still feel guilty for what happened to Rebecca. Plus, having her go through that trial couldn't have been easy."

I walked back to the stove to pour myself another cup of coffee. "Would you like another? I asked, holding up my cup."

"No thanks. I have to head to the livery to pick up a harness I had repaired. I teased, rubbing my stomach, "Next time I'm in town, I'll stop by with some of Enedina's churros."

"Oh man, thanks. I would love some. I hear they're the best around."

ᦰᦰᦰ 77 ᦰᦰᦰ

Benjamin

NOT LONG AFTER Rebecca and Nathaniel left, I heard screams coming from the direction of the mercantile. Freeing my revolver from its holster, I hurried to the open door and stopped short. As a precaution, I scanned the boardwalk from right to left before exiting. I couldn't risk being surprised by a knock on the head or, worse, shot.

A stagecoach parked in front of the mercantile blocked my view of the north side of the street. I thought it strange that the boardwalk and street were empty. Something was definitely not right. I only hoped the woman I'd met earlier, Maeve, and her daughter Fiona, were somewhere safe.

Another scream, louder than the first, wrenched the desert air. I picked up my pace, crossed the street, and stepped onto the opposite boardwalk one store down from Angus McLaughlin's mercantile.

My steps faltered when I saw who was standing there. I couldn't believe it. I'd recognize that man anywhere. With his back turned toward me, thank heavens he hadn't noticed me yet. I was shocked.

He had one arm wrapped around an older woman's neck and a pistol held to her temple.

Oh, God, no! I recognized the woman as Pearl, and the man holding the gun to her head was Elliot Ackerman.

How had he escaped? I hadn't seen Sheriff Johannson since he volunteered to escort Elliot to prison. Where was he now? I would have thought he would go straight home to his wife, Abigail, and their infant daughter, Noel. If anything had happened to him, I couldn't live with myself. I'd walk away from this town and never look back.

I grabbed Samuel, the barber shop owner, by his sleeve as he came out to check on the commotion. Luckily, he didn't scream at my touch. I leaned down and whispered in his ear, "Sam, go around back and get Caleb. Tell him to come armed and tell him Elliot is back." Staring directly into his eyes, I asked, "You got that?"

Without a word, he shook his head in circles and hastily moved down the alley to the back of the buildings. I only hoped he would find Caleb in time.

◦◦◦◦◦

I made my way in Elliot's direction, carefully taking each step to lessen the creaking of the boards on the walkway.

Elliot jerked his arm back and screamed in Pearl's ear, "You old hag, where's my wife and boys?"

Pearl didn't reply but instead tried to pull Elliot's grip from around her neck. Her movements only caused him to tighten his hold. No wonder she couldn't answer him.

Hang on, Pearl.

I motioned to those on both sides of the street to get back inside their stores. I knew Elliot had a short fuse, and his volatility was now at its peak. Out of the corner of my eye, I caught a glimpse of Maeve, but I didn't see Fiona. She was standing alone in front of the hotel, watching me. Though we had only spoken for a few short minutes when she arrived on the train earlier today, something about her had captured my heart as no other woman had.

I couldn't have her hurt in the chaos, so I motioned for her to go back inside. But the stubborn Irish woman stood there defiantly. Knowing I couldn't watch out for her and concentrate on Pearl and Elliot at the same time, I could only hope that Maeve would come to her senses and return to the safety of the hotel.

When this is all over, I'll have to talk with her about her obstinate attitude. *Like that will do any good, Ben.* Returning my focus to Elliot, I could see Pearl's legs were weakening. I had to act fast, or Elliot would strangle her to death. Keeping my revolver down at my side, I moved closer.

My speech wavered as I yelled, "Ackerman! Let Pearl go!" At the sound of my voice, Elliot jerked Pearl around, using her as a shield. Damn him! We wouldn't be in this mess if the judge had just sentenced him to be hanged.

Sinisterly, Elliot snickered. "Well, if it isn't the town's crippled new sheriff. Come to arrest me, have you? Despite despising this man with every fiber of my being, I wouldn't let him intimidate me. I wanted to shoot him outright, but as the sheriff, I couldn't. I had the law to abide by.

But neither did I want him to harm Pearl, and he would, without giving it a thought. "I said, let Pearl go!" My gut told me to shoot him, but what if he moved and I hit Pearl instead?

Once again jerking Pearl back, he replied, "I don't think so, sheriff. I came back to get my wife and boys, and this ole' hag here knows where they are."

At Pearl's whimpering, I started to lose my patience. As yet, I hadn't raised my gun. I just hoped Caleb would arrive soon, stay out of sight, and take the deadly shot without Elliot ever knowing what hit him.

The silence surrounding us was eerie, and the tension palpable. I could feel the people watching from behind the safety of their doors. It was as if we were the only three people in town.

"Elliot," I added calmly. "There's no way out of town for you unless it's by the undertaker. Just let Pearl go, and we can talk about this."

Elliot let his head fall back, boldly laughing.

Caleb, now is the time to take your shot. It didn't come, and Elliot remained standing with Pearl in his clutches.

"Sheriff, the only one going to need an undertaker here today is you."

My gut told me from experience that this standoff couldn't last much longer before Elliot shot Pearl. Again, I asked, "Elliot, let Pearl go. Let me take her place."

Pearl shook her head from side to side as much as Elliot's grip would allow.

"No! he screamed. "I want my wife here, now!".

Stomping their hooves and snorting, the horses attached to the coach were spooked by all the yelling and creating a screen of dust, making it difficult to see what Elliot was going to do next. Where were the drivers who could hold them in check? I had my suspicions. For all I knew, Elliot probably shot them. This had to be the way Elliot made it back into town.

Gone was his prison garb. If they didn't know who he was, no one would question his grubby attire, looking like any coach driver who came through town.

⁓⁂⁓

Playing right into her husband's hands, Rebecca called out, "Elliot, I'm over here."

No. It can't be. Rebecca is supposed to be at the dress shop. Turning my head in the direction of the voice, Rebecca was standing on the boardwalk across from us.

My first instinct was to scream at her, *What in the name of heavens are you thinking?* She was going to get herself killed. Think Reynolds. Think! Is it possible for Elliot to kill Pearl and Rebecca before I take him down?

Damn him. He's going to make me choose between one of these women. "Elliot. Look at me," I yelled, calling his attention away from his wife. I shrugged and rolled first one, then the other shoulder, to ease the building tension as rivulets of sweat ran down my back like a waterfall.

What a mess this was turning out to be. "Elliot, you don't want to hurt any more people, especially the mother of your boys."

Rebecca called out while taking one step off the boardwalk. "Elliot, please let Pearl go, and we can talk."

"Not until you come over here," he yelled, indicating with his head.

"Alright," Rebecca replied, holding out her hand. "Just don't hurt her, please."

Time had run out. Where the hell was Caleb? My mind was rapidly playing out the scenarios on how this would end when a little voice in the back of my mind whispered, *Reynolds, this is going to be a bloodbath. It's just like the war. You can't save them all.*

That nagging doubt snuck its way into the back of my mind. *Maybe you're not cut out to be a sheriff, Reynolds.* Stop it! Don't think that way! With my focus back on Elliot, I moved forward to take his attention off Rebecca. It worked.

Hanging by my side, I cocked my revolver. I was ready to die if it meant saving Rebecca and Pearl. After all, it was my job. My only regret would be I couldn't spend time with my new enchantress, Maeve.

Hearing me cock my gun, Elliot instantly looked my way and pointed his revolver in my direction, which allowed Nathaniel, who seemed to come out of nowhere, push Rebecca down in the street.

It all happened so fast that I didn't have time to think about the consequences. Elliot and I raised and fired our revolvers at the same time. I thought I heard two more shots ring out, but from where or by whom, I couldn't tell. I was too busy grabbing my chest and dropping to my knees.

All I worried about was whether Elliot had killed Pearl and Rebecca. At this point, I guess I would never know.

Damn, this hurts! I know I said I was ready to die, God, but I didn't really mean it. Looking down at my blue plaid shirt, a circle of scarlet began to move out from the fabric-printed squares, becoming larger as the seconds ticked by.

I gave in to the searing pain and collapsed sideways in the dirt. In a pain-induced fog, I desperately tried focusing on where Elliot and Pearl had stood, but my vision was too hazy. Pressing my hand against my chest was the wrong thing to do. It hurt far too much. So, I let go, knowing bleeding to death was a slow and tortuous way to die.

Please, God, let this be quick.

It's funny what you think about when you're dying. I had survived years in a war only to be killed by a madman.

I dug my heels into the dirt in an attempt to sit up but failed. Instead, I rolled in a ball from one side to the other as the pain intensified. More screams surrounded me. I wanted the noise to stop. I wanted silence while I died.

My hearing was still intact, and in the distance came a familiar woman's voice yelling my name, "Sheriff Reynolds!"

Surprised yet grateful for her presence, she knelt beside me in the dirt. It meant I wasn't going to die alone. "Benjamin, it's Maeve. Can you hear me?"

"Maeve," I barely whispered. My sweet enchantress was here. I leaned into her hands as she ran them down my face. I was going to miss her and her spunky daughter Fiona. Now, I can die peacefully in her arms.

Wait, she called me Benjamin. Earlier, I'd introduced myself as Ben. I hate being called Benjamin. Only my mother and the Army called me that. Why was I thinking this?

Reaching up, I grasped her hand and rasped out through a shaky breath, "Where's Pearl and Rebecca? Elliot. Is he dead?"

Now wasn't the time to be having lusty thoughts as Maeve tore my shirt open and yelled at me, "Pearl and Rebecca are fine. Elliot's dead. But damn it, Reynolds, don't you go dying on me!"

She's a bossy little thing. There's no fooling around with my Maeve. I'll have to remember that for the future. I huffed and remembered it wouldn't be necessary. But I wanted to take her in my arms just one time before I left this earth. Then I'd die knowing I held her soft sweetness close to my heart as I breathed my last.

Suddenly, drawing back, Maeve yelled louder to the people surrounding us as she pressed on my chest.

I don't know if I actually spoke, "Maeve dear, that hurts. Please stop."

Each time I tried taking in a breath, pain so intense surged through my lungs. I couldn't breathe.

I really was going to die.

There was my bossy Maeve yelling again. "Someone get me a stretcher and tell the doctor he's needed. Tell him the sheriff's been shot."

"Momma. Momma," I heard a child call out. I recognized the voice as Fiona's. We had gotten off on the wrong foot earlier today, but I was glad she hadn't been hurt.

"Momma, what happened to the sheriff? Is he going to die like Papa did?"

"No, Fiona. He isn't. Now, please go to the hotel and fetch my medical bag from our trunks."

Don't lie to Fiona. You don't have a crystal ball. Whether I live or die isn't up to us.

"Yes, Momma, I'll be right back."

Medical bag! Wait, was Maeve a doctor? Suddenly, I was being lifted and jostled from side to side as I heard people yelling more instructions. "Hurry. Get him to the clinic. He's losing a lot of blood, and I can't hold his chest forever."

No, you can't, my sweet Maeve. You have to let me go.

78

Nathaniel

I HAD JUST left the livery when I heard screaming coming from out front of the mercantile. My eyes fixed on Rebecca standing in the middle of the street, speaking with that madman husband of hers. How in the name of the heavens did Elliot escape? He was supposed to be on his way to prison.

I didn't have time to think as shots rang out. Panicking, I jumped off the boardwalk, landing on top of Rebecca and pushing her forward with my body. Letting out my breath in a whoosh, we tumbled in suspension to the ground. I looked up just in time to see Ben and Elliot drop lifeless to the dirt.

As panic set in, I closed my eyes and held tightly to the woman I loved. I couldn't lose her. Not after all we'd been through. I yelled louder than I probably should have while running my hands over her body. "Rebecca! Rebecca, are you hurt?

Looking up into my eyes, she placed her dirty gloved hand on the side of my face and softly replied, "I'm fine, Nathaniel. But, Pearl? Benjamin?"

Was it possible for a person's heart to ache because they loved someone so deeply? I couldn't answer that question for anyone else but myself. And the answer was yes. Especially when you thought you would lose them forever.

The shooting over, I heaved a sigh of relief and whispered in Rebecca's ear, "I love you." I managed to stand and hold out my hand to assist her off the dirt. I didn't care that we were both covered in dust. At least we were alive.

As Becca turned to look at Elliot's body, I placed my hands on the sides of her face and said, "Don't look. There's nothing to see there."

Surprising me, she stoically answered, "Yes, there is. I need to check on Pearl and make sure Elliot is really dead.

Despite her body quivering, I walked beside Rebecca as she took one slow step after another. Standing over Elliot's body for mere seconds, satisfied, she turned to Pearl without saying a word.

I could only imagine what was going through her mind at seeing her husband dead. Was she sorry, or was she relieved? I hoped she was relieved because I knew I was.

Rebecca made her way toward Pearl and engulfed her trembling body in her arms.

"I've never been so scared in my life. I was afraid he was going to shoot you again," Pearl said.

I stood aside, feeling like the luckiest man alive, as I watched the love these two women shared for each other. I might have died in a previous life, but I was here now, grateful to breathe in the cool desert air and be with the woman I loved.

"I'm fine, Pearl," Rebecca said, nodding her head. "It's finally over. I'm free. We're all free. I only wish I could have been the one to shoot Elliot," Rebecca added boldly.

"Oh no, my dear," Pearl answered. "You wouldn't want that act to hang over your head the rest of your life. Besides, how would you tell the boys that you killed their father? No, how it ended is for the best."

"You're right as always, dear Pearl." Hugging her tightly, Rebecca added, "I love you so much. Don't you ever think of leaving us!"

"After today, I have no intentions of going anywhere. This is where I'll stay until the day I die."

Coming up next to Rebecca and Pearl, Rebecca placed the palm of her hand on the side of my face and declared, "We'll all stay here in this dusty town and make a fresh start."

My heart was content for the first time in a long while. I finally could make the woman I loved a part of my life.

"Nathaniel, we have to go check on Benjamin. It doesn't look good. I can see his shirt is covered in blood, and I'd feel awful if he died because of me."

"Rebecca, he's not going to die because of you. Ben was doing his job as Sheriff."

Patting her hands on my chest, she said, "I know you're right, but still."

❦

A large circle of people had surrounded Ben as he lay in the dirt. Becca was right, his condition didn't look promising."

He's a good man, God. Please don't let him die.

A woman I'd never seen before was kneeling next to him, yelling at him not to die while putting pressure on his chest and shouting out orders simultaneously.

Bless Angus McLaughlin. He came rushing out of his mercantile with one of the doors he kept in stock. I waved my arms and shouted for people to stand back and give us room. Then, on the count of three, Angus and I lifted Ben onto the door.

Thankfully, several other men pushed forward to help us carry him to the clinic. Ben wasn't heavy, it was the door that added the extra weight. I knew Angus to be a strong Scotsman, but even he was breaking a sweat as we rushed down the street to the clinic.

We were met at the clinic door by both Doc Emily and Doctor Mathew, who directed us to where to take Ben. The door he was on wouldn't fit through the surgical suite, so we all shifted our positions around the door so Angus, with his brute strength, could pick Ben up and place him on the operating table.

The woman who had been with Ben in the street pushed her way through the door without a 'pardon me.' I heard her introduce herself to Emily, but I couldn't hear what she said, and I didn't think this was the time to ask, so Angus and I returned to the parlor.

"Ach, man, the sheriff looks to be in a bad way. I feel terrible I couldn't get to Pearl and help sooner, but my gun was under the counter, and I didn't dare move from the doorway."

"You did right, Angus. You had to think of your pregnant wife who was in the shop. Who knows how many people Elliot could have killed."

"Thanks, Nate. I'm going to head back to the mercantile, check on my wife, and clean things up outside the store. Then I'll come back later to check on Ben."

After Angus left, I headed back into the clinic's parlor, where Rebecca and Pearl waited in conversation with the elder Doctor Sweeney. Rebecca looked up at me, and I said, "You were right. Ben is in a bad way. Doc Emily and that lady I've never seen before is with him now."

"What lady?" Doc asked.

"A lady who appeared out of nowhere. She took control of the situation and began shouting orders right and left after the shooting. I must say we all jumped to her task. I think she may be a doctor because she asked some small girl to get her medical bag from the hotel."

Doc Sweeney paled, then started to walk away while saying, "I need to check on te sheriff and see if my granddaughter needs help."

"Thanks, Doc," I called out. "We'll come back later to see if you need anything. Then Rebecca and I will happily take turns sitting with Ben throughout the night."

"That be kind of ye," he answered as he rushed down the hall.

79

Nathaniel

REBECCA CAME TO stand beside me, putting her hands around my waist, and leaned her head on my chest. Looking down at Becca and Pearl, I asked, "How are you ladies holding up?"

Pearl was the first to reply, "I must say I've had better days. I'm just glad this is all over, and Elliot can't hurt us anymore."

"I agree, Pearl. It could have turned out worse for you both. I'm just sick about what happened to Ben. He doesn't deserve this."

Like I had in 2016, Ben had only been doing his job and had paid a price.

I was shaking inside. I'd felt helpless in a critical moment. As a former police officer, I should have been the one to take Elliot down. But who could predict that he would escape? He'd almost succeeded in coming between Rebecca and me again.

The nightmare was finally over as the three of us embraced. Standing there quietly, hugging each other, I let today's events sink in. We were the only ones in the clinic parlor, but I wouldn't have cared if the whole town was there watching us.

"Ladies, I need to check with Caleb and see what's been done with Elliot's body. Why don't you two head to the casita and get some rest."

"That's a good idea. And I need to check on the boys. I have a difficult discussion ahead of me."

I asked, tightening my embrace around Becca's waist, "Do you want me to come with you?"

"Thank you, but I think this is something I need to do alone. Pearl will be there while I take the boys into the parlor to explain what happened to their father. They've been with Clarice all this time, and I doubt they know what's transpired."

⌘

Why we chose to exit through the front door was anyone's guess, but I'm glad we had when my attention was drawn to the corner of a building next to the mercantile. There, leaning against the grayed siding, looking bloodied and pale, was Sheriff Anders.

The street was now empty, and no one seemed to have noticed him. "Rebecca, hurry," I shouted, pulling on her hand. "It's Anders."

All three of us ran across the street. Getting closer, I heard Anders groan in pain as he slowly slid down the side of the building, leaving a trail of blood on the wood. Rebecca and I dropped to our knees beside him. "Anders, can you hear me," I called out.

"I'm not deaf, man. I'm shot," Anders growled, holding his left arm across his chest. Eyes wide, he suddenly grabbed the front of my shirt. "Where's that jäkel? Did I hit him?"

Taking hold of his hand on my shirt, I answered, "If you mean Elliot, yes, he's dead."

Letting out what I only imagined was a sigh of relief, Anders went into a coughing fit.

"Calm down, man," I said. "He won't hurt anyone ever again unless he takes up a fight with the devil. Which I wouldn't put it past his evil spirit."

While attempting a feeble laugh, Anders patted me on the chest.

"Anders, do you think you can walk to the clinic?"

He nodded a silent reply.

"Rebecca, help me get him up," I asked, placing my arm behind Ander's back.

Letting out a booming groan and muttering words I believed to be in Swedish, Anders managed to stand with our help.

"Abigail. I need te see my wife," he whispered, leaning into my side.

"Don't worry. I'll have one of the men fetch her from the ranch and meet us at the clinic."

"Tell her and Noel I love them. Please." Coughing, he added, "I'm not as young as I used to be. What if I die? What will happen to my family."

"Stop talking foolish, man. You tell them yourself. You're going to be fine."

One on each side of Anders, Rebecca and I carefully walked him the short distance to the clinic. Pearl, having gone ahead, held the clinic door open as we were met by the elder Dr. Sweeney.

"What in te name of all that's holy is going on in this town? He asked while doing a quick exam on Anders. "You'll be fine, son. Just a shot to te shoulder. I've tended ye for worse over te years as sheriff."

"See, I told you you'd be alright," I whispered in Ander's ear.

Pointing down the hall, he instructed, "Take him to te first exam room, and I'll be in shortly."

Rebecca and I made sure that Anders was comfortable before leaving him in Pearl's care. I knew she'd be a mother hen and fuss over him until Abigail arrived.

Once I closed the exam room door, I took Rebecca's hand and led her to the kitchen in the back of the clinic. Finally, we were alone as I swung her around to face me and watched her dusty gown billow in a circle behind her.

Bringing her into my embrace, I kissed her as if my breath depended on her touch. Gone was the inhibition of a once-married woman. "Let me just hold you," I said. "I don't ever want to let you go."

Her arms slipped around my neck as she pulled me down for a deeper kiss. I rushed out, "I love you, Rebecca, with all my heart. I'll never hurt you or lay a hand on you or the boys the way Elliot did. You have to know that I will love you till my last day."

Placing her palms on the sides of my face, she looked at me with her bewitching eyes that had captured my heart the first day we met. Speaking softly, she said, "I love you too, Nathaniel. Nothing and no one can ever keep us apart again."

I didn't have a ring in my pocket, but that didn't matter. I got down on one knee and declared, "Rebecca Young, I love you. Will you do me the honor of becoming my wife?"

The silence between us seemed to go on forever, though it was only seconds before Rebecca burst out crying. Throwing her head back, she yelled, "Yes! Yes, Nathaniel, I'll be your wife."

Taking her in my arms, I wanted to shout it so the world could hear how happy we finally were, but neither of us spoke for several minutes. We just stood there holding each other, thankful for the moment. Nothing could have made me happier. I finally had what I wanted all my life: a loving woman and a family all my own.

80

Maeve Sweeney O'Reilly, M. D.

I HAD NO idea which direction we were heading, but I had to trust those carrying the sheriff knew what they were doing. Stopping, someone opened a white picket fence surrounded by dying and dead roses. I looked from Ben to the doorstep, where a woman with long auburn tresses stood. She looked very familiar. But I couldn't place where or when I'd seen her before.

With her hands on her hips, she raised her skirt and white apron before rushing down the stairs. "What's going on? Who've you got there?"

"It's Sheriff Ben, Doc," one of the stretcher-bearers answered.

"Quick! Bring him inside and take him down to the surgical room," she instructed, standing back out of our way.

"Yes, Ma'am. I mean Doc."

"Never mind about formalities, Hunter. Just get him down the hall."

As we made our way through the door, I had to release the bloodied hand I held over Benjamin's chest since we all wouldn't fit through the door together.

I stood back and remained silent as this doctor took control, ignoring me and calling out orders. I watched out of the corner of my eye as a colored woman hurried down the hall and into the surgical suite. She, too, had on a white apron over her dress. Choosing to ignore me, she walked straight to a table full of instruments as if she'd done this many times before. Both women seemed competent in what they were doing, so it was better I didn't interrupt their thought process as they went to work on saving Benjamin.

⁓ ❦ ⁓

I stood unnoticed in the corner, watching the two women work with a precision I admired. I'd never known of a black woman being allowed as part of surgery, but she obviously knew what she was doing, and I admired her skill.

The one they called Doc Sweeney chose her instruments carefully as she waited for the black woman to administer the ether. Benjamin's injury was life-threatening, and all I could do was stand here and pray that he would survive.

My heart ached since his survival was doubtful. Had our chance meeting this morning been all I would have to remember him by? In the charity hospital where I last worked, we saw so many patients come through the doors that we would have put little effort into saving someone with a similar wound and instead would concentrate on making them comfortable till their end came.

Although I'd long since abandoned my religious rituals, I still believed in God and prayed that Benjamin survived. It was all I could do at the moment.

I saw this as an opportunity to watch and learn if I wanted to be a part of this community. Hearing heavy footsteps approach the only door to the surgical suite, I held my breath. Now wasn't a good time to meet my Da after all the years we'd been separated. But it would have to happen, whether now or later.

All the memories of my past came rushing at me as soon as the man I would recognize anywhere walked through the door. Despite aging, a head full of wavy gray hair, and the stress of being a doctor, time had been kind to him.

I couldn't help but smile. He was still the handsome Irishman I'd always loved and always would. He hadn't yet seen me standing in the corner. I hoped it would remain that way until the surgery on the sheriff was over.

In his still present Irish brogue, he said, "I heard te sheriff's been shot. Let me wash me hands, and I'll help."

"His right lung has collapsed," the female doctor declared to my Da. "Can you please prepare the supplies for a thoracostomy?"

She piqued my interest. How could she treat a collapsed lung out here in the middle of nowhere? Unknowingly, I found my feet moving me closer to the table, which caused the young doctor to look up.

"And who might you be? she asked. "You shouldn't be in here." Without looking at me again, she pointed a bloody instrument toward the door and said, You'll have to leave."

I mumbled. I didn't want to cause a stir during the operation, but obviously, I had. "I'm, um, a doctor," I replied. "I arrived on the train this morning. The sheriff and I met earlier at the depot."

Hearing my voice, my Da turned from a table holding instruments and looked at me with a stunned expression. His color turned ghostly pale, and the glass bottle he was holding slipped out of his hands and shattered across the floor.

"Maeve! Is tat you? What in heaven's name are ye doing here, girl?"

"Hello, Da. It's good to see you.

EXCERPT FROM

I Can Love You the Best

Book Three
Desert Hills Trilogy

NEW YORK CITY, 1881

Maeve Sweeney O'Reilly, MD

IT WAS THE middle of the night, and the wailing of patients and their mourning families echoed down the dark hall—a sound I would never get used to despite it being a never-ending occurrence.

I was exhausted. But admitting to such would only give my male counterparts an excuse to have me dismissed. These so-called hallowed halls of medicine were a world where the male species dominated and believed a woman didn't belong, no matter how educated or talented she was. I had invaded their sanctuary, and they ensured my life here was unpleasant, if not miserable.

In my one quiet moment this night, I sat motionless on a hard bench in the hall outside my patient's room. With my head leaning back against the wall, I closed my eyes momentarily until I heard the rustling of fabric along the wood floor.

Nuns who had dedicated their lives to caring for the sick and infirm silently moved through the darkness at a rapid pace creating an ethereal picture. With my Catholic upbringing, I knew the black to be a symbol of repentance and the white veil covering their coif to represent them as the Bride of Christ.

I wondered, did they go back to the convent, leaving the worries of their day within these walls? Or did they take them back with them, like I did, only to have sleepless nights?

What I would give to be a regular person, living my life free from constant death. But I had chosen this path and loved what I did despite the dispiriting days.

The acrid scent of ether and dying patients filled the air around me and brought me out of a dream-like world that didn't exist. I had been here so long I didn't think I would ever recognize the sweet fragrance of a rose again. I needed to get away. I needed life, not death.

It was an unpleasant fact in the city's charity hospital that more people died than survived to walk out its doors. Maintaining some semblance of cleanliness was a twenty-four-hour work in futility as disease traveled quickly from one patient to another.

Most people were afraid to come here, preferring to suffer and die at home than alone amongst strangers. I couldn't blame them. Surviving the hospital was a rarity.

⁓⁂⁓

Fiona's father, the small child sitting next to me, lay dying of consumption in the bed behind us as his racking coughs passed through the open doorway.

Surprising me, since she didn't speak much, she asked without turning her head my way. "Are your parents alive?"

I didn't look at her when I answered. "Yes. My father is. At least, I think he is. My mother passed away quite some time ago." I hadn't thought of my father in years since he'd left me with his sister after my mother died, and he decided on some crazy idea to run off to the Arizona Territory to practice medicine.

"Fiona, do you have any family in Boston you can stay with?"

"You mean when Da dies?

"I'm sorry, I didn't mean to imply your father's." I couldn't finish because I didn't know how much she understood about her father's illness and impending death.

Looking at me with the bluest eyes I've ever seen, she asked, "You know he's going to die, don't you? You're a doctor, and doctors should know these things. Can you tell me when?"

Turning to face her, I replied truthfully, "Fiona, yes, your father will die soon. But exactly when, I can't tell you. That's not something doctors have the ability to predict. That's up to a higher power."

"You mean God, don't you?" Shrugging her shoulders, she added, "I don't believe in God. If there was a God, why did he make my Da sick and my Ma die?"

"Oh, Fiona. Please don't say that," taking her small hands in mind. "I know it's unfair that he's being taken away from you. Life can be cruel sometimes. But you should never give up believing."

I was asked these same questions daily but didn't have the answers families needed. It was out of my hands.

I took a long, deep breath, knowing my faith was frequently challenged. "Fiona, why don't you stay here and rest while I check on your father? You haven't left his side in days. I'll have one of the Sisters bring you something to eat."

Fiona nodded, then looked down at her hands folded in her lap. Her tattered brown dress was so thin I didn't know how she kept warm other than the old woolen shawl one of the Sisters found in the charity box where we kept clothes of patients who passed.

⤶⧖⤷

Mr. O'Brien's rasping breaths were evident from the hallway as I walked to her father's bedside. His once muscled and strong body, I'd known from early fall when he came to the clinic, was now a fraction of what he used to be. Now frail and gaunt, lying lifeless in the bed, his skin held the gray transparent sheen of impending death.

Gently touching his hands, I didn't want to break his fragile skin. "Mr. O'Brien. Can you hear me? I'd like to listen to your lungs."

"No use," he whispered. "Going to die."

Those few words sent him into a fit of coughing, producing bloody sputum. I reached for a damp cloth on the stand beside his bed and wiped his bloodied lips. His time to leave us was nearing.

His frail fingers wrapped around my hand in an attempt to pull me closer. I leaned down to hear what he had to say. Holding his hand, I patiently waited.

"Fiona," he gasped out.

"Yes, she's in the hallway," I nodded toward the door. "Would you like me to get her for you?"

"No. Don't want her to watch me die." He struggled to continue, "Doc, promise me something," as he gripped my hand tighter.

"What is it, Mr. O'Brien?" Something in the back of my mind told me my life was about to take a dramatic turn.

In a whisper, barely audible, he said, "Take care of my Fiona. She has no one else. You'll be a good mother for her."

A good mother! He couldn't possibly mean that.

I tried not to look stunned when, in truth, I wasn't. I had a feeling this question was a long time coming. The first time I met Mr. O'Brien, we formed a bond over his daughter. He obviously trusted me with his most precious possession.

Was I crazy to believe I could step in and be Fiona's mother? I had no experience with children, let alone lessons from my own mother, who died when I was a child. Although I'd loved my aunt, who raised me after Da left for Arizona, we had a strained relationship.

About the Author

DEBORAH SWENSON is an award-winning author who writes from an island in the Pacific Northwest. After an extensive and rewarding career in health care, she now focuses on writing Western Historical Fiction and adding a dash of romance and time travel, a pinch of suspense, and a skosh of medicine.

When she's not writing, she spends time with family and friends, spinning fiber, traveling (glamping), quilting, and reading.

She is a member of the following: Women Writing the West, Western Writers of America, and Pacific Northwest Writers Association.

Deborah loves to hear from her readers. Connect with her online.

Website:https://deborahswenson.com
Facebook:https://www.facebook.com/deborahswensonauthor
Email:deborah@deborahswenson.com